Druids of the Faerie

Gather the Champions
Book One

By:

Lewis G. Gazoul

© 2015 Lewis G. Gazoul

All Rights Reserved.

No part of this publication may be reproduced, stored in a retrieval system, or transmitted, in any form or by any means, electronic, mechanical, photocopying, recording, or otherwise, without the written permission of the author.

First published by Dog Ear Publishing
4011 Vincennes Rd
Indianapolis, IN 46268
www.dogearpublishing.net

ISBN: 978-1-4575-3339-6

This book is printed on acid-free paper.

This book is a work of fiction. Places, events, and situations in this book are purely fictional and any resemblance to actual persons, living or dead, is coincidental.

Printed in the United States of America

for

my lovely wife Therese

and

my beautiful daughters Claire and Camille

Chapter 1

WHAT *lay beyond the Narrow?* thought Baytel, looking northward toward the mountain pass he was never allowed to enter. Beyond it were lands and towns and people and challenging new experiences, all of which were so close, yet unreachable under his father's eye.

"Cyr, I cannot live like this anymore," he whispered, feeling as if he spoke any louder his father's spies would surely report back every word. "Life will not prosper and grow under my father's reign and I am afraid he will never allow me to, either. At least not the way I want."

Cyr said nothing. Prince Baytel took this as a sign to continue. That was Cyr's way in their frequent talks. Baytel decided to fully declare his view of the situation, hoping that Cyr would enable a solution.

"My brother is becoming nothing but evil, Cyr. Since Ravek witnessed our father practicing his magic in the deep crypts he has been obsessed with the thrill of conjuring the dark art. He has changed terribly – or the magic has changed him."

Baytel looked at Cyr, knowing the Tree Faerie's own magic to be powerful even though he had never seen Cyr perform anything stronger than making a plant grow from nothing.

"Have your magic powers changed you, Cyr?" Immediately regretting so personal a question, the young prince stopped walking. "My apologies, Cyr. That was out of place."

Cyr smiled sympathetically and said in a voice that flowed to the prince's ear like a melody: "We are much too close for such formalities anymore, Baytel. And their magic and ours is entirely different. The One Land gave the magic of the Faerie to us. We treat the gift with reverence and employ it only for the good of the land and sects of humanity. Practicing magical powers for other purposes will sooner or later consume the practitioners and destroy themselves, especially those who conjure magic with evil intent. No one can obtain by force or coercion that which the land has given freely and only to the chosen."

"Then my brother and father will destroy themselves unless someone shows them a reason to change their ways?"

"Eventually, yes."

1

"And what, then, will become of the people of this realm?"

Cyr resumed his silence.

The dawn exposed the morning dew that lay frozen upon the meadow from the frigid night, blanketing the valley in colorless white. Prince Baytel shaded his eyes while the sun rising over the east arm of the Fork Mountains touched the low meadow of the Middle Fork, turning the terrain of frost to a glistening field of crystals escorting in the new day.

Turning, Baytel followed the bright shafts of light across the valley toward the castle. Even in their brilliance they never seemed to illuminate the structure's walls, battlements and turrets. He reflected aloud, "Dark, formidable and threatening; as if the blackish stones of its construction rejected light. And happiness." Such had become life at his home, the realm of King Vokat.

Resting high upon the middle arm of the Fork Mountains, positioned perfectly to meet any opposition from the northlands, his father's lofty castle spire towered impossibly skyward, offering King Vokat the ability to oversee his vast realm from a haughty precipice. The black stone structure with its strangely shaped observation platform gave the appearance of a menacing bird of prey poised to fall upon those who dared venture into its sight. No truer statement could be said of the king.

With a sigh, Baytel brought back to mind how the morning had begun, how shortly after he went out upon the meadow he watched a bright spot appear against the backdrop of the dark castle. That was how the petite figure of the Tree Faerie Cyr had come into view. The prince never tired of admiring Cyr's delicate features. His pointed ears, somewhat like Baytel's own but smaller, his soft child-like face, his twinkling blue eyes that slanted upward and his lacy transparent wings fluttering behind him were all entirely fascinating.

The youthful appearance of the Tree Faerie was something Baytel learned not to take for granted, for these magical creatures in fact lived for hundreds of years, accumulating a vast store of knowledge. Plants, animals, the rivers and lakes, the soil and terrain were all subjects Cyr had taught him. Cyr was his only tutor outside of King Vokat's military advisors. Their relationship went beyond that of tutor/student. Cyr was his friend, companion and confidant.

The only person I trust.

On their morning walks, Baytel found it entrancing how Cyr's feet would barely skim the damp grass while his wings beat silently, propelling him forward. Today in particular Cyr's silvery-blond hair gleamed in the sunlight, further emphasizing the darkness of the castle behind him.

How can one so tiny be so powerful? And why did he stay in this place? His powers surely could overcome any obstacles to gain his freedom from my father's imprisonment.

"Cyr, how can I bring any change to the direction King Vokat takes his realm?"

"So often you call him King rather than Father."

"I find it a necessity to keep a guarded view of him when contemplating the state of affairs within the realm. Considering that my contact with my father is minimal and his concern for me appears casual at best, I prefer to keep familial titles to a minimum."

"Is your bitterness the result of hearing your father's announcement?" asked Cyr.

Baytel felt a pang of unease deep in his stomach. "All I heard was my summons to his council meeting. What announcement?"

"King Vokat has named Prince Ravek as his new Military Commander of the Realm."

The peace Baytel had felt from the morning evaporated. Abstractly, he had known that his brother's elevation to the highest rank under king was just a matter of time, but this sudden reality unsettled Baytel.

"Promoted over Lord Lezab?"

"It seems so."

"Well, the king finally has the person to deliver his form of justice." Baytel did not attempt to hide the bitterness from his voice. "The choice was obvious, Cyr. He's the anointed one."

"Your father taught him well, Prince Baytel. That is the station Prince Ravek has sought his entire young life. I am sure Lord Lezab would disagree with the choice, but he is getting old and was never of the same mind as the king in the ideas of the realm's ultimate direction."

"A good man and leader. Lord Lezab's influence will be sorely missed. In his place will be my twin brother, though you would never know our twin-ship by looking at us now. His strength and cunning will build the army into a fierce force. Ravek will apply harsh measures to those who do not adhere to his designs—just as the king does."

"I wholly disagree with Prince Ravek's methods. Nevertheless, he will no doubt become a powerful adversary to those who oppose your father's realm," said Cyr.

Baytel heard a small degree of distaste in his piping voice. He felt no jealousy toward his brother. It was right he be elevated to the position. Though young, Ravek was the most powerful man in the realm, aside from his father. As for himself, Baytel's only ambition within the realm was to work toward peace and harmony for all subjects.

Whether on the battlefields or in their sphere of sway within the realm, the prince had witnessed too many deaths and numerous lives destroyed in the wake of his father's and brother's military campaigns. He wanted none of it. He wanted a realm where there was no fear and people could live in happiness and look upon their liege lords with appreciation and contentment.

Cyr noted: "Prince Ravek proved his might most effectively in the recent conflict against the Pithean Goblins. His victory in that far West Fork range secured the entire Fork Mountain region under your father's complete control."

"Yes, but Ravek nearly destroyed the Pitheans while doing so. The horror and waste of it we should be ashamed of."

Baytel pounded a fist into his hand. "Every effort I made toward a way to bring that conflict to a peaceful resolve was thwarted. The same can be said for everything I have suggested to improve the region."

Cyr floated higher off the ground, high enough to pat Baytel's shoulder. "You did your best, Prince Baytel. You had too many factions against you, especially when the council has no desire to oppose your father. He is too powerful."

They walked down the slope toward the heart of the meadow at the base of the Middle Fork. Upward, the broad heights of the East and West Fork curled toward one another, nearly touching at the north end of the valley—silent sentries and permanent barriers to the lands beyond, pierced only by the Narrow, completely isolating the Southland realm from all the lands to the north. Baytel's yearning to see beyond the barriers seemed to halt time in the valley. He thought of what life might be in the north and what the people were like.

Were there realms with evil kings and lords? Were the people under the heavy weight of despotic government? Or were there good kings and were people free to go where they pleased?

Cyr gently tugged at his sleeve, interrupting his silent repose. "What is it, Baytel?"

He gave a half smile, still staring northward. "You do not often ask what is on my mind. Usually you allow me to formulate my thoughts and then say my piece when I am ready."

"Yes I do, young prince. Nevertheless, there are times when you must express yourself, not only to be understood, but also to gain personal clarity. I believe this to be one of those times."

Baytel turned toward his father's dark castle and then back to the Narrow. He felt he was at a crossroad and wanted to shout to the heavens what he had in mind, knowing it would shake his foundation and change all he was accustomed to. Yet, suppressing his desire would surely destroy him. He needed change and freedom to create and mature.

If I do not act upon this, all my hopes will be dead to me.

Slowly, he drew in a deep breath, feeling the clarity of his decision, as though his body and mind were finally in accord. "It is time for me to leave the Southland. I have known this for some time. I believed I could make a difference, make it a better life for those here. My ideas for an enriched kingdom have been ignored again and again. It appears I am a prince in name only, dismissed as just a dreamer. Cyr, I must learn how to be effective in my beliefs. How realms other than this one are led. If I stay here,

I will surely perish or become like my brother and father. The northern lands are where I believe I will find the answers. Then I can return to show my father and brother that there is another way, a better way to rule other than by war and autocracy."

Baytel paused as the thrill of his declaration made his heart pound faster. Excitedly, he continued, "Cyr, all my life I have felt an irresistible draw toward the lands beyond. I sensed it early in my childhood, like a calling. Through these years under Vokat's darkness the desire had been methodically dampened but now I feel it stronger than ever. It is time I answer that call."

With his desires rekindled he found himself speaking with complete commitment and enthusiasm. "Cyr, you have often spoken of the Citadel, the fortress of learning in the wild. That is where I want to go. With the knowledge you say I can attain there, I can return to guide this realm toward peaceful reign."

Cyr smiled warmly and began to partly stroll and partly float ahead of him toward the forest edge. Birds tweeted from the high grass, darting after insects as they went. Baytel felt liberated and almost light enough to float as Cyr was. But no sooner than acknowledging the sensation he heard the gallop of horses approaching. Spinning on his heels, he felt all his relief dashed as Prince Ravek and his guards thundered down the slope and reared to a halt.

The massive horses' long dark manes swayed as they fidgeted beneath their riders. The horses glistened with sweat, their panting breath steaming.

Baytel felt his brother's gaze rake over him. It was always the same; his slow peruse to study his features, resting first on his pointed ears and fairer skin, then over his body, which was more slender and less muscular than Ravek's. Finally his stare stopped at Baytel's blue eyes, and as usual Ravek's gaze hardened. Baytel knew his softer features always bothered his twin.

Ravek turned and glared at Cyr. In his harsh, rasped voice, he asked, "Where are you off to with my brother, Tree Faerie?"

One of the guards cantered uncomfortably closer. Baytel flicked his hand at the stallion's eyes and the horse reared, throwing its rider to the ground. The guard jumped to his feet and grabbed the hilt of his sword.

Baytel ignored the guard and addressed his brother. "What business is it of yours, Ravek? You are not my keeper, or my master."

Ravek stayed motionless on his steed, eyeing Cyr with contempt. Baytel studied his brother in turn. He had changed much since last they saw one another two months ago, much darker and larger. His narrow raven-black eyes deep set in his angular face and his protruding jaw gave him a frightening appearance. He had an indomitable physique accented with full battle dress, a black steel chest plate, leg and arm mail, and a black helmet, parading his new command for all to observe. His flowing black cape draped from his shoulders across the back of his stallion; his shield and sword hung ready at his side.

"I have been the tutor in your father's service for nearly sixteen years," Cyr replied; his musical voice had a sharpened edge. "During this time I have had the liberty to venture through the castle and its grounds without petition. What is your purpose to know where I go? State your business, Prince Ravek, so we may continue with ours."

"Everyone's business in the Southland is my business, Tree Faerie, especially yours, which in my opinion is most suspect. Perhaps someone should remind you that you are a prisoner here. If it were not for your good favor with my father I would have you rotting away in our deepest dungeon along with the rest of your Tree Faerie sect. The sooner your kind is removed from the land the better."

Ravek edged closer to Baytel, turning his anger that way. "Brother, whatever your business was with this pest is ended. I was summoned to our father's private chamber to report on the attendance at council and had the unfortunate task of informing him that his wandering son was the only one not in attendance. Did you not receive notice that you are required to appear at the king's council?"

Baytel shrugged and looked nonchalantly across the valley, knowing this would infuriate Ravek. Indeed, a scowl formed across Ravek's face, deepening his frightful appearance. Even his steed beneath him felt his anger as it stirred.

"I was dispatched to retrieve you. All the council awaits the king, who awaits full attendance."

"Why does he summon me, Ravek? He has no desires for me as he does for you."

Ravek motioned to his guards. Two brutish soldiers jumped from their horses and grabbed Baytel by the arms. "You question the king when you should obey. I am losing patience. What will it be, Baytel? Do you go under your own power or do you need a physical escort?"

Baytel turned to Cyr. "We shall speak later, my friend." He shook off the soldiers' grip and walked toward the castle.

Chapter 2

THE walk from the valley, through the serf yard, past the castle yard and ward apartments, up numerous flights of stairs and through long corridors took Baytel above the level of the battlement and into the war tower, where he entered wearily only to recall to mind that there were more steps to traverse.

The tower was so dark he slowed his pace to allow his eyes to adjust to its meager light. Embrasures were cut far too high to cast significant light upon the stairwell.

Not having visited the war tower often as he was never before invited to share in these council meetings, he was struck by how many of the tower's levels were used to store weapons and other instruments of war. A ramp ran along-side the narrow spiral stairs for ease in transporting large weaponry. The highest point of the war tower was the observation platform on the thirteenth level. The king stationed sentries at constant watch, for they had the ability to see all the lands surrounding the castle.

Finally Baytel was on the twelfth level, the assembly hall, and the only habitable level of the tower. He stopped in the foyer to catch his breath but his rest was cut short as Ravek came up behind him and propelled him between the heavy wood doors into the hall.

The assembly room looked like the tower itself, constructed of cold, dark stone found in the West Fork that seemed to absorb any light. Stone pillars and wood beams supported the octagonal ceiling. Lighted candles fixed on the pillars threw ominous shadows about the walls. Rows of seating ran along the walls, under lit chandeliers, but they were empty; no audience would sit this day.

In the center of the room a long oaken table stood where the entire congregation of councilors rose to their feet at the princes' appearance. The scraping of chair legs against the stone floor echoed in the vast chamber. A fireplace, tall enough for a man to walk erect into, stood behind the head of the table, flames darting from crackling shards of hardwood, leaving fiery embers upon the stone floor. Near the fireplace a lone door stood, his father's private entrance to the chamber, which on the other side led to places unknown to the assembled, though Baytel knew they led to the deep crypts.

Baytel decided not to conceal his discord with his brother, and moved away from Ravek before he reached the table. The councilors and lords took their seats and resumed their whispered conversations.

He stopped at the end of the table while Ravek sat to the left of the head, next to his father's place, whose seat was raised two steps higher than the others. To the right of the table head sat Hectus, Chancellor of the Realm and Vokat's trusted advisor. Hectus stood and offered his place at the council table. Baytel smiled and silently declined, preferring a place at the far end.

Hectus's duty was to the king, but he was a good man. As the only person in the realm allowed to travel into the northlands for political purposes, the chancellor was the prince's source for information about the realm as well as about the northlands and the people who lived there. Hectus maintained his own philosophy about the northlanders and he and Cyr debated many subjects of concern that filtered in from spies and reports about the north. Although Hectus witnessed faerie activities, he still had his doubts that the Tree Faerie tribe was meant to oversee the workings of the land outside Vokat's realm. What Hectus really thought about powers beyond Vokat's borders were a mystery to Baytel.

The whispered conversations ceased as Ravek sat and a dreary silence commenced. He had gained the reputation of an adversary rather than a comrade to the lords and councilors, too often employing his short temper and swift acts of vindication. Ravek's presence might be disconcerting, but he was in line to be king, so those in attendance had learned to be politically tolerant toward him.

The hall became so quiet the only sounds were the rustle of garments, the snap of burning candlewicks and roar of the fireplace. Suddenly Vokat appeared at the head of the table as though materializing from the air. Startled, the council members awkwardly dropped to one knee as the shocked Hectus, gaining his composure, stood and announced the king. Vokat stood with the blazing flames behind, which seemed to stir with new vigor in his presence, giving the impression of encircling him in a mandorla of fire.

Studying his father, for he had not seen him in months, Baytel noted they were nearly the same height. His father was dressed as usual in his red military garb. His black hair fell to his shoulders and his keen hawk-like eyes seemed to cut through the assembly room and take in every detail as he gazed at each kneeling council member one by one. When Vokat's attention finally focused on Baytel and they met eyes, his father did not hide his displeasure. Baytel looked away from the dark, somber eyes that always seemed to bore directly into his soul.

Vokat was a slender man and Baytel always thought him almost graceful to watch. However, his gracefulness was the last attribute that came to the minds of most people encountering the king. Instead, a sullen evilness seemed to provoke a sense of malice in a most unnerving way.

Vokat stood a moment longer than usual, making sure no one flinched. Baytel had learned this tactic of intimidation early in his youth at every disciplinary action his father took with him. It was Vokat's way of reading those under his stare and thus revealing any form of disloyalty that might be occurring in his realm. If someone broke under his silence, he was surely a traitor.

Satisfied, he sat and all followed. With a voice barely a whisper, yet reaching all councilors as though he sat at their side, he said, "Hectus, announcements, please."

Hectus stood, his face a constant blush as red as his disheveled hair. Using the chair to balance his heavy body while nervously adjusting the robes of his station, smoothing the loose fitting clothing he always wore to conceal his girth, the chancellor appeared as an oddity among the other lords of the realm, Baytel reflected, yet Hectus had the unconditional trust and ear of the king.

"King Vokat has appointed Prince Ravek the new commander of the military." A roar of approval rang through the chamber. As the shouting subsided, he continued. "Also, the region of Pithe has come to join the Southland as an ally to King Vokat and the realm. Welcome, Pithe."

Hectus gestured down the table to the representative of Pithe, Lord Plet. He was a large, dark goblin, muscular and rigid with formality. The goblin stood, nodded to the polite applause and sat back without a word.

Hectus met Baytel's eyes. He knew what Hectus wanted to do. Announce him. He returned the silent request with a slight shake of his head that stopped the chancellor, and with announcements ended he sat down in a relieving *thump*.

Vokat resumed his intentional gaze at each again, resting slightly longer on Baytel. The king spoke without standing. "We have peace within the realm now that all regions of the Fork Mountains are under the Southland flag and my rule."

Baytel listened to his father exorbitantly boast of the acquired regions to the very lords he had conquered, now at the table. The representatives from the two other Fork Mountain regions, Pithe and Azkar Rol, writhed angrily in their seats.

"Now is a time for healing and rebuilding," he proclaimed. "Gentlemen, please relay to me your reports on the current situations under your commands. Let us begin with you, Lord Lezab."

The oldest in the council, Lord Lezab had been until recently the Military Commander of the Realm, and was now Regent of the Southland. Tall, strong, and lean, he stood in one motion, using muscles disciplined by his rigid standards of command and soldiering. His black hair was streaked with gray; his cold green eyes showed reserve, intelligence, and keen instinct. Baytel had never seen Lord Lezab without complete composure. As a king's advisor, his devotion to the Southland was beyond compare and question. Whatever bitterness he may have felt at losing his command to Ravek he held in check.

"I speak for all Southland regional lords, sire," he stated with a confidence achieved through years of experience. "The war with our new ally, Pithe, was costly in both men and property. In my estimation rebuilding our regions and the military will take three years, perhaps more. Shall I offer specific details, sire?"

"Your statement will suffice, Lord Lezab," answered the king. "Are the other lords in agreement with your assessment?"

Lezab and Vokat looked to the lesser lords, all of whom nodded in agreement. Baytel had never heard of anyone questioning Lord Lezab's assessments. All knew his attention to detail was surpassed by none.

"Pikus. What of Azkar Rol?" Vokat asked.

Baytel gazed coldly at the high lord of Azkar Rol, the volcanic region up the Middle Fork under the Azkar Rol volcano. Lord Pikus was the tallest at council. His hair was long and white, though not from age, and tied behind his head. He wore the uniform of Azkar Rol, a black mail cloak with a red flame embossed into its iron ringlets. His eyes showed no love for the Southland or the king. Baytel believed those who claimed that had Vokat not conquered Azkar Rol in the early years, Pikus would be as powerful and evil as he and would now have rule over the Fork Mountains.

Lord Pikus slowly rose, which made Baytel quickly look at Ravek, seeing him seethe at the arrogantly deliberate and dispassionate posturing Lord Pikus displayed. "We have sustained little damage to our fortress, but our army took many losses. It will take one year to rebuild the fortress and another to restock the army with new recruits. Maybe less."

"And your assessment, Lord Plet?" asked the king of the Pithean.

The goblin lord rose quickly, feet spread in near battle stance. His burly, muscular frame filled the end of the assembly table. Lord Plet was dark as night, with large black eyes and long arms and legs. His face showed weariness, yet emanated strength and confidence, even in defeat. Baytel found a deep appreciation for his composure and gained a high respect of the goblin lord.

"Sire, our lands and troops, as most know, sustained the most damage and devastation from the war. The rebuilding, using our own resources, will take at least five years."

Baytel admired the Pithean's restraint. He knew that without the aid of the Southland, the people and lands of Pithe would never flourish again, and Lord Plet had subtlety asked the king for assistance.

Hectus rose to he heard. "Sire. This situation could have been avoided had the Southland army not been overzealous in their battles with the Pithean army and uncontrolled in their destruction of their lands." He looked disapprovingly at Ravek. "In order to gain the trust of an ally after defeat, Prince Ravek, we must be compassionate to the defeated and not so reckless as to destroy without regard."

"When waging a war campaign, Chancellor, there is little time to consider who we spare or what we destroy." Ravek spoke defensively, clearly uncomfortable with being lectured to, especially in front of council and king.

Hectus was not to be thwarted and replied firmly. "A good commander whose leadership is based on a loyal following should be in total control of his troops and contemplate all consequences of their actions before he acts. This is the essence of a good general." He paused, then added, "And a lesson for those who covet wisdom."

Ravek flushed with anger and appeared about to rise when Vokat raised his hand. Hectus sat down, wiping the perspiration from his forehead.

"Lord Plet," the king said in so soothing a voice it was almost feminine. "You are now an ally of my realm and as such are entitled to our assistance."

Baytel noticed the slight squint as his father calculated what to say next. Then a small uplift of a smile twitched his lips. "Lord Pikus, because your lands have been spared most, Azkar Rol will aid in the rebuilding of Pithe." Before Pikus could object, Vokat continued. "As for your realm's military, I decree that both Southland and Pithe are to join forces under one command. Pithean training and recruitment will coincide with our own."

Vokat raised his hand as Plet was about to object. "Sacrifices to the realm, however unpleasant at the time, are always for the betterment of the state and shall be remembered."

Plet took a deep breath, folded his hands upon the table, and stayed silent.

With no objections voiced, Vokat addressed all in attendance. "Whatever the cost of rebuilding the fortresses and armies is insignificant and must be accomplished as quickly as possible. Now that the Fork Mountains are under my rule, we shall begin a new order. Prince Ravek will take from all armies your strongest fighters, then, along with the Southland castle guard, begin training them to be the ultimate warriors—an elite troop. This troop will then train the divisions and the battalions until our forces will be the most powerful in all the land. Once this is accomplished, together we shall march north with a force of unquestionable power."

Baytel was shocked at the announcement. War with the northlanders was an enormous undertaking. It also seemed ridiculous and foolhardy. The clamor in the room rose as excitement grew among the lords. It was inconceivable to think they were for war.

"This will take time. You all will have tremendous responsibilities. The onus of what I order will rest not only upon the commander of the military, but upon every one of you. I require your absolute unquestioned loyalty."

Vokat waited until everyone in council had nodded in the affirmative. "Hectus will coordinate Pithe and Azkar Rol with Pikus as advisor. Lezab will coordinate the Southland. Prince Ravek, of course, is in charge of all military operations and all will report to him."

Baytel watched the burden of Vokat's orders now fall heavily upon the lords and councilors. Some faces became grave, while others showed somberness and concern. They all were veterans of battle and understood the severity of a long campaign of war and the deaths that always followed. Nevertheless, he could see the majority of councilors were impelled by the king's building mania to conquer more lands and subjugate the masses to his will.

"Now, lords, councilors, and friends, tonight, at the ballroom of my Keep, I offer you all a royal ball. We shall dine, dance, make merry and toast a new age to the Southland Realm. Go back to your homes and prepare, for this evening we rejoice."

Baytel sat up in surprise along with all in attendance. Never before had his father hosted a formal ball. With much revelry they all departed, cheering the king and the Southland on their way out of the room.

"Baytel." Vokat motioned him to stay, along with Ravek and Hectus.

He remained standing as the assembly hall doors closed and the exuberant voices echoing until they faded into silence.

"Why did you not come to council when summoned earlier, Baytel?"

Baytel replied defiantly. "May I ask why I was summoned in this instance?"

"You are the son of the king," said Ravek. "You do not question or object to such a summons. Your duty is to obey it immediately."

Ignoring his brother's scorn, Baytel looked only to his father. "Father, you never asked my counsel before. Why is it you now require my attendance in these matters?"

Vokat ignored the question. "Ravek tells me your studies with Cyr have taken a direction outside the agenda I directed him to take. Is this true?"

So Ravek has me watched, and probably Cyr as well.

"I find nothing wrong with what Cyr has been teaching. It has been consistent from the beginning of my tutelage, all fifteen years."

"Then it is worse than I imagined, Father. Cyr obviously chose to ignore your agenda completely and substituted his own," said Ravek, shaking his head.

"Cyr has taught me everything you asked, Father. Only through my inquisitiveness was I taught other matters."

"I have spoken with Cyr of this, sire," said Hectus. "Some subjects we quite disagree on. However, in my opinion, there is nothing wrong with the topics being taught to Prince Baytel. These discussions expand his mind."

"Are the king's lessons and the realm's affairs of politics, business, and the military not enough to fill your mind, Son?"

"Of course these subjects are challenging, Father, and intriguing, but there is more to our world than the Fork Mountains and Southland realm. I am curious about what lies beyond our borders."

Baytel was slowly approaching a subject he did not feel ready to bring up. Fortunately, Ravek interrupted.

"Nothing is more important than that which is within these borders. You spend too much time and effort on outside matters, Brother. They are a disruption to your lessons and show disloyalty to the realm and your father."

"And you spend too much time and effort in the deep crypts, Ravek," he countered, knowing this would quiet his brother. He understood that the king knew Ravek practiced with the dark art, but not that Ravek visited the crypts where the dark magic thrived.

Vokat's eyebrows rose and he glanced at Ravek, who sat fuming. "Baytel, sit down." As he did, Vokat cleared his throat. "Your studies, it seems, are important to you. You have no experience in fighting and war, though you seem to have the strength for it, and the mind for its strategies once learned, but not the desire. It is my wish you end your lessons with Cyr for it is time for you to take a responsible position with my realm. I have decided to give you an appointment. You are to be the Liaison of the Realm. It is your responsibility to keep track of the progress of the regions in the rebuilding and report back to the council. Your duties will be . . ."

Baytel's mind was racing. The king was still speaking, but he was not listening. He felt his world, his dreams and his aspirations, collapsing at that moment and he had to stop it or his life would crumble with them.

"Father," he interrupted so sharply the anger rose on the faces of his father and brother. "Have you discussed this appointment with anyone else?"

"Why, Prince Baytel? Is something wrong?" asked Hectus, edging his chair forward. He was clasping his hands together, squeezing his chubby fingers with nervous anxiety.

Baytel wished he had prepared for this. He had heard no rumor of this appointment; no notion had occurred to him that his father was interested in his participation in the realm. His father was not even a part of his life except for an occasional royal dinner where he wanted to parade both his sons for the lords and families of the realm to see.

At what cost would his rejection of the appointment come? What cost would acceptance mean? The more he pondered both, the more he needed to convene with Cyr. He decided to test the waters and see what they thought of the idea of travel.

He cleared his throat. "To answer your questions, Hectus, no there is nothing wrong. I have been giving much thought recently to the idea of travel."

Laughter shook the room. Vokat and Hectus seemed completely amused and Ravek's uproarious laughter ended with him choking for air.

He spoke through exhausted guffaw. "Travel? Where?"

"North through the Narrow. I thought to travel through villages and towns to see..."

Ravek interrupted him, the glee of laughter replaced by a scowl, replied, "You are a Southlander, boy. You will be welcome nowhere. Nevertheless, how would you get by? You know nothing of living on your own, especially in the wild between these villages and towns."

"I can take care of myself," Baytel said, mustering his dignity. "I have spent many days and nights hiking and have camped in the Middle Fork numerous times."

Ravek sniffed and said, "Child's play, Baytel."

Hectus asked, "Where would you go, Prince Baytel? The villages you think are out there are many weeks travel from the Southland, months even."

Baytel answered cautiously, remembering the king's plan to rebuild an invincible army. "It is not only towns and cities, Hectus. I want to study the land on the way also. I am sure there is much to see and learn. I have always been interested in nature."

Ravek's voice took on a bitter tone. "You are the son of a king. You cannot run about the land studying and daydreaming. We have responsible work for you here, important work."

Baytel felt his face redden. He stood and slammed his fist on the table and then immediately regretted the outburst. He did not want them to know the passion he had for his plans. Collecting himself, he sat and said, "It is my own council I will yield to and not yours, Ravek."

Ravek replied as if reprimanding a schoolboy. "You sit here at the King's council chamber and have the audacity to say to your father and liege lord that it is your council you yield to and no others?"

"This is my life, and I alone will decide what is important and what is not."

Vokat had remained quiet during their heated debate. His eyes never left Baytel for a moment. He raised his hand to stop the argument.

"Baytel, I understand you are feeling the lure of adventure. Many young men your age do. However, due to your lineage, not many would act on such an impulse at the cost of their station. You were born into nobility and have obligations to your title and claim to this realm. This appointment means a great deal to me. It is my wish you take this appointment."

Baytel sat back, feeling his dream fading further from reality. The full realization of the hierarchical line of ascent as the second son settled upon him. He was not more than any other councilor or advisor. Truly, he was no different than a serf of the realm or a servant to do his lord's bidding.

They will not allow me to leave the Southland.

"It is that Tree Faerie," Ravek said. "He twisted your mind. You belong here, Baytel, not in the land of fools. It is a fool's dream, Brother."

"Your place is at my side, Baytel," said Vokat as both Ravek and Hectus nodded their agreement. "You are a prince of a kingdom that does not adhere to the politics of the lands to the north. Your brother is correct; you will not be welcome no matter where you travel. Inexperience and other hostilities will rear up. You will be targeted by anyone who finds it an advantage in using you to get to me. All this nonsense will eventually cause you an early death and trouble for my realm, Son. Let wisdom take root here with me. This appointment will fill your mind with enough to do. I am certain of it."

Baytel stared at the floor while they waited in silence. He needed time to speak to Cyr, but he could not leave the room without deflecting their concerns.

"Father, may I call upon you at dusk tomorrow? I see the truth in what you say. I am a Southlander and, as your son, I surely do have a sense of duty to you and the realm. The post you have appointed me to is a tremendous responsibility and I want to make sure that I will be the correct one to lead it."

His father smiled and nodded his satisfaction and said, "Good, Baytel. We will convene at dusk tomorrow. Ravek, I will supply you with the details of your post tomorrow morning and Baytel's duties as Liaison. These you will thoroughly review with your bother after our meeting."

Vokat rose from his chair and swept from the room. Baytel sighed silently and stood with the others. He met Ravek's scowl and said, "Tomorrow morning then, Brother?"

"You act like a schoolboy instead of a prince, *Brother*." Ravek strode toward the doors and over his shoulder said, "Meet me at dawn in my chambers, fool." He slammed the doors behind him.

Baytel walked with Hectus out of the assembly hall and, before parting company, Hectus stopped in the foyer.

"Prince Baytel, remember your station. The romance of travel will come eventually once your father's plans are put in place. Do not be foolish to cross him now. He is on the cusp of enormous greatness and nothing will get in his way of achieving it. Take this post. Accolades will be forthcoming and fulfilling. You will see, young man."

Dark gray clouds had replaced the morning sunshine and the weather had turned inclement during the day as a freezing wind laced through the Southland from the north. Baytel was cloistered with Cyr in his chambers all afternoon in the upper level of the east tower looking down upon the serfs hauling in cut wood to the furnaces. He already felt the hot air flowing into the intricate system of flues within the walls and under floors, transporting heat throughout the castle.

"Understand, Baytel, that if you leave the Southland you will be forsaking your father's wishes. In his eyes you will have abandoned the realm. Your title and claim to the kingdom will surely be forfeited. This is an absolute. King Vokat will never back down from anyone showing disloyalty to his rule, even his own son."

"I do not believe that, Cyr." He had debated these points for hours with Cyr and remained steadfast that his father would not abandon him or his worth to the realm. He felt justified with his idea that when he returned, what he had learned would surely eliminate any acrimony between him and his family.

"Cyr, losing my claim to the Southland is not enough to convince me to remain. What is it to be the second in line to the throne when we both know Ravek is not only favored but the first born, be it by only a moment. My father has chosen him as his ascending heir, not me, and that is fine. I want no part in the rule of the realm, Cyr. And who is to say that if I gain the knowledge and bring it back, he will not welcome me?"

"Perhaps, though I believe you should at least talk with Ravek. Learn the liaison's duties and the prospects the post could offer before you decide your course. Maybe this appointment could be the very conduit to change your father's realm into something more civilized."

"No, Cyr. I will see Ravek only to tell him of my departure."

Cyr conceded. "If that is your decision then be mindful of Ravek. If you tell him of your plans he may not allow you to leave. According to what you said was discussed at council the king will likely close the borders. Speak with Ravek about the new post. If things are not going your way, stop and say you will call on him when you have a thorough understanding of the appointment. Then take your leave."

"Ravek is expecting me tomorrow morning, but I will see him at the ball tonight. We can talk there."

Cyr's face showed a concern crease Baytel had never seen before. It made him smile.

"Do not worry, Cyr. It will be fine. I will call upon you later tonight, after the ball."

Chapter 3

BAYTEL stepped out from the safe obscurity of a curtained alcove and entered the ballroom. A hum began across the large chamber and spread from one end to the other. A tide of color flowed toward him from all over the ballroom. As the multi-hued gowns of the ladies of the court converged to vie for his favor, he likened it to a coursing river with boulders in its midst, its waters flowing around the rocks, only to merge once more downstream, and he was its delta.

Happy greetings and salutations piped at him in diverse tones and exaltations. Beautiful faces presented an array of blushes and facial paint. Some ladies were all smiles while others, who had been edged out of proximity failed to conceal nasty expressions creasing their beauty, and a few displayed leers of envy. The sweet perfumes of the flock made the ballroom smell of a flowering spring meadow.

"Good evening," Baytel replied, over and over, bowing politely and continuing with his deliberate crossing of the dance floor, making it difficult for the ladies maneuvering to follow. He had seen and talked to most of the young women before and thought them beautiful and polite, but not true to themselves. All their parents were lords, officers and councilors to the realm, and because of this the young ladies thought they had status and a certain power. At times the power was applied, for a whisper into a father's ear occasionally had a lesser young officer suddenly promoted—or a seasoned officer broken down in rank—depending upon the lady's pleasure.

The king stood at the far end of the ballroom surrounded by officers competing for his attention, perhaps to mutter a word or two to enhance their position in the new power movement. Baytel met his eye and they nodded.

Baytel made his way forth as the braver ladies followed, carrying on snippets of pleasant conversations and falling politely quiet every few steps as they realized he was headed toward the king. His way toward his father was interrupted a number of times on the dance floor when greeted by a councilor or officer. He negotiated through the dancing guests in a princely manner, graciously conversing with each.

As he approached the Pithean, Lord Plet, Baytel bowed with full formality, showing him the utmost respect and knowing it would not go unnoticed by all in attendance.

Baytel greeted the goblin. "Sire, it is a pleasure seeing you again."

Plet bowed stiffly and replied with the same kindness. "A grand gathering and most colorful, Prince Baytel."

He leaned toward the goblin and whispered, "Yes, it is. And it is the first in my lifetime."

Lord Plet smiled knowingly, bowed deeply in appreciation and stepped back to allow an opening for the ladies who followed.

Along the way Baytel noticed the extra care his father must have taken to create the joyous setting. Flags hung from ceiling beams fluttered in the breeze from the opened high windows. Chandeliers illuminated the ballroom with an intimate glow. The black and white marble dance floor shone at the center of the room encircled by carved stone support pillars. Its intricate interlaced pattern strained his eyes. On a stage wedged between two pillars was the orchestra playing a merry tune.

Surrounding the dance floor, dining tables bore heavy crystal candelabras lit with many candles. The tall bay windows were elegantly framed with draperies of deep crimson, the favorite color of Vokat the Red King. He deserved the nickname more for his bloody campaigns than for the decorations, Baytel reflected.

His father had moved from the place he had last seen him and the prince decided not to go looking for him at the moment and turned his attention to the ladies who still followed. They pressed toward him with deliberate pleasure in their eyes and hand fans fluttering. He was drawn to a young woman he had seen following the entourage, but not in fact a part of the clamor. She was modestly attractive, not of the beauty of most of the ladies around him and much younger, yet her poise caught his eye. She wore a simple blue gown with a white lace ribbon that held her brown hair behind her head, revealing the unpainted rosy coloring of her face.

"Good evening," he said, bowing slightly. "I do not believe we have met. I am Baytel."

Her green eyes widened at his attention, and she quickly curtsied. "Prince Baytel. Good evening. I am Della."

He smiled at her and, seeing it returned, asked, "Would you care to dance with me?"

Surprised, her rose color now red, she answered, "Yes."

Baytel offered her his arm and escorted her to the center of the dance floor, to the disappointed sighs of the other ladies of the court.

The musicians' melody changed to a slower rhythm, and Baytel smoothly curbed the tempo of their dance, with Della following without awkwardness.

"Thank you for asking me to dance," she said.

Her voice was a medium pitch and pleasant. "It is I who should be thanking you for accepting and getting me away from the crowd."

"I would think you would be pleased with so many ladies more your age awaiting your pleasure."

Baytel looked into her eyes. "Were you awaiting my pleasure, Della?"

Her cheeks glowed further. She missed a dance step and then, regaining her composure, declared, "Oh, no! Please do not think that way of me. I am not like that."

Looking over her shoulder he could see the group watching them intensely, so he guided Della farther away.

"Prince Baytel, I am—"

"Please. Just call me Baytel." He watched her face change with a surprised look. Then she nodded to him curiously.

"Baytel." She giggled. "I am glad to be here with you. You are a wonderful dancer and a gentleman." She paused, drawing a breath. "My intentions are just to have fun. My father said to enjoy the festivities while I can, for it may be the last for a while. Though it is my first."

"My first too. Your father is wise to note that it indeed may be the final such ball. All because of my father and brother and their lust for more power."

He spoke with more of a bite than he had intended, making her hesitate in his arms. "I am sorry, Della."

"It's all right, Baytel."

"I do not agree with my family's policies for the realm. There are other ways of improving our kingdom. Most have nothing to do with the military conquest or war."

Baytel pointed his chin to the northern windows of the ballroom. "Out there are the answers, Della, if only we would offer a hand of friendship to the northlanders. Perhaps we could open a dialogue to forge a peace."

Della opened and closed her mouth in surprise, and then gathering herself, said, "Baytel, you are unusual."

"Unusual? Well I have been called many things, Della, but not that."

Della smiled sweetly. "Some councilors and officers would consider that kind of talk treason."

Baytel nodded, and then grinned mischievously. "Let it be our secret, then. But it is a belief I cling to."

"My father hopes the same thing," said Della.

"Who is your father?"

She smiled shyly. "Lord Lezab."

After his own moment of surprise, Baytel said, "Well, perhaps I should have guessed that, Della. You carry yourself with great poise. I find your father to be a man of dignity and honor. He goes about his tasks for the realm with honesty, sincerity, and integrity. I admire and respect him exceedingly. A great man and I am certain a great father."

Della glowed at his praise. "He is the best of men. And" –she looked about to make sure they were still not being overheard- "my father says that this direction the realm is going has no specific purpose except to fill the vanity of those who crave power. Peace through diplomacy is what he would like the realm to pursue."

With deepening admiration for his dancing partner, Baytel whisked her gracefully across the floor as the music changed again to a sweet flowing melody. She followed exquisitely with never an inelegant step, nor did she stammer in conversation, although she was younger than most at the ball.

"How is it we have never met before?"

"My father does not approve of the officer gatherings, so we stay to ourselves."

"And your mother?"

"She died when I was younger," she replied in a sad quietness.

"Mine too."

The music stopped and the dance floor began to clear. Baytel saw the crowd of ladies walking toward them. Behind Della he could see his father approach. "I must excuse myself, Della. I enjoyed our time together. Perhaps we can dance again later tonight."

She curtsied and said, "Yes, Baytel. If time permits for you, I would be honored."

Baytel bowed formally and, as she swished away, skillfully avoiding the bevy of envious ladies, she walked directly to her father, took his arm and exited the ballroom.

Baytel turned to the king and bowed. "A fine celebration, Father."

"Surrounded by so many beautiful women, how could it not be?" answered the king.

The musicians began again with a waltz. Vokat grasped Baytel's arm and guided him off the dance floor, leading his son through the ballroom as if on parade, passing their subjects as they bowed, some even stopping their dancing to do so.

Baytel felt uncomfortable with the attention but kept his deportment, knowing his father felt it necessary that they were seen together at the ball.

"Have you seen your brother?" asked Vokat.

Baytel scanned the ballroom. "No. I have not looked for him. Would you like me to send the castle guards to physically escort him to attend?"

The corners of Vokat's mouth turned upward at Baytel's remark, probably having heard of the episode in the meadow. "He is no doubt on his way late enough to make a grand entrance."

They stopped at a window and he followed his father's gaze out toward the Narrow, though unseen in the dark. His face seemed oddly melancholy.

"You cannot have remembered your mother, Baytel," said Vokat. "You have her look and demeanor about you. Her poise and quiet intelligence always made me feel inadequate. Pren was the only person who could take me off my guard."

Baytel turned to see his father's face and the edges of its hardness had melted away.

"I may not show it, Baytel, but a day does not pass without my thoughts turning to my Pren. Your face is a constant reminder of her for me."

Baytel nodded slowly, feeling unaccustomed warmth from his father. He stood in silence, unsure what to say.

"Pren was my queen. My subjects loved her and no one shined brighter."

"You have never spoken at length of her before, Father."

"It was just before her death—your birth—that we had our last royal ball," he said. "Tonight is a reminder of easier times."

"Do you believe she would have supported your plans?" Baytel asked.

Vokat stiffened, then inhaled slowly, and sighing, turned toward him and looked into his eyes. His expression of peace had disappeared. He was the King Vokat again.

"Your position as Liaison for the Realm means a great deal to me, Baytel. Your place at my side is important. Your advice differs from the council and I need it from time to time."

"To advise you properly, I must learn how we are looked upon from the outside and how governments are run beyond these borders. Then, I believe I will best be able to serve the realm," replied Baytel.

"You have Hectus and Cyr to assist you with what lies beyond the Southland. No need to risk your life to find it for yourself. The time for adventure and learning about the northlanders will come sooner than you think. Baytel, the timing of our solidarity is at a crucial point. My kingdom must show this from the nobility to the highest ranking officer to the lowliest soldier."

"But Father, the position of Liaison can be given to another until I return," Baytel pleaded.

Vokat raised his hand sharply. "Enough of this!"

Baytel stepped back, knowing nothing he could say would change his father's mind.

Softly, Vokat added, "Enjoy yourself tonight. Put your concerns to rest. Dance and make merry. Tomorrow we will talk of the campaign. Now go find your brother so we can share in the celebration—as a family."

Baytel made his way through the keep, his thoughts turned inward. Cyr was correct, of course. Telling Ravek of his plans will do him no good. He decided to step lightly and just bring him to the ball.

He reached the third level and walked out of the keep, passing through a long hall that ran underneath the battlement and into the south tower where, at the top, Ravek kept his quarters. The tower was dark and cold; candles barely lit the stairway. Small windows inaccessible from the landings at each level offered little ventilation and the corridors smelled of overpowering decay.

Baytel's heart raced, anticipating a confrontation, despite his hopes the meeting would pass without incident. He worried that his behavior would scream out his intentions.

He finally reached Ravek's level. No door or vestibule separated the stairs from his quarters and Baytel walked into a large open chamber. Normally a castle guard was stationed in the chamber to announce visitors, but no sentry was present now. No partitions divided the room except at the back, where a gloomy hall led toward Ravek's sleeping quarters. Heavy animal hides adorned the dark wood floors and crimson brocades lent the walls the appearance of being washed in blood. Torches burned at the top of the stairs and at the back hall, but offered little light.

He called out to his brother as he made his way through the room, stepping over the discarded clothes Ravek earlier paraded at the council. Nearing the back hall he was about to call out again when he heard a faint groan.

He paused and listened. Another groan filtered toward him from down the hallway. He called out again but the only reply came in short gasps. Then a shriek of pain came from the bedroom.

Ravek is in trouble!

Baytel looked around the room and, finding a short sword, grabbed it and ran down the hall. Another shriek held him back. He readied himself outside Ravek's door for whatever was causing his brother to yell out in pain.

He peered in and saw Ravek was on his hands and knees writhing in pain. On his naked back his skin was festered and blistered beyond recognition. Ravek shrieked again and the horror and dismay drew Baytel's breath away as he backed against the cold hallway wall watching the cocoon-like membrane on his brother's back split before his eyes.

Baytel swallowed down his disgust, trying to hold onto some self-control as black wings quivered free from the torn membrane. Ravek's human form had metamorphosed into some type of evil incarnation of the dark magic he wielded.

Sickened at the sight, Baytel edged away from the ugliness that was once his twin. He bolted from the chamber, down the stairs of the tower, not once looking back to see if he was found out. He ran wildly through the corridors until he finally stopped and crumpled against the wall of a vestibule in the ground level of the keep in a massed ball, sweating and overcome with nausea.

Realizing he was still holding the short sword, he threw it down, repulsed by knowing it was Ravek's. Baytel had witnessed the darkest of magic and now he knew for certain that none of his abilities could stop the demonic alteration in his brother. Hearing a sentry approach he straightened himself and hurried off to find Cyr.

They made their way silently through the corridors, ducking in and out of the many halls and vestibules to avoid detection. They secreted past the interior gate and crept along the dark recess of the outer wall and took a rest in the shadows of the livery stable near the main portcullis.

A sentry stood at the portcullis, his attention drawn to the patrol approaching for that night's guard change. Among the six patrolmen was the sentry's relief. A surly older soldier stepped apart from the patrol and the sentry immediately brought his hand to his dagger.

Baytel felt sweat roll down his back. He shook with fear, not from the sudden chill of the night, or the nearness of the patrolmen, but from the hurried packing and harried clandestine exit from his home.

If our plan is to work, I need to depart without being seen. If I am discovered, all will be for naught!

"Change of the guard," he heard the captain of the patrol say.

The sentry and his relief stepped forward each eyeing the other, each waiting for the other to make the first move to fight.

Baytel watched the exchange in annoyance. They were in the way of his escape.

The captain stepped between the two sentries. "You two put a halt to this. You both will have a position in the new army. No need to kill yourselves over it."

Word had already spread of the rebuilding of the army and talk of an elite corps was on everyone's lips. Most soldiers desired selection to this special force, and arguments ensued as to who among them should be selected.

The old soldier spat at the sentry. "Not this one," he said. "He'd just make the force weaker. Prince Ravek wants the best. The stronger ya are, the better."

"Shut up! Change stations, soldier," barked the captain.

Baytel withdrew back into the shadows of the stable. His heart was beating so fast, he could barely keep his wits. He commanded his mind to try to think of something other than his escape but all that came to mind was the unknown ahead of him.

I am leaving everything behind. The convenience of being cared for every day, never needing to worry over when my next meal would be, or wonder if a turn about the castle yard will be safe. The privileges I have taken for granted my entire life, I am abandoning. What will this step bring me in the wild?

He took control of the wayward thoughts and soon his breathing slowed. Calm, he thought of Cyr and what would be in store for him once Baytel was discovered as missing.

I am leaving without conferring with my father or brother. They will blame Cyr! What punishments will they create for my friend? Torture? Will my brother and his powers cause him pain? Death?

"Vokat and Ravek will accuse you of being the instigator of my departure. I should not go," he whispered.

"No. I will tell them of your leaving tomorrow afternoon. This should give you the time to put a fair amount of distance between you and the castle. As for what they will do, I do not know. Learning the news from anyone else, or simply through your prolonged absence, would only add a degree of disloyalty to my already compromised position in the realm. I am your tutor and advisor, so they will know I would have had knowledge."

Baytel shook his head to remove the dark thoughts. "Let's go back. It is a tremendous risk, Cyr. Vokat's favor toward you will be jeopardized, and with Ravek growing in power your life may be in danger. Perhaps I should try to make the liaison office work?"

"You must go, Baytel!" said Cyr. His voice was so stern it surprised Baytel. He had never seen the Tree Faerie this way. "It is no longer safe for you to be here. You have dreams of a better life for you and others here. You must follow this path. Do not worry about me, for there are ways I can lighten the burden of your leaving for myself and your father and brother. As for you, it may be a while before they forgive you for abandoning your appointment and the realm. Nevertheless, we shall see what the events of today will create for tomorrow."

Baytel held his head low. "I feel lost, Cyr. I know I could help my father's realm toward a better future. I just do not know how to get through to him and Ravek; or where to begin."

"Whatever you attempt with them now will surely fail," Cyr replied. "Too many complexities are at work here. You must learn of new ways to change what takes place here. Your desires must be properly channeled for you to cure the ills of your family."

"I do not want to leave you, Cyr. How will I survive without your help?"

Cyr smiled and said, "The northlands are not like here, Baytel. Help will be there when you least expect it."

Baytel heard a commotion outside and they slipped out of the stable into the shadow of the gatehouse. The young sentry had lost his senses, unsheathed his knife and charged the old soldier. The old soldier sidestepped the sentry and met him blade to blade. The patrol backed away, giving them space as their fight moved farther into the ward and away from the post.

Baytel and Cyr slipped past the gatehouse through the portcullis and out into the night beyond the castle. They kept low until they passed outside the reach of the gate lamps and ran toward the tree line to the northeast.

The sky was dark with low clouds and a chilled wind came from the north at a steady pace. At the tree line they looked back at the castle. Satisfied no one had followed or detected them, Baytel stood with his back against a large pine, catching his breath from the run and the excitement of his flight.

"This may be the beginning of many difficulties for you, Cyr."

"I will be fine."

"How will you get back into the castle, Cyr?"

"I will get back undetected," the Tree Faerie said matter-of-factly.

Baytel felt a wave of sadness. This was a parting of their companionship, a union of fifteen years. He looked into the forest and then back to the castle. "Come with me, Cyr. Come with me and escape the danger. We can travel together. You can teach me things as we go."

Cyr smiled at the offer and said, "You have learned enough from me, my friend. The path you embark on is for you alone to take. Let the land teach you and let its magnificence burn into your soul."

"Please, Cyr. Come with me."

Cyr shook his head. "I must stay."

Baytel could not hold back his tears as they rolled down his face. "I will miss you, Cyr. You are a friend, brother, father and mother all in one. It hurts to leave, yet when I think of the lands we spoke of..." He sighed, gazing into the face of his teacher. "This is farewell to you, my Tree Faerie friend."

They embraced. Cyr took a last look at him and said, "Do not travel through the Narrow, for the town of Weyles is unsafe. Keep to the east and climb up and over the East Fork. The eastern land will open to you."

Baytel nodded and embraced his friend again.

Cyr's wings began to beat as quietly as the rustle of leaves and he rose off the ground. Baytel was astonished, for he had never seen Cyr fully fly in all their years together.

"Travel northeast up the slope and you will see a bright light behind you. Keep the light behind your left shoulder through this night. Stop for no one. Keep out of sight and travel swiftly. Farewell, my brave and fine Baytel." And Cyr rose into the night sky and flew toward the castle.

Baytel turned and ran into the forest. When he stopped he was in a clearing far up the incline of the East Fork. He looked over his shoulder and saw the castle of his father dimly lit by tower lanterns. But the top of the north tower shone a light as brilliant as a star, and knew his friend was guiding him to sanctuary.

Cyr stood atop the tower, the light from his body bright in the dark night. Upon his hand sat a red-feathered hawk, the color of blood. Its black piercing eyes darted back and forth, waiting restlessly for a command.

"Go my friend and hurry."

Cyr launched the red hawk into the dark sky and watched the powerful predator fly from the tower with an ear-piercing screech until it disappeared, but with Cyr's faith that it would reach its destination in time.

Chapter 4

"WHERE is he, Cyr?" repeated King Vokat, scowling, barely holding back his anger.

Cyr remained standing before the seated king. "Again, Sire, I am not sure."

Vokat shifted in his throne irritated by Cyr's nonchalant answers and calm demeanor. "My son was missing and you know where he has gone, Cyr! I want answers!"

"I cannot offer what I do not possess," he countered.

Ravek paced behind Cyr with demanding boots upon the stone floor, impatient with Cyr's unemotional responses. He seemed unable to form newer questions, and burst out again in his gruff voice laced with venom, "What direction was Baytel headed, Tree Faerie?"

"Prince Ravek, if I do not know where he is, how would I know what direction he was headed?"

Vokat could see Ravek's anger swelling through his body at Cyr's sarcasm and queried, "We know how long he has been gone. He must have departed late last night; less than a full day."

"And you were the last person known to be in his company. He must have mentioned his destination," asked Ravek, his voice bordering maniacal heights.

Cyr shrugged. "If he did, I do not recall it."

Ravek pivoted away in frustration. His cape whipped about him as he vigorously stalked up and down the king's chamber, stirring the dust into small whirlpools on the stone floor. Cyr followed the cape up to Ravek's shoulders and detected sharp protrusions bulging from beneath his cape, confirming Baytel's report of his mutation. He wondered what Ravek would eventually become.

Thankfully, their estimation of Baytel's departure was off by an entire day. Baytel had a two-day start on their search patrols and the longer they questioned him, the farther Baytel would distance himself from his father's and brother's wrath.

Cyr casually said, "The only inkling to his whereabouts I can share is with regard to the recent discussions we had of life in the north regions. If I were one to wager, I would risk my stake toward that direction."

"So you gamble he is in the north?"

Cyr bowed his head slightly in acknowledgement. "The chances are very good he has departed your realm, Sire."

"Why did he leave?" asked Vokat.

"You already know, Sire. He mentioned that he spoke to you of his desires. I have observed your son for years, Sire. He was suffocating here. He departed to learn of the land and the sects of humanity, to be a wiser prince and to better serve you and your realm."

Vokat leaned back on his throne and exhaled his reply. "His departure will cause a controversy I care not to explore. Our borders are closed, Cyr. At council we planned for the preparation to reestablish our military and formulated the beginnings of a war campaign against the northlanders. My son's actions will be seen as a betrayal to me, and to the realm."

Cyr testified, "Yes, Sire, I spoke to him of that very thing."

"He is a dreamer and useless to the realm until you drove him to this ridiculous dream, Faerie!" Ravek barked. "Now he could destroy our strategies and upset our realm!"

"No, Ravek!" he replied with as much strength as his piping voice could muster. "I did not cause his dismay. Not me. Prince Baytel wants nothing more than to improve this realm, to help build a more peaceful existence for all here. You..." he pointed to Ravek, "and you, Sire, would not listen. So he searches for ways to better understand what the land and humanity can offer and bring this knowledge back to you."

Vokat edged forward. "He would have been useful as Liaison to all our regions of command. He would have had a voice in council, Cyr. What better way to express your sensibilities? Instead, he deserted this post and, moreover, abandoned his duty to me. He is of royal blood, damn him! Not a common serf! The whimsical needs of this dream are nothing compared to the responsibilities of his duties as my son."

Ravek chimed in. "Baytel is weak, Father. Once the northlanders identify who he is, they will break him. Then, I am sure, they will exploit him further."

King Vokat stood and grabbed Ravek, stopping his irritating pacing. "Baytel will not do that. You made it quite clear at the council meeting that his being a Southlander would thwart any welcome in the north. He is intelligent enough not to disclose his origins." He let go of his son and suggested, "Nevertheless, I do not want to take any chances."

Cyr stayed silent while they disputed Baytel's loyalty. It was during this debate that he realized they would stop at nothing to find Baytel and either return him to his rightful place among them, or Ravek would kill him. His fate rested in King Vokat's decision, and he hoped with all his heart that Baytel was far enough up the East Fork where they could not touch him.

Vokat strode right up to Cyr, looming, but Cyr did not so much as blink. The king seemed to recognize his undaunted reaction and quickly stepped away.

Vokat had never physically challenged the Tree Faerie and would be unwilling to do so in the presence of Ravek.

Vokat shook his head. "Cyr, you disappoint me greatly. I have treated you with the highest respect and have given you ample freedom of the realm even though you are its prisoner."

"I am remorseful you are displeased with me, though I have done everything you have asked of me, Sire. All of the lessons you ordered me to teach, I have taught Baytel. Only his own inquisitiveness, intelligence, and desires have driven him to act outside your designs for him."

"Cyr, I want to believe you but I cannot. Therefore, you are confined to your quarters until further notice."

The king gestured to Ravek and he called out to the guards outside the doors. They entered with their heavy boots reverberating in unison off the stone chamber. They stopped a few paces away from the throne and, with quick bows to the king and heir, awaited their orders.

"Guards! Take possession of this Tree Faerie!" Ravek said with the same venom in his voice as before.

They were obviously Ravek's men, as they were quite rough in their grasping of his arms.

Vokat slumped onto his throne as if finally feeling the weight of his son's departure. "And you, Ravek. Find your brother and return him to his home. Use any and all devises and deception you can think of to wring information out of anyone who has seen him."

The sinister smile that played across Ravek's face would have frightened the strongest constitution. "Does that mean I can start with this Tree Faerie, Father?"

"No. Gain your information through your spies, informers and lackeys. Report back as soon as you find anything. I want to know where he is headed. Make sure Cyr is escorted directly to his tower and lock him in his chambers. I will deal with you, Cyr, when it is my pleasure to do so."

Chapter 5

REST was the farthest thing from Baytel's mind. His only concern was extending his distance from the Southland castle. The wind whistled through the dense forest of the East Fork thick with cold. He left the quiet valley behind him that night and hiked up the slope veering northeast until dawn. His leg muscles burned from the strain and the higher he traveled the steeper the incline and the unaccustomed activity and he struggled into the morning glum and exhausted.

The fallen leaves from autumn's passing coated the foothill with a blanket of scarlet and gold that made his passage soundless. The forest was sparsely populated but woodcock, pheasant and scarlet grouse jumped from their unseen cover, causing him to recoil from their sudden pounding feathered flight numerous times.

His mind soon wandered to what his father would do to Cyr. Despite Cyr's confidence that no harm would come to him, Baytel was apprehensive that some form of punishment would be inflicted upon him. How long would Cyr hold up under the devices his father and brother had at their disposal? Would Cyr keep secret his intention of seeking out the Citadel? He reckoned they would call on Cyr and ask him of his whereabouts this evening. Then, having been informed of his certain departure, his father will order patrols to search the countryside. Baytel figured they would search the castle grounds first and then the outer regions surrounding the Southland. Next would be the Narrow. He was counting on their recalling his wish to travel into the northlands. The Narrow will lead them to the town of Weyles. After that, he was not certain where they would look. Eventually they will be inspired to search the East and West Forks. This encouraged him to pick up the speed of his climb.

He rested when he could no longer climb and slept in short intervals for the day was pleasant enough to not set a camp. When night passed beneath his feet and another morning arrived it brought cold blustering winds. At the height of afternoon snow broke from the clouds. The flakes fell heavy and accumulated quickly hampering his pace and footholds became difficult to grip as the leafy ground became slick and treacherous.

The higher he hiked the deeper the snow became and quite rapidly the snow was well over his shins. His progress was slowed further as the young foothill forest was congested with an abundance of poplar, beech, and maple trees with only a few mature pines, leaving more open sky to drop snow in his way as opposed to mature forest with a thick canopy.

At twilight the wind changed and blew out of the north with such ferocity he stopped, wet, tired and cold, and found relatively flat ground where he could pitch his tent. Crawling in, he collapsed into exhaustion and sound asleep. At dawn he woke refreshed and found the same cloud cover, but no snow. He ate a small bite of biscuits and cheese and broke camp and commenced his upward hike.

From morning to dusk each day, he kept a steady pace and something occurred to him as time went calmly by. He had lost most of his apprehensions and felt free of the confines and obligations of the realm and his kinship, and he it made him feel more confident with his decision to leave his home and as the days passed without alarm, the climbing became routine. He took in the sights of the high range of lands he would never otherwise have seen. Baytel felt the carefree peacefulness of solitude, something he had never truly experienced in the imperious oversight of the Southland.

On the eighth day up the East Fork, his buoyant confidence turned to concern as he had discovered his food supply had shockingly diminished. He felt the fool for not rationing his foodstuff from the beginning and upon further assessment of his provisions, he figured what remained would last, at best, another ten days.

The following day was met with extreme cold air. It had snowed overnight and he was high-stepping the incline wishing for snowshoes and chastising himself again for his hurried departure. Mid-day, Baytel reached the boundary of the timberline. Cloaking himself in all his clothing he collected as much firewood as he could carry in his pack, knowing he would find none in the barren highlands near the peak.

The terrain above the timberline was bleak and more rugged than below. Leaving the protective cover of the trees he met a terrain of ice and rock tundra that had been etched by the unceasing winds and mountain storms through the ages. A few uprooted trees lay about, overpowered by the weather, the bark ripped off their trunks that were bleached white and smooth by the sun and ice particles carried by the constant wind. Massive boulders were scattered about the barren highlands, upheaved long ago by the forces of the land, which he gladly used as brief shelter from the incessant ice winds and to rest his weary legs. The ground beneath the snow and ice was a loose crag stone and jagged-edged rocks threatened his shins at every step. So often Baytel encountered thin layers of ice covering narrow crevices that offered the promise of a broken leg if he stepped too carelessly.

In the distance along a far ridge he could see mountain goats and bighorned sheep balancing on the sides of the sheer cliffs withstanding the height and brutal weather, sentries of the mountain range as steady as men would be on flat meadows. He thought to himself, witnessing the magnificent feats of the animals, that only the wild untamed creatures with stalwart hearts could survive in this land.

He forged on, day and night, up the desolate dreary slope ever mindful of the low rations and the fatigue that was setting its hooks. Occasionally he came across a wide outcrop of rock or sheer that he had to scale up to reach the next level of the heights and did so with the hope he would see the summit, but found that the peak was nowhere in sight. Reflecting back on the night he departed from the castle full of excitement and promise, he realized how unprepared he was for the East Fork far exceeded what he had anticipated.

Past the midnight hour, fourteen days out from his home, he finally reached the summit of East Fork. He was at an elevation so high he was inside the snow clouds. The wind had died and the snow fell soft and light as he stood atop the peak peering into the darkness. Baytel thought he should be more elated at the prospect of reaching such a height, but his fatigue was complete and he barely remembered setting camp and did not recall the moment he fell asleep.

Chapter 6

VOKAT could barely see past his outstretched arm. He stood with Hectus on the outdoor platform on top of his tower oblivious to the swirling, angry snow. Ice had formed on his shoulder length hair and the wind bit at his face, leaving it tender and inflamed. Snow had fallen continuously for days, restricting the activities of realm to inside the respective fortress and courtyards.

The incessant drone of Hectus's voice irritated him more than the contents of the subject matter, but he listened, impatiently, to the chancellor's report. "We have enough food and firewood to survive the winter as well as Azkar Rol and Pithe," said Hectus, his nervous fidgeting always a constant.

Vokat changed his mind; it was the continual movement of Hectus's fretful behavior that was the cause of his impatience.

Hectus kept on speaking, entirely absorbed in his report and not noticing Vokat's irritability. "Needless to say, when spring returns, we will need to stock our cellars with more extra supplies than usual for more will be necessary to building and sustain the military."

"What of the Narrow?" Vokat asked, of the only access to the northlands where, through the gap between the East and West Fork the border city of Weyles rested, turning his mind to the only subject that mattered to him: finding Baytel.

Hectus must have picked up on his mood and said with an unnaturally calm voice, "The Narrow was nearly impassable at my last report. The final shipment of supplies from Weyles had to turn back due to the accumulation of snow."

Vokat turned hearing the platform door crash against the wall. Prince Ravek stomped onto the platform and paced angrily before him.

"Well?" Vokat asked, entirely impatient with his son's antics. Everything about Ravek seemed to irritate him since Baytel left.

"We could not find him!" growled Ravek. "The snow covered too much of the valley. I have now searched throughout the Southland, all the Fork Mountains, and through the Narrow and in the town of Weyles. No one has seen him."

"What about Tridling Del and the outlands?" asked Hectus pointing to the far-off town well into the northlands.

Ravek shook his head. "No way Baytel could have got that far. If he had tried for that far off town, he would not have made it and for all we know, he is dead under a blanket of snow!"

"And is the Narrow traversable?" asked Hectus.

"Impassable. We are here for the winter," said Ravek.

Vokat could see the prince's exhaustion. He had done everything in his power to find his brother, but still, Vokat's anger remained. The king sensed there was something more to Baytel's departure, but could not grasp it. He felt off-balanced as if something else were being orchestrated—a ruse or conspiracy from forces unknown. It deposed his mind to distraction.

"Come spring, Ravek, you search the lands and bring him back. If he is dead, then bring me his bones. Do whatever it takes. I will not have the northlanders know I have a son who has abandoned me. Find him at all costs. Am I clear?"

"Yes, Father," said Ravek.

Vokat dismissed them and returned to his quarters. He entered his private library outside his sleeping quarters and stood before the painted portrait of Pren, still hanging seventeen years after her death. He regarded her face; the artist's brushstrokes brought out her beauty so vividly, it was as though she still lived within the canvas.

Pren's mysterious and unknown origins fascinated him. Her features were so delicate, so soft—her violet eyes slanting slightly upward, almost like those of the Tree Faeries, had always caused him pause. Her white skin, slender and graceful body, lovely blond hair and pointed ears were perfect in every way. Illuminated by the candlelight in his chambers the portrait seemed to pulse as if it breathed. He reached out to it, but stopped before his fingers could touch the canvas.

"Baytel's likeness is so much like yours, Pren," he whispered, longingly. "Your keen looks were always difficult to read. I wonder, my dear, did Baytel inherit more than your looks? Did he acquire your magical talents as well?"

Vokat looked away, he sighed. "Where are you, Baytel?"

Chapter 7

BITTER winds whipped across the summit plains, their wicked song, along with his hunger pangs, filling Baytel with foreboding. He built a small fire behind a large outcrop of rock for warmth and ate a meal of stale biscuits and dry cheese. He assessed his supplies: foods to last perhaps two to three days, and wood for one more fire. *But then what?*

From the vantage point atop the East Fork, he was able to survey the entire Fork Mountain Range. Far to the south was a barricade of ranges called the Forbidden Boundary, an unexplored region of mountains sweeping in procession formation like colossal rock soldiers, one after the other; uninhabited and impossible to traverse.

As legend had it, ages before, the only barrier blocking the lands beyond the Forbidden Boundary was the great mountain Azkar Rol. When the mighty earthquakes rolled across the lands they collided against the great mountain from the east and west. Yet Azkar Rol did not move, standing strong-willed against the unrelenting pressures until the lands on each side succumbed to its power and pushed upward, forming three new ranges. This was the birth of the Fork Mountain Range. As it was then, so it was now that he observed in the distance Azkar Rol, Fire Mountain, belching flame and molten rock from its inner core, its power supreme.

His thoughts went to the Southland castle and wondered: Had they sent out search troops to this region? Could the search parties have attempted the same climb up the East Fork? No. Even if they did, surely the snow had covered any evidence of my passage by now.

Baytel was jarred out of his thoughts by a high-pitched screech. Overhead, flying upon the swirling winds was an enormous red hawk. He watched it coast effortlessly circling upon the air current, turning its head back and forth scanning the range. Then, with a tilt of its wings, the red hawk banked to the east diving down the slope and out of sight. It was a magnificent maneuver and all he could do was look upon the memory of the flight wishing the red hawk could have carried him upon its back.

With too much physical exertion with too little to eat, sleeping had no revitalizing qualities to him so he broke camp and started down the opposite side of the East Fork, anticipating a faster, less taxing trek.

With an inviting sky, clear vision and taking no rest, Baytel traveled farther the first day of his descent than he had in the last five up. The east was open to view as far as his eyes could see, but only the blanket of snow was visible, peppered with the greenery of the tall pine trees that dotted the lower landscape from his height.

Night came quickly, which also reminded his stomach of the time, and he set up camp, lit his last fire and ate a rationed meal. Perusing the star-filled sky, Baytel felt a sense of calm settled upon him and clearer thoughts of home came unbidden, not of longings for its comforts, but of his father and brother and the hope the scorn they might feel toward him would subside in time. He felt a compulsion to return and make things right with them as every so often the guilt of leaving them filtered into his mind. But he always rejected the thoughts for nothing would change unless he brought back what he will learn of the northlands and the sects of humanity; of their governments, traditions, and customs. *Or I will never be able to help govern my father's realm.*

The night was filled with dreams of solitude and quiet. No restless song in the wind penetrated the serenity of sleep. The quiet was so profound he felt it could go on forever—but a spark of awareness lit in his slumber, a warning that entered his subconscious, and he woke from his dream to soundlessness.

He sat up and immediately his head rubbed against the sagging interior of the tent. He pushed at it but found it heavier than expected. Moving to the flap, his opened it and snow fell inward at an alarming rate, and he realized he was buried. Panicking, Baytel grabbed his little remaining food, clothes, and pack and began digging through the drift. He burrowed like a badger, transferring the snow before him to the rear of his upward dig. Finally, his head popped out of the snow tomb meeting the blinding light of the sun that reflected off the snow. Breathless and unnerved, Baytel propelled himself out of the tunnel and, forgetting the slope, rolled downward until he thankfully slid into an outcrop of rock.

Shaken, nearly blinded by the brilliant whiteness, he secured his clothing and tried to get a bearing east. The sun seemed to be everywhere and he could distinguish nothing. The angry wind scratched his face with ice particles. No matter where he placed his hands and arms for protection, the ice found an opening. Calming himself and recalling the last vista of the clear day before, he sensed the bottom was within two or three days of his position. With no wood for a fire, he put on his remaining clothes and ate the rest of his store and advanced down the East Fork.

He stumbled and slid more than hiked, heedless of the rocks and crags in his path. His eyes stung from sun blindness, his legs and ankles ached from twisting them on the uneven terrain beneath the snow. He longed to reach the base of the range and the happiness of seeing a homestead farm or hoping a town was nearby.

The wind freshened stronger; it mercilessly scourged him at every step, penetrating his clothes and chilling him to the bone. The menacing drifts shrouded the land from sight and touch. More than once he lost his footing and plunged down a wide crevasse, uncertain when he would meet ground, but with extreme effort, was always able to climb out of the breach and continue. There was no sense in halting, for there was no shelter or food at hand; only the desolate mountain range and the demon wind.

He welcomed the night like a lost friend as his sight returned. He knew it could be temporary but he was thankful as he scanned the twilight of the mountain to map out his descent.

Morning brought the return of the blinding sun and his descent with useless eyes. Weak from hunger and exhaustion by what seemed to be midday, he found refuge against another outcrop of rock. He felt his way around a huge protrusion to retreat from the wind when the ground disappeared beneath his feet and he tumbled helplessly down; body flailing in the open air. He bounced off the side of what he assumed was a ravine; the ice and rock cut across his chest and ribs. He came to a crashing halt as the pain of collision knocked the breath from him.

He lay on there, catching his breath, not wanting to move or discover more injuries from other places upon his body. Warmth rolled down his forehead and he touched the liquid. It was thick and he knew without seeing it that he was bleeding. He dared moving onto his hands and knees; the pain throbbed in his head and chest. He propped himself on his knees and with the aid of the wall of rock beside him got to his feet.

Balancing against the wall, he edged along its interior and felt the ground sloped at a lesser rate of descent than above. Even through his pain, he was grateful as the chasm he had absently discovered gave him shelter from the biting wind. Uncertain of the direction the sanctuary might lead, nor caring so long as the relief from the storm continued, he moved with the decline.

By touch, he traversed along the jagged chasm interior, keeping one hand brushing against the interior walls and the other in front to identify any barrier before him. Through the day and what seemed like night, as his eyesight had not returned as before, he staggered on. At times, he took a fall over unseen rock or slid across a plain of ice. Occasionally, he would rest where he fell sleeping in short intervals only to be awakened by his pains.

Cut and bleeding, sightless, hungry and teetering on total exhaustion, he emerged from the protective chasm only to return to the unyielding brightness and wind.

Another night came bringing blistering cold. Delirious with fatigue and unsure of where he was, what he was doing, or where he was going, he felt he was walking in a nightmare with a lone companion—the howl of the storm.

Then he stopped as he thought something was materialized before him. Then there was Cyr, standing in front of him in the snow. *Am I dreaming?*

"Cyr!" He reached out to his friend hovering in his subconscious. The Tree Faerie quickly dissolved. Baytel, shaking his head to unfasten the mirage, re-focused his mind back on his waking nightmare. He increased his pace with a reckless abandon. Nearly at a run, he plowed into the teeth of the storm, challenging its fury. Mustering the little strength remaining, feeling each step could be his last, he pushed his aching legs to move. But with muscles numb, his lungs burned ready to burst and gasping for breath, he began to falter. He dropped to his knees and crawled forward, gulping air as if it were his last breath. Then he could go no farther and Baytel collapsed.

The sounds of the storm faded. He could barely feel the cold anymore. The plush snow was comforting and he felt he could finally rest.

"No. Not this way!"

Baytel shook himself awake. To sleep was to give up and perish. Finding strength he did not know he had, he stood erect and resumed his trek through the maddening storm. Though laboring for air he screamed his anguish at the wind. Then his knees buckled and he fell into unconsciousness.

He stole through the deep crypt beneath the castle; the only sound was his footsteps, hollow off the dim, confining walls. The stale air smelled of rotted flesh that permeated the darkened maze. He convulsed from the stench, but did not halt his downward trudge, the urgency of which was a mystery to him.

Finally he reached the antechamber. Peering through the dim light he saw two grotesque beasts, evil seeds of unknown origin, huddled over a table. The larger one moved to one side revealing a scene so horrible, he gasped.

Strapped to the table banded about his arms and legs, was Cyr, with his eyes open but fixed on nothing. His gaping mouth emitted no sound. Dead.

Rage swept him into the chamber, sword in hand, and leaped at the monsters. Their swords rang out in the antechamber, bringing other demon servants forward. He was thrown down, kicked and beaten. They grabbed him. He struggled to free himself but was wrestled to the stone floor and was bound and gagged.

The evil demons shouted, "Kill him!"

They dragged him to another table and chanted, "Death to the traitor! Death! Death! Death! Death!"

Ice pelted his face, jarring him back to consciousness and relief swept over him, as he realized it was just a nightmare. Then he heard a prolonged howl in the distance as a bona fide nightmare was approaching.

Zekawolves!

He struggled to his knees barely finding the strength to move. Crawling forward until he found a purchase of rock he hauled himself to his feet.

The howling drew near. He turned to see if the howl was coming from behind, but he lost his balance and sagged across the boulder and fell. He tried to rise but he had no strength. As he lay in the pillow-like snow, its comfort lured him once more and all went blank.

37

Chapter 8

BAYTEL sensed that he was floating outside his body, detached and free from any sensations save the dream-like state. In the unearthly atmosphere, he peered through a fog upon his prostrate body resting on a split log bed. His face was bruised and swollen and a bandage was wrapped around his head.

Then a flash cut through the fog and the curious sensation vanished, replaced by an unyielding pain that bombarded every muscle and joint in his body. Excruciating coldness raced across his skin and he knew he was with fever. His entire being wanted to race toward a return to the floating dream and never to wake again, for the reality of the pain was overwhelming. Instead, from time to time, he fell into unconsciousness only to wake with pain and panic over having to live the rest of his life in this agonizing state.

Baytel, through the many wakenings, sensed the passage of time and felt the spark of warmth penetrate the frigidity of his body. A hand slipped behind his head and lifted it until his lips met a hot cup that was tipped and a dense liquid was passed through. The thick liquid lay in his mouth; its sweet taste and scent evoked a composed air. He gulped the brew down and felt it flow outward from his stomach, searching into the depths of his body, infiltrating his blood, washing over the pain and carrying the radiating warmth of tranquility.

His many attempts to rise caused him to fade in and out of consciousness. When awake, he found he was still without sight, and he despaired at the prospect of a life without sight. Awareness was fleeting. He was unable to grasp what was real and what was illusory. At times he could hear the distant shriek of a hawk and the lonely howl of a wolf that brought his mind back to the mountain and the tribulations of the trek. The inescapable nightmare of recurring pain and fatigue tormented him.

More time passed. The crackle of a fire and the warmth of his surroundings drew him into the present. He was hesitant to open his eyes, anticipating darkness. Unable to move without enormous pain shooting through his body, sightless and afraid, he cursed at his vulnerability and helplessness as if he were a newborn. Yet, there was solace to it all; someone was caring for him. But who was it? Where was he?

Another lift of his head and another dram of the bolus rushed down his throat. It was unwanted for he knew from experience the drink would press him back toward oblivious sleep. The prospect of not being able to escape from that unwelcome place of dreams was distressing. His head was brought to rest on the pillow and no sooner than it touched its softness, he plunged into deep sleep.

Darkness enveloped him at every turn. Smoke and fire had scorched the corridor black, its heated ashen air singeing his face. Creatures in the shadows grabbed him and dragged him toward a pit of fire where a beast awaited. The dark beast taunted him; his outstretched arms promised doom.

Sweating, gasping for air in the heated chamber, he struggled to escape, but was held tight. The closer he was dragged to the pit, the hotter and fouler the air became.

Then he was before the beast. Fire was all about him as they held him over the pit. Flames licked at his body burning his skin. He looked into the face of the beast and death returned his gaze. The beast's scaled skin was like that of the charred remains of the dead; its gaping mouth revealed horrific dagger-sharp teeth and its breath was fire itself.

The beast grabbed one of his arms. He cried out in pain as his skin blistered from the creature's fiery touch. His attempts to break free only caused the beast to tighten his grip, its clawed fingers biting into his flesh.

The beast clutched his other arm, drawing him close toward his gruesome face. Fire emitted from the beast's mouth, scorching his face. Suffocating flames engulfed him as he struggled to breathe. Then, through the flames he recognized the eyes of death that held him! Ravek!

Baytel awoke gasping for air. He tried to rise, but was pushed back into his bed and securely lashed. He lay still as exhaustion set in. He felt uncomfortably slick with sweat and his immobility was a private agony as the nightmare had turned to reality. His brother had finally found him and he mourned for himself that his end was near.

A cold cloth was laid upon his forehead and from this small gesture he found a glimmer of hope. Then a voice spoke softly in his ear. "You are safe from harm and need rest. Do not move. All is well."

The voice sounded as if coming from the depths of serenity and it drew him back from the abyss of the world of nightmare and back onto the comfort of his bed and the care of his keeper.

"Sleep," the soothing voice said. "Be at peace. All will be well when you wake."

The darkness returned except it was one of quiet, peaceful slumber.

Consciousness slowly returned and his first physical senses were of soft cotton blankets smelling of fresh outdoor air. He opened his eyes and to his joy saw rafters on a ceiling instead of darkness. A brief scan showed he was lying on a feather bed inside a roomy cabin constructed of stone and wood.

The pain of the past days had profoundly diminished and his internal time-piece discerned he had slept for a long period of time. He propped up on an elbow to look about the cabin and was met with vertigo that sent his head to spin. He slowly rested back on his pillow to quell the tempest.

He reviewed his journey that had brought him to this strange cabin. The long climb up the East Fork and blind trek down came flooding back to his memory in rapid procession. The cold, hungry, blind and painful recollection ended with the chilling howl of zekawolves. But here he was alive and warm, lying in comfortable surroundings.

The smells of food stirred his stomach to growl. Recalling the last meal he had taken, the day he woke after being buried beneath the snow...that paltry meal of old cheese and stale biscuits seemed like an eternity past. Gingerly he turned his head and focused on the far corner of the room, where small flames stoked the base of cooking pots on the stovetop that emitted the delicious smells.

A door opened and closed somewhere in the cabin; he attempted rising but again failed miserably. Twisting his head in the direction of the sound he was met by two silver eyes staring back at him across the room. His heart skipped a beat as he stared into the face of the largest zekawolf he had ever seen.

The zekawolf's coat was black as night with a silver stripe down his back from head to tail, his paws were wide as a large man's hands. The moment passed slowly as the animal seemed to be assessing whether he stared at a friend or a foe.

Having decided, the zekawolf trotted toward Baytel; the nails on its paws tapping lightly upon the wood floor. When it reached his bed it nuzzled its head into the crook of his arm. The wolf's eyes turned trustingly toward him as if saying hello and brought a smile to Baytel's face. It backed away and jumped up on the edge of the bed, towering over him, wagging its tail.

"Get down, Thor!"

The strong voice came from outside the room and then a man followed the voice in. "Good evening, Baytel. I see you have made acquaintances with Thor."

Baytel stared back warily. The stranger was tall, dressed in brown pants, green shirt and a leather tunic. Having discarded a green cloak across a bench by the door, he approached, carrying a stool, and sat at the foot of the bed. The tall man carried himself like a proud warrior would. His hair was long and brownish-blond, eyes steel-blue; with an ageless quality about them, and looked as if they could command a stampede of horses to halt with a glance.

Baytel tried to speak and found he had no voice. His attempt at rising off the pillow again sent his vision whirling. Lying back down to stop the room from spinning, he realized the man had spoken his name.

As if the man read his mind, he said, "Yes, Baytel. I know who you are and where you came from."

"How...?" was all he could squeak.

The man smiled, relieving Baytel's apprehension. He braved another attempt to speak and said, "Where am I?"

"You are where few have been and where none can find, save by accident."

The more he observed the man the more he thought he carried himself not so much as a warrior, but more like a nobleman, or even a king.

"I do not underst—" his throat closed upon his words.

"Do not talk, Baytel. All explanations and understandings will come in time. Know that you are safe and will live. We found you eight days ago at the edge of the pinewoods at the base of the East Fork. Your journey over the mountain range was very courageous and successful, but you were near death."

I made it down! I am out of the Fork Mountains! Out of the Southland!

The man continued. "I have kept you alive with an herbal drink until you awakened. Luckily you did, but you are still weak and need nourishment. Since you are conscious, broth and small amounts of root stew will bring your strength back. Then we will get to your questions." He stood, and then added, "I am called Calidor."

Baytel's mind raced as he recalled memories of a legendary great warrior named Calidor. Many tales were told of his heroic deeds and bravery. Yet, this could not be the same man. Those tales date back hundreds of years.

Over the East Fork and out of the Southland, eight days safe!

In his joy, Baytel started to rise. Pain shot through his body as the room jostled before him, once again sending him back to his pillow.

"Easy now, Baytel, try not to disturb yourself. It will only cause you harm. Rest to heal is the course to take," said Calidor returning with a tray of food. "If you follow what I say you will soon be on your feet."

Calidor firmly propped him up against the headboard and went about carefully serving him spoonfuls of broth. This gave him the opportunity to view the man closely. He had a familiar look to him, as if he had seen him before, but no occasion came to mind. How could it, being sequestered by the Fork Mountains his entire life?

The man's face was bright with intelligence. The small crow's feet at the corners of his eyes showed him to be a middle-aged man, though his eyes gave evidence of someone who has experienced abundance of life. Even seated on the squat stool, the figure of the man named Calidor was imposing.

His spooning was nonstop and the warm broth went down gratefully, mouthful after mouthful, and all he could manage was to dutifully swallow. The flavor of the herbal drink lingered in his mouth as the spoonfuls finally stopped. His eyelids became heavy and he felt his head being lowered upon his pillow once more. A thought occurred before he surrendered to sleep, still puzzled over how the man called him by name, he fell off into forgetfulness.

Baytel woke from a restful sleep and propped up with no difficulty or dizziness. Resting against the headboard he was able to look out the window. The cabin must be situated on a rise as his eastern view of the outdoors showed an undulating terrain covered with snow rolling on until meeting a sparse population of trees that ended far away against a span of mountains. He looked about the immediate grounds, seeing a stable and holding yard, and fields that spread around the cabin until he lost them from view.

A crimson sky above the snow-covered horizon presaged the morning sun. Shafts of light reached the vast lands and began moving across the plain as the sun rose. The silence and tranquility of the moment felt like perfection and he sensed that all was in its proper place and the new day in this strange but secure cabin would be a means toward his desires and dreams.

A silhouette on horseback appeared as a mirage between the sunlight and radiating white of the snow. Mesmerized by the figure lit from behind, Baytel then saw it was a magnificent black stallion he rode. As this vision neared he recognized Calidor and the zekawolf, Thor, running beside him. He must have gone to hunt for strapped across the back of the stallion was a mountain stag whose girth was only slightly smaller than the stallion carrying it.

An odd trio to be seen together. Had he not been introduced to the wild wolf, he would have taken them as dangerous and terrifying; unapproachable and to be avoided at all costs. He wondered if Calidor practiced a form of mysticism to control the animals.

Arriving at the cabin yard, Calidor jumped off his horse with the vigor of a young man and removed the strapped carcass, allowing it to fall to the ground. He loosed the stallion in the holding yard beside the stable. Baytel leaned forward to see across the angle and found it was built into the side of a rock hill.

A few yards away from the stable stood a deer pole; two vertical logs secured in the ground supporting a horizontal pole across the top fastened by 'v' shaped joints to the vertical risers and wound in place by rope. In the center of the crossbar, about ten feet off the ground hung a leather harness attached to a rope and pulley.

Calidor dragged the stag to the deer pole and lifted the large carcass off the ground, fastening the stag's antlers to the harness. Then he heaved on the rope, hoisting the carcass off the ground, and secured the rope to a spike on the pole. The stag hung, swaying in the wind. Calidor was a large man, though not with the bulky build and muscle of a Ravek, and displayed surprising strength. His physique was most likely encased with tight muscle and sinew, somewhat like Baytel's own.

"Good morning, Baytel," the hunter said, entering the cabin. "Beautiful sunrise."

"Good morning," replied Baytel. "Very serene."

Calidor dropped his cloak on the bench and stomped about the cabin, replacing his bow and arrows in a weapons cabinet against the wall beside the door. "Do not let this passive morning delude you to distraction. A storm is headed our way; a nor'easter from the smell on the breeze. Once it hits us, it will blanket us for the season."

"Blanket us in?"

Calidor pointed out the window at the hanging game. "That stag will put our stock to full capacity. Our foodstuffs should last through the next few months."

"A few months? I do not have a few months. My travels take me—"

"Get away from there, Thor," Calidor yelled at the zekawolf, who was on his hind legs licking at the stag.

Baytel was about to complete his protestation when he realized his manners were not quite proper. How impolitic to question the man without so much as offering his thanks for all he had done for him.

"I do not know where to begin, sir. You saved my life and have cared for me in a most kindly fashion. You have helped me tremendously and I want to thank you. I am sincerely grateful and I am in your debt."

Calidor waved a hand at him nonchalantly. "There shall be no talk of debts here, Baytel. I merely saved you to tell you what a fool you were to travel the mountain range so late in the season; especially being as ill-equipped as you were."

"It was my time to leave, so I did," the prince said with more bite in his voice than he meant to express and immediately regretted the outburst. "Well, the reason for my hasty departure does not matter. I am here and alive thanks to you."

A quiet moment fell between them. He studied the man closer and again felt a familiarity but was still at a loss where it came from. Calidor left the room for a moment and returned carrying a platter with steaming bowls of stew, a loaf of dark bread and tea. Seeing the food brought forgotten hunger pains. Calidor pulled an end table to the bed with his foot and set both bowls down. He passed out the utensils and they ate without talking. It was delicious but there was not enough to fill Baytel.

Before he could ask for more, Calidor said, "Your body must adjust to solid food again. Small portions will sustain you for now, Baytel. And these root vegetables are just as filling as the venison hanging outside."

Again he asked, "Calidor, how is it you know my name?"

As soon as he asked he felt the air leave the cabin. Calidor seemed to be mulling over a thought. His eyes became hard, searching Baytel's face with an intensity that made him uneasy. Sweat sheened Baytel's brow and upper lip and he wiped it away with his napkin, regretting asking the ill-timed question. If this man was the same as that named in legends, he surely had powers beyond Baytel's comprehension.

Calidor began to clear the bowls away and while he stacked them in the basin, with his back to Baytel, he ended the silence that seemed to have lasted an eternity. "I know more about you than you can imagine, Baytel. I know you are Vokat's son. I know you escaped your home for a good reason. Most of what I know has come to me from discrete sources, which at this time shall remain nameless. However, I will tell you that most of my familiarity with you is partly due to your hysterics while unconscious. You talked in your sleep, Baytel."

"My sleep?"

"Yes. You have been in my care for nine days, Baytel. You have been delirious with fever and pain, unconscious the entire time. You were babbling and incoherent, but at times quite clear. So there you have it."

Smiling at the simple explanation, though clearly hearing the comment about *discrete sources* in his statement, Baytel knew there was more to it than Calidor was saying. Nine days of rambling on about himself without censure to a complete stranger; so much for being anonymous. "Am I to be relieved at the prospect that I am safe with you knowing so much about me?"

Calidor shrugged. "That is entirely your decision."

Baytel had not felt threatened by the man at all and sensed no danger from him whatsoever. But who was he?

"Calidor, are you the one that legends speak of?"

"You have many questions, Baytel, and you are wanting information that, at the moment, I choose to not convey. Nevertheless, as we continue our association with one another, eventually your questions will be answered in due time and, entirely at my leisure. For now, your stay here will be for some duration. Winter has come and will last for a few months."

Baytel mumbled an objection and was about to continue with his protest when he was stayed to silence by Calidor's cold stare.

"Take heed, boy. I did not pull you from the clutches of death to push you back into its grasp."

He could not disagree with this wisdom, especially when he recalled the nightmares of the trek, but was perturbed at the evasion of his question. Resigned not to ask anything more about the subject, he asked, "Sir, where is here?"

This time Calidor smiled. "An excellent query to begin our finial alliance. You are in my home and everything as far as you can see around it is my land."

"I have never been outside of the Fork Mountains and am unfamiliar with this region. What is that distant mountain range to the east?"

"That is only a gateway mountain range that leads to the Treldor region, the lands far to the northeast. One must know how to survive the wild to travel in such a place as Treldor. As far as I know, that land beyond that small range and into Treldor is uninhabited."

Treldor Reach; another territory of the land he knew nothing about. He turned from the window only to see Calidor looking intently at him. He was still uncomfortable under his scrutiny.

"Baytel, I have surmised by your appearance and the condition I found you in that you are unaccustomed to travel and lack most of the necessary skills for self-preservation and survival out in the wild."

Baytel nodded respectfully, looking down on his body as evidence of the truth of this statement. What a sight he was; thin, cut, and bruised from head to toe, and weak beyond measure.

"Well then, I feel obliged to improve your lot. While you are here I will strengthen your body and advance your mind. Heed what I say. Watch what I do and learn from it all. The knowledge you gain under my auspices will best prepare you for what is to come when you leave."

"I was on my way to the Citadel," he said, hoping it would impress him.

Calidor was unmoved by his declaration. He stood up, grabbed his cloak and walked to the door. "Then you will need all that I teach you. Your first lesson begins after you dress." Calidor pointed to the sideboard where a pile of clothes lay ready for him. "I have some preparations to complete. Come to the storage house after you dress."

An avalanche of questions raced across his mind, tumbling over one another like debris being swept within a landslide, loosening numerous queries until his head ached. Calidor's pledge to prepare him for what was to come made him wonder if the man already knew of his desires to attend the Citadel? He probably knew everything else about his life, having listened to his delirious ramblings for nine days and nights. He is a deliberate man and careful with what he says, as if concealing some fact that would be a revelation, but choosing not to draw attention to it. An exacting man and not one to cross, especially if he coveted being *prepared;* whatever that meant. Truthfully, being instructed by someone of Calidor's caliber was enticing in and of itself, and the more he contemplated it, the prospect became most desirable.

Resolved to move forward as if Calidor knew everything about him he found there was no use hiding anything from the man, especially being holed up through the months of winter together.

He stood and walked into a large room with a ceiling vaulting high and supported by chiseled wood rafters. A fire hearth built of multiple colors of stone climbed the west wall to the height of the vault. The kitchen was on the north side and his room was on the east. All about the walls of the lodge hung animal hides, old hunting equipment and the tools of a farmer—hoes, sickles, shovels, a harness for a plow horse and numerous picks and axes.

Decorative forged silver plaques depicting scenes of men and places hung at the sides of the hearth. They appeared to be in a particular order. Comfortable furniture was arranged before the fireplace where a blaze roared. His study of the cabin had not uncovered anything about his strange host save for his partiality with hunting and farming.

He turned back to his bedroom and the sideboard. The clothes were perfectly folded on top of the wood and leather sideboard, as was a towel beside a wash-basin. He washed, feeling good to throw water on his face, and slowly dressed. The clothes were a comfortable fit—brown pants, stockings, shirt, green wool sweater, soft leather tunic vest with multiple pockets, heavy leather mountain boots and a green hooded cloak like the one Calidor wore, which drooped past his knees but was incredibly light to wear.

The dressing exhausted him and he returned to his bed to rest as his head again began to spin. He laid back down to rest his head and before he knew what happened, he had settled into a warm sleep.

Chapter 9

THE afternoon sky was cerulean, its depth of color equal to the brightest sapphire. The sunlight reflected off the snow with less ferocity and more warmth than that of the demon storm of the highlands. The air was crisp with winter's bite. Baytel breathed deeply the cold air and it replenished his spirit with pleasant freshness.

He glanced back at the cabin and nodded in appreciation of Calidor's confidence in stating no one could find this cabin except by accident. It stood alone in the high plains and blended perfectly with the surrounding terrain, for the cabin, stable and storage room were excavated into the stone of a rising mound, built with the natural tundra of the surrounding land. The skilled hands to create so perfect a setting were extraordinary. Both the stable and storage room looked the same—perfectly fitted stones that looked as though they had been etched by time. Windows and doors were built low to the ground and inset to avoid reflection and discovery. Only the chimney stood above the rock mound but concealed enough to go unnoticed by a passerby. So naturally hidden were the structures that from fifty paces away the untrained eye would not be able to distinguish a dwelling.

Calidor stood before the storage house at a raised marble slab where cleaver and carving knives rested. He waved Baytel forward but his pace was slow as he was still weak and hurt.

Without greeting or elaboration, Calidor said, "Your first lesson is how to skin a stag, tan its hide, butcher, smoke, salt and store its meat. Since you are still too weak to be of any use, watch and learn."

First he removed the stag's hide by peeling it off the carcass as easily as removing a garment. He then stretched the hide onto an octagonal board until it was taut. With a sharp, thin knife he scraped the excess fat that lined the inner layer and set it to rest in the sunlight. Then the butchering of the stag began with him cutting the major parts off piece by piece while the animal hung from the pole. He laid them out on the flat stone and, identifying each, either boned, left whole or filleted the meat. The minor pieces he cut into thin strips and soaked them in a mixture of herbs to make jerky from. All the finished pieces he placed in cold storage.

All during the time he butchered, salted and smoked the meat he talked of the hunt, the kill, the untamed land surrounding his cabin. It was a dialogue filled with passion for the wildness of the land and animals that shared it with him.

His zekawolf companion was drooling for a scrap of venison a few paces away from the marble table, not moving from his seated position; a veritable example of patience. "Sir, how did you befriend Thor? Zekawolves are known to despise man and they usually hunt in packs."

"Most hunt in packs," he said as he sliced through another shank of meat. "The territories that provide for their existence they aggressively protect. Only the large, independent zekawolves hunt alone."

He finally tossed Thor a small portion of the meat, which was devoured in seconds. "Thor here was a young pup when I found him while hunting the Forbidden Lands south of your homeland. He had been trampled by a herd of deer and his leg was broken. He would have died had I not brought him back here and nursed him to health. He travels back there at his leisure."

"He is as large a zekawolf as I have ever seen."

"The harsh winters in the Forbidden Lands take their toll on the dens and packs. Thor gets his nourishment in those lean months here with me. But yes, he's big; the largest I have seen, too. He is my companion, my warring cohort and friend." He tossed him another piece of the stag, which he happily ingested.

"You go to battle with him at your side?"

"At times. He seems to know when to show himself, as all good warriors do. He is no different than marching into a fight with any soldier in any fiefdom or kingdom."

Baytel thought of the many regions of the land he was unfamiliar with and the probability that the Southland was preparing to go to war against them. "Are there many kingdoms and fiefdoms in the northlands?"

"Many of them, and entirely spread out from one another, with the dangerous wild lands between them all."

"Are they on good terms with each other?"

"Some are, some not at all. Animosities and jealousies have developed through the years caused by stupidity, bad judgment and incompetent leadership. Skirmishes that ignited between the sects and fiefdoms have escalated into wars. The deaths that result from any of such events afterward are difficult to forgive. This, in turn, causes delicate balances of the power. With the help of the Druids of the Citadel and the Tree Faerie tribe, a peaceful balance exists among the many sects of humanity. Man, gnomes, dwarfs, goblins, imps, whoever and whatever they may be live in somewhat harmony due to their efforts."

"Were there many wars between the sects?"

Calidor paused in his butchering and his face took on a thoughtful pose. "Long ago, deep in the histories of the ancients, humanity was quite abusive both to the land and to humanity itself. Through greed and war the ancients nearly destroyed the land and the people that cared for it. Yet they did not realize that the land was and is omnipotent. It can create and destroy. Eventually, the land destroyed the ancients and wiped their stains from existence. Through the dark years that followed, the land transformed itself, healing the wrongs the ancients caused and creating a new land upon the old earth. Then the faerie tribe came, received magical powers from the land and aided in the healing process.

"They directed the growth of new elements which commenced the growth of all you see before you. The magic of the land breeds life every moment of every day—trees, plants, foods, beings of the seas, forests, mountains, valleys and plains."

Calidor's passionate words flowed over him like a fresh spring breeze. This was the very thing Baytel had been seeking and suddenly, the veil that clouded his mind with doubts about leaving the Southland was gone, and it its place grew an excitement of what might come from his acquaintanceship with Calidor.

Calidor continued in a reverent tone: "The magic of the One Land and Faerie is a part of but a few of us. We must use this gift to strengthen all the sects of humanity to bond with the land. It is a tremendous responsibility. Peace is the greatest cure for the land. Humankind is in its early stages of development and is most vulnerable. The errors of the past—greed, suspicions, despotic fiefdoms, tyrannical kings—invariably show themselves. They will seek more power without consequence and humankind will struggle to survive."

Calidor went back to butchering the stag, allowing Baytel time to think. What Calidor had said pointed directly to his father and brother and their thirst for power and ultimate reign over all. After hearing Calidor speak, he was distressed over what he knew could come to pass from the Southland.

"You said war, death and destruction cause the land to perish, while peace, harmony and tranquility among the sects will keep the land prosperous. Yet there are always wars. Since my youth, the talk of war and death has been on everyone's lips. How can you avoid them when the sects of humanity are so different?"

For a moment Calidor appeared to study the tip of his butchering knife. Then he said: "Human beings must learn to live amongst one another—learn of one another to achieve a harmonious state. This re-creation of the land and those who live upon it is in its infant stages. The sects need to be guided along the proper path. The great kings, feudal lords and magnificent lands and castles that they oversee, they really do not own. Sure, they have possession of them, but truly, the land itself has ultimate power over all. It is the responsibility of the faerie tribe and other factions like the Citadel and its druids to help guide them. Yet they can only point to the right path, it is up to the sects themselves to accept that peace is a good way of life."

Baytel nodded. "So only a few people throughout the One Land possess the same magic as that of the faerie tribe? The magic given to them by the One Land itself? I ask this because my father has magic abilities. When I was younger, my brother and I happened upon him at practice in the deep crypt of the castle." As soon as he said it, he felt ashamed of what he was revealing. Calidor did not hesitate in the least bit from cutting on the slab and Baytel sensed he had previous knowledge of it. So without prodding Baytel disclosed that his brother had also practiced the magic.

Calidor's expression then turned cold. "Your brother is practicing this also? That I did not know. I do know of your father's abilities, Baytel. The magic they wield is no craft. It is not the magic of the faerie they practice, but an evil that originated in the time of the ancients. Be wary of it, Baytel. This dark art influences the mind and most often captures the practitioner's soul."

Baytel was silent while Calidor continued his stern but compassionate lecture about the evils of the dark art his father and brother wielded and realized that the dark art truly had taken over their lives. The changes he had witnessed through the years in his father and brother were frightening and he wondered what kind of family he would find on his return. *Would his father see the changes in Ravek? Would he be wary of his powers? Will his brother's power grow stronger than his?*

He suddenly realized that with his knowledge of their plans and powers, his brother and father would stop at nothing to find him. He kept peering over his shoulder to the west, wondering if any had found his tracks in the snow upon the East Fork and how close they were to discovering him. The safety of Calidor's land was suddenly suspect and his anxiety at possibly being discovered made him shiver. "If they find me here, they will send the entire army to bring me back."

Calidor had stopped talking and was staring at him. "Baytel, they have not the slightest clue where you have gone and would not consider venturing onto or over the East Fork. So let me assure you, you are quite safe."

He breathed a sigh, trusting Calidor's conviction. Reassured of his freedom from the Southland and its oppressive existence, he suddenly felt sadness as he realized that in leaving his father and brother, he had removed a peculiar balance to their strange family. He felt, especially after the last conversation when his father finally opened some of his heart to him, that he was the counterweight to the family scale. However, had he not left what would he have become?

With the thoughts of his family and their magical practices in mind, he asked, "What are the differences in faerie magic and that wielded by my father and brother?"

"The Faerie magic is enlightenment." He paused at a thought and continued looking up at the sky, as if reading the gathering clouds for his next words. "Faerie magic is complex, overwhelmingly chaotic and extraordinary; it is in actuality the power of the land. The faeries that wield it can create as well as destroy. To fulfill its force in life, the magic encompasses the mind, body, and soul of those who practice it. It is virtuous and good.

"Yet there are those who attempt to twist the magic to their own need. History has shown that those who tempt this fate fall to the power of the dark magic and eventually are consumed by it."

"I have met only one tree faerie—Cyr, my tutor. He did not speak of his magic to me."

"Cyr's wisdom was guided early in his life. It was fortunate you had such a tutor. To be taught the faerie way will help you in your studies at the Citadel, as well as what you will learn in my care. Cyr prepared you to open your soul to the land's teaching, did he not?"

"Yes, that was the premise of his lessons."

"Then the talk of magic can wait. You have much to learn before we speak any more about it."

The feeling that Calidor knew more about him than he was saying ignited more uncertainty but before the prince could ask another question, Calidor held up his hand. "All in time, Baytel."

He looked skyward where the gray clouds that had swept from the northeast covered the sun. The air immediately became cold and the winds seemed to increase, blowing the top snow across the plains. A stillness settled upon the vicinity. The chirping of birds fell silent as the chill warned that severe weather was approaching, and he returned to the cabin feeling cold and confused.

They ate a meal of the venison and wild mushrooms whose flavor lingered in his mouth, and after another draught of the bolus he felt warmer once more.

The evening darkness was intensified by the very storm Calidor had foretold. Dark clouds gathered above the cabin. Calidor was outdoors, climbing atop the rock roof of the cabin and securing extension pipes on the chimneys. He had hauled up hollow metal ducts that he attached on the roofs of the cabin and stable. He explained the piping would allow fresh air to circulate freely throughout the lodge.

He had explained during supper the workings of the air flow system. "Because the fireplace and stove create upward drafts, a suction effect will draw fresh air down through the ducts into the cabin. So as heat rises out of the chimneys, fresh air is drawn in."

Still physically weak, fighting exhaustion, Baytel did what he could to help. He placed the stallion in the stable and put Thor in the cabin to keep him from being underfoot. He set about securing the window boards to the interior latches in the stable and cabin and then re-stoked the fire in the hearth. He sat beside the hearth with the hide of the stag and began conditioning the hide while recalling Calidor's lecture.

Reflecting, he realized that his new tutor had purposely chosen precisely what he wanted him to know and dismissed pointed questions throughout the day with a hand gesture or sideways glance. He resigned himself to trust that the questions formulating in his mind would eventually be answered without having to be raised.

With this accepted insight, Baytel put down the skinning knife, settled into a soft chair and fell asleep to the crackling of the embers.

Chapter 10

THE snowstorm had arrived before Baytel woke. Great clouds had gathered from separate fronts converging strong from the north and east and together deposited heavy snow across Calidor's land. Throughout his young years, Baytel had never seen a snowstorm of this magnitude. Unlike the whiteout he had experienced upon the East Fork, this snowstorm was so thick that he could not see past the cabin.

Baytel's only companion in the cabin was Thor. Calidor was outdoors blazing a path from the cabin to the storehouse and from there to the stable. By midday the snow had drifted over the north side of the lodge so high he could not see the other structures from the cabin, and still Calidor toiled on. Only once, at nightfall, did Calidor come in from his plowing to take nourishment drinking the herbal dram he had administered to Baytel that had offered such wonderful recuperative powers. Calidor drank heartily and quickly returned to his labors.

Witnessing him against the elements Baytel identified in Calidor a fierce determination to the task at hand. Earlier he had wondered at why anyone would choose to live in a land so desolate and wild? Observing the man's toil at the path, he came to the conclusion that this land wholly represented who Calidor was as a man; strong, wild, dangerous, unforgiving and yet, peaceful and generous to those who are their loyalties.

The dark of the night slowly faded to gray and, as dawn arrived, Baytel feeling stronger and wanting to help Calidor dressed and stepped outdoors upon the path. Now the path was flanked by snow walls so high, the wind swept falling snow across the top, allowing little to fall all upon the path. Walking farther up the path, Baytel found that the storehouse and stable were completely covered save for the air ducts and chimney extensions.

Calidor emerged from the storehouse with two ladders, and said, "Good morning, Baytel. I see you are up and ready to work. Good." He set up the ladders against a wall of firm snow. "Watch what I do and repeat the process. You start at the base of this wall and work your way up as high as you can. I will start on the other wall until I see you have moved forward and will finish the upper part of your wall following behind you."

Calidor started at the cabin entrance and began packing and smoothing the path wall from base to crown, forming a solid ice façade. Following his instructions, Baytel worked rapidly but soon fell behind. Before he realized it, Calidor had completed his wall to the storehouse and returned to the cabin entrance adjusting the ladder to reach the height of the wall and began shaping the crown inward, sculpting a lip that would extend over the path. As another layer accumulated, he repeated this fashioning until an ice canopy covered the path.

They ate when they were hungry and worked with quick pauses to eat until the first tunnel was completed and darkness informed them the day was ending. Baytel then followed Calidor through the storehouse to the path between there and the stable, repeating the process with tunnel number two. At intervals, Calidor dispatched him to bring hurried meals, sharing the hot brew whose properties he was wholly amazed with, as the draught seemed to sustain an energy level that defied exhaustion.

Finally completed with the second tunnel, they returned to the lodge, replaced their wet clothing with dry and repaired to the kitchen where together they prepared a hot meal. Calidor left the cabin through the tunnels to the storehouse and returned with a demijohn of a dark liquid. He poured the dark brew into two stone flasks. "Stout ale from Tridling Del. You cannot find heartier anywhere in the land. Drink up."

Calidor had left the door of the cabin open. Baytel looked into the dark tunnel and an unwelcome feeling of detention set in and the prospect of being stranded in a snow cocoon for the winter, without the freedom he sacrificed so much for, was weighing on his mind.

"How long does the winter season last here?"

Calidor wiped his mouth with his napkin as he finished with his meal. "A few months. Some years longer, some not so long."

"It will be strange not seeing the light of day or knowing when it is day or night."

Calidor let out a short laugh that made Baytel angry. "What is so funny?"

"Baytel, what time of the day is it now?"

Baytel rolled his eyes, too tired to hear a lesson about the telling of time. "It's just after dusk—twilight, I suppose."

"Correct. So when we wake from our sleep, it should be morning. Is that not so?" Calidor's grin was mischievously widening.

Baytel did not answer, knowing he was being made fun of.

Calidor shook his head. "Do not look too far ahead, Baytel. You may miss something directly in front of you."

Annoyed, Baytel looked around the cabin as if it were the first time. The walls seemed closer, the ceiling lower and the candlelight less luminous than before. "Shut in within these walls for months, finding things to do will be challenging."

Calidor looked up from his plate. His face appeared tired but his eyes were lively and stern. "There will be enough activities within these structures to fill your mind and body with challenges. Tomorrow we will begin with the first, which will be to learn patience and see beyond your nose." He drained the flask of ale, slammed it down on the table and went to his sleeping quarters.

Baytel's first sensation upon awakening was his hot feet and looking down to the foot of his bed found Thor lying on top. He gave the zekawolf's head a scratch and sat up. It had been a dreamless, deep restful sleep. The night passed without sound reminding him of the night he spent in his tent under a blanket of snow that almost caused his death. He walked from his bedroom into the great room and saw that the fire in the hearth had burned low. Heading toward the door to gather wood from the storehouse, he noticed a faint line of light beneath the closed door of the cabin. He opened it and the wonderment of the view caused him to catch his breath. The storm must have ended during the night for the morning sun had risen and set aglow prisms of light through an ice canopy that cast brilliant beams through the tunnel.

Baytel put on his boots to retrieve the logs for the fire and along the way to the storehouse he recalled Calidor's reprimand the night before of his statements about their confinement. Realizing everything Calidor had said last night had a purpose behind it, he resolved to be entirely committed to all Calidor had to teach him.

His winter confinement lasted three months but it felt nothing like detention for Calidor had kept him busy day and night filling the time with tasks and activities. As the ice and snow that concealed their existence began to melt, Baytel could hear the singing of birds again and the scent of early spring was in the air. The sky was blue and the sun bright, refreshing and uplifting.

What he was most excited for was to put Calidor's lessons into action. Through the long months they talked of many things and with spring blossoming, he was shown the physical elements of his teachings. Calidor pointed out and identified the foods and herbs, the wild greens, nuts, grains and roots, instilling the knowledge that they can keep him alive and strong. He found water to drink from plants, crags of rocks and spring wells.

Calidor instructed him in the hunting and trapping of game, the use of the longbow and short, knife and garrote traps. Baytel learned to make fire out of what the land offered. He soaked up lessons in tool making, shelter and boat construction, snowshoe and mountaineering—skills that would allow him to traverse and scale the highest peaks.

He listened to Calidor pontificate over and over again about the land and how to hear signs where you least expected. "The forest, birds and animals will be your allies," Calidor said. "They know more about your surroundings in strange lands than you do. Listen, learn and decipher their messages. Most often they are warnings of possible dangers unseen."

Calidor instructed him in the deer walk, practicing with him for days observing and mimicking the silent wanderings of the forest deer. Baytel imitated their passage until he was as quiet as a light breeze through the woods. Stealth was the lesson Calidor stressed, to be one with the surroundings, flowing with the landscape.

"You must become part of the geography of the land, whether in rivers, forests, mountains or passes. Even in towns, cities and territories of one of the many sects in the outlands. You must be invisible until you know it is safe and choose to show yourself."

He taught Baytel of the healing herbs the land supplied at every turn, of their proper drying, the preparation of mixtures and healing ointments, and how to treat illnesses and injuries.

Most importantly, Calidor taught him swordsmanship, enlisting Thor's aid in teaching him balance and strength while training him to fight, from horseback and on foot all within the close confines of the stable. The small area inside the stable provided a perfect setting for Baytel to feel the horse as part of his own body; two beings as one complete warrior. The hours spent with the sword, repeating maneuvers and strengthening his body and mind to the point his sword became an extension of his self. Calidor stressed defensive tactics, countermoves, continuous balance, coordination and, only when the perfect situation happened in battle, offensive tactics.

As they worked together through the spring and summer, Baytel realized that all the elements of Calidor's teachings complimented each other and he achieved harmony of mind and body. If one element was missing, then the whole would be disturbed and the balance of this harmony would be lost. He suspected that Calidor had a motive behind teaching these things and waited patiently for the hidden purpose to be revealed. He sensed it not as a foreboding, but more as an awakening of a sort.

The afternoon sun had been sinking lower in the sky earlier than usual foretelling the shortening days to come. The breeze was light and a little cool blowing over the amber-green grass at the base of a towering rock outcrop they had just completed climbing. He coiled the ropes and lines while Calidor packed the clips and pins.

"It's time we talked of the Citadel," said Calidor, leaning back against the column of rock.

Baytel stood up surprised at his announcement. This must have been the reason for all the lessons and instructions throughout the winter.

"Baytel, you know of some I will say about the Citadel from Cyr, but listen to me and understand. The Citadel is a mystic fortress in the wilderness that attracts people seeking knowledge of the ways of the land. Eventually, if they have the aptitude, the students are admitted into advanced education levels and some even become Druids of the Citadel. Thereafter they quest in honor of the land and sects of humanity."

"Is this why you have taught me all this these past months?"

"Yes. That, and you were horribly in need to learn how to survive in these dangerous times."

Baytel could not disagree. "What should I expect when I arrive there?"

"Much of the same that you have been learning here, and other teachings which will become an intrinsic truth within you. Everything that is taught at the Citadel has a purpose. Do not ignore the mundane, for in your travels, it may save your life or that of another."

Baytel had grown used to the fact that he never received a direct answer. Calidor always left him needing clarification. This was his way of prompting him to think deeper of things and not take the simplest explanation as the best and proper resolve.

"Baytel, if you commit to the Citadel and its teachings, it is a obligation for life. You will be one of the few who are responsible for the well-being of the land and its sects. You will learn many things that are essential to the care of all walks of life. It will be your bound duty to be a nurturer of the land and its people, to protect them with your knowledge and skills, to make sure they are on the true path to keeping them and the land unscathed. The land's magic must endure and you will be responsible for keeping it from being harmed and misused."

"Will I learn magic there?" asked Baytel.

"The magic of the land cannot be taught. Its power will reach out to those who are most worthy and no other," Calidor answered sharply.

Baytel smiled, having become accustomed to such sharp replies. "How is it you know so much of what I will learn at the Citadel?"

Calidor met his gaze. "All in good time, Baytel, all in good time."

Calidor had used that expression so often through their time together that Baytel came to know that each time he used it, the answer usually was not far off.

As they went back to packing the mountaineering gear, Calidor added, "You leave within the fortnight."

Without a word Baytel nodded, threw the packed gear across his back, and walked toward the cabin.

The fortnight passed quickly. Baytel and Calidor woke with the sun behind thick fog rolling down the mountaintops. Baytel had packed his gear the night before and found his bag at the door; Calidor's way of telling him it was time to leave.

They ate a small meal of scones and cheese and drank herbal tea, passing the time casually, trying not to show too much enthusiasm for the journey to come or sadness in parting.

Baytel glanced once more at the marble plaques on the wall. Though he had lived nearly nine months with him, he had never asked about them. "Did you sculpt those plaques?"

Calidor rose and sat next to the fireplace, lighting his pipe. "No, an old companion and dear friend carved them."

Baytel walked over to the wall and looked at each one carefully. "They tell of great deeds from the past, if my translation of the rune markings is correct," said Baytel with a smile, for Calidor had wrestled long in teaching him the many different dialects of rune. *"Of great wars and acts of bravery."*

Calidor nodded.

"The era, according to the plaques, was when the land was young and wild. It is written here," Baytel pointed to one plaque, "that a fellowship of men traveled throughout the land, offering assistance to those in need. *A band of gallant men carrying out heroic acts,*" he read aloud.

Calidor was sitting in his chair; a peaceful faraway look was on his face. "Back then there were only small towns, villages and upstart fiefdoms spread far and wide from each other. People wandered the wild to build homes and farms and live free. The wild was not for the weak-hearted. Then the lords of fiefdoms wanted to establish more lands and set laws for those trailblazers to abide by."

Calidor stood and leaned against the stone hearth. "There was discourse, fighting and a few fiefdom battles. As it happens, there was no one to protect the innocent. The Faerie tribe, Citadel Druids and a band of men united in thought and deed joined forces and held back the marauding fiefdoms and sects from starting war campaigns. This band of warriors helped the weak, protected the trail blazers and allowed the sects of humankind to survive, and thus the land was pleased."

Baytel absorbed Calidor's reminiscing. They were silent for some time when at last the tall man concluded: "It was a romantic and chaotic beginning for all."

Calidor walked out of the cabin, grabbing Baytel's bag. Baytel followed him out. The sun was high and had burned off the fog, showing a clear blue sky. Thor trotted up to Calidor and sat at his feet for a strong scratch behind his ears.

Calidor's face was strained but his eyes showed sorrow. Baytel would miss him greatly, as he missed his Cyr. However, he was proud to begin the last leg of the journey to the Citadel having known and learned from these two amazing people.

"Learn as much as you can from the people and situations you encounter along the way to the Citadel, Baytel. Remember, not all sects are harmonious with one another. The wounds of past wars and conflicts are ingrained in their cultures, traditions and histories. The battles may no longer be in the field and forests, but are still waged in the minds and beliefs of the sects. There exists an abundance of hatred and dismay. Be very careful with what you say and to whom."

Calidor's eyes bored into him like spikes of heated steel. "Baytel, you must remember, your homeland is not well loved. Do not disclose where you are from until you reach the Citadel. Only then should you speak of it."

"I will, Calidor."

"My last bit of advice I cherish to this day I offer to you—You have eyes, ears, and a mouth. If you keep the latter of these closed, you will learn much about life and be a wiser man for it."

"I will keep that pearl close to my heart."

Baytel smiled, thinking of the day he had departed the Southland so excited but so foolishly ill-prepared. He felt his heart fill as he gazed at Calidor, who had been more a father to him than the king. Except for the time with Cyr, he had never been happier than when being here with Calidor.

"When I first woke and found myself in this cabin, I remember saying to you that I was in your debt and you said you would hear no talk of debts." He paused, swallowing in a dry throat. "I owe you my life, Calidor. You have given me what I was seeking when I left the Southland—a new life and a purpose for it. I owe you everything and although I have nothing to give you, I will offer you this: I pledge to you, Calidor, that your teachings, kindness and wisdom shall not be wasted. I will strive to work with the land and its people for the betterment of all. This is my pledge to you, Calidor, my friend."

Calidor smiled and said as he embraced him, "You are wise beyond your years, Baytel. I accept your pledge."

Baytel stepped back, throwing his pack over his shoulder he set off northeast, only once looking back, seeing the great zekawolf atop the rock cabin. Thor pitched back his head and, with a powerful howl, sent Baytel on his way.

Chapter 11

EASTWARD from Calidor's land, the beauty of the dense forests and plush meadows lay open in their splendor at every turn and over every hill. Travel was fair and the weather mild, and Baytel encountered little difficulty through the wild countryside. Upon reaching the well-traversed roads, he found quaint country hamlets dotting the landscape. A sense of true freedom unfolded for Baytel in all its glory.

Summer's heat had retreated long ago and the scenery changed with autumn's turning of the leaves. Brilliant hues of red, gold, orange and brown were the milieu as if an artist had spilled an array of paints across the horizon. Baytel hiked through golden valleys covered entirely by the fallen leaves of the sugar maple. The roads and paths were not beaten down with gravel and dirt; they were blanketed in the multiple colors of the season; a cornucopia of Mother Nature's autumn tears.

Baytel ventured through numerous villages and found them all charming. Most were farm communities with hardly any central town area, save for the lone mercantile establishment that stocked necessities for the handful of settlers, and a blacksmith shop. The people had found their peace in the cultivation of food and serenity among their own families and small circle of friends.

Though Baytel found that most of the settlements were wary of strangers, they still greeted him with kindness, and despite the fact that his visits were short he discovered the people were pleasant, polite and good-humored. At every hamlet he found a farmer needing an extra hand with chores. His offers of assistance were welcomed and Baytel gratefully took his pay in the forms of food and lodging.

His pleasant and genteel conduct, he realized, was seen as welcoming, and although the families were not as educated as he was, he found the common folk sociable, amicable and excellent company. At the end of his stays, he always departed the homes and farms better than he found them and with the impression that he would be welcome back, and had formed good friendships.

Autumn was in mid-season and the rains became more frequent. Even though the land offered enough shelter and food between the settlements, he decided to rest before the last leg of his journey to the Citadel and so entered the town of Balmoral. The town was larger than any he had yet encountered and he walked the main street slowly, taking in the sights that paraded before him. A crowd had gathered in front of a hardware store, all watching the owner barter with a farmer over a load of cut wood in exchange for an upgraded plow. In the storefront next to the hardware store, textiles and grains decorated the windows, as did weaponry for the traveling warrior and hunter.

The deeper into town he walked, the more Baytel felt eyes upon him. A tanner poked his head out of a stable, staring forwardly with suspicion. At the barber and the bathhouse, patrons stared out at him from behind the windows as he passed. He began wondering if his clothes were not the right sorts for traveling. He had assumed they were, for Calidor supplied them to him. He was in front of a butcher shop as the butcher walked onto his wooden porch, cleaver in hand and blood stained apron resting on his enormous belly, Baytel, without a second thought, headed his way.

Baytel hailed the man. "Excuse me sir, I am new in town and ..."

"New isn't the word, boy. You look as though you are as lost as a hare in the mountains," said the butcher. His face was speckled with freckles and his rosy cheeks glowed.

Baytel nodded politely and continued, "I have been on the road for some time and was wondering if you could recommend a place to stay?"

The butcher smiled, showing a full set of white teeth that further brightened his face. "Hungry and thirsty are you?"

Baytel smiled back and placed one foot on the step of the porch, leaning on his leg. He was tired and didn't mind showing it to the affable butcher. "Both, and a bath would also set me to rights. Do you have anything in mind for me?"

"Well young man, you seem to be of a good sort. Polite, seemingly good disposition, though nameless. I can recommend an inn for you."

The butcher paused before disclosing his recommendation. Baytel took the pause as a hint and responded. "Pardon my impoliteness, kind sir. My name is Baytel. Whom do I have the pleasure of speaking with?"

"Ahh! Such distinction! I am unaccustomed to so polite and eloquent behavior. Allow me a pause and savor this moment," the butcher said with a friendly grin, and holding himself still as a statue for a short moment, said, "So, Baytel, since you expressed yourself in such a refined manner, I believe you are worthy of our finest establishment. I am Pat Spry and I believe you will get on swimmingly with the inn's proprietor. I can say without reservation that you both are cut from the same cloth."

The butcher Spry pointed down the road. "Just keep walking that way, and just after where the road veers north you will find the Green Goblet."

Baytel looked down the street, seeing more heads peering out of storefronts and businesses. "Do all strangers draw this much attention, Mr. Spry?"

"As a matter of fact they do. We here in Balmoral try to make all visitors feel special."

"Special? I feel undressed with singularity."

"Hahaha! Oh Baytel, you will get along fine here with such wit. Hahaha! Now clothe yourself and off you go to the Green Goblet."

Baytel waved him good-bye and took his time walking through the stares until at the bend he found the Green Goblet standing magnificently in the center of the north side of the street. It stood four stories high where all other buildings were no more than two. A covered porch was elevated four steps off the street and wrapped around three sides of the building. Double doors were opened enough to display the entrance foyer. Entering the establishment he stepped onto the marble floor cut in diamond harlequin fashion and grained in hues of burgundy and alabaster. The enormous goblet stood at its center made of the deepest green marble he had ever seen. In the goblet were displayed fresh fruits and vegetables of various shapes and colors that rivaled the leaves of autumn. Beyond the goblet stood a winding staircase that led, he presumed, to the boarding rooms and baths. The foyer then split the interior's carved wooden walls in two; one side was the dining hall and the other the tavern and lounge where in the center was a stone hearth with a chiseled stone seat surround.

The Green Goblet had such a refined atmosphere even nobility would be convinced of appropriate comfort. All the same, Balmoral was a trading town and destination of wayfarers from every sect of humanity imaginable, which seemed to be currently patronizing the tavern. After checking in with the day manger at the reception desk, Baytel was led to a room on the third floor above the tavern end of the Green Goblet.

Through the days Baytel spent in Balmoral, he took his meals in the tavern or dining room alone and casually listened to the patrons and travelers from all regions of the land. Most stayed only a day or two, urgent to continue on with their travels. Dwarf, gnome, imp, tall man and the like all circulated within Balmoral, sometimes in harmony, though in most instances with indifference. Their banter, as a rule, was of their lands and stories of woes and triumphs. Tensions when patrons interacted were inevitable, as exchanges between the different sects became personal and offensive in the closed settings. An innocent or imprudent word quickly interpreted would cause a slight and, at times, erupt into violence. Each party prepared to receive a gesture of peace or insult, and if neither was put forward, they remained adversarial but in a delicate balance, only a minor infraction away from collapse.

The proprietor of the Green Goblet was a cordial and reserved sort named Juliard. He was as large and strong a man as Baytel had ever seen. Yet for all his obvious physical strength, he was affable in nature and quick to humor, with a laugh that started as a low and convivial throat rumble turning to an outright guffaw. His counsel was often called upon and generally appreciated.

Being a boarding patron, Baytel spoke often with the big man and found Juliard to be an exceptional resource of information. He seemed to have seen and heard plenty in the Green Goblet. He kept a neutral pose when at his work. He had a good, established business and wanted to sustain it that way so he kept his opinions to himself on the more heated subjects that crossed his way.

Instead, Juliard's conversation tended toward his stories of past times and noble places. These his patrons welcomed as a respite from the hard lives the travelers lived. Baytel sat at the tavern many nights sipping dark ale, listening to the big man speak and observing him interacting with the patrons as if he had known them all the days of their lives.

Early one evening, after a long-winded version of a past battle in a region he had not ever heard of before, Baytel asked, "Why did you choose Balmoral as a home?"

Juliard took the question as a cue and a welcome change of subject, answering in his deep baritone voice that carried throughout the tavern, as if reciting verse to the crowd. "Balmoral is the city of travelers where journeymen, rovers, adventurers and all of the people of the land stop to refresh themselves, rethink their journey, and go about their concerns without the burden of anyone telling them what to do, where to go, and when. Balmoral is a way city where wanderers can rest. It was my time to rest, Baytel."

"How did Balmoral become an established city?"

He stopped wiping the bar, threw the towel across his shoulder, and began his oration.

"According to some of my older patrons, this spot on the map was just a trade road. The route meandered from Treldor Reach to the northern fiefdoms. This is the halfway point. A few merchants built small cottages where they could rest and replenish themselves and their stock. As time went on, these traders saw an opportunity and constructed meeting houses to barter their goods. Some decided to stay permanently, opening establishments like this one. Then came the farmers and the town was born. No one sect of humanity claimed *This is our land* or stated himself or herself to be the founder of Balmoral. It became what it is from the sects' common need to use for a short stay—or for a lifetime."

Though the majority of the patrons and travelers were from the northern regions including the great cities of Kilhalen and the dwarf headquarters of Ctiklat, men and women from far eastern Treldor frequented Balmoral also. Most traveled in caravans with their goods to barter piled high on the backs of their burden animals. From the northwest came wines from Glenilon; from the north grains from Kilhalen. The eastern provinces brought teas and herbs, scented oils and spice. The dwarves traded hand-fashioned farm tools to farmers and weapons and warring equipment for soldiers and for protection in the wild. The western territories traded fine rugs and clothing and foods from the outland farmers that the merchants passed as they traveled, trading along the way.

Baytel found most spoke the same language with minor adjustments of dialect, and when there was a speech barrier, trading goods for goods was still as common a language as his own.

Baytel was unsure where Juliard was originally from. He did not have the looks of any of the sects Baytel had encountered yet on his journey. He towered above all, and while his face was strong and firm it had an undistinguishable age to it. Juliard's eyes were as steel-blue as Calidor's and his frame had similar mass.

Baytel found himself alone with Juliard the morning he had decided to depart. His stay had been longer than he expected but he had learned so much from patronizing the Green Goblet that the delaying was well worth it. It was the first opportunity he had to speak with the man in a private setting since he arrived.

"So, Baytel," Juliard said with his usual cheerful demeanor, "you have resided in my establishment for much longer than I thought a young wanderer would. I was of the mind to the point of offering you employment, but since I see your bag packed and resting in the foyer, I surmise you are on the wing."

Baytel took a stool at the long oak bar and accepted the mug of tea Juliard offered. The brew smelled floral; he tasted hints of ginger too. "Yes, Juliard, it is time for me to go."

"Where are you off to?"

Baytel remembered Calidor's warning not to disclose his destination until he reached it, but he felt he could trust Juliard with anything. He leaned forward, as did Juliard at his movement.

"I journey to the Citadel," he whispered. He scanned Juliard's face. He saw no change.

"Do you know anyone there?" asked the innkeeper.

The question surprised Baytel. He had expected the man to ask a more direct question, like, *"Why do you go?"* or *"What is it you seek there?"*

"Well no. I will not know anyone there. I expect others will be in the same circumstance, not knowing a soul, but there to learn of the land."

He fell silent, sipping his tea and wondering if his statement would be true once he arrived at the Citadel. Since leaving Calidor, he had a vision of what he expected to see, similar-age people seeking the same things he sought. Though he would know no one, he hadn't thought if others would be from familiar regions and be acquainted with each other.

He broke the silence. "Thank you for making my stay here comfortable and enjoyable. Balmoral is truly a way city and I have learned much and achieved a good feel for the people who live throughout the land. Mostly, I appreciate your kindness answering all my many questions."

Juliard nodded. "Your soul is good, Baytel. I could tell the first day you came into my tavern that you were not like the usual traveler. You seemed to be at the beginning of seeking a purpose to your life. I believe you will fare well with this quest, my friend, and when you are upon its path, remember this place and let it be your sanctuary if trouble arises." He leaned forward and with a wary eye warned, "I caution you, Baytel. Being a Druid of the Citadel can be dangerous."

Baytel gazed at the man and smiled, "You speak like a good friend of mine. I wish you two could meet one day."

Juliard stepped toward the kitchen door. "Well, you never know. I may have already met this friend of yours."

Baytel saw a knowing look in the man's eyes before the kitchen door closed behind him but took it as a jest. Juliard came out with a bag filled with food and handed it to him across the bar. "Remember, you have a friend here in Balmoral."

"Thank you, Juliard. Good-bye."

He walked out of Balmoral with the bag Calidor gave him stuffed with Juliard's offerings and headed northeast. A screech from high above brought his attention to a red hawk drifting on the wind high in the morning sky. He banked and then soared away at tremendous speed. It was odd to have never seen a red hawk before, and then to see two since leaving his home. He watched it fly south, probably to seek out its mate.

The autumn's brilliance departed, leaving the forests and land depleted of color. Preferring no interruptions during this last stage of the journey, Baytel appreciated not seeing a soul since leaving Balmoral. The natural sounds and quiet of the land enhanced a peaceful reverie as the environs greeted him with mild weather, though the ubiquitous northerly wind hinted of the winter to come.

Unknowingly, he had walked into a forest so enormous that days after entering it outside Balmoral he had not exited yet. The continual forest dominated the land with massive aspen trees intertwining with one another and almost closing off the sun even though leafless in the post-autumn time of year. Through the dark forest, day or night, he never encountered any form of danger, or reason to fear. Nor did he find a worn path for easy travel, blazing his own trail the entire time.

Clearings dotted the forest where tall grass and smaller birch trees shared the same sun. He stopped regularly in the dells to mark his passage by the sun's position. Keeping a constant measure of direction and distance he was able to maintain his bearing northeast with little adjustment of direction.

The days passed pleasantly, the forest and fields rich with wildlife all preparing for hibernation, foraging and scurrying about. Yet during his passage, he began to feel the impression that the forest was closing in behind him. As this feeling grew, finally Baytel stopped in the center of a dell and looked behind him. He saw no evidence of the trail he had just blazed through the tall grass. He moved through another difficult clump of foliage he had to cut through and, stopping again, he turned to look at his path and was amazed by what he saw. The dell seemed to have mended the damaged bushes and broken bramble, and all looked entirely undisturbed.

Curious, he knelt and broke a fern leaf from a plant and was astonished as it instantly mended itself. It was magical. He placed his palms to the ground. He felt it pulse. He had never known of such a thing as this. The magic of the land was strong in these woods. Baytel wondered if it sprang from the Citadel.

These thoughts exhilarated him to new heights. They also humbled him into focusing deeply on the teachings of Cyr and Calidor to better prepare for what was to come. As he thought back to his ill-prepared departure from his home, the teachings of his two tutors and his experiences during travel deepened his awareness of the land and sects, giving him a profound confidence to enter the next stage in his life.

He walked from the dell after a lengthy hike through the woods with strong strides, meeting the land beneath his feet with purpose. Entering another clearing Baytel met the sun and walked onto an undulating terrain of tall grass baked to a golden hue. The immense trees surrounding the clearing blocked the early winter wind and, in its stead, soft breezes rolled across the grass, giving rise to the illusion of golden swells upon a sunlit sea.

Baytel stood in the center of the tranquil clearing absorbing the heat of the day when his peruse over the bordering treetops caused him pause. High on the horizon stood a magnificent edifice. It was the Citadel.

The structure seemed to ripple like a heat mirage as the brilliant sunlight played upon the castle. Massive turrets, tall merlons, and foreboding battlements adorned the fortress and emanated a power he felt overwhelming. All the resolutions he had made and all of Cyr's and Calidor's teachings were inadequate to what he was feeling at the sight of the Citadel. He felt suddenly insignificant and fearful. Mesmerized by the resplendent image, he found it had abruptly disappeared behind the trees. He realized he had been involuntarily stepping toward the fortress as if some unseen force was drawing him in.

Back into the dark of the forest and away from the view and lure of the mystical castle he felt more at ease. The ground began to rise on a gradual incline and the air became cooler as the sun sank. Thinking he needed a fresh start if he were to reach the Citadel the next day he decided to rest for the night and set camp.

After a fitful slumber he was welcomed by the new day with a thin layer of snow. He shook off his belongings and ate cold portions of dried venison and biscuit, the last of Juliard's supplies, and set off up the foothill of the mountain where the fortress stood. The forest thinned as he climbed and soon he reached the timberline meeting the open highland where, high upslope, the Citadel came to view. The sense of being drawn toward the edifice returned and Baytel accepted it and continued on.

Nearing the ominous castle he was taken aback by its construction— masonry of enormous limestone and marble blocks precariously placed in an unusual pattern by the architect, designed with deliberate angles to the sun that created the spectral image he had witnessed the previous evening. Flags flew on top of every turret and tower and banners hung along the entrance and high over the gate.

The distance was farther than he thought and as dusk came again to the mountain he finally reached the castle entrance. The gate was a bright metal glowing even in the poor dusky light. Pushing against the cold metal he found it locked. Up the portcullis structure a single light glowed from the gatehouse portico. Somewhere deep in the gatehouse a shadow moved across the lighted area.

"Greetings, gatekeeper."

His voice seemed to die against the stone wall.

"Gatehouse. Is there anyone there?"

After a long wait a harsh voice resounded from deep within the portico. "Who hails there? State your purpose."

"I have traveled far and seek admittance for study and learning. I am Baytel," he declared, trying to speak in a strong voice. It sounded flat against the stone.

A shadowed figure Baytel could not distinguish appeared and looked down upon him from the portico. The figure said nothing, and after a long pause retreated back into the room. Baytel remained silent while he waited for another response, and when the figure came back to the shadowy portico the gruff voice solicited, "Who is your sponsor?"

Baytel was surprised to confusion by the query. He had expected the gate to be open for all who traveled to the Citadel. Now after the long journey he might be refused admittance. Not certain what the proper response would be, he counted on the truth. "I have no sponsor. I came at my own desire. I journeyed for a full year to learn of the teachings of the Cit—"

The voice cut him short. "Where did you come from, young man? Who sent you?"

His frustration and fatigue threatened his demeanor. Calming himself, he asked as politely as he could, "Kind sir, as you can see, I am alone and one person cannot cause any harm to so formidable a castle as this. It is night, I am weary, and if you allow me to enter I promise to answer any and all questions you may pose."

He felt, rather than saw, the dim shadow staring down at him. Then a flicker of light touched the figure's features; his face looked more kindly than his voice presented. The man retreated from the window and a few moments later Baytel heard the locks behind the stone portcullis activate and then the gate slowly opened on its own power. He walked into the fortress and onto a stone floor that led to a large vestibule where an old gnome stood flanked by six guardsmen. The guards were in all-white uniforms and wore at their side dagger and broadsword.

The gnome stood half Baytel's height, unusually tall for a gnome, and was heavyset and muscular. His eyes were large and dark, his black hair and beard specked with gray and cropped close. He wore brown pants and a green shirt with a leather tunic and mountain boots, the same as Calidor except, of course, smaller. His face showed nothing that would be mistaken as welcoming or friendly.

"Greetings again, sir."

The gnome eyed him. "Greetings, young man. Where do you come from, and who sent you?"

"As I stated, no one sent me. I learned of the Citadel from friends and desired to learn the teachings of the land. I came here of my own accord."

"And where are you from?" the gnome asked again.

He hesitated, which he knew was not lost on anyone there. The Southland borders had been closed to the north for many years, since before he was born. Calidor had warned him not to mention his homeland until he reached the Citadel. With strength carrying his voice, he stated, "I come from the Southland."

A murmur sounded through the guards and one drew his sword. The gnome raised his hand at the guard, who then immediately sheathed his weapon.

The gnome stood confident and in control. "The Southland, you say. We have not seen a Southlander for many years." He paused, assessing the situation. "May I inquire as to your friends who initiated your desire to come here?"

"Well, it is a long story about why I am here."

"Young man, it is I who will be granting you admittance. Or not. I do not have the time to hear long stories, nor the inclination. Who are these friends you speak of?"

The gnome waited impatiently and he felt the tension in the vestibule increase. He noticed the guards stood like Calidor had taught him to when confrontation was eminent. Their eyes moved from him with suspicion to the gnome, waiting for the signal to attack.

"Very well. My tutor is of the Tree Faerie tribe. His name is Cyr. My other friend, whom I have a short acquaintance with, is a man named Calidor. He prepared me for my journey here."

Another murmur swept through the guards and this time the gnome raised a questioning eyebrow.

The guard who had drawn his sword spoke. "Lying will not gain you admittance, Southlander, only death."

Baytel replied quickly, and with directness. "I have no purpose in lying. I have stated the truth. I seek the learning of the Citadel. I do not seek to fight for entry, but to be welcomed."

The guard stepped forward, drawing his sword once more. Baytel stood his ground, unfazed, subtly balancing himself for battle.

The gnome stared back. Just as the guard was about to lunge, he stepped in front of Baytel and held up his arm. "Hold! Remember your place!"

Baytel had not moved and the guard looked at him with regard and then stepped back into line, sheathing his sword. It was decided.

The gnome stepped closer to Baytel for a closer look. His eyes seemed to linger on Baytel's pointed ears. Then, smiling, the gnome asked, "What did you call yourself?"

"Baytel."

"I am called Stilar, steward of the fortress. Welcome to the Citadel."

Chapter 12

RAVEK felt uncomfortable in the light of day and disliked the little man who stood shaking in fear before him. The search of the outskirts and border town of Weyles was complete and once more Ravek was aggravated at not uncovering any evidence of his brother's whereabouts or death.

The interrogation had not gone well. The town constable bled from his mouth and ears after being repeatedly cuffed by Ravek's guards but had divulged nothing. This was his third search of Weyles and the surrounding region, in spring and in summer and now with fall in its final stage, and with the same results; Baytel was not known to have traveled through Weyles.

He nodded to a guard and the bulky soldier cuffed the man, knocking him to the ground once more. "Constable, how is it you could be so uninformed of the comings and goings of people in your town?"

"No more! Please, Prince Ravek. No more. I have not seen Prince Baytel any-where. No one has. Our postwatches at the Narrow, and at the outskirts of the town road, have never left their posts! Ever! Not one day and night. I personally thoroughly searched the entire town and questioned our citizens many times over. We looked through storage sheds, houses, farms, and fields. We sought him out far into the forests around Weyles. Strangers and wayfarers were questioned as to his whereabouts. Not a soul has seen Prince Baytel! Not a soul upon my honor!"

"I do not believe my brother could walk through the Narrow at the begin-ning of winter and go undetected by all in Weyles. It was the day before the first snow. With practically all the citizens standing vigil at the north mouth of the pass watching the snow accumulate, how could no one see a lone man walking through from the Southland?"

"Sire, that snowstorm lasted over ten days," reasoned the man desperately. "That night the storm began the traders carrying the last shipment had to return to Weyles after almost being buried alive in the Narrow. The entire town was holed up in their homes until the skies cleared. No one except our watch guards went out of their homes. Perhaps Prince Baytel became disoriented in the storm and wandered off in the wrong direction. Forgive me for saying, Prince Ravek; it may do well to look off the common trails and roads for his bones." The consta-ble bowed apologetically.

Ravek paced, circumnavigating the marble fountain that adorned the center of Weyles. No one was in sight as all of Weyles had withdrawn behind their doors and curtains fearful of even witnessing the interrogation that took place in plain sight. That was all well and good as far as he was concerned. Their fear was just the catalyst he needed. The city of Weyles was his to control and it will become his primary post and first advance into the northland territories.

He contemplated the constable's reasoning. Could Baytel be dead? After taking inventory of his bedroom in the keep, he found that the gear and supplies Baytel had hastily packed when departing were insufficient to survive the winter. Truly, inadequate to even survive the storm. For certain?

He halted abruptly and glared down at the little man. "Constable, inform your townspeople that King Vokat will be commissioning a large garrison to your town. Have them prepare proper housing for three hundred soldiers. I believe you have storage houses at the end of town. Those two buildings will do temporarily until new quarters can be built. Two of my officers will be in Weyles tomorrow at noon to coordinate the occupation."

"Occupation? A garrison? Why?" asked the shocked constable.

Ravek answered the man in a pleasant manner. "Weyles is now under the protection of the Southland." He mounted his horse and his guards followed. "Back to the Southland!"

Baytel is not dead, and my search for him is far from over. There are other ways of searching for him. My skills are wasted in this town.

The deep crypt echoed with the roaring flames emitting from the cauldron. Ravek stood so near the fire his skin tightened from the heat. Amid the cauldron's alien fumes, he became transformed into the receptacle of the dark magic.

With newfound power, he accepted the dark art with all its evilness and raised his arms to the cauldron, causing the flames to leap to the ceiling. Fire and heat snapped the air; the magic infused into him, now transforming him from a mere receptacle to the complete possessor of the dark art.

He spread his black wings wide as the magic pulsated through his body. Bathed in fire, he turned his attention to the Pithean goblin chained to the stone floor. He lowered his hand and fire shot forth, striking the helpless Pithean.

The creature writhed in pain, swallowed up in flames, yet the fire did not burn its flesh. The scalding onslaught of magic set off an alteration of the Pithean's body. Muscles and bones changed visibly. Its mouth grew wide and predatory sharp teeth filled its void. Its feet turned to talons. It stretched its arms outward and, as it looked upon its hands, the Pithean screamed in revolted dismay, watching its fingers grow long and gnarled with nails morphing into sharp claws. Muscles rippled and expanded upon its back, forming membranes that rapidly cracked and freed black wings unfolding from its back.

As the final alteration was complete, the creature's moans transformed from screams of pain to shrieks of evil.

Ravek lowered his arms, folded his wings and reveled in hideous joy at what he had created. The Pithean no longer resembled its former self. It rose from the floor and stood transformed to a monster. Its body flexed muscles that protruded angrily from its dark skin. Then the creature bowed to Ravek and said in a snake-like hiss, "Master."

Ravek held back his elation at what he had created—a new-formed creature to do his bidding. His magic had been so powerfully ingrained in his underling that if he ordered it to turn its weapon upon itself, it would be powerless to disobey.

This is the beginning. I see an entire army of these creatures, unstoppable in battle.

"Go! Bring another Pithean to me. No! Ten! Bring me ten! But you must stay out of sight of others. Let no one know your change."

"Yes, Master." The monster bowed and left the crypt.

He glared into the cauldron of fire. It felt wild and horrific and he savored the sensation.

The ten will soon be hundreds, then thousands, and my army will be unlike any force upon the land—superior fighters with unsurpassable strength and drive.

He peered around the crypt, paranoid lest someone hear or see what he had created. He whispered to himself, needing to hear his own words.

"For now they will travel at night, spying on the northlanders, finding where their strengths lie. My creatures will search the lands for signs of Baytel, if he still lives. If he does not, so be it. Now that Vokat's power is nothing to mine, he will eventually weaken further and I will rise above his limitations and take his throne and lands. Then nothing can oppose me. Nothing!"

Chapter 13

BAYTEL counted twenty acolytes with him in a straight line standing at attention in the cold outdoor amphitheatre somewhere in the Citadel, all men and women about his age. All wore blue pants, white shirts and heavy cloaks bearing on the breast an embroidered insignia of the Citadel—a silver sword pointing up and a green vine with crimson roses entwined around it.

Before him upon the stage stood four druids dressed the same except in all blue. The three men and one woman were all tall, separated by one pace; their only movement was in their eyes as they scanned the recruits. He felt they could see directly into his soul. On the lower stage stood Stilar, the steward, who as Baytel came to find out was a Shôrgnome whose province was a region where the mighty Awär River flowed. Baytel turned his head slightly to look down the line of acolytes. He was one of the tallest among them.

"Eyes forward, Acolyte Baytel!" ordered one of the druids. He snapped back to attention.

In niches around the oval theatre were marble statues, each signifying the different seasons of the year. Many other marble figures were carved into the perimeter walls. Between the marble columns were etched rune markings in the alcoves and walls everywhere. Outward from the stage where he stood, he counted thirty rows of seats up.

The cool morning bit at Baytel's nostrils as the steam from the acolytes' and druids' expelled breath was the only movement in the amphitheatre. Snow and ice lay upon the stage and marble statues. The swish sounded behind him and he fought the urge to turn to see what it was. At that moment a Tree Faerie flew over his head and hovered in front of their line for a moment, its wings beating softly until it floated down and landed lightly upon the stage.

Baytel immediately noticed the familiar face of the Tree Faerie and nearly ran forward but checked himself, realizing it was not Cyr. He stared at the tiny silhouette against the blue marble backdrop of the stage. The child-like face, his twinkling slightly slanted blue eyes clear and crisp, the pointed ears and translucent wings formed as near a likeness of his tutor as he could imagine.

The intake of breath from the acolytes beside him proved to him that none had the privilege of ever seeing a Tree Faerie before. The faerie raised his small

73

DRUIDS OF THE FAERIE

hand. He felt the calm of him and knew the other acolytes had also, as all expelled the breaths they were holding.

"Greetings, Acolytes. Welcome to the Citadel," said the Tree Faerie with the same piping sweet voice as Cyr. "I am Yar, Master Tree Faerie, and I am at your service and, may I add, I and all here are in the service of the One Land. This is a statement you all should understand as the motto of this place and something to remember as long as you shall live. We of the Citadel are always and will forever be in the service of the One Land and all those who walk this great earth. If there is the slightest hesitancy in your minds and hearts of the commitment to the duty to the land and its sects of humanity, speak now."

Baytel listened to the silence that followed Yar's statement. He did not hear a shuffle of hesitation from anyone.

Yar continued, "Then repeat these words: I shall forever uphold the teachings of the Citadel and adhere to the will of the One Land."

Baytel repeated his words and made a promise to himself to uphold the oath for Cyr, Calidor and himself.

"Thank you for your pledge. You men and women have traveled to the Citadel from all points of the compass with ideals and designs of bettering your kingdoms, your lands or yourselves. You twenty begin your candidacy as equals. None is better than the other. Nevertheless, each of you has talents, abilities and strengths that will expedite the teachings we offer. Some of you are older, or wiser, or more educated than the others. Know this. These attributes you believe to be helpful may be a detriment. Do not judge yourselves against those among you. Judgment will come naturally as the lessons unfurl.

"Some of you belong to great kingdoms or fiefdoms and are of hierarchy birth. You will soon see that this means nothing. The way of the druid is the way of the land. Titles are man-made as the castles that house them. They are easily torn down and forgotten. The land is everlasting and shall always reign. It does not forget even when the sects of humanity fail to remember what is offered to them.

"Every waking moment here in the Citadel is a study to open doors in your mind and soul. Your sleeping moments may also be of some enlightenment. Take heed in whatever form of teachings that come. Absorb them all so entirely that they become instinctive.

"Here before you are the Druid Scholars. Druid Vernol, Druid Anise, Druid Roen, and Druid Karmen. These men and woman shall be your mentors as well as your friends. I leave you in their care. May you all fare well."

Yar's sheer wings began beating so quickly snow blew off the stage. He flew high over their heads and with a turn of his wings darted across the sky to the west and disappeared in the clouds.

"Acolytes," shouted the Druid Vernol. "Before I am your friend, you will follow and learn."

Baytel saw Vernol jump off the stage and run up the stairs of the amphitheatre, exiting between two pillars. He looked at the acolytes beside him, tall young men like him. He nodded and they ran quickly after the Druid Vernol and the others followed.

Baytel caught up with the swift Vernol and slowed to a steady pace a few steps behind. The stomping of their passage reverberated against the stone walls and floors of the outdoor passages. Baytel stole a glance behind and to his surprise saw only three other acolytes following the druid. The others must have been diverted to another group.

Druid Vernol turned toward a turret tower and entered, bounding up the steep stairs. They were in the keep of the Citadel. Upon reaching the top and without stopping, Druid Vernol started back down. Baytel's legs burned as the druid repeated the trek over and over. Labored breathing and the heavier placement of feet dominated the enclosed staircase.

Finally the druid exited the keep and they followed through the west ward and through the portcullis entrance and were outside the Citadel. Deep snowdrifts made the run difficult. Head down, blazing through the drifts, Baytel's attention was diverted and when he looked up the druid was much farther ahead. Then the druid turned the corner and was lost to sight.

Baytel increased his speed though his legs were weary. Turning the corner he found only footprints in the snow where Druid Vernol had passed. Following the footprints led them into the east forest and he plunged in through the thicket. No sooner had Baytel entered the woods than the druid came into view standing at the base of a small clearing; his hand held up for a halt. Baytel had been running for what seemed like hours and as he stopped beside Druid Vernol out of breath he could not help but notice the druid's breathing was steady, barely taxing. He thought back to the months of training with Calidor, thankful he had encouraged him as hard as he did.

"Acolytes Baytel, Areus, Sezon and Ekar," announced Vernol. "Within this forest is a latent path. Upon the path are markings to find its end. At the end of the path shall be your only meal of the day. Once you nourish yourselves, return to the Citadel using your skills of overland navigation."

"What kind of markings are we suppose to look for?" asked the acolyte Ekar.

Ekar had a shorter, muscular, bulky physique; his blond hair was matted down with sweat, and his brown, bulging eyes darted back and forth uneasily. He still panted severely from the run. He was a curious young man, and even though Baytel tried not to pre-judge those at the assembly, he had a predisposition about Ekar as a difficult person to be friendly with.

Druid Vernol looked coldly at Ekar. "You shall see soon enough, Acolyte." The druid turned away from Ekar, his displeasure at being interrupted evident. He pointed toward a copse of pines and said, "The path lies ahead and will show itself after you enter between those two trees. Now, are there any questions?"

It struck him that Druid Vernol was using the same form of speech as did Calidor when offering a lesson. Remembering the patience he practiced in his questions and lessons, knowing that no question ever received a direct response and that all answers unfolded in time, he remained silent, figuring at this juncture it was part of the test.

Ekar spoke again: "I have no weapon. What if there are marauders? I will need to defend myself."

Baytel inwardly cringed hearing Ekar ask more questions. The others remained silent, probably with the same discomfort.

Druid Vernol turned to Ekar. His earlier cold expression altered to a scowl. "Acolyte, you use the word 'I' too frequently for my tastes."

Ekar visibly stiffened. He fidgeted and shuffled his feet in the snow. The display was a sign he was unaccustomed to being disciplined.

"Acolytes, the Citadel is your destination. The trial before you is only as arduous as you make it. Good luck and I hope to see you safely back at the Citadel."

With that being said, Druid Vernol turned and walked briskly back where they had run and disappeared from view.

The momentary pause after the druid departed left a strange silence to their group. It was lasting longer than was comfortable and finally was broken by Areus, the tall and dark-haired acolyte who had stood beside Baytel at the amphitheatre.

"Gentlemen, let's go!" Areus said, slapping his hands together and stepping toward the trees.

"Wait! Do we go together or should we separate?" asked Ekar.

"Well, since we have been together from the beginning and placed here in this clearing and directed as a group to those trees, I see no reason to separate," replied the acolyte Sezon, a wiry thin man with deep-set soft eyes that suggested reflective intelligence. He immediately fell into place behind Areus.

Baytel followed them and heard Ekar fall in line behind him. They broke through the two trees and found they were in an open wedge of the trail that showed through to a narrow path. The branches of the pine trees were blanketed with snow and seemed to wall them in. Ten paces into the wedge they all stole a glance behind. The forest had closed in around them.

Ekar ran forward but found only thick brush. Breaking small branches, he frantically sought where the path went. Snow and branches flew as he flayed away at the wall of trees. "What treachery is this? A few paces in and we are lost? I don't like this!"

Having understood this type of lesson, Baytel decided to offer advice. "Calm yourself, Ekar. We have to remember that everything that is put before us has some purpose. It is all a test. The intent of this exercise is to reach the end of the path, eat, and then return. The place where we started is not necessary to our objective. It is the path beyond the two trees we must focus on."

"Don't tell me to calm myself, boy. I know what the objective is," he said, defensively.

"Easy there, Ekar. No need to get unsettled. Baytel only meant to put the situation in its proper perspective," said Areus, who apparently was always of a cheerful disposition. "We will get through this together."

Baytel put aside Ekar's behavior and took to studying the surrounding woods. The tree branches thick with snow draped low but Baytel stepped forward and discerned a path ahead.

"Wait!" shouted Ekar, as he stepped in front of Baytel. "Who made you leader?"

Baytel looked to Areus and Sezon. All shrugged. He turned to Ekar. "You can lead if you like."

"Good. Follow me," he commanded and stomped ahead with a satisfied smirk.

Ekar kept a fast pace through the snow-canopied woods. At times, the others hailed after him to slow down as they diligently searched for markings. Occasionally, Baytel heard Ekar shout from far ahead, in his sharp, squeak-pitched voice, to keep up.

Ekar was so far ahead that Baytel asked Areus and Sezon to keep seeking signs while he hailed and then caught up.

"Ekar, you need to slow down. We may be passing signs that lead us to the right direction."

"I am on the path! It is right at my feet, Baytel." Ekar turned and shouted, "Hurry up back there!"

Sezon and Areus walked up and stood next to Baytel, their expressions grave.

Ekar reacted, "What? I know we are on the right path. You all move too slowly. The faster we travel this path the sooner we find our meal and get out of this wretched cold."

Baytel ignored Ekar's rant and looked back along the path they had traversed. All signs of their passage had been wiped away. No evidence of their being in the woods showed as the snow lay upon the ground and branches as if they had never passed this way.

In a passive calm voice, Baytel asked, "Gentlemen, could you please look behind us?"

Sezon gasped and exclaimed. "We walk upon magical ground!"

Recalling the small clearing before his arrival at the Citadel, he replied, "This same phenomenon occurred in the forest I traveled through on my way here. It is magical, so all the more reason, Ekar, to slow our pace."

Areus concurred. "Ekar, your forerunning is reckless. While we are looking for signs and markings, you are disturbing the area ahead before we can inspect it. For all we know you may have covered our first clues."

77

"Quite right," said Sezon. "Either slow down or let Baytel lead."

Ekar's face turned toward him, as red as a cardinal, and his eyes blazed with hatred Baytel had never before witnessed in another's eyes.

"Let a Southlander lead? Never!"

The ugliness of Ekar's condemnation unsettled him. He was about to defend himself but upon quick thought realized there was no reason to. Instead, he posed a question: "How does my homeland have anything to do with this path and our objective, Ekar?"

"Absolutely nothing! I do not trust you, Baytel. I heard one of the sentry guards say a Southlander was among the acolytes. I presumed right, didn't I? It is you! After all the pain and death your homeland has inflicted, why they accepted you is beyond reason. It is an outrage!"

Ekar was not concealing an ounce of bitterness or hatred. "I think you are a spy sent by whatever evils that come from your land and, therefore, you will not lead us. Not as long as I am in this company."

Baytel took a calming breath. He knew there would be people who would be prejudicial once they learned of his origins, but this disclosure had come sooner than he anticipated.

"You judge and admonish me for no reason other than an inner hatred of events that happened before you or I were born? This preconception that all Southlanders are bad is unjust. I am here to learn to serve the land and the sects of humanity just as you, Areus and Sezon."

"No, Southlander. You will use the Citadel's teachings to destroy us all. Just as your forefathers did."

Ekar's accusations bit deep. His father surely did harm to the people in the last war. There was no doubt that Vokat was known as a tyrannical king bent on destruction and domination. Baytel, silent, felt unable to counter the hatred Ekar spewed.

"Enough of this nonsense, Ekar," said Areus. "Baytel is one of us. He accepted the oath, just as we all did. So let's not deliberate further about it, shall we?"

"You come to his defense too often, Areus. Are you loyal to the Southland?"

Areus shook his head, not in the negative, but rather in an annoyed response. "I am losing patience with your accusations and prejudices, Ekar."

"That coming from a pampered elite Kilhalen man means nothing to me. You and your region are holed away from the real dangers this Southlander has caused. So be aware then, Kilhalen man, this Southlander's oath means nothing to me."

Sezon pushed past him and pointed an angry finger at Ekar. "You are wrong, Ekar. The oath, whomever recites those reverent words, means everything! We are all in this together. We all spoke those words before Yar! So enough of this nonsense and either lead properly or step aside."

"Never! I will make the end of this ridiculous path without you all."

He bolted forward, crashing through the woods. Baytel could hear him far up the path breaking the winter-dried branches until all sight and sound of him were gone. Immediately, the branches mended and snow covered Ekar's passage.

Baytel asked, "How will we find him now?"

Areus replied, "He is on his own, Baytel. Let's learn that hatred and prejudice are impertinent and cause those who harbor them to make poor judgments and asinine decisions. Now, if you will, Baytel. Lead the way."

Baytel glanced at Sezon, who nodded his agreement. He walked ahead and immediately something caught his eye.

"What is it, Baytel?" asked Sezon.

Baytel knelt down and lifted a pine branch away from a sapling. "Something is etched across the bark of this birch tree. Look here."

"The marks look as if they were made with the tip of a blade," remarked Sezon.

Areus bent low and studied the scratches. "It does not look familiar to me."

Baytel squatted beside the others. "It is rune sign."

"Rune?" they asked, simultaneously.

"Yes. These rune marking origins are in the tongue of the ancients," said Baytel.

Sezon and Areus looked at him with questioning faces. "You know the tongue of the ancients?" asked Sezon.

"Yes."

Both men nodded their acceptance and Sezon asked, "What do they read?"

"Two idioms, but only three words. Point north ascend."

Sezon looked questioningly at Baytel. "Ascend, point, north? What does that mean?"

"No, Sezon. Ancient rune reads in locutions, or catchphrases. There are two utterances in this rune. *Point north* is the first. Then the lone word *ascend* is the second phrase. In that sequential order. The ancient rune is a very specific tongue."

"It must be something up the path," said Areus.

"Let's take it slow then. No sense in rushing toward an enigma."

He stalked the center of the path while Areus and Sezon followed two paces behind, flaring out to the sides of the path. They moved slowly, methodically seeking any sign or clue to the strange rune message. Snow began to fall and the air filled with white flakes the size of chestnuts. Barely visible in the thickening snowfall, the path curved and widened into a cluster of pine trees where it forked into two directions.

"We would have missed this had the snowfall started earlier. Now I presume *point north* means we take the north path as the rune read. But what is the *ascend* part?"

"To ascend to something? Maybe we are to scale up one of these trees," contemplated Areus.

"It also means to rise, but rise to what? Or on what?"

He edged forward gingerly onto the northerly fork and a lesson from Calidor flashed through his mind.

"When advancing into the unknown, prepare for the unexpected."

Suddenly, the ground beneath his feet became unstable, rising and falling like waves on the sea. Baytel shouted, "Stay back!"

As the vacillating accelerated, he looked for a branch or limb for support. Nothing was in reach. He teetered forward. The snow was heavy and he sensed that if he fell, he would drop deep into an abyss. Then the sounds of a landslide reverberated all around him. It became louder.

"Baytel there is a branch above your head!" yelled Sezon, over the noise. "Jump up to it! To ascend is to rise up! Jump!"

Baytel jumped and found and grasped the limb. Clinging to it, he was suddenly propelled upward through a chute of snow and branches. The flight was exhilarating. He could hear Areus and Sezon shouting after him; their joyous cries filled with wonder and amusement.

Then their voices faded and the sounds of the chute and breaking branches followed until his own shouts of excitement filled his ears. Accelerating to a speed never experienced, he was suddenly thrown from the chute into the snowdrifts at the top of a cliff.

He freed himself and was met with the sight of Areus in mid-air shouting, "Whoooohooo!"

Directly afterward, Sezon was propelled through the air, landing beside Areus in a puff of snow.

Baytel peered down the chute at their course up the cliff. Massive trees filled the landscape below him. He was astounded that with the intricate channel that twisted and turned upward, they never collided with any of the trees and rocks along the way up the cliffside.

Areus cried, "What fun! But what was the ground doing beneath our feet down there?"

"Whatever it was nearly took my boots off," said Sezon with a grunt. "I need a little help here."

Baytel pulled Sezon out of the snow bank he was deposited in, and said, "Thank you, Sezon. You saved us all down there."

"We would be nowhere without your knowledge of the ancient rune, Baytel," he replied.

"Well, onward we go gentlemen. Baytel, lead the way," said Areus, pointing toward the newly discovered path atop the cliff.

The camaraderie was a euphoric physic to Baytel. Never had he experienced such companionship, and though they were far from the end of the path with more signs yet to decipher, he was thankful to be among them.

Hours later, at the Citadel, Druid Karmen had finished a lecture on the many forms and symbols of rune and their multiple meanings. It was late. Brilliant stars filled the night sky. Baytel sat between Areus and Sezon. All acolytes were present except Ekar.

A sound came from the rear of the amphitheatre. Marching down the stairs to the stage were the Druids Anise and Roen. With a look of stoic disappointment they joined Druid Karmen. Behind and appearing where they had come from was Druid Vernol with Ekar in tow. Ekar was wet from head to boots, his clothes torn, his face cut and bleeding. He looked disheveled, exhausted, and abased, having been lost in the forest all of the day and most of the night. No one made a sound. The statues that surrounded the theatre looked as if they too were disappointed. Their vacant eyes stared out as if in judgment, like the druids upon the stage.

Druid Vernol left Ekar to stand below the stage and pointed toward the acolytes for him to join his classmates. Druid Vernol addressed the assembly. "You are all individuals with certain conditioned behaviors, preconceived ideas, and ideologies. Forget them. Here and out in the lands beyond this fortress you must adjust to the elements, the participants, and the situations you find yourself in. They will dictate your conduct and demeanor. Wisdom is a virtue that can come naturally if you keep the common good in mind. Ekar did not and thus a lesson hard learned."

Baytel turned and met Ekar's eyes staring back as incensed as they were in the forest. Baytel turned away from his hate.

Areus leaned toward him, having seen Ekar's loathing, and whispered, "Do not be concerned with Ekar. He is wrong in the head."

Baytel nodded appreciatively. He liked Areus and Sezon and it warmed him how naturally they had become friends. Nevertheless, the cloud manifested by his father's and brother's past deeds and their current thirsts would never be completely absent from his mind.

Chapter 14

BAYTEL gazed out upon the landscape from the turret window. The view stretched away from the Citadel grounds to where the tops of the forest and distant fields of green were open to the warmth of the summer sun. The movement of the trees and the swaying of the tall grass from the ever-present wind sent his mind adrift to how much he had absorbed since arriving at the Citadel.

A dwarf appeared below, exiting the fortress through the north postern gate. The dwarf leaned heavily upon a walking stick as he made his way toward the forest. Baytel recalled the day the dwarf had arrived. It was deep winter and the dwarf had crawled for some time to reach the fortress. His leg was twisted awkwardly and broken in two places from a battle far to the east. Upon examination, the dwarf had other serious injuries: His arms had been ripped and clawed by a pack of wolves. He was near death.

Throughout the winter and spring, gnomes, dwarfs, imps, and even trolls arrived at the Citadel, sick and injured, and all received treatment and medicines from the druids. Once healed, the injured or sick departed, leaving nothing except their thanks. Most were frightened to stay even though the druids were nothing but accommodating. The visitors mostly kept to themselves. They felt fortunate to be healed, but the mysterious fortress with various legends attached played on their sensibilities, and once healed, the patients left the Citadel with unqualified relief.

For Baytel, the months while at study had gone by fast. The druids offered no time for loitering or daydreaming. His occasional respite took the form of early-morning foraging ventures with the beautiful Druid Anise. Most acolytes avoided this additional study, but he found the morning routine a solace that allowed him to assemble his thoughts and put into perspective all he was learning. Druid Anise would lead those who participated into the land about the fortress to collect stem roots, leaves and bark of all varieties, and special minerals from riverbeds, soil and rock. As they harvested she imparted her knowledge of their healing properties. Each leaf, stem, root, growth, or crushed mineral contained an element that, once mixed in specific measurements and combinations, formulated a curative substance.

Master Yar and Druid Anise instructed him on the proper ratios and administration of the many remedies for specific ailments and Baytel stood beside Yar and Druid Anise while they administrated to those who came to be healed. Eventually, he mastered the medicinal properties of the land as he, Areus, Sezon, and another acolyte, Podius, having progressed faster than the others, advanced from the medicinal schooling to the study of physical healing.

Examining the various physiques of sects of humanity and absorbing the skills and techniques of the mastery of surgery, Baytel and his acolyte companions assisted in all surgeries, each taking a turn in the diversities of operations, post treatments, and healing processes.

Baytel's gaze followed the dwarf until he disappeared beneath the fluff of branches and leaves, leaving a feeling of gratification. Though Baytel knew eventually his life would take him away from the medical tower of the Citadel, the healing knowledge and talent would go with him.

He snapped out of his reverie, realizing the time of the daily lecture was near and the lecture was on the far side of the fortress where he had not been yet. He hastened through the maze of passageways, recalling the confusion of the first days in the fortress, taking wrong turns that deposited him into corridors unknown. Baytel turned right, then left down a long corridor and right again and found the study room without loss of time. Tables and chairs were placed in rows. Over each study table an oil lamp hung from the beautiful ceiling mural. All the acolytes were seated awaiting the lecturer. But before he took the last chair, Baytel's eyes fixed upon the far wall where marble plaques hung. He stepped toward them and inhaled sharply, recognizing the plaques as the same as those adorning Calidor's cabin.

"You are surprised by something, Acolyte Baytel? We, however, are not surprised by your tardiness."

He whirled about, hearing Yar's piping voice, not expecting him as the lecturer—and from the murmur within the study room, neither had the others.

"My apologies, Master Yar. I am quite taken aback. I have seen plaques like these before in a friend's cabin. These are of the kind from which I was taught to read and write the ancient rune."

"Yes, Acolyte Baytel, Calidor is a fine scholar and a great man. You are fortunate to have been taught by him."

Another murmur swept the room and with more volume at the mention of Calidor and Baytel's acquaintance with him. None of the acolytes' lessons had mentioned Calidor before.

Questions that had burned inside his mind for over a year ignited. One burst out: "Master Yar, is he the Calidor of legend?"

"He is, Acolyte Baytel, and much more. Calidor's ancestry dates back to the kings of the ancients during the Golden Era of Man," he replied, and glided to the wall of plaques. Yar turned to the acolytes and said, "The history of the land is vast..."

Baytel heard Yar stop talking and he turned away from the plaques, giving Yar his full attention.

"Be seated, Acolyte Baytel," directed Yar, pointing to his study table.

He took his seat with greedy anticipation. His eyes riveted on Yar, awaiting the full story of the man he spent a year with and learned so much from.

Yar began: "Many millennia ago, far beyond our comprehension of time and history, the land was much different than you see it today, as was humanity. It was bountiful and young, and tranquility was at every turn. Ancient man and animal existed harmoniously. Peace and serenity ruled the days and the people cherished what the land offered them. In return, humanity cared for the land and returned the love a parent would a child.

"From this nurturing by humanity, the land offered seeds to sow that yielded crops to harvest, and with the purest waters to drink, the populace multiplied. Left to their desires the people enhanced their civilization by mining rich minerals and creating sciences of its matter. They forged tools and built objects of need and desire.

"It was the Golden Era of Man. The population steadily increased and so the mind and body also advanced. Great intellectuals and astute colleagues of high learning created incredible devices that altered how people lived, making their toil less and their lives easier. Enormous structures were built and classes based upon privilege developed. Soon, however, prejudices arose and members of the populace turned hostile toward one another. Aggression spread across the land as the privileged forcibly seized possessions, and overpowering of the weak became commonplace.

"This, as the histories tell it, happened so rapidly it caused widespread discord. Ancient man gathered forces to prevent further chaos. They founded nations, drawing the populace into separate regions. The population swelled disproportionately and land became scarce. Industry spread farther outward, suffocating more of the land. The air became congested with illness and waters were fouled. These factors affected the growth of crops and food shortages became prevalent. Nations could no longer support the lives of all and people perished in vast numbers. Consequently, wars arose between the nations over food and power.

"During this turbulent era a race of man emerged and came to the aid of the weak and set to right many regions of the land. They were kings among men and their leader wielded a mighty magical sword. This sword was forged long before and in its steel was infused the magic of the land itself. The sword had been held back for just such a time when its powers could be wielded by those worthy to do so. These Kings of the North were the chosen among all mankind, and the Sword of the Kings was theirs to wield.

"Nevertheless, their triumphs were few and their hope was fading as most of the populace remained under the power of the warlords of the nations. Crestfallen, the good kings set upon an alternative ambition. Seeing, in despair, what humanity had become and recognizing its eventual collapse, they embarked upon the collection of all knowledge, wisdom and writings of ancient mankind and safely stored them for the future ages. Then they disappeared from the land to wait for a new and better age of humanity.

"With no one to enforce peace for decent societies, the warlords, unrestrained, escalated their horrible wars and designs. Greed, violence, pestilence, the defiled waters, the rape of the land and its unrepressed ruination became overwhelming and unforgivable, and the land finally retaliated. Earthquakes opened vast crevasses and fissures swallowing entire cities. Volcanoes spewed molten rock and fire, destroying edifices of evil. Safe havens were fought over as the people scattered from the onslaught. When the destruction ended and humanity was near extinction, the rains came and darkness descended to reign alone.

"A millennium of time passed before light returned. The first to venture out of the darkness were the Dwarfs of Minion. They ascended from the depths to take their rightful place among mankind. They had been hidden away throughout the Golden Era deep in their mines. When finally emerging from life underground, they found no people or civilization.

"Then the Kings arrived shortly after, having sailed the seas from their land far to the north. They befriended the Minion Dwarfs and together they combined to search for the scattered. Soon, people emerged from their sanctuaries, yet remained as stubborn as before the destruction and commenced to mirror the previous age. They disregarded the urgings of the Kings and the Minion Dwarfs and set upon battling for territory.

"Dark forces led by warlords wielding a magic they conjured during the millennium of internment enslaved all who defied them. Opposition was futile for the dark warlords brought forth the old weapons of war that no one could combat. The Kings and the Dwarfs tried to rally the people against their folly but few joined the cause. So there commenced a horrific war that lasted many years. When the Kings and the Dwarfs finally destroyed the evil lords, their hearts were low because many had been lost in battle, as was the Sword of the Kings.

"Yet still, humanity did not adhere to the wisdom of the Kings and the Dwarfs. So the good Kings said their farewells to Minion and with great sadness, sailed back to their lands. The Minion Dwarfs, having discovered the precious metal Pintél at Ctiklat Mountain, decided to abandon Minion and went to ground under Ctiklat Mountain, heeding the warning from the Kings that destruction was eminent.

"And once more, the earth shook and ripped apart all that remained of that horrible civilization, and humanity scattered and darkness returned. Years passed and nothing remained of the previous eras but a few remnant structures in regions long forgotten. The land, however, was reborn. Mountain ranges were transformed with high peaks sloping down to verdant valleys where strong rivers and serene lakes dotted the landscape. However, all this restructured youthful land was barren of life.

"Then the land created us, the Faerie tribe. We were birthed by the One Land and given magical powers drawn from the very essence of the land itself. Our assignment remains to this day to be the custodians of the One Land. We worked our magic and life sprouted from the earth. Trees, grasses, flowers, plants of all kinds, fish from the waters, animals from the forest, as life sprang forth where none was before. Fruits and other foods blossomed and wildlife flourished once more. Our work was not toil but a reward for being given life.

"From Ctiklat came many dwarfs, after years beneath the mountain, and they built upon their mountain a castle of unsurpassed magnificence. Some of the Kings, seeking their lost talisman, the magical sword, stayed among us faeries in the west forest.

"During this time the Kings beheld the magic of the One Land and offered their alliance to us, which we happily accepted. They commissioned the Ctiklat Dwarfs to build a fortress as their home. With our magic and the dwarfs' extraordinary abilities of construction, we built this structure you now have the privilege to live in, with its strength, beauty and magic infusions that will withstand any onslaught. The Kings brought their storehouse of knowledge of the ages and placed it within these walls. To further their commitment to the Faerie way and to the One Land, they became the first Druids of the Citadel.

"Man began to venture from hiding, but just as the land had re-created itself through years of chaos, physical changes also occurred to humanity. Different sects of humanity emerged. Man, gnome, troll, goblin, pixie, ogre, imp and more, all desiring to establish a land of their own. This time they tried to establish their territories without warfare.

"Most of the good Kings departed, seeing humanity co-existing peacefully. However their leader, the Druid Calidor, chose to remain for the sword was still lost. Vowing to find the sword of their father, Calidor gave his crown to his brother who with the others sailed back over the vast Great Sea to their lands far away.

"A small number of the Druid kings stayed with Calidor. These strong and tall men scouted, reported and recorded the progression of the many sects of humanity to the Citadel. They became known as the Grey Riders and they accomplished all this by keeping their ancestry secret as they continued their search for the sword.

"During one of the last conflicts among the sects, a war where the pixie sect fought the gnome tribes, the Grey Riders were called upon to intervene, and attempt to negotiate peace. The pixies-fierce fighters despite their size-interpreted the gesture as the Citadel taking sides against them and attacked the negotiating group. The few Grey Riders were outmatched as the pixies swarmed the conference. The Citadel reacted, sending out the remaining Grey Riders who, allied with the gnome tribes, took arms against the pixies. Their combined forces drove the pixies south, beyond Azkar Rol, pursuing them deep into the Forbidden Territory.

"The pixies avoided death by escaping underground, deep in the region. The Grey Riders followed them into grottos and cave basins that reached far and deep. It was there, in the depth of the Forbidden Territory, that Calidor and the Grey Riders found their lost talisman. How it came to that place is unknown. If you recall, the land had reformed itself during the dark days, and perhaps it was its way of keeping it safe for the Kings to recover.

"With the pixies driven to ground, and as time passed without major conflicts, the populace grew and became more adventurous and the outlands became dangerous. Factions broke off from the populace, acquiring weapons and began an era of terror in the outlands. Many did not survive as these tyrants took advantage of the weak and alone. Calidor and the Grey Riders, seeing farmer, villager and wayfarer being attacked, assembled a troop to protect the innocent. Grey Riders, dwarfs and gnomes rode with Calidor, following him and the power of his sword against the tyrants. Calidor serves the One Land in his own way to this day."

Baytel shook his head at the luck he had in being found by the very man Yar lectured about.

"What is it, Acolyte Baytel?" asked Yar.

"Master, I have asked Calidor hundreds of questions and had as many discussions and I always wondered why he knew so much about history and the Citadel. The only question I never asked him was if he was a druid."

"Yes, asking could have saved you time in study," said Yar. "The Grey Riders remain in our service to this day, reporting the happenings of the land and recording its history."

An acolyte raised his hand and asked, "These Grey Riders must be hundreds of years old. How is that possible?"

Yar replied, "These men and women are most extraordinary in that their sect has always held a special bond with the land, even before the scattering of humanity. Their sect has a rare propensity of longevity, and other talents, some of which were gifted by the One Land for their altruistic and unyielding devotion and service. Their bloodline is of a hierarchy beyond time. They are the true royalty of the land, descendants of the Kings of the North—but have chosen a different way of life for the betterment of all."

"Are all the Grey Riders still druids?" asked Sezon.

"Yes, they are. However, let me point out that throughout the Citadel's history, not all Grey Riders were Kings of the North. Dwarf, man, and even gnome rode with these champions."

The acolyte asked a follow-up question: "Why are they not here among the other druids?"

Yar replied, "Although they remain steadfast in their duty, they have no part of the teaching arm of the Citadel, which is why none of you have been in contact with them."

"They sacrificed much," said Areus.

"Really?" asked Yar. "What did they sacrifice, Acolyte Areus? Land rights? No one really owns the land. To be bowed to? A ridiculous practice. Riches, power or material objects? These are fleeting desires. The good kings see none of these as sacrifices in the service of the land. Which brings me to you, Acolytes, and your service to the Citadel. It will be this sort of duty that is required by you all; to serve the sects of humanity and the One Land. That is the function of a Druid of the Citadel. The rewards may be small to some, but if you are true in your commitment to this institution, the recompense shall be enough to saturate your souls beyond humanity's yearnings and desires."

During his lecture of the history of the kings a spark seemed to ignite deep within Baytel. Every word Yar spoke created urgency he could not comprehend. He remained seated as Yar and the other acolytes departed the study. Something was missing from the lecture that left a hollow sensation, like a door that remained closed but within reach. Perplexed, and unable to shake the feeling, he walked from the study room, wobbly and uneasy.

Chapter 15

BAYTEL faced upward, his vision split between the sight of rock inches away from his face and the upward view of the vastness of the blue sky. He could barely feel his hands and feet, as the chill of the early morning air and the cold rock penetrated deep. The shadow of the east mountain sheer blanketed the escarpment he clung to; however, its dark outline ended a few maneuvers above his reach.

He re-chalked his hands and, extending one, worked his fingers into a small fissure. He tested the hold with his fingertips and judged it firm enough to support his weight. Drawing his right knee up and securing a foothold onto a protrusion, he hoisted up to his hand level and adjusted his position, placing his left foot onto a flange for further balance.

Glancing down he could see Areus and Sezon, joined on his line. They had experienced no problems taking his direction of ascent, showing the same skill as he. Starting before the day began, the climb in the blackest part of night was a challenge. Now, even with the light of day high above them, the shadowed escarpment in no way seemed to lighten.

He called to Areus ten feet below. "Beneath my foothold is a jetty of rock. Use it for your finger hold. You are almost face to face with the left foothold. Beside it to the right, three feet, you will find a wide crease for your other foot."

"Hand at the jetty; foot three feet below to the right. Got it," he answered.

Baytel continued to climb and a few minutes later heard Areus communicating the same holds to Sezon.

His assignment was to lead his team vertically up the escarpment. Each step and heave up must be secure enough to support his team and to clearly convey direction to them. He was careful and precise. The instructions to his team had to be exacting, or they all would plummet and die.

The next maneuver was not so good. The ascent brought him to a position on the façade that he found would traverse over a surface that looked fragmented and weak. He needed to move to the left to avoid the compromised surface. He took his time evaluating the new line of ascent. From his position the surface showed promising holds, many far superior to those he had experienced the previous one hundred feet.

He checked his ropes and straightened his position. The next maneuver would be a rather difficult one. He spoke down to Areus. "We need to move our ascent position. I need more slack."

"How much line do you want?"

"Climb another five feet. That should do it."

Once the message was relayed to Sezon and both his climbing partners prepared the necessary line, Baytel took a cleansing breath and extended his left arm at a 45-degree angle and grabbed a small outcrop of rock. He tested its strength and discovered it firm. Transferring his right foot to share the foothold with the left, he found another finger grip and released his feet. Now with his right hand holding his entire weight, he swung left, finding another left hand hold. He dangled for a few seconds stretching his muscles. Then he pulled his legs up toward his hips, using his knees to search for the protrusions he knew were there. He felt the jagged escarpment run coarsely across his legs until his knee found a lip where his upper thigh was. "There it is!" he whispered to himself and placed his foot upon the hold and rested to catch his breath and work out the maneuver in his mind. Retesting the position for sturdiness and satisfied in its security, he relayed the maneuver to his team.

Baytel briefly glanced north at the progress of the second squad of climbers on a parallel line. Ekar's voice echoed off the escarpment, shouting down directions for his team, he being their lead climber with Podius and Druid Roen below him.

Ekar's line had little difficulty and his team had ascended at a swift pace, though they remained at about the same height as Baytel's.

Leaning into the sheer, balancing easily on his footholds, one at a time, Baytel blew warm air into his cupped hands. His fingertips and hands were raw with abrasions, but on the whole, he felt fine. He placed his face against the escarpment; its coldness was so uninviting he forewent the rest and extended his arm upward, feeling for the next purchase.

His hand met warmth. He stole a glance upward. Sunlight bathed his hand; its warmth penetrated the chill in his fingers. Baytel smiled to himself and let his hand hover over the hold for a moment. The warm sensation was rapture. Continuing with his climb, he grasped another hold. It was damp with dew. Making doubly sure he had a proper grip, he drew his legs up, finding footholds, and lifted his entire body up, breaking free from the shadow. He pressed his face against the escarpment, feeling its wet heat rejuvenate his spirit.

He exclaimed loudly, "Ahhh! I could stay in this spot all day. What beauty. The sunlight gives me such a feeling of warmth. Gentlemen, you should be up here. The warm breeze passing about reminds me of being in a field of tall grass; warm and pleasant as a summer day."

"Cruel, Baytel. Very cruel," replied Areus from below. "Sezon, Baytel says he's too warm up there in the sunshine."

"Show-off!" said Sezon, his voice strained, as he pulled himself to another hold. "If I were near him, I'd loosen his line!"

Their laughter was interrupted by Druid Roen's voice from across the escarpment. It was not a pleasant tone. Baytel paused to listen in case the second squad needed assistance.

"Acolyte Ekar! You must wait for your line mate below. If you cause your connecting line to tighten too much this pulls the entire line away from the escarpment and possibly the entire team with it. Also, it taxes the climber's strength and will create premature fatigue. Remember the lesson, Acolyte Ekar, and do not repeat it."

"Enough! I understand." Ekar's reply showed his impatience. He sounded agitated, not the proper attitude to lead, Baytel thought, especially on an escarpment hundreds of feet above the earth floor.

Ekar's disregard for Druid Roen's reprimand continued and he shouted down to Podius, "Step it up faster, Podius. Baytel is near the top!"

Podius countered, grunting his reply. "This is not a race, Ekar. Relay your positions and holds properly. I have been forced to find my own since we began the climb all while remaining on your line of ascent."

Being at a higher elevation at that moment, Baytel could see their line was headed toward an eroded ledge where a shrub had taken root in the escarpment. Seeing the potential danger within reach of Ekar's next maneuver, he hailed across, "Ekar. Ten feet above your line of ascent there is a plant growing out of a ledge. The ledge looks too worn to support your weight. If you veer slightly toward my line, you can avoid it and find solid rock and superior positions all the way up to the top."

"Keep to your own squad, Southlander! I will direct my team without your help," replied Ekar with his usual biting tone.

"Acolyte Ekar! If another climber sees a problem it is for your safety and those on your line that you adhere to the warning and take their direction to avoid a potential danger. Being higher, Acolyte Baytel is in a better position to view your ascent. I recommend you follow his suggestion."

Ekar's cursing could be heard across the façade. Finally, Ekar veered and resumed his climb.

"Ekar! Hold up! You are climbing too fast!" yelled Podius.

"I cannot wait forever!" yelled Ekar. "Speed it up, Podius."

Podius was struggling against being pulled away by the line. One hand snapped away from the façade. His other had a mere fingertip hold keeping him from being entirely detached from the escarpment.

Baytel couldn't keep silent. "Druid Roen, Podius needs help! He is pulling away!"

Druid Roen acted quickly. "Acolyte Ekar, climb down a few feet. Podius needs slack."

"I am nearly equal to Baytel's team!" countered Ekar.

"Climb downward, Acolyte! Now!"

"Just have Podius pick up the pace!" Ekar pleaded.

Druid Roen was beside Podius and secured his feet to holds and moved up toward Ekar.

"Podius, cut your line attached to Ekar's! You are taking over as the lead climber," ordered the druid.

"No! I can do it!"

"Acolyte Ekar! Slack! Now!"

"But.... A few more feet," he pleaded.

"That's it! Acolyte, wait for me at your position! Podius, I am cutting my line from you and am climbing to Ekar. Just continue on as you have. Veer more toward Baytel's team. Baytel's team, secure a hold and wait in position."

Druid Roen free-climbed toward Ekar, who had continued to climb, which infuriated Druid Roen so much he shouted so loud at him to stop that it echoed off the escarpment.

As Druid Roen reached Ekar, he pulled out a spike, wedged it into a small crack in the escarpment, took his hammer out of his belt and, with one swift accurate hit, drove it deep and secure. He reached into his knap and pulled a length of line out. Tying it to the clip and securing it to the spike, he sent the other end falling down the façade to the ground.

"You're done, Ekar. Belay your line and set your rappel. You are off the mountain," said Druid Roen.

Ekar's voice came across the distance in chopped phrases. "You can't do this to me! I am almost to the top! It is not fair!"

"You are not climbing as part of a team. As always, you concern yourself with individual effort. This is a personality trait you must rid yourself of, Acolyte Ekar. It is not part of the resolve of a druid to think only of oneself."

"Druid Roen, let me reach the summit. I will lead better. You will see."

"Not today, Acolyte Ekar. Belay your line. Your climb is over."

"But Druid Roen…"

"Druid Anise is below. She sees the line and knows there is a problem. Descend, Acolyte Ekar. We will speak of this later."

Baytel felt uncomfortable watching so private a reprimand. Since early on, Ekar had had trouble adapting to the discipline of the Citadel. The druids had put forth more effort toward him than anyone else in the advanced acolyte stage. They were losing patience and Baytel could not blame them. Ekar seemed to cause trouble and concern at every turn.

Ekar shouted across the façade at Baytel with the same venomousness as in his first outburst those many months ago. "What are you looking at, South-lander? Are you taking amusement in my situation?"

Baytel ignored Ekar's slight against his homeland, all too used to it by now. "Not at all, Ekar. I only wanted to see you reach the summit safely."

Ekar grabbed the spike, attached the line to his clip and rappelled down, disappearing in the dark shadow below. The only sound heard was Ekar cursing Podius as he passed.

"Podius, climb up to me. You are doing fine," ordered Druid Roen.

As Podius made his way upward, the druid spoke to them all as if he were in a study room rather than clinging upon a sheer escarpment.

"Gentlemen, a Druid of the Citadel must have purpose, drive, integrity, presence of mind, patience and a duty to the task at hand. He must be able to recognize a problem and have the courage to deviate for the betterment of their charge and show determination to see the task to its end at whatever the cost. No man or woman is perfect.

"Experience is the origin of wisdom. An oath is the genesis of desire. Your education here at the Citadel offers awareness of the situations you may find yourselves involved in after you leave. The missions ahead shall challenge these virtues daily. You must strive to learn from these challenges, meeting them with full intentions to better the circumstances where your involvement is needed. Only then will you carry out the event to its proper conclusion."

Finished with his lofty lecture, he said, "Carry on, Baytel. Podius, you shall lead me up to the top, as you have all night and day."

Shortly after the incident, Baytel pulled himself over the lip and onto the summit and stretched to relieve his tense muscles. Seated, he looked all about the region. Treldor Reach was far off to the east. He followed the green plains that rolled to the far foothills of Treldor, and felt drawn toward the mountainous barrier, unsure why, sensing a desire to travel there. He sat down and stared at the cloudless sky, not thinking of anything except the horizon and what it offered.

A hand reached over the lip of the sheer and Areus pull himself onto the top. He said, "Baytel, as usual, your guidance up was perfectly executed. It makes us all look good," and collapsed beside Baytel.

Moments later, Sezon reached the top, panting from the excursion. Baytel pulled his line, assisting his last heft up. He was truly relieved to see Sezon on the summit. Sezon was physically the weakest among the acolytes and Baytel had doubted he could reach the top. But Sezon's heart was good, and he never gave in.

"Good man, Sezon. You've done well," said Baytel.

Sezon dropped next to Baytel, and said, "Good thing..." he paused to catch his breath, "there is a top to this escarpment. Does anyone have any water?"

Baytel looked at Areus, who was assigned to haul the water for them, and saw him shrug in his usual nonchalant way. "Sorry. Forgot. But I remember where I left it, so I can get to it when we descend." It was always something like this with Areus. A care-free attitude, even when against difficulties. But they all were used to his ways. Free-spirited and happy with everything and everyone and always lighthearted.

Podius climbed over the edge and stood with his arms up, shouting at the sky, *"Eeeaaoo!"*

Finally Druid Roen appeared over the lip of the sheer. He clenched a finger hold and jerked himself on top and rolled clear of the edge on his stomach and came to his knees smiling.

"Good execution, Gentlemen, especially you, Podius. You adjusted yourself to your inefficient point man, relaying to me a proper climb without jeopardizing both our positions. You called for help when necessary. A lesson, Acolyte: Never be too proud to ask for assistance. You are all men of higher skills than most, but you are not omnipotent, or omniscient. Others, from the lowly educated and weak of mind and body, to those of highest esteem and character, can offer astuteness and strength."

Baytel liked Druid Roen. He found him to be a fair man whose physical presence never overshadowed his intelligence. Even upon the escarpment, disciplining Ekar, the druid never showed anger, but when he said something, Baytel listened, as they all did, and obeyed without question.

"Congratulations, men. By reaching the summit, you are entitled to a reward," said Roen.

"I will trade my reward for a simple drink of water. That will do me fine," said Sezon.

"Ah, Sezon, you opened your mouth too soon, rejecting the reward I am about to offer. But that is alright, there shall be more for the rest of us," said Roen, laughingly.

Roen walked over to Sezon, turned him around and removed Sezon's knap. As he placed it on the rocky floor of the plateau, they heard a liquid jiggling from within it. Roen reached in and removed a demijohn filled with a deep reddish-brown ale.

Baytel touched the glass container. It was cool and his mouth immediately salivated. Sezon stood on the opposite side, unable to see the ale. Baytel asked, "Sezon, are you certain you want to forgo the reward?"

"It's not water, but I believe it is an adequate substitute," said Roen, placing it in front of Sezon.

Sezon jumped up, seeing the glass demijohn filled to the top. "Druid Roen. Perhaps I have misspoken. If I may, I would like to use the excuse of exhaustion for my recent outburst. I was not myself as I was overcome with thirst. And after all, I did, unbeknownst to me, haul it up the mountain."

"Come, Sezon, you get the first drink," offered the druid, handing Sezon a flask.

"Easy now, Sezon," said Baytel, seeing him quickly gulp down the ale. "Save some for the rest of us."

"Thank you. I will never reject any reward from you again, Druid Roen," he said, handing the flask to Baytel.

Baytel drank and sat watching the others drink and laugh, jostling each other back and forth with wise remarks and repartee. He felt a deep bond of friendship with them all. They were his comrades and there was nothing any of them wouldn't do for one another.

"You were excellent on the rock today, Baytel," said Druid Roen, sitting beside him. "You have made me proud."

Baytel was humbled by the compliment, and nodded, "Thank you, Druid Roen. I just love what I am a part of here. The Citadel has taught me so much; it filled a void in my life that I cannot describe."

Roen rose, offering a hand up to Baytel, and said, "You are and will be a credit to us all, Acolyte Baytel."

Baytel patted him on the shoulder. Something about the way Roen looked at him gave him the impression they were equals, and that liberated something within him and the feeling that he could conquer anything.

Chapter 16

DRUID Karmen's voice had failed him well before the last two acolytes began to spar. His commands and directions lost their forcefulness, having been expunged upon those who had battled throughout the long day. Now all who had been defeated watched the finalists and he was not concerned about instructions, for the two sparring were flawlessly executing their swordsmanship.

Karmen had begun the challenge early that morning. Elimination was a strike or stab in what would be a fatal point upon the body. The observing acolytes stood against the wall, all soaked in sweat. The two finalists were in full ringlet mail armor. Neither had scored a strike, matching one another's maneuvers with precision and proficiency, neither able to break down the other's defense.

The Master Tree Faerie Yar and all the other druids stood in the balcony above the sparring circle, observing and judging the acolytes' skill levels and styles. Both young men were well trained prior to arriving at the Citadel, and with Karmen's education the two had reached so high a level of skill they could probably out-joust most of the judges, himself included.

Finalists Baytel and Areus were drenched with sweat. Their performance was truly a joy to watch. However, their strikes began to slow as fatigue was setting in. Karmen looked up at the gallery, seeking out Yar, and his unspoken words were answered with a nod from the master.

Karmen called out with a cracked voice, "All quiet! Hold arms!"

Panting and resting on their swords, the two men smiled to one another and shook hands. Two years ago they had arrived as strangers; now they were the truest of friends. Karmen remembered how it was when he came to the Citadel, many years ago. Nothing has changed. Though the Citadel was closed for many years for training in the druid way, since taking Yar's advice to recruit and set in motion the school once more, they all sensed a change—the implications that more druids were necessary—so long as they proved worthy.

Karmen addressed the acolytes: "Good sparring, all. You all proved your skills with the sword most surprisingly well. Please adjourn to your quarters, bathe and prepare for dinner. Formal dress, if you please."

They all shuffled out, and as the last departed the druids and Yar came down from the gallery. Karmen said, "My training is complete for this session. It is my honor to recommend the following acolytes in swordsmanship for your award approval: Areus, Baytel, Podius, and Ekar. Also among the acolytes, I give Sezon an honorable mention."

"Very good, Karmen, you have done quite well; remarkably well with some of the younger acolytes," said Yar. "And congratulations to each druid for the effort you put forth the last two years. Your tutelage and training have been exemplary and you have completed all sessions with superb results. You should be proud of yourselves."

Yar paused a moment and paced across the sparring circle. Karmen knew what was to come next. They all did.

Yar looked up from his musing and spoke with so sincere a tone it was as if his entire tiny body let out a sigh. "I believe it is time for you to judge who of these fine men and women are eligible to receive the full accolades of this institution. Karmen, please do your duty."

Karmen nodded and, with stiff formality, asked, "Are there any nominations from this class of acolytes for bestowing with the distinction of Druid of the Citadel and to receive the Laurel of Academia and Healer?"

Druid Anise stepped forward and addressed Yar and the druids in her clear voice, "I nominate Acolyte Candidate Baytel."

"I support Druid Anise's nomination," said Vernol.

"Is there any discussion of the nominee?" asked Yar.

Anise continued, "He is the strongest, and has shown numerous times throughout his training his patience and fortitude in battle. His skills as a healer are exemplary. His leadership skills are superb. He chooses the difficult tasks, does not shy away from responsibility and unselfishly supports and assists the other acolytes when they are in need."

Vernol spoke again. "I support Baytel to be a druid. He is everything we could wish out of an acolyte candidate and deserves the Laurel. We have analyzed his ancestry. Pren, his mother, is evident in all his mannerisms. He has her calm resolve. I have seen nothing of his father in him."

The murmuring acknowledgements of satisfaction rose among them but Karmen was not fully satisfied. He asked, "Master Yar, you do not have a vote; however, we would like your opinion on the nominee."

"I am entirely confident in Acolyte Candidate Baytel's abilities to bring honor to the position of druid and to this institution," said Yar.

"Let the nomination stay and move forward. Are there other nominations?" he asked, closing discussions on Baytel.

"I nominate Candidate Areus," announced Vernol.

"Support," added Karmen. "Discussion of the nominee."

Vernol stated, "As with Baytel, so it is with Areus. He shows talents in all areas of academics, healing, and strength. He is not as serious as Baytel and is a bit fun-loving, but we all do not have to be cut from the same cloth."

"Are there any other nominations?" Karmen asked again, and then answered his own question: "I too, have a nominee. I nominate Candidate Podius."

"I support Karmen's nominee," said Roen.

Karmen liked Podius. "He is a powerful man but does not use it ill. Podius has a talent for finding the truth in things. He is the perfect example of a loyal servant to the land. Being the most traveled of the acolytes, doors will open to him from all different sects of humanity."

"On to the next nominee," Yar said.

"I nominate Acolyte Sezon," said Roen.

"Support for Acolyte Sezon," acknowledged Anise.

Karmen was reluctant and felt uneasy with the nomination. "Sezon is weak with weapons. I am not sure he can properly defend himself or others in the wild."

Roen responded, "Karmen, no one exerted more effort, nor labored at the tasks to the fullest extent, than Sezon. Yes, he has limited physical abilities, which may be a shortcoming, but there are other talents that Sezon can offer the sects of humanity."

Anise cleared her throat and took up the defense from Roen. "He is the smartest student among the acolytes. His knowledge of flora and fauna, their healing properties, and the discoveries he personally found of new cures proved an advanced physiological awareness, adding to our own knowledge. Also, his surgical abilities are second only to that of Yar."

"Without the strength to position yourself to heal, his talents may not be able to be used," said Karmen.

Anise smiled and said, "You all remember when I was an acolyte. I was weak in weapons, also. I traveled the land in its service, healed those in need along the way, and defended myself numerous times. Sezon is certainly stronger than I. Karmen, your weapons training is far ahead of the training others outside this fortress could receive and much more advanced than what I had been taught. Besides that, would you want Sezon's healing talents to be holed up here for another year, or let him touch those in need? Do not waste his talent because his muscles are not like the others. Like Vernol said, we are not all cut from the same cloth."

Her passionate and defiant stance touched memories of their candidacy together and her struggles to achieve the Laurel. Karmen nodded to Anise. "I withdraw my opposition to Acolyte Candidate Sezon and support Roen's nominee."

Karmen then asked, "Are there any other nominations for the Laurel, and distinction of Druid of the Citadel?" and hearing no one voice another, said, "I move we accept the nominees. All in favor say *aye*."

Hearing all ayes and no nays, Karmen said, "Motion carries."

"Your choices are excellent," said Yar. "Nominees will be awarded their Laurels tonight. Anise, you will do the honors. Karmen, gather the acolytes in the amphitheatre after dinner."

The night sky was aglow with vivid starlight. The amphitheatre was cold. The early spring night still felt like winter. Colored-glass oil lanterns hung along the columns waxing the marble in multihued radiance.

Baytel stood in a line with the rest of the acolytes below the stage where the druids and Yar stood. No sound from acolyte, druid or even wind could be heard, as all in the amphitheatre was silent. He leaned toward Areus, and whispered, "What is going on?"

Druid Vernol declared: "Acolyte Candidate Baytel, you stood in this exact place over two years ago, at which time I had to remind you to be quiet. Please show us that you have learned something here by remaining silent."

Baytel heard Areus whisper, "He doesn't forget anything."

Druid Anise walked across the stage to the podium, her posture and fluid stride perfect. She was clothed in a blue formal dress, the crest of the Citadel embroidered in a white wrap that draped over her shoulders down to the stage floor. She looked more beautiful than ever. Her vibrant violet eyes ran across them all, not resting on any one acolyte; her black hair tied with a white band behind her head set off her alabaster skin, intensifying her stunning beauty.

Areus leaned toward him again and Baytel cringed, hoping Druid Vernol would not notice. Areus whispered, "I once knew a girl who looked almost as beautiful as Druid Anise. Perhaps afterward, you can come and visit Kilhalen so I can introduce you to her, or any number of girls."

Baytel smiled and nodded, knowing only too well that Areus could without question come through on that promise, him being so flirtatious with Druid Anise through the years at the Citadel, even in the constant face of rejection and absolute disapproval by Anise and the rest of the druids. He could only imagine what Areus was like at his home in Kilhalen.

"Gentlemen and ladies." Her voice carried softly. "We are proud of all the efforts you have put forth and the ambition you have shown to strive and grow to become druids. You have demonstrated a commitment few would accept, especially voluntarily, and praise of this comes from our deepest feelings and affections to you all."

Anise continued in a stronger voice. "We are all here tonight to honor four of you who have successfully mastered the teachings of the Citadel. By no means does this diminish anyone's efforts, for some of you are only short lessons away from the honors these four will receive. In the spirit of the One Land and its teachings, let us give tribute to them and celebrate their successes and hopes for their continued efforts for the good of humanity."

Baytel breathed deeply, his muscles tense as anxiety pulled at his nerves while Druid Anise stood silent at the podium looking again at all the acolytes, now resting her gaze on each one in turn. Who would be among the four he was not sure. This was so unexpected that he had not thought of who was deserving. His mind ran swiftly through the class, finding fault and praise, weakness and strength in everyone present. Never one to consider himself better than the next person, Baytel discounted any possible chance of being named.

"When your name is called, please come forward onto the stage."

The steward Stilar entered from the rear of the stage with small wreaths on one arm and blue garments draped over the other.

Anise continued, "The Laurel of Academia and Healer and cloak of Druid of the Citadel are awarded to Druid Sezon!"

A cheer rose from the assembled group, Baytel cheering loudest, knowing Sezon's work ethic was strongest among them.

Sezon climbed the steps to the stage and Druid Roen approached him with a blue cloak. Sezon removed his white acolyte outer garment and, with Roen's assistance, put on the blue of the druid, and stepped to the podium where Anise placed a wreath of laurel upon his head, saying, "Druid Sezon."

Another cheer rose from the acolytes. Baytel looked down the standing row of his classmates, seeing smiles and cheering all the way down the line until he came across Ekar's face. His unmasked scowl showed displeasure and he applauded with little enthusiasm.

The Druid Sezon stood to one side and all eyes turned to Druid Anise. "The Laurel of Academia and Healer and cloak of Druid of the Citadel are awarded to Druid Podius!"

Again applause echoed off the marble of the amphitheatre as Podius received his honors.

"The Laurel of Academia and Healer and cloak of Druid of the Citadel are awarded to Druid Areus!"

Baytel shouted, embracing his friend and patting his back as he headed to the stage. Seeing his friends wearing the blue cloaks standing next to the other druids upon the stage was fulfilling, and whether or not he was chosen he felt content with selections of druids.

Time seemed to stand still. The aroma of the laurels wafted throughout the amphitheatre, sending his head spinning with their scent. He looked down the row, left then right. All seemed to be holding their breath. All looked on with happy anticipation. All but Ekar, who stood on the balls of his feet as if readying for battle rather than an award.

"...Druid Baytel!" announced Druid Anise.

A shout rose up louder than the others and Baytel stood, unmoving, looking at Anise. He had not heard the beginning of the announcement. Acolytes were slapping his back with congratulations. He was numb with emotion, unsure if he actually heard his name after he heard the title Druid. He felt someone push him forward, pointing him to the stage. As he came out of his numbness, he walked toward the steps. His feet tangled and he fell forward. A commotion surged through the ranks of the acolytes, some laughter, some shouts of dismay.

Baytel rose to his feet and looked back. Ekar's face showed all he needed to see, the expression twisted with shocking hatred after his intentional trip.

Ekar sneered and spat, "A Southlander as a druid? What an atrocity!"

Acolytes began shouting rebukes at Ekar. The druids shouted from the stage for all acolytes to re-form their line. A young acolyte patted Baytel on the shoulder and pointed to the stairs. Baytel nodded his thanks and disengaged from the ruckus and looked up and saw Druid Vernol waving him forward. He climbed the stairs and walked toward the druid, his mind still on Ekar's reaction.

Vernol smiled at him and said, "Druid Baytel, I will not hesitate to say this before all here, for I know all here can wholly acknowledge that you have shown unremitting loyalty and intelligence in all tasks, and have proven leadership abilities beyond expectations. You truly are deserving of these accolades. Now, Druid Baytel, as it is not proper for a druid to be wearing the cloak of an acolyte..."

Baytel hurriedly removed his white cloak and, with Vernol's assistance, put on the blue. He embraced Vernol and stepped to the podium where Druid Anise stood. His eyes misted over seeing her eyes tear. He lowered his head and she placed the laurel upon it. The wreath's sweet scent would be one he would never forget.

"Congratulations, Druid Baytel," she declared in a softly mellow voice.

Baytel embraced her and stepped into line with his friends. He thought of Cyr and Calidor and his time together with both. It seemed like only moments ago he was at their side. Now he was a druid, and he knew it would make them both proud.

Yar stepped forward and turned to the new druids. "Congratulations all. The ideals of the Citadel and the ways of the One Land are ingrained in you. May they not tarnish unused. Now, your charge is to go and wander the land. Learn its beauty. Become its conduits. Meet the sects of humanity and assist those in need. When you can, come back to us here and teach us what you have learned."

As Yar lifted off the stage and flew into the night sky, Baytel felt his own sense of lightness and enlightenment—free to accomplish anything he set out to do.

Chapter 17

"SURVEILLANCE of the lay of the land or settlement prior to drawing notice to yourself is essential to your safety and potential actions demanded of you."

The lessons had become so ingrained in his mind that anything outside of those specific behaviors was foreign to him. Baytel moved so naturally into his role as a Druid of the Citadel that his previous way of approaching a town was lost to him. There were now responsibilities in everything he did and he was not one to shirk any duty that he came upon, which was why he quietly entered Balmoral shortly after dusk and sat still as a statue in the shadows of a darkened porch of a closed shop across from the Green Goblet Inn, Juliard's establishment.

The storefronts and houses were difficult to distinguish, as early spring could not break through the late winter snow falling thick on the town. A few townsfolk gathered under covered verandas and terraces gestured fixatedly at the snowfall, shaking their heads and then hurrying off to home or tavern.

While in the dark recess unseen, Baytel eavesdropped on a group gathered in front of the mercantile shop next door. He learned that the townsfolk were troubled about a strange creature recently spotted lurking about the town and forest edge late at night.

One of the men, a tall, broad huntsman with a large jaw and keen eyes, spoke with familiarity of the creature. His deep voice carried through the falling snow.

"Just three days ago I rode into town well past midnight and I saw it."

"You saw it?" asked an excited young dwarf.

"Aye, I saw it. It looked like a beast, I say. Its skin was the color of soot; gray/black. And his arm muscles enormous with gnarled hands at their ends. Its face was ugly with sharp, fanged teeth; demon-like it was. It caught sight of me at the same time and it scampered away from me up over the Goblet's rooftop. I tried to follow it, but it leaped into the trees and disappeared."

"Where is it from?" asked a second, older dwarf. His beard was long, yet not the length to gain the status of an elder. Both dwarfs were less than half the size of the huntsman, with muscular stocky frames and serious expressions. They were dressed in green pants and cloaks and white fleece caps.

"It's up to no good," said a plump merchant, stepping off the porch after locking his store for the night. His bald head shined from the flame of the lamp overhead. "You say it was leaping from roof to roof, eh?"

"And fast as lightning."

"This kind of creature has been here before," said the storekeeper. "Looking for someone, I gather. The trade caravans will be arriving soon. If the merchants get wind of any dangers, they will set up their shops in another town."

"Stop your worrying. The caravans will not go anywhere else," the old dwarf said. "But this creature may already have been the cause of harm."

"Aye, you are talking of young Essin. Died he did, mutilated beyond recognition, I heard. Everyone trying to keep *that* secret. Maybe at the creature's hand?" the huntsman said.

"Perhaps it killed others we don't know about," said the young dwarf.

"Best we just be on our guard and leave it alone, but keep a watchful eye and hope it moves through town and is gone with no troubles," said the older dwarf.

The others all agreed, and as they walked away together chatting, their conversation changed to the weather and where to take their dinner.

Baytel stayed in the shadows observing the twilight of Balmoral until just before closing time and then entered the Green Goblet and took a dark booth away from the small crowd of patrons by the hearth. He wore the travelling cloak Calidor had given him and was concealed under its hood. The Citadel's druid cloak was for other occasions of a formal nature.

Juliard was not among those in sight, although when Baytel peered through the window earlier he had recognized the big man animatedly gesturing and entirely engrossed in one of his stories of the past. The man had not changed at all in the two years Baytel had been away. But he did not fool himself about his own appearance. Juliard would surely notice the changes in him.

He was in deep thought pondering the creature when a thin waiter cleaning a nearby table noticed him.

"Oh! Where did you come from? Startled me, sir. It's just about closing time but you still have time for a wet. What'll ya have?"

"A flask of ale will suit me fine," answered Baytel barely above a whisper, keeping his face hidden beneath the folds of his hood.

The waiter returned with the flask, stepped back attempting to get a glimpse, and, failing, went about his work.

As the night grew late only two other patrons remained at closing time, heavy with drink, hunched over the bar demanding ale. "You skinny whip of an old man, another flask! And don't drag your feet when you deliver'em!"

Juliard suddenly appeared from the kitchen, grabbed each one by the collar and dragged them out the door to the street, with the skinny waiter behind him, yelling, "Try yer smart mouths 'ere again and I won't be so easy on ya!"

Juliard and the waiter returned and the waiter, still feeling brave, yelled across the room. "You, it's time to leave. Let's go."

As Juliard glanced to his booth, he said, "Closing time, fellow. Time's up for the drink tonight."

Without a word, Baytel pulled back his hood and revealed himself. A moment passed before Juliard recognized him and his broad smile acknowledged the detection, and then just as quickly, his features turned to a stone gaze.

Baytel took that as a warning and replaced his hood. "I need a room for the night, sir," he said as if they had never met. "Is there a bed available this night?"

Juliard walked away toward the bar without turning back. "Timmons, give the traveler what he needs to lodge. Set him up in the back room on the second floor. Then clean up and go home. And no loitering about drinking tonight. Straight home after you clean." Juliard left the room.

Grumbling, the waiter led Baytel up to a back room. It happened to be the farthest room from the noises of the inn and near the upper level back stairs.

"Breakfast is served a little past dawn. Water is in the basin." He unlocked the door, handed him the key and departed still grumbling.

The room was neat and clean. A feather bed rested against the far wall. A chair was beside the sideboard with washbasin, and a settee sat beneath the window overlooking the east end of town and the forest. He sat and waited in the quiet room. Shortly he heard a gentle rap at the door. He opened the door to the big man.

"I figured you to be hungry," said Juliard from the hallway. He handed over a plate of sausages, cheese and bread. "You can eat while coming with me."

Baytel followed Juliard silently through the inn and to the back corner of the kitchen where the proprietor removed floorboards, revealing an opening. Descending a wooden ladder to the sub-floor, Juliard struck a flint and lit a lantern. It made visible a tunnel high enough for both to walk erect. Along the sidewalls were crates of wine and spirits aging in the damp. After a long stretch they reached the end and another ladder leading to a trap door above. Baytel put down his now-empty plate; Juliard extinguished the lamp and pushed his weight against the door.

Baytel found they were deep in the woods, surrounded by pine trees.

"Stay low and keep hidden," said Juliard, and they stalked back toward town directly behind the Green Goblet.

"I want you to see something," Juliard whispered, crouching low. A few moments later he said, "Look," and pointed to the roof of his inn.

Baytel's eyes grew wide as he studied the dark figure moving atop the roof, nimbly negotiating the tiles and leaning into the wrought iron window frames, peering inside each room.

"He comes every night, looking for someone," Juliard said.

Baytel couldn't take his eyes off the creature. At first glance and from that distance, it resembled a goblin, perhaps from Pithe. But after a second glance, he saw something strange and twisted about it. Very agile and strong, its claw-like hands and feet held the creature's balance upon the snow-clad roof tiles and stone façade of the building.

"It has the size of a goblin, but not the look. Have you tried to capture it?"

"Twice we attempted it. It's a slippery, strong creature. It is intelligent and its senses are quite acute. One man was killed two weeks ago, but we kept his death quiet. No reason to panic the town just yet. A few know about the creature, but keep it to themselves and watch their own."

"What or whom does it look for?" he asked, afraid of what the answer might disclose.

Juliard did not answer. When the creature had gone over the roof and disappeared into the forest, they slipped back into the tunnel. He re-lit the lamp and both sat upon wine casks. Juliard took a long look at his houseguest. "Baytel the Druid, I presume," he jested.

Baytel returned the jest with a smile. "It is good to see you, Juliard. Yes, I am a Druid of the Citadel and I am still the one you met two years ago."

"Ah yes, but older, wiser, stronger, and with purpose. This is good and it makes me glad," said Juliard. Then Juliard raised the sleeve of his cloak, exposing his forearm where the mark of the Citadel was tattooed.

Baytel raised his, showing the same silver sword entwined with a green vine of crimson roses, but freshly rendered. He embraced Juliard. "I knew there was more to you than just tavern owner!"

He sat back upon a cask, smiling at Juliard, who had opened a bottle of spirits. They toasted his achievement.

"Was the Citadel all you anticipated, Baytel?" asked Juliard.

"Yes, all that and more. I never knew the vast resources the Citadel had to offer. My hopes were met at every stage of learning I experienced. It opened my mind and helped me understand so much more than anticipated. It was nearly overwhelming at first, but I adjusted and here I am ready to move among the many sects of humanity for the good of all. But what did surprise me was how few people there were. I was expecting the Citadel to be crowded with people like me, all wanting skill and knowledge. Only thirty guards, six druid scholars, twenty acolytes, the steward Stilar and the master Tree Faerie, Yar, were there."

"You should feel privileged to be among those there."

"No one more so, I assure you."

"How was the training?"

"Plenty of reading, study and discussion, the ways of the sects, their different cultures, beliefs and ways of living. I came to understand why our existence upon the land—each of ours—is so extraordinary."

"Yes it is, Baytel. If only others could realize this gift," said Juliard. Then he asked, "Did you like learning from Yar?"

"That was the most fascinating learning experience of all. The elements of the land and the physiology of each sect, from the faerie, gnome, pixies, to the goblins, trolls, dwarfs, to man were at my disposal. Yar's lessons in the healing art were most satisfying. I have practiced, cured and saved life and limb of all walks of humanity. Yar instilled this knowledge to us in such a way, it grew within me to the point I felt it was always there awaiting an awakening."

"As it had with us all, Baytel," said Juliard.

"The druid scholars taught the different forms of government and the choices of rule the sects made for their realms and territories. Among the acolytes were men and women from the great cities to the small towns and villages, all with diverse theologies, all seeking what I sought upon first arriving—though we found so much more."

"How is Vernol?" asked Juliard, smiling to himself.

"A taskmaster! He ran us into the ground. But he is a great man, and a good friend," said Baytel.

"That good of shape, eh?" said Juliard shaking his head. "He was always the best athlete among us. Go figure him taking the youth to task, probably due to living within the walls of a magical fortress."

"I can believe that. I could feel the magic of the land throughout the fortress and country surrounding the fortress. Yar and the druids never spoke of the magic except to say its power is omnipotent and gives life," he said.

"You sound disappointed," said the big man.

He shrugged. "No. My tutor told me earlier that the land seeks out on its own to work its magic. I do not know what that means, but it is not something I am seeking answers to.

"They educated me and took my mind to places I never imagined possible, Juliard. The land is still young and unexplored. Many new and fascinating things await those who venture out, but fear keeps the sects among themselves. My charge is to travel the land, offering assistance and direction to those who are in need, and to observe."

"A worthy charge, Druid Baytel, one I see you have embraced. Nevertheless, be cautious. Being a Citadel Druid also may keep doors closed to you. We druids are considered mystical and capricious. Let those you encounter see only Baytel. Let the druid part unfold in the natural course of exchange. Your soul is good and you will be welcomed by those who see its decency."

"I will be careful, my friend."

They both smiled, taking a moment to reminisce. Then, as if each read the other's mind, their smiles faded.

"How long has the creature been roaming the town?" Baytel asked.

"I first heard of their kind just short of winter, soon after your departure two years ago. Not here in Balmoral, but from travelers in the outlands. Until the summer of last year, these creatures were never seen around here. First sightings were only in the forest on the outskirts of town. They disappeared again when winter came, but they arrived about a month ago."

"You say they. I saw only one. Are there more?"

"I have distinguished four different creatures, but cannot get close enough to identify what they are," said Juliard.

"Have you found anything that would lead you to what they seek?"

"No." Juliard eyed Baytel closely. "Where are you bound, Baytel?"

Baytel answered frankly. "I go back home, hopefully to help guide my father's realm upon the path of the One Land." He paused. "I go back to Southland, Juliard."

Juliard nodded. "Then I have ill tidings for you, Prince Baytel."

He felt mildly surprised that Juliard had addressed him as prince and sensed the man had probably known two years ago.

"For many months now, word of trouble has come out of that region. Patrols of Southland soldiers have been reported ransacking the communities north of the Forks. Some say this may be a prelude to another war."

Baytel stood and paced the cellar. "I may be too late, then. I had hoped to have time to spread the teaching of the Citadel to the realm before . . ." He stopped himself and sat on a dusty barrel. The cellar felt damp; the smell of fermenting wine permeated the air. Juliard had not moved, seated opposite in the narrow aisle between casks.

"These creatures, many believe, come from the Southland. They may be looking for you." Juliard's tone was very serious. "Baytel, I know you departed under strange circumstances. Have you thought of the possibility that you may not be welcomed back?"

He nodded his reply, unhappily disposed to accept that his father and brother still hunted after him. "Yes, that seems more of a possibility than I thought, but I must go back. The reason I left was to find ways to better the realm. Now that I have attained the knowledge, am I supposed to turn my back on all of it at the first sign of opposition?"

"The threat may be more lethal than you think."

"It could very well be. Nevertheless, I have a personal objective that I must attempt to fulfill. This is the reason I left the Southland."

Juliard was adamant in his reasoning. "Military activities have increased and advanced outside your father's realm. They have garrisons in Weyles and patrol deeper northward at their leisure."

"Even though I ran out on my duties to him, he is my father and I do not see him being opposed to my return, especially when he learns of the knowledge I have gained."

"I do not see Vokat being that amicable, or magnanimous, and I did not even mention your brother," said Juliard. "I advise you not to return home, Baytel."

Many scenarios paraded through Baytel's mind. All were conclusively dangerous, running from acceptance to imprisonment to death, with the last the most prevalent. Yes, Juliard's concerns were astute and he would be misguiding himself if he did not heed them.

"If there is a way in which to gain an audience without causing alarm, I feel I can convince my father of a better way of life. Then we both can work on Ravek."

"For that to happen, you will need to secrete your way through Weyles and infiltrate your father's castle undetected," said Juliard.

"That would be necessary if what you say is true."

"Everything I said is truth." The big man stood and paced where a few moments ago he contemplated the same ground. Then he nodded, as if ending a thought. "There is a tavern on the north end of that town called the Cleaved Oak. The proprietor is a young woman who has my trust. She is a high-principled woman and will be discreet. Carefully make yourself known to her. Tell her I sent you. She will find a way to help you into the Southland castle."

"What is the woman's name?"

"Her name is Tira. She is in my protection. Your identity will be safe with her. I trust no other person more."

Curious, he asked, "Who is this special young woman?"

"She is my daughter."

"Daughter! You have family in Weyles?"

"Only Tira."

"Dangerous place for a young woman. Why is she there?" he asked, then felt he was being indelicate.

Juliard's voice dropped low with sadness. "She serves her duty to the land in her own way. She and I stay in communication and she gets word to me frequently saying that, so far, she has not been affected by the Southland occupation."

Baytel could almost feel his discomfort in the situation. "How would you like me to approach her?"

"Approach her watchfully and with careful prudence, Baytel. Be cognizant of the fact that you are a hunted man and she is in my protection. Keep well hidden for Southland and Azkar Rol soldiers are in abundance. Find a way to contact Tira without calling attention to your meeting. The rest is up to her and you."

Baytel stared into the flame of the oil lamp and speculated again on what kind of welcome he would receive from his father and brother. *Two years without word of my existence and they may still be hunting me? Are they using these strange creatures to locate me?*

"Juliard, I will sleep here tonight and slip out through the tunnel into the forest at noon tomorrow."

"Time is very short for you now, Baytel. Have you a horse?" Juliard asked.

"No, Juliard, but I—"

He held up his hand and said, "When you exit the tunnel, go straight south until you reach a clearing. At the base of the clearing you will see a line of pine trees. Once in the pines you will see your steed, fully provisioned. Release him before entering Weyles. A man on foot is less noticeable than one on horseback. The horse will find its way back to me."

Juliard extinguished the oil lamp and climbed the ladder into the kitchen light. "What you learned at the Citadel the last two years will be put to use now. Be wary and use all your senses wherever you go. Keep off the paths as much as possible." He grabbed Baytel at both shoulders. "So begins the life of a Citadel Druid. I know you will fare well."

Juliard stared at the hoof prints in the snow leading south through the woods behind his inn with a heavy heart. He liked the young man and hoped whatever was to come he would survive.

High above the treetops screeched a red hawk circling in the steady wind. Juliard stepped into a clearing and held out his arm. The red hawk lazily swooped down and landed with an upturned flush of its powerful wings, talons clenching Juliard's leather glove.

He whispered to the magnificent red hawk, its black eyes cautious and strong. With a shriek that echoed through the forest, it took to the sky with a great leap from his arm, flew fast and disappeared beyond sight, bound with urgency toward its destination.

The snow was deep but not enough to prevent Baytel from riding in the highlands of Calidor's land. The russet-coated stallion trotted steadily up the mountainside with little difficulty. The moment he mounted it he knew it was no ordinary horse. The stallion must have been from the northeast tanning town of Daleshire, as was Calidor's black stallion. He recalled the stories circulated among Southland officers of the gifted horses raised by the Daleshire breeders. They told of how the mighty beasts had been as adroit as their riders in the last war, and drove the Southland armies back to their borders with menacing efficiency.

The stallion's gallop was swift and smooth. They reached Calidor's cabin ten days out of Balmoral.

He found it deserted, with no sign of tunnels to the barn or storehouse ever being shaped. Calidor must have left some time before the first snowfall.

He entered the cabin and found neither clues to where Calidor had gone nor any evidence of foul play. Everything was in its place as the day he had left for the

Citadel. He stabled the stallion, finding feed there and brushed him down for the night. He was not surprised to find the storeroom empty of foodstuffs. He returned to the cabin, built a fire and sat at the hearth and warmed water, making himself a drink of an herbal tea.

Baytel was disappointed that Calidor was not there. He wanted to tell Calidor how much his teachings had helped him at the Citadel and to show how much he had changed. He wanted to share in the camaraderie of being like him, a Citadel Druid, a learned scholar, and a custodian of the land.

Instead, he concentrated on the next stage of his journey, to Weyles and then home.

Here I am. I have come almost full circle. But what will I find upon my return to my home?

Chapter 18

WEYLES was no longer the town of Tira's youth. Gone were the comforts and quaintness of the small village nestled just outside the towering mountain range beyond which lay the Southland.

Her distant memory was of cobblestone lanes and pretty clapboard cottages where a quiet people sat on their porches greeting one another as they passed. The outskirt small farms supplied the town and region, sustaining a contented simple life for all. Now, as she walked gingerly around the torn-up cobbles on the road, avoiding the spaces now filled with mud from the lack of maintenance, she wistfully yearned. Passing abandoned cottages and a few boarded shops where at one time fine country folk worked, Tira found she did not recognize many of the proprietors who manned the few that took on new shopkeepers. Most likely they were disguised soldiers of the Southland, spying on any possible threats to the Southland.

She walked quickly past the new barracks that housed Southland and Azkar Rol soldiers assigned to the town. Unlike the carved limestone structures with embellished facades of the older buildings, the barracks were made of simple mud-brick and mortar; cold, unattractive, oppressive and filled with rude and intolerable men. The townsfolk lived under the turbulent atmosphere where the friendly were ostracized and the aggressor heralded. And at the few businesses still owned by townsfolk, Southland soldiers and officers elbowed aside the peace-loving townsfolk.

Tira reached her tavern, unlocked the front door, and stepped inside, leaving the noise and dirt of the streets behind her. The afternoon sun was rapidly sinking and soon the stores would close before the patrols of the occupation force ended and her evening customers would begin to wander into her place, the Cleaved Oak.

Fortunately, the reputation of her tavern was well established prior to the occupation, and most of her customers continued to be townspeople. She glanced about the interior and smiled to herself. She thought it a somber place; rustic enough for a backwoodsman to appreciate, but also with a few frills and fancies that the gentle women and proper men could enjoy. The unruly found it too quiet; that helped the regular customers to eat and drink in peace.

The Cleaved Oak did have its intrigue. Regular clandestine encounters happened frequently and, speaking in whispers was commonplace. But the crossroads village of Weyles had not always been a whispering sort of town. Always first to be drawn into wars they did not want and last to be rid of what remained afterward, the residents' only desire was for a peaceful existence. Unfortunately their small town had been settled on the cusp of two divergent realms, the Kingdom of Vokat and the northland sovereignties.

Tira had established that common soldiers were not welcome at the Cleaved Oak. This she accomplished all in one night during the beginning of the occupation. A Southland officer had been directed to her tavern by a local merchant with compliments to the food and quiet ambience. As he was finishing his peaceful meal, soldiers infiltrated the Cleaved Oak after drinking at another establishment, thus ruining a perfectly peaceful evening for the officer. The following morning the officer decreed the Cleaved Oak off limits for lower-ranking troops. Thus the officers of the Southland regiment took their meals at the Cleaved Oak while the common soldiers overran the other taverns. She knew the townsfolk were pleased about this, but the arrangement exceeded what she wanted as the Southland officers arrived at her tavern in droves. She always welcomed them, and they showed their respects, not wanting to risk forsaking the only decent place that remained in town.

Opening the windows, Tira welcomed the fresh afternoon air, which blew her long red hair behind her. She inhaled deeply. The late-day sunlight warmed her fair skin. She stretched her arms skyward, then turned to the dining room and smiled, pleased that she had cleaned the night before. She placed the upturned chairs back around the tables. Retrieving a utensils tray from the service station, she arranged them upon the tabletops. Behind the carved mahogany bar she inspected the kegs of ale and casks of wine, testing the taps and spouts, and found the bar was fully stocked and prepared for the dinner crowd. The sound of clanging pots came from the kitchen as she entered.

Whomp! A puff of flour swept off the counter in a rolling cloud, engulfing the large man and woman as they kneaded the bread dough once more to rest and rise in its final stage, and then to the ovens. Tira found the cooks, Dault and Emma, had arrived well before her.

"Good morning, my dear," greeted Emma, her fists deep in grainy dark dough. "We weren't expecting you this early, seeing the dining room clean."

Tira replied, "I ran out of things to do at home and the sun was so warm, I felt I had to start my day. I believe spring is finally here."

Both Dault and Emma nodded and Emma said, "It is a fine day."

"Dault, thank you for stocking the bar."

Dault stopped his pounding of the dough and laughed. "I needed to get away from Emma! I suppose I was not working quickly enough for her this morning. The dough is rising faster, that is for sure."

"He had nothing to do, Tira, and you shouldn't be lifting those heavy kegs, anyway," said Emma.

Dault pulled another tray from the dough rack and began kneading what was to be black rye bread, a customer favorite.

"Dault! Stop that kneading and stoke the ovens. How are we to bake these loafs if there is no fire! Customers will be arriving soon!" ordered Emma.

Tira backed away from the ovens, knowing that when Emma—whose frame nearly matched Dault's muscular bulk, and for that matter most men in the village—ordered her man about, he would hustle to the task. Both were up in years, graying, and slowing some, but their strength and work ethic kept them active and they took pride in her kitchen.

Dault rolled his eyes and Tira grinned in return. They had no children and often called Tira "Child," and in their own way looked after her as their own.

"What is the menu tonight? I have not been to the stock room."

Dault answered, "Venison steaks, cheese rice, pickled beets, and honey scones. Also pheasant in an herbal cream, with sweet yams. And for those who crave something heartier, a venison root stew."

Tira nodded her approval. Aside from her famous breads, she always offered a selection of dinners to choose from and never the same dishes as the previous night. "Do we need anything?"

Emma smiled mischievously. "We are all prepared."

Tira followed Dault's gesture as he pointed to the roasting pans on the stove where the venison sat soaking in her very own marinade. She saw the pheasants, plucked, cleaned and rubbed with a mixture of herbs, ready for the ovens. "What is it with you two?"

"Like we said, the dough rose quickly this morning and we had time on our hands," said Emma.

Tira heard the entrance door chime announcing her first customers. She poked her head out of the kitchen and saw six townspeople enter and seat themselves. She winked at Emma and Dault and backed out of the kitchen saying, "Customers. Let's go!"

Tira cupped her chin in her hands and leaned on her elbows resting on the bar. She had served the last few customers a final round of spirits, then watched them linger, delaying their departure. Finally, after their drams were drained, she smiled warmly to them, and said, "Gentleman and ladies, it's closing time."

After their departure, she finished cleaning the last of the tables. Satisfied, she left the tavern as clean as the day before, locked the door behind her and walked toward home. Passing the other taverns, she noticed they were open later than usual, and the noise seemed louder, with many a drunken soldier loitering outside. Upon reaching the last on the road, she let out a sigh of relief.

Walking alone at night with only the light of the moon and stars had once been serene, but since the soldiers had arrived and their nightly activities increased, the walk home was wrought with fear. Tira reached the outskirts of the town and left the main road and town noise behind her, and turned toward her lone cottage in the hillside of the forest along a lane that ran alongside its grade. The lane was smooth dirt and the forest bordering the lane on both sides was filled with the soft hoot of an owl and the chatter of birds still awake—signs of the change of season, which filled her with pleasant thoughts of spring.

The woods were damp. Snow had melted from the warm day and the leaves from the previous autumn lay soggy on the ground beneath the elms that hung over the lane that turned to a path leading up the hill.

No sooner had she left the lane for her cottage path than the birds stopped their songs. The shuffling of the leaves she kicked up were the only sounds. She paused a moment to listen, her senses alert. Total silence in the forest was uncommon and she recalled a lesson from her father:

"Listen to the animals of the land, for if they are silent, a predator is nearby and trouble will soon follow."

Tira had had many happy days, as all children should, living in the northlands away from the hateful King Vokat and his swift heir of vengeance, Prince Ravek. She missed her father, only seeing him when he could covertly cross the Southland lines for a short visit, for in the war that Vokat had waged long ago, Juliard had commanded one of the northland armies,. Now if seen near or within Vokat's realm he would surely be captured and killed.

Snap! A twig broke and her fears rushed back. Her senses grew fully aroused when she heard a second twig crack behind her. Without hesitating she bolted uphill as fast as her legs could carry her toward the cottage. She stole a glance behind and saw two men jump out of the woods in pursuit.

The grade of the hill was steep, but her legs were accustomed to the climb, yet as the men raced toward her, it seemed they were unaffected by the slope. The men were hollering and shouting after her and she ran faster, but still she did not gain distance.

Suddenly, she was pulled backwards as one grabbed hold of her hair. She fell back and scrambled to pull away. Clutching a handful of dirt and leaves, Tira threw it at the attacker's face, twisted from his grip, and tumbled free. She drew the dagger she kept in her boot and, in one motion, swiped it across the man's knee. She ran uphill, ducking into the woods and hopping over brambles in the hope they would slow her attackers. Then a hand appeared like a flash, slapping her across her face and sending her sprawling.

Dazed from the blow, she tried to rise but fell back down. Tira tried to rise again but this time she was pushed down by someone's boot against her back.

One of them took the dagger from her hand. She was rolled onto her back and saw her attackers standing over her, though her vision was still unclear.

One of them exclaimed, "The wench from the Cleaved Oak!"

Tira tried to focus on the raspy and uncouth voice but her head was spinning, still reeling from the blow.

"Always t'good t'notice us foot soldiers, eh?" said the ruffian.

Tira shook her head and found it helped her eyesight to clear. She looked up again and saw only one man, but another was coming up the hill toward her, limping with a bleeding leg.

"Get away!" she yelled, edging away on the ground.

"Yeah? Well, Miss Pretty Red-haired Officer's Wench, ya'll notice us now." The injured soldier wrestled her up, bracing her against a fallen log.

"The more ya struggle, girl, the more it'll hurt."

Both soldiers converged toward her. She screamed and was struck again across the face.

"Let the woman go!" a voice boomed from the night forest.

The wounded soldier let go his grip and she dropped to the ground. The soldiers wheeled about, their swords flashed out of their scabbards and the two ruffians found they were face to face with a stranger. Tira could not see him beyond the two men in the way but his silhouette was tall and he was cloaked in darkness, giving off a sense of menace.

"Be gone you two and no harm shall come," the tall stranger said.

The men laughed. "Get lost, ya fool!" said the bleeding soldier. "This ain't none a yer concern. Off wit ya, or feel our steel in yer gut."

"Let the woman be and go sleep off this night's drink," commanded the stranger.

Tira did not move; could not move. The dizziness and her fear left her immobile. The stranger's face was hidden within the folds of his hood. She could just barely make out his eyes, as they seemed to glimmer deep in shadow, making her shudder with fear. Like all Southland soldiers, her attackers were brave when battling those less powerful than them. However, she could sense their fear, for the tall stranger had come to her aid from the soundless dark forest and stood motionless and terrifying.

"I advise you to reconsider and yield this nonsense," said the stranger, his voice strong as if he were used to command.

The limping soldier moved first, swinging his sword at the cloaked stranger's head. The hooded one leaned back as the blade swept past, then stepped closer and slammed his elbow into the soldier's ribs, doubling him over. The other soldier lunged at the stranger and stabbed at his heart. The man pivoted at the last moment, leaped over the fallen soldier, rolled, and bounced up wielding a fallen branch. The soldier lunged again, but the stranger swung the heavy branch down with a crash on the drawn blade, pinning the soldier's hand to the ground under the hilt of his sword. Then the stranger kneed the soldier under the chin, sending him backward.

Brandishing the branch before him, the stranger blocked the first soldier's thrust, then kicked him in the stomach, and with a full-speed pivot slammed the branch against the soldier's head, knocking him unconscious. He turned to the other stunned soldier and, with a boot to the temple, rendered him senseless.

The man stood over the fallen soldiers as if inspecting their condition. Then he turned and looked calmly toward her. Tira was trembling and tried to stop the shakes but could not get them under control. She glanced unsteadily where both soldiers lay unconscious at the stranger's feet.

"Are you hurt?" he asked, his voice now calm and soft.

"No!" She burst into uncontrolled tears but immediately straightened herself, wiped her tears and regained control. The stranger gently lifted her by the shoulders and helped her onto a fallen tree. She sat and saw that his hood fell back slightly from his face. He seemed to shine in the darkness; the perfection of his skin caused a shiver of warmth to run through her. She wrapped her arms around herself to restrain the sensation.

"Are you cold?" He touched her shoulder tenderly.

Tira blushed and was thankful it was dark, and replied, "I am fine." Then she realized this man was an outlander and should not be trusted so readily.

But he saved my life!

"Here, take my cloak," he said.

Before Tira could object he removed his cloak and placed it across her shoulders. He was young and beautiful and strong. Nothing about him looked threatening and there was something familiar, almost recognizable, in his steel-blue eyes, causing another tremor of warmth to course through her.

"Why are you following me?" Tira heard her voice sound raspy and barely above a whisper. She rubbed her neck; her throat was sore from screaming.

The man picked up her discarded dagger and handed it to her, haft first. "I was not following you. These men were up to mischief and it was them I followed, watching them follow you."

The man's voice was calming and it soothed her fears away. Tira tried to stand and took a step but fell to the ground, grabbing her foot. "My ankle, it's twisted."

The man once again helped her to her feet. Tira tested her ankle again but the pain was too much.

Still holding her upright, the man asked, "Do you have a home nearby?"

Helpless and still shaken, Tira replied, "Up the path a bit. If you would let go I will take myself, please. Thank you for your kindness." She spoke in the authoritative tone she used in the tavern on disruptive customers and the man immediately released her arm.

Tira felt the warmth of him leave her and for an instant was sorry she had dismissed him. She replaced her dagger in its hidden sheath within her boot and took two steps before falling again in pain.

"Your face is bleeding and you are hurt," the stranger said gently. "I do not want to be a bother and your home is probably not far. With your permission."

Without pausing to hear an objection, for her words were stuck in her throat, the man swept her up in his arms and walked up the path.

Soon, her small stone cottage with a thatched roof appeared. He stepped to the door and Tira grabbed the handle and pushed the door open. She watched him as he perused the one-room cottage, its fireplace mantle and hearth of marble, the kitchen area with a small storeroom and the hewn logs supporting the dwelling at its corners and in the center of the vaulted ceiling. The man stepped into the room and placed her upon a woven rug in front of the fireplace.

Surprisingly, there were a few red embers deep in the ash and he soon had a fire going. He turned back to her and began removing her boots and gently tending to her ankle and abrasions. Tira studied the man's face while he helped her. His mane of dark blond hair fell across his broad shoulders, setting off his handsome features and kind eyes. *How young he was!*

The silence was deafening and Tira felt she had to say something. "You look less menacing in the light."

She rolled her eyes at her comment, feeling silly, and tried again. "Thank you again for helping me. It is not often anyone comes to a person's aid around here, especially when Southland soldiers are involved."

The man finally looked up, not for what she said, but to dab her cuts with a salve from a bowl in which he had mixed healing herbs from a bag he carried. He said nothing as he cleansed and treated the scratches on her face and forehead. She looked to his eyes and found them staring back at her as if suddenly noticing her and she blushed.

"I am Tira," she said. "Are you a healer?"

"Yes," he replied.

"Weyles does not often see strangers these days. Will you be here long?"

"No, not long at all."

Tira looked at him again and this time when meeting eyes it was the stranger who blushed. "Were you really following those soldiers?"

"To be honest, I had been waiting a few days for the opportunity to meet you. Unfortunately, this was not my preferred method of getting acquainted."

She frowned. "So you *were* following me."

"Please do not be alarmed, Tira," pleaded the stranger. "I have been in Weyles for four days observing the patterns of the town. I thought you might be able to help me."

"Who are you, stranger, and why are you in Weyles?" she asked, defensively, thinking it was a mistake getting too familiar with this man.

Ignoring her first question the stranger replied, "I am in Weyles trying to find a way into the Southland."

"Get into the Southland?" she asked, surprised. "Most people want to escape the Southland. Why would you want to enter it?"

"I—I have unfinished concerns that must be allayed." The man paused, as if wondering how much to say. "I must enter the Southland castle undetected."

Frowning, her suspicions were rekindled. Tira asked, "You look too familiar but I cannot place you. Who are you?"

The stranger met her gaze and, with a crooked smile briefly appearing across his face, said, "I am Baytel."

"Prince Baytel?"

He nodded in the affirmative. Tira sat motionless before the king's son, her emotions running from shock to fear to disbelief and finally settling on apprehension.

He saved my life! Treated my wounds! The evil one's son?

Recovering from her depth of thought, she said, "I know where I have seen your face. It was on handbills passed out by those that hunt you. They say you are a traitor to your father and to the Southland."

The smile faded and he nodded as if confirming for himself a thought of his own.

"I have been away," replied the prince.

"Where have you been?"

Prince Baytel was about to say something, then stopped and looked away from her to a corner of the cottage. He seemed to stare at nothing in particular, moving his head slightly, as if calculating some internal dilemma.

She resumed: "I assume you came to me for assistance? Why me?"

Tira waited while he contemplated, patient to hear the story, for there must be one behind the son of the king disappearing three years ago only to resurface and want to sneak into his home.

The prince returned his attention from the corner gaze and said, "Your first question was where have I been? I have been at the Citadel."

His direct disclosure surprised her on so many levels she became silent herself. Almost to herself, she replied, "How? Why?"

"I had hoped to instill the Citadel's teachings within my father's realm. It seems I may be too late, though."

Tira's mouth dropped open. "You mean you are a Citadel Druid?"

"Yes, and yes to your previous statement, I need your help."

Being a Citadel Druid would explain both his fighting talent and his healing skills. However, she was not quite convinced as to why he was trying to contact her. Before she could ask another question, he answered her thoughts.

"Your last question: Why you? Your father sent me to you. He sends his love and regrets not being able to visit."

It was as if she had been struck by a blow. Her father's association with the Citadel and him being a druid were not common knowledge and she became more suspicious that a Southlander—!—claimed an acquaintance.

"You know my father?"

"Juliard is my friend," he said.

Juliard would never communicate with her by note. He used other forms of contact. Tira was still skeptical and wanted some proof that this man was who he claimed to be. "How can you prove to me what you say is truth?"

The prince pulled up the sleeve of his shirt, exposing the mark of the Citadel. No other evidence was needed. Whoever bore that mark was what they said themselves to be. She blushed with excitement, both at the fact that Baytel knew her father and that both were friends and druids. "How is my father?"

"Juliard is in excellent health and keeps the travelers through Balmoral quite entertained," he said.

Tira wiped a tear that had run down her cheek. She smiled at Baytel at the remark and, with the acceptance of mutual acquaintance, her comfort in allowing Prince Baytel into her life was agreeable.

"Well, my father must feel a great regard for you, Prince Baytel, to trust you enough to send you to me. That alone is all I need to trust you myself."

"Thank you, and please call me simply Baytel."

"So I shall, Baytel. How can I help you?"

"You can help me by finding a way for me to return to my home without being seen. I have spent the last few days hidden within the shadows of Weyles studying its movements. I have watched when the soldiers eat and drink, at what times they patrol and who the commanding officers are. I have identified the messengers from the Southland castle, their arrival times and contacts, heard their exchanges and know most of them report through their commanders directly to my brother, Prince Ravek."

"If he or his guards find you, they will kill you."

"Perhaps, but I must go."

"Why?"

The prince sighed. "I spent the last few years learning the teachings of the Citadel, of the land and its people and the good it will do if we would just embrace them. My whole life seems aimed in the direction of these teachings. I must see my father and find a way to convince him of this. It is something I must attempt. It is the reason I departed in the first place."

He spoke with such simple sincerity that all Tira could do was nod in agreement. He spoke from his heart and his passion and ideals were what the Southland needed. But he must be told of its dangers.

"Baytel, your brother will never give you the chance to reach your father. He has guards at all possible places inside and outside the castle."

"I need to get past the perimeter only. From inside the castle, I can find a way to my father's chambers," said Baytel.

"Prince Ravek has vowed to kill you. I heard the talk of the officers when you disappeared. They said he was mad with fury and hate and that he hunts you now in ways they do not mention for fear of losing their own lives."

"I have seen evidence of this," Baytel acknowledged.

"He will imprison you and then execute you as a traitor to show his followers that none will have designs against the king or himself."

Baytel smiled gently and placed his hand on her shoulder. "Tira, the outcome of his desires may be quite different than what he expects."

She felt his confidence—and something more. Her heart raced when he touched her and she shyly drew away, not wanting to expose what she felt.

"There may be a way." She paused and shook her head at all the thoughts floating across her awareness. Her ankle throbbed and all she wanted to do was sleep. "It is late, Baytel, and I am quite exhausted. Weary minds don't formulate plans properly."

Baytel nodded. "Yes, it is late and you have been through enough tonight. Let me keep watch while you sleep, just to make sure those soldiers go back to town."

Tira sleepily agreed, yawning her acceptance of the situation. How odd that she trusted a man she had just met, yet there was something about the prince that felt right. It was not the fact of him being one of the privileged, but something more; something hidden away within him she could not grasp yet.

She stood, balancing herself on one leg while nursing the other. "Goodnight Baytel. Sleep will bring me good judgment, and perhaps an opening into the fortress for you to slip through."

Chapter 19

TIRA steered the wagon on a steady course, keeping off to the side of the road to avoid the deep wheel ruts made by other carts that delivered goods to the Southland and Azkar Rol. Clearing the Narrow by dusk, her lone wagon filled with foods and supplies was a common enough sight, and it was a certainty she would come across someone on the road to the postern gate of Vokat's castle.

As if having knowledge of her thoughts a large contingent of horsemen exited the gate. She pulled sharply on the reins, steering the oxen team farther away from the road to give way to the mounted troop as they made their way to the Narrow and toward their regular evening patrol of Weyles. The patrol galloped by without a second glance at her or Dault, who refused to let her deliver the goods alone. Tira, in turn, had to take him into her confidence, and then Dault absolutely insisted on accompanying her.

Tira guided the wagon toward the postern gate and hailed the post watch, "Delivery from the Cleaved Oak!"

The post watch looked down and acknowledged her with a wave. She heard him shout something below the upper tier of the gatehouse and the mechanics of the gate activated and the postern gate opened. She steered the oxen through and into the outer ward of the castle. The gateman gave a nod to Dault and looked longingly at Tira, winking his greeting.

She pretended not to see his forwardness and said, "Delivery for the kitchen. Can you call for the victual quartermaster?"

He smiled up at her and perused the wagonload. "Always glad when the ale arrives. You are in luck. He is in the kitchen. Go straight to the storehouse, Missy."

Tira smiled back nervously and turned the team of oxen toward the barracks ward where the kitchen storehouse was located. It was quiet in the ward after the evening patrol was dispatched and she reached the storehouse without another encounter.

Dault jumped down off the wagon, meeting the kitchen steward, and together they attached the ramp-boards on the back of the wagon and began unloading the cargo, rolling the barrels slowly down the ramp and into the storehouse. Tira stayed on the wagon, seated on one particular barrel, using the lofty view atop it to oversee the delivery and the activities in the ward.

The gateman had returned to his quarters inside the gatehouse and the post watch resumed his attentiveness on the road. Dault entered the storehouse, taking with him the steward of the kitchen. With no one in sight, Tira opened the barrel beneath her, freeing Baytel. They jumped quietly down off the cart and ducked to the rear of the stable.

Three days had passed since she was attacked in her woods and during that time she had so enjoyed Baytel's company she felt akin to his ways. She had fallen in love with him, perhaps an impossible love, but she did not care. He came to her and filled a void she had no idea was there. The morning before their departure she begged him to reconsider the venture, fearing it was a hopeless situation and would surely cause certain death. But her wishes were unanswered, as Baytel's mind was made up.

She crouched beside him in the dark shadows. Baytel's shoulder and leg pressed against her. She could hear the rumble of the ale barrels and the voices of Dault and the kitchen steward as they finished unloading. Her heart pounded in anguished urgency. Peering around the corner for signs of a sentry watch or patrol and finding none, she longed to delay the moment when he left her, but could not.

Baytel stood, pulling her up with him and took her hands in his and kissed them. "Tira, we must part ways now."

Tears flowed down her cheeks. "You may go to your death, Baytel. It is not too late to come back with us."

Baytel shut his eyes as if in pain. "It could be so easy to walk away and forsake this, but I cannot. I must do this. Please understand. If my plan goes badly, I will know before it is too late. Do not worry for me, Tira. All will be well. Just make certain you return to Weyles quickly and safely."

The torment in Baytel's voice wrenched her heart. She threw her arms around his neck. "You have made me so happy, Baytel. Our three days together feels more like a lifetime. Come back to me. Promise me!"

"Tira, I will return to you, I promise."

She kissed him deeply and pressed against him as if reassuring herself it was all real. Then she completed the kiss tenderly and without a word ran back to the wagon.

Darkness engulfed the stable yard and a layer of fog descended from the cool night air dulling the blackish walls of the castle, allowing Baytel to scurry from the stables, past a sleeping sentry and into the inner ward. The moon had not risen quite yet and he took advantage of the dark to gain ground toward his father's quarters. The evening lanterns had been lit throughout the inner ward, their meager illumination straining to reach beyond their placements upon posts and walls in the ward and high along the battlement. Quietly proceeding, weaving through the darkened lanes of the vacant ward, Baytel stopped at an intersection of alleyways to observe the castle guard at his post near the keep. The guard was slack in his vigil, probably nearing the end of his shift. Resting in the shadows of an entryway of a minor officer's residence, Baytel waited for the post relief to arrive.

He timed his movements precisely, making his way into the guard tower, up the steep stairway, across a battlement and into the main keep. He secreted through the serpentine hallways, gliding in the shadows between the lighted sconces, concealing his progress by way of the dark recesses. Patrols passed by within feet of his locations many times, but no one noticed his presence. How long it would be before he was discovered he did not know but he hoped to make it into his father's quarters without triggering an alarm.

It all came back to him—the halls, corridors, passageways and hidden rooms. He had spent his youth exploring the castle, finding tucked-away corners and crevasses, alcoves unused throughout the keeps and towers. It was his home and the discoveries were secrets he disclosed to no one. The memories of these places were warmhearted, yet underlying those fond moments were recollections of a lonely boyhood entwined in secrecy and at times fear of his family. As he later learned in the northlands and the Citadel, those fears were shared by many outside the realm.

The more he thought of these, the more he urged himself forward to reach his father and speak to him of other ways—ways of less death and destruction.

An instant after he ducked into an alcove, the night patrol turned down the lane he had previously traversed to gain the keep. They were six strong marching in unison two abreast, from post watch to post watch, substituting the standing guards with the new post watches. While they changed guards, he decided to risk the officer's residence. Opening the door of the entryway Baytel slid along the wall and slipped into a tower. Running up the stairs he reached the battlement that extended from the residence to the keep. Along another battlement and through another stairway he reached the keep.

Baytel maneuvered through the intertwining hallways of the north tower, bounding up the many levels to the last flight of stairs. As expected, there were no sentries posted, for high in the north tower was Cyr's chamber. The door was ajar, as it often was. Baytel called out, but Cyr was not there. Walking inside and taking a quick glance, he smiled. Nothing in Cyr's quarters had changed since his last visit. He found quill and paper in its usual place on Cyr's writing table, and sat down and drew the mark of the Citadel, like the tattoo that was inked upon his forearm. He left the sketch upon his table and withdrew.

Back down the stairs and across the eastern battlement, through the turret and over the high walkways that surrounded his father's tower, he encountered no guards or post watch patrols. Entering a vestibule, he stayed hidden in a darkened alcove before ascending. A small embrasure window was within the alcove. He peered out across the vastness of the castle grounds. The fog sat so thick it cut off all but the high walls and turrets over the yard. The high walls with their dark menacing peaks of black stone embrasures looked as though they were foul teeth that filled the gaping mouth, with the king's tower rising high above as the head of a fell beast.

As with Cyr's tower, Vokat's tower had no sentries. *Who would dare infiltrate the evil one's tower? One who knows the lay of the castle.*

Baytel moved slowly up the stairs, recalling long ago when he and Ravek adventured through the castle seeking hidden corridors and secret antechambers. He sighed wistfully at the past, wondering why his brother took so readily to his father's magic prowess and he did not. It was not fear that kept him from the crypts, rather the vulgarity of the practice. It seemed too dark, foul, and somewhat dishonest.

Reaching the top of the stairs, he turned into the corridor hall of the king's chambers and stopped as he immediately was hailed by a demanding voice from the far end of the hallway.

"Who goes there? Show yourself!"

Baytel stiffened, silently chastising himself for daydreaming. A guard posted at the king's chamber door was new, but what was more astonishing was the other three soldiers at the far end of the corridor guarding the opposite entryway. From their uniforms, Baytel knew them all to be from Vokat's personal elite force, the Kings Guards.

Baytel remained at the entrance of the stairwell, undecided whether to retreat or move toward the guards. Turning to flee would bring them to pursue, whereas facing the guards in the corridor and claiming a wrong turn would keep his discovery contained where they all stood, and where he could control the situation before anyone could raise an alarm. He had not acknowledged the guard yet and that brought the guards marching at a quick step toward him. He decided on the second option and steadily made his way forward, keeping his face concealed deep within his hood.

The guard at the king's door had not moved but the three others were on their way. "Who are you?" barked a guard. He was wearing a captain's uniform. The other two guards stopped and stood beside their captain, who unsheathed his sword and the others followed his lead.

Baytel stopped a few paces away from the pointed swords. Seeing the condition of their weapons, he surmised the guards were accustomed to violence and were ready for a fight. Running was out of the question, as was the lame excuse of a wrong turn. He decided to speak the truth, but not entirely.

"I seek admittance to the king. His nobleness will know me. Would you be so kind as to announce a visitor? I shall wait for his summons downstairs."

Baytel turned toward the stairway but the captain ran past him, blocking his exit at the point of his sword.

"Do not move, stranger," he demanded. "How did you get up here?"

Baytel held his composure at the point of the guard's blade. "It is not my intention to cause disquiet, Captain. I seek an audience. If King Vokat is not here then I will call on him tomorrow."

Ignoring the captain's sword, he walked past him and made his way toward the stairs and was fast approaching the stairwell, thinking he would gain it, but he heard the heavy boots of the guards running hard and they quickly overtook him. Again, standing at sword point, he was resigned to the fact that the situation would not end well.

The captain snarled, asking again, "Who are you? And how did you gain access to this tower?"

Baytel edged away from the guard and wall, creating the space he needed for maneuverability. "I am a mere servant to his master, King Vokat."

"Yes, aren't we all. But who let you in this tower? The castle is shut down for the evening."

The guards spread out, encircled him, their faces grim and battle worn. Baytel thought out another two options from the situation: Talking his way back to the stairs and an amicable exit, or fighting his way back. The latter prospect would dash all his hopes of a peaceful meeting with his father. It all depended upon the reasonableness of the four soldiers before him.

Baytel bowed to the captain, his hands in the folds of his cloak, face still hidden. Bending slightly, inducing a benign posture to show a more diminished countenance, he said in a humbling voice, "It seems that his majesty is preoccupied. My audience with him can wait until he has time for one as low as myself."

Baytel edged backward toward the stairwell but a guard grabbed the hood of his cloak and pulled it back. The soldiers did not react immediately. It was as though they were shocked to silence and disbelief seeing his face. Then at once, their recognition of him took form in a unified cry. "Prince Baytel!"

Their expressions changed from shock to hate. "The traitor prince!"

"Seize him!"

The guard closest sprang for him. Baytel evaded him, grabbed his outstretched arm and accommodated his momentum by directing him into another guard. He sprinted past the fallen guards toward the opposite end of the corridor, but the captain anticipated his retreat and cut off his escape.

"Hold right there, Prince Baytel!" The captain had to shout over the loathsome calls emanating from his guards as they picked themselves off the floor. He had not heard such vehemence since Ekar's profaneness at the Citadel and he could not believe the same was being directed at him in his home.

Rising from the floor, disregarding his captain's command, the first guard swung his sword at Baytel's head. Again the prince sidestepped the unbalanced guard and with a vise-like grip on his wrist twisted the sword free and confronted his attackers with sword in hand. Baytel positioned defensively and addressed the captain. "Captain, I do not want to do battle with you. All I want is to speak with my father."

The captain hesitated and was about to speak when the other guards attacked in a flurry of wild strikes. Baytel met the attack with exacting effort, deflecting their sharp blades while trying not to cause the guards any harm. Then one of the guards produced a dagger and attacked two-handed. Baytel shifted his position, bringing the inept soldier to move in front of the other guard's line of attack and, engaging both, forced the captain backward, tumbling him over the fallen soldier still upon the floor. The guard maneuvered away from the cluster of fallen bodies and hurled his dagger.

The blade produced a superficial arm wound. The guard lunged with a second dagger in hand. They sparred and Baytel deflected many a fatal strike, all the time trying to avoid bloodshed. But the guards were insistent; they wanted him dead. Unable to forgo blood being spilled, and knowing the battle now inevitably would turn deadly, with regret, Baytel buried his sword in the guard's neck.

With one guard dead at their feet, the two other guards engaged him simultaneously. Baytel spun away from one and ducked under the second's lunge while sweeping his sword across the guard's stomach. In the same motion he brought his blade up, meeting the next guard's sword. The captain, recovered from his fall, joined in the fight.

They battled long; thrust and parry, Baytel using shifty moves to intercept their assault while leading the foray toward his father's quarters in the hope that the king would hear the commotion and appear. However, as the battle continued, his hopes ebbed and escape became the only other possibility before more soldiers arrived. With two guards down, Baytel knew the captain and other guard would fight to the death. In their eyes he saw frantic struggling, fear, and even wonder at his fighting skills. He did not want to kill them but the alternative would be to surrender and that was not a prospect he found welcoming.

As the sounds of their battle rose to a pitch that would surely bring more soldiers, he knew he needed to contain this battle to the corridor and keep the two before him from calling for support.

Baytel pivoted, dropped and rolled, and surprised the captain with a slash across the arm. The captain's sword crashed to the floor. Baytel and the last guard exchanged violent blows. He met each deftly and with a power that surprised even him. He moved across the hall, kicking the guard across his left knee.

Then he saw the captain dart for his father's door. Baytel tried to reach him before he entered but the guard before him was too persistent and the captain gained the room and slammed the door. Baytel turned into the aggressor. With a swift maneuver, he ducked under the guard's thrust, causing the guard to buckle and lose his balance. Baytel finished him with a thrust to his rib cage.

Seeing the three guards dead on the floor outside his father's quarters, he knew his cause was lost. His visions of a better Southland ended in a corridor of clashing steel and blood. *It will never be.* Then he heard it. Bells sounded in the tower. The captain of the guard had raised the alarm.

Chapter 20

PRINCE Ravek looked down at the bleeding guard and asked, "Why did you sound the alarm?"

"Baytel is back," panted the bleeding soldier.

Ravek leaned forward on his seat beside his enthroned father. "What did you say?"

The soldier, a captain of the king's security force, knelt below the raised dais. "He killed three of my men and I barely escaped with my life. He is within the castle walls."

"Impossible!" shouted the king.

Ravek bolted from his seat, nearly stepping on the harlequin lounging upon the footrest at King Vokat's feet. He turned and glared at the unfazed jester, still playing his flute without losing the rhythm of his tune.

Ravek seethed silently. *Had it not been for those early season storms that winter, I could have tracked Baytel down and killed him. Now he is killing the king's guards. It was madness!*

"What is being done, Captain?" asked Ravek while he paced the throne room, not knowing quite what to make of it all.

"The castle guards have been made aware of the situation and are searching for him as we speak," said the captain, wincing as he rose.

"Where is Cyr? Has anyone checked his chambers?"

"Yes. I sent a post watch patrol to search Cyr's chambers. I took the liberty of ordering him to report here, Sire."

Ravek heard footsteps hurrying toward them. A guard burst into the chamber and approached the throne, dropping fearfully to a knee. "Sire, Prince Baytel was not in Cyr's chamber. Neither was the Tree Faerie. But I found this on his writing desk."

"He is no longer a prince, post watch," Ravek said, tearing the paper from his hand. It was a sketch of artwork. He handed it to his father. "What is this?"

"That symbol! I saw that tattooed on Baytel's forearm when we battled," said the captain.

"This is the emblem of the Citadel! He has the Mark of the Citadel on him?" shouted King Vokat. "If that mark is upon his person, then he has mastered their teachings and has become a Citadel Druid!"

The court harlequin jumped up from his footrest and began to dance around the chamber. Ravek could not believe the jester would choose this moment to entertain. He was dressed in bright colored fineries, his face covered by a mask of feathers and jewels. Ravek frowned at the annoying interruption. The harlequin recited as he leapt about.

> *The young prince returns, his body full of life.*
> *The brother prince a ruffle, the news causes strife.*
> *Strength and cunning learned abroad.*
> *Gone the innocent, the weak and withdrawn.*
> *Behold the prince's shroud unveil.*
> *The brother's might to all is shown.*
> *His Laurel affixed against family, alone.*

Ravek had heard enough and stomped toward the jester. The nimble harlequin danced away, evading his grasp, and maneuvered out of the chamber.

"Baytel is a Citadel Druid!" exclaimed the captain. "That explains it."

Ravek heard the harlequin's jingling bells recede down the hall, finding himself disturbed by the jester's taunts though not knowing why. He had never trusted the harlequin; always masked, his eyes concealed and difficult to judge.

Ravek spun on the hapless guard. "Explains what, Captain? That he killed three guards and injured one of our officers? He is a fool and a weakling. You were caught sleeping at your post!"

"No, Sire. No! Those men were my best guards. He attacked us at the post outside King Vokat's chambers!"

Vokat glared fiercely, dividing his displeasure between the captain and Ravek. "He came to my chambers and attacked my guards?"

Ravek ignored his father's anger. There was no satisfying him anyway. "Answer your King, fool! And give an account of what happened."

"Yes, Sire. It was not a surprise attack. We were all alerted to him when he entered the corridor. We were not certain who he was at first. Without identifying himself when ordered to, Prince Baytel tried to retreat back down the stairs but we blocked the way out. He stated he wanted an audience with you, King Vokat. The prince was unarmed and still managed what he had done." The captain paused as if he were back in the corridor. Then concluded his report: "These druids are dangerous men."

"Druids? Bah! They are meddling nuisances who live off the reputation of an age past." Ravek's irritation mounted at the prospect of his brother returning and killing seasoned guards. *How is it he can be this skilled? Baytel was good at nothing before he left, always in study and in the company of that faerie.*

"Father, you sit there and say nothing?" he barked, losing patience again with his father's silent regard. *Why was it he had the need to deliberate on all subjects brought before him? Why is he not angry? His son had returned and attacked his guards outside his quarters!*

Vokat answered with sinister calm. "What do you wish me to say? You said you were hunting him. It's been three years and you have reported no sign of Baytel? You said he was *probably* dead. Well, he is not! He is killing my personal guards, no thanks to your efforts; and right outside my own chamber!" He picked up the sketch and flung it at Ravek. "This piece of *artwork* you so classified it to be, and the evidence reported by the captain of my personal guards, no less, proves that your brother has attended the Citadel and mastered its teachings. This means their power is once again ignited, a power that should not be underestimated. If Baytel is truly one of their druids, he is indeed dangerous and a formidable threat to our plans."

Ravek felt the blood rise to his face. In his father's eyes he had failed, again, and he did not want to show him any weakness. "My brother was a weakling; his nose was in books rather than battle. If this Citadel could do this to him, then they all must be destroyed." He strode to the captain. "Find him! Search every corner of the castle day and night, inside and out, until he is found."

"Yes, Prince Ravek."

"Start by looking for that Tree Faerie. Find him and it will surely point the way to the other."

"When you find my traitor son, kill him," commanded Vokat. "And Captain…do not fail me."

The chamber quickly emptied, leaving Ravek alone with his father.

Surprised by his father's death sentence for Baytel, Ravek said, "Your precious son has gone heretic, Father."

"Just find him and be done with this business," said the king, and he left the chamber.

Would Baytel's return upset the Southland's invasion plans? Ravek dismissed the question from his mind, for he had plans of his own. His power was reaching new heights daily and soon it would be unleashed. Then nothing could stop it— not Baytel, not the Citadel, not even the king himself.

Chapter 21

BAYTEL withheld a sneeze, nearly bursting his ears. In a forgotten alcove in the southeast turret undisturbed since he last was home, the slightest movement caused a stirring of dust. In the tiny enclosure, the only opening was a lone embrasure slit that allowed daylight and fresh air in. It was his secret sanctuary where, as a boy, he hid away to put his troubles out of his mind. He had built shelves that lined the walls where his collection of novels and manuscripts rested. Pathetic candles with wicks spent low rested on the sill and floor from what seemed like years of nights reading and in deep contemplation. Keepsakes and mementos hung on the walls or lay in corners or on shelves. He picked up a lucky stone he had found and kicked along a corridor when saddened at something his father had said, and the gold-jeweled chalice found where the stone had come to rest after his final kick. A piece of multi-colored deep-grain driftwood in the shape of a resting bird he found on the banks of the high river south of Azkar Rol, at a place where he and Cyr camped for days on end while the young prince was taught about the habitat and tendencies of the wild forest creatures.

Dried flowers of still-brilliant colors lay pressed between glass panels. The flowers were from a pasture off the East Fork where he first realized that he was a being capable of wielding magic, though slight in comparison to his father. What joy he experienced after mastering what Cyr taught him, capturing the powers in a rainbow and using them to transform the grassy pasture into a bountiful meadow of wondrous flowers of astonishing colors.

He kept his mind on these things while ensconced throughout the night, listening, with extreme anxiety, to the running footsteps of soldiers passing by and the shouted orders from officers whose frustration over not finding the *traitor prince* was being unleashed upon their men.

The turret alcove was on an elevation where he, peering through the disintegrated mortar, was able to watch patrols sweep past. Every few hours, Ravek passed beneath him. As he came near, Baytel felt an odd sensation take root within him that caused a deep discomfort and near sickness. Ravek's appearance, strong and fierce as ever, was sharply altered from three years ago. The black art he wielded had rendered his physique almost unrecognizable.

There was a moment once when Ravek passed by that he hesitated below in the vestibule of the turret. At once Baytel felt the unseen connection between them, somehow affecting only the two of them. But then Ravek walked on, the sensation subsided and Baytel remained undetected.

Baytel's thoughts returned to the corridor where he killed three of his father's guards. *I have death upon my hands. The act of killing was so simple. I learned to do such a thing throughout my stay at Calidor's cabin and trained for it at the Citadel. It was an important part of preparing to become a druid. Is it a necessary skill? Yes. Was it necessary in this situation? Yes. But why do I not feel regret or remorse for taking a life? Am I immune to feel sorrow over causing another's death? Do I have the right to claim someone's life and consider it justified because the act advances my objective? Am I not so different than my brother? No, I am not like Ravek! I offered the guards a reasonable alternative and attempted to withdraw from the situation. They forced the fight and fought to kill me! I had no choice but to return the aggression.*

Exhaustion seeped into his body as he came to terms with the inner turmoil of the need for killing. Then the realization came to him that he will likely have to kill others to escape from the castle. And once away, killing will become a necessity in his chosen way of life, being a Druid of the Citadel. He nodded to himself, accepting the fact that death was another part of the "just cause" in his duties, and in the quiet of his alcove sanctuary he fell asleep.

As dawn approached and the patrols were less frequent, Baytel dropped from the alcove into the shadows and made his way through the ward. The morning air was crisp and cool. The warmth of the early sunlight was not yet penetrating the fog that still hung over the castle. Reaching the tower in time to duck into the shadows as a patrol turned the corner from the corridor, from the window he could just discern the eastern postern gate where a post watch of two guards stood at their duty. Outside the castle, the area now thick with gray mist, he pictured his escape route into the foothills of the East Fork. All he need do was avoid detection and get past the two guards manning the gate.

Baytel saw no one behind him or along the walkway so he strode in quiet solidarity across the high walk he hadn't set foot on in years. His happy remembrances in the alcove were gone as the bleakness of the castle brought him low and wary. Stopping at a turn, he peered down the corridor that led to the stairs down to ground level. At the end of the corridor a figure emerged. It was a woman. She had an easy, willowy loveliness in her stride. As she gracefully drew near, he recognized her and smiled. It was the girl, Della, with whom he had shared the pleasure of the dance at the royal gala the night he departed the castle.

She wore a white walking gown covering the frills of a lace nightgown. She had grown taller and refined. She would be almost sixteen years by now. Upon stepping into the corridor, she immediately knew him.

"Prince Baytel!" She began to run toward him, nearly tripping on the hem of the robe. She gathered it up and shot forward and jumped into his arms, embracing him without the least embarrassment. "I'm so pleased to have found you. So very glad to be able to warn you!"

After returning her embrace, he took her hands in his. "Della, you look all grown up and beautiful. Now what do you have to warn me of?"

"Your father, Prince Baytel, he has a death call upon you," she said in a whispered panic.

"Della. What is this you speak of?" Smiling, trying to calm her by pressing her hands gently, he said, "A death call is to kill upon sight. Why would my father do such a thing?"

"Oh but he has done so; a death call is on the lips of all the soldiers throughout the castle, Prince Baytel."

Tears ran down her worried face and he wiped them with the sleeve of his cloak. "Calm yourself, Della. The King would not do such a thing. I am sure you are mistaken."

"No, Prince, I am quite sure. My father confirmed it. Oh, no harm must come to you. Please, please go. Leave the fortress and never return for they will—"

She gasped, her eyes wide with sudden terror. He caught her as she fell forward in his arms. He gently lowered her to the floor and noticed a bloodstain growing on her robe. He tore a swatch of her nightgown away and saw an arrowhead had pierced her body from behind and through, protruding just above her breast. He laid her on her side on the floor. Her breathing was erratic and she was in shock, but she was not coughing blood, so the arrow had not pierced any vital organs.

Baytel whispered in her ear. "You will be fine, Della. Now lay still, do you hear. Move not an inch and I shall attend to you shortly."

Another arrow whistled past his head from a bowman down the walkway. Anger swept all care aside as he dashed down the corridor after the archer. So fast was his approach he was able to reach him and, with drawn sword, cut off the man's arm. The archer screamed as he gawked in horror at his severed hand still clutching his bow. Baytel let him view his detached limb and feel his agony a moment longer for piercing one so innocent, then stabbed him through the heart.

Movement behind the dead archer brought his attention to the tower door where the harlequin stood staring at him. He leaped, grabbing the jester around the waist and dropping him to the floor. His bells jingled until stilled by his submission under Baytel's grasp.

The harlequin's mask had fallen from his face and his sightless eyes stared back. Baytel fleetingly wondered how the blind jester got around the castle so well.

"Young prince, I mean you no harm," said the jester with no excitement to his voice.

"So be it, then, Harlequin. Come with me."

Baytel pulled him to his feet and practically dragged him to Della's side. She had risen to a seated position against the wall of the walkway, causing more blood to flow from her wound. "I told you not to move, Della."

"I needed to sit," she said weakly. Her face was paler and her eyes dilated wide.

Baytel dropped to his knees, gripped the shaft of the arrow and broke off the arrowhead. "This is going to hurt, Della." Without allowing her to think past his comment, he pulled the arrow out. Her intake of breath kept her from screaming out. He cut strips of cloth from her robe, placing one on the entrance wound on her back. He took her hand and placed it against the wound.

"Press hard," he whispered gently. "You'll be fine." From the corner of his eye he could see the harlequin nodding, as if judging his work.

He looked into Della's eyes; her fear for him still pervaded. Her breathing was out of control and she shook from fright. He held her as she trembled beneath his embrace. "It's alright, Della. It's alright."

Then her breathing slowed and she raised her hand holding the bandage against the wound. "I will recover, my Prince."

From the bag he had carried from the Citadel Baytel removed a small parcel of ground herbs and slipped them into the harlequin's hand. "Clean the wound with hot water. Then mix these with a small amount of water until they form into a paste. Spread it over her wounds and then wrap them in clean cloth and make certain you immobilize her arm. Repeat this twice a day. She should heal quite rapidly. I am entrusting you with her safety, Harlequin."

The harlequin nodded, sending his bells tingling once more, confirming acknowledgement of his task.

Baytel rapidly scanned the walkway and saw no threat, yet. "The guard's screams will surely bring more soldiers. I must go, Della. Tell your father I meant harm to no one."

Della watched Prince Baytel run into the tower. Guards emerged from around the opposite end, running toward her. She looked at the harlequin. He seemed wary of the soldiers. He dropped the angle of his face low as he pressed the cloth against her wound, staunching the flow of blood. His agitation continued until he took a deep breath. As the harlequin raised his face, she took a sharp breath as the face she had seen only moments ago began to move like the surface of a brook whose current was disrupted by a protruding rock in midstream. His features were altering before her eyes. His nose rounded, his formerly clouded eyes were now clear blue orbs. His hair turned black and his body seemed to grow taller and wider. Transfixed upon the fluidity of movement, she realized she was in the presence of a magical being. As the transformation ended, the figure before her was no longer the harlequin, but a man who looked like most soldiers in the Southland.

Astonished, she could only form one word. "How?"

The harlequin gently covered her mouth as soldiers ran past in pursuit of Baytel. One soldier slowed but, seeing she was attended to by another soldier, ran on into the tower.

Della sat in shocked silence while the harlequin cut another strip of cloth from her robe and wrapped her wound at her back and above her breast. He said, "We must get you to your quarters and to hot water to clean these wounds."

She nodded and tried to rise, but she was dizzy from the loss of blood and the confusion of all that had occurred in so little time. She felt herself being lifted and carried away only to be set back down against a wall.

Della focused on the form before her. The soldier began to change his appearance and, as quick as before, the harlequin had transformed back to himself. He found his mask and placed it back on his face, but not before she looked into his vacant eyes.

The harlequin turned his masked face toward her and said in a tone that displayed accustomed authority, "Mind me, girl. Keep what you see to yourself. There are subterfuges and contrary powers here that go beyond your knowledge. Exposing them will do more harm than good."

Having lived under King Vokat's reign her entire life, she understood the need for silence. And if Prince Baytel trusted this harlequin, surely she could not object. "Your secret is safe, Harlequin."

"Good girl. Now, let us get you to your quarters without attracting attention to ourselves so I can administer Prince Baytel's poultice."

Still reeling with lightheadedness, she acquiesced and taking his arm, allowed the blind harlequin to guide her, though wondering how he was ever to do so.

Avoiding capture by deception, through the open wards, up stairs, across battlements and into towers through his knowledge and abilities, Baytel frustrated the patrols and king's guards to incompetence. Comfortably back in the long-neglected turret alcove he rested and measured the time intervals between passing patrols once more. They had escalated and their frequency caused him much concern. His hiding place would not last much longer. Whatever his escape plan would be, he would surely draw the entire Southland military his way.

The escape route had not changed, as the need to reach the East Fork was paramount. From the East Fork, he could curl across the foothills, veer north and make his way back to Weyles through the Narrow. If the Narrow were manned, he would double back and climb over the East Fork as before and return to Calidor's cabin and hope to find him there.

His mind turned to all that had just happened. From the battle in the corridor outside his father's quarters, through the trek of walkway and tower, to encountering Della and the Harlequin, his confidence and poise between chaos and death was a revelation to him. He killed men, took lives with little remorse and no hesitation or fear. His method was exacting and cold, as though he had been born to battle. The lives he had extinguished seemed deserving of the deed. But was he to be the one to judge? His upbringing was temperate; his education gave him a perceptive degree of righteousness and the Citadel taught him a corresponding answer to the injurious behaviors—all qualities ingrained in the training and mastery in becoming a Druid of the Citadel. It was what he was meant to do, he concluded affirmatively.

Vacating his short-lived misgivings and returning to the present, he heard another patrol approach. As the guards passed beneath his alcove, he recognized them, which confirmed their repeated visit. He calculated the patrol schedule and quickly exited the alcove.

With the patrol heading in his desired direction, he quietly shadowed their progress through the castle. Upon reaching the east tower, they moved down the stairs and disappeared into a low corridor. He had plenty of time to reach the outer castle grounds and figuring the way out became a matter of timing and not chance, and he stepped out onto the walkway that led to the northeast wing of the castle.

No sooner had he challenged fate than, from across the courtyard below the walkway, a shout of alarm from a guard in the ward echoed across the quiet morning. He turned to duck back into the east tower when he noticed a tiny figure in the center of the opposite walkway. He stopped and fixed his gaze across the ward to the petite figure shining in early light.

Cyr!

Baytel ignored the congregation of soldiers below and their shouts of hatred as Cyr, finally seeing what the tumult was about, met his stare. They waved to one another, smiles and happiness filling the space of the courtyard. The urge to sit in peace and talk as they once had was crushing, but it was not to be. Their brief delight ceased as the commotion below increased. Seeing Cyr nod his regret with tears of sadness mixed with joy upon his face, matched only by his own, Baytel broke the reunion and was away into the east tower.

The tower was dark. The open windows showed the outer yard where flags flew on the outer wall. Reaching out through the window, he grabbed the poles and ripped away the flags. Tying them together, and with one of the sturdy flagpoles propped across an opening, he threw the flag rope out the window and scrambled down into the yard.

No sooner had his feet touched the ground than a shower of arrows followed. Running to distance himself from the projectiles, he made for the postern gate, but seeing a post watch charging after him, changed direction and ran into the stable. Horses and mules whinnied and nickered, stomping and snorting with agitation. He opened the gates, freeing the animals, and urged them out into the courtyard. In the confusion of wild galloping and flying hooves, he ran with the animals, steering them toward the unmanned gate.

"Hold!"

Before him a guard stepped out of the darkness and diverted the animals. He stood his ground, holding a mace at the ready as his large form blocked the exit. Baytel unsheathed his sword and crouched, prepared to defend himself. He studied the guard's eyes and stance and saw that though the guard was positioned solidly, he was favoring his left side, the weaker side. The guard was not so aggressive, but more satisfied to await help than to initiate the fight.

The guard began swinging the mace round and round and Baytel waited to respond to whatever moves came his way. Watching the revolving mace, he calculated the rotating spiked sphere's speed, the length of its chain, and the distance it rotated around the guard.

Behind, Baytel heard the storm of more soldiers. The guard glanced at the advancing soldiers, his first and only mistake. Baytel swung the sword so it caught the chain between the sphere and handle and let go. The revolution collapsed and the sphere and sword converged into the side of the guard's head, killing him instantly.

Past the dead man-picking up his sword-and through the gate Baytel gained the outside. The castle guards were at his heels. Baytel ran north toward the sloping fields that cut between the castle and cliff, but stopped as he spotted Ravek and a contingent of his guards on horseback galloping into the field barring his northward route toward the Narrow. Behind, another contingent of soldiers converged cutting him off to the south. Caught between two factions in the field and the castle to the west, he could not slip past any of them. With only one alternative available, he bolted eastward through the tall grass of the high field until it ended at the edge of the cliff that sloped severely until reaching a mire of unknown depths at its base.

Without a second more of deliberation, Baytel dropped over the cliff edge. Loose rock surrendered under his feet, causing him to slide. After a momentary hectic descent his feet found solid outcroppings and coming to an abrupt halt, shielded his head from the cloud of dirt and loose stone engulfing him.

An arrow whistled past. Then numerous arrows rained down about him. He paused at a foothold for a moment and looked up to see if anyone had followed. No one. The commanding voice of his brother floated down. "Break the rock at the cliff edge and throw the pieces down the slope! Let's make sure he does not reach the bottom on his own power! I want him dead, you hear? Dead!"

Baytel was nearly halfway down the cliff when the first rocks dropped past his head. He plunged faster down the slope. *If just one of those boulders strikes me, I am dead!*

He changed his line of descent, maneuvering horizontally, and found an improvement in holds, leaving behind the rain of rock and debris.

The sun broke over the East Fork. He no longer could hide, and the hurling resumed with greater force. Cascading stones, dirt and boulders careened off the cliff on both sides of him. Losing his balance, he grasped for a hold but lost his footing and plunged downward. He felt his clothes rip and skin tear as he scraped against the cliff face. Blind from the debris, he desperately snatched for any handhold available, tearing his fingers against the rock until finally they held.

Supported by his fingertips, he reached his foot sideways until he was surprised to find a shelf protruding from the cliff face. Then rumbling shook the façade and he knew the face of the cliff above him had come apart.

Chapter 22

A massive cloud of dust rose from the base of the cliff as the tumble of tons of rock ceased. Coughing slightly, Ravek waited for the cloud to clear. The soldiers were silent beside him along the new edge of the cliff, all gazing down at the tomb of debris from the avalanche.

"He is dead, Sire," said the captain, still bleeding at the arm from his injury the night before. "No one could survive this."

Ravek looked down in triumph. "Citadel Druid Baytel indeed," he said, barely above a whisper. "What have your studies gained you, Brother? Only death and disgrace."

A murmur spread among the guards, who stared at the pile of rocks.

"Druid?"

"Prince Baytel?"

The soldiers and guards in earshot muttered, gesturing superstitiously to ward off what evils they could.

"Shall we search for his body?" asked a castle guard. "The King may want to see his son?"

"I want nothing to do with the body of a druid," said the captain, signing to ward off any ills that might be travelling up the slope from below.

"Enough of your ridiculous superstitions and irrational beliefs, you fool. He is dead and buried. Leave him in his rock grave. He deserved nothing more."

"Yes, Sire."

Ravek turned away from the crumbled slope and walked toward the castle, taking all with him. "Captain, call ahead and have all the lords and commanders summoned to assemble in the weapons arsenal."

"Sire?"

Ravek still fumed over the way his brother had avoided capture, killed guards and disrupted the castle with the mysticism of his newly acquired druid status. It all had to be put down. "This Citadel must be destroyed before word gets out of their powers. I will not allow the threat of druids interfering with our plans. The northlands will be ours for the taking, and I will not rest until the Citadel and its druids are eliminated from the land."

The castle lanterns cast a yellow light upon the field outside the postern gate, their illumination barely reaching the cliff. The Southland castle was asleep except for the pre-dawn patrols and gate watch.

Della stood at the top of the cliff looking down upon the wreckage. She hugged her arm that hung in a sling, ignoring the pain from her wound. The dark horizon began to brighten above the East Fork peaks, bringing another day to the Fork Mountains, yet her sadness could not be lightened.

Grief welled in her heart as her tears returned. She tightened her fists, gaining control of herself and wiped her face. No comfort from anyone came her way for no one knew the depth of her affection for the fallen prince. She knew, in the brief moment of time together in the corridor, he felt the same bond.

He was kindness and warmth, not traitor and assassin. And even though all under the dark cloud of Vokat's land was against Prince Baytel, especially since the word of his being a Citadel Druid was known, she was steadfast in her alliance to him.

So wasteful life was, in this land and under the rule of such evil beings that I do not know if I can live among…

Della heard a sound come from down the slope of the cliff. As the sound continued she edged forward, carefully testing her footing along the edge to make sure it was not loose. Peering through the darkness into the shadowy depth, she could distinguish only patterns of blackness with gray fringes.

Then she saw something move but lost it. There it was again, movement far down the slope. Squinting, as if it would help her eyesight, she could barely make out a shadowed figure moving slowly across the rock wreckage. The longer she looked at the shadowed figure, the smaller it appeared. As it moved downward toward the base of the cliff, it was fading quickly. Then the silhouette reached the edge of the mire and the shadowy form stepped with deliberate movements until, silently, it disappeared deep under the foliage.

She scanned the topside of the cliff and the field about her. Two sentries on patrol marched past by. A post watch at the gate stood silent in his perch. The normal activities of the morning were undisturbed. And though she had not seen his face, her heart would not allow her to think differently.

Baytel lives!

Chapter 23

WHATEVER mineral deposits there were mingling in the mud and slime of the mire Baytel had traversed seemed to have a medicinal effect upon his condition. He felt barely any pain and the abrasions and scraped skin seemed to be healing more rapidly than he could imagine. He trudged as quickly as possible through the forest swamp. Gaining time and distance from the cliff was imperative if he wanted to survive. Baytel kept his fatigue at bay, still unsure if he had been detected and followed.

The first glimmer on the horizon was a dim red cloud, confirming he was headed eastward. He finally reached the end of the mire. Standing on solid ground, where the mossy tangle of the mire changed to cedars and oak trees, Baytel found himself renewed vigor. Putting his fatigue out of his mind he traveled until midday and he came upon a rambling brook. Resting along its sandy shore, he leaned back against the trunk of fallen oak, the base of which had been gnawed and felled by the indigenous beavers. Looking about the wilderness, he found the beavers had ingeniously constructed a maze of dams and waterfalls that altered the stream in so many places that the flow of its waters seemed to defy the logic of gravity.

Stretching his legs, easing muscles overused, he listened to the forest. The continuity of the small waterfalls and the trickle of the brook calmed him. The undisturbed peeping of chickadees flittering about him while collecting insects brought a feeling of safety.

Looking down, he saw he was covered in slime and mud. Pebbles from the cliff had embedded themselves in his clothes and he smelled of dank, rotted foliage and sulfur from the mineral prevalent in the mire.

The limestone ledge he had climbed under on the cliff had saved him from being buried alive. Just before he had scrambled to shelter, a boulder grazed his head. Luckily, his momentum brought him under the ledge and then all went quiet. He woke after what seemed to be forever, and found it was late night, and silent. The evident destruction of the cliff and the lack of patrols upon the unstable slope told him that he had been given up for dead. After gingerly descending off the cliff face and into the mire, he found his sense of alertness to sound and movement more heightened than ever, and his survival skills came to the fore-front of his being.

His head ached. Feeling his face he found dried blood and followed it up to a gash along his hairline. He disrobed and washed both his body and clothes. Still in possession of his Citadel bag with a supply of healing herbs, he cleansed his cuts and prepared a poultice and administered along his forehead. Immediately he felt better.

The sun had risen and shone down onto the brook through the thick canopy of boughs overhead. Baytel was uncertain what region he was in, or where to go next. The decision to return to his home sifted through the haziness of his mind. Knowledge was power. He could have changed many things for the better. Yet it was not unnoticed to him that everyone he talked to about the notion of his return was against it. Even looking back and knowing the results, the idea that he could change his father's realm and government seemed plausible at an academic level. *If only I could have talked to my father before all was lost in battle and deaths.*

But he had underestimated his brother's influence and the advancement of his evil magic, as well as his father's desires to hold rule over all the lands. What Baytel had counted on was perhaps more than his family was capable of: caring for one another. *If only I could have been able to speak with my father. Maybe all this would have turned out differently.*

But he summoned a death call on me!

Baytel's anger jarred him out of his myriad of thoughts. Just then he heard the trot of a horse somewhere in the forest.

Where had it come from?

The sunlight showed through the trees and he could see fairly deep through the thick oaks. Crouching low and away from the sound of the horse, Baytel lis-tened to the intermittent canter. Something moved into the sunlight deep in the trees far up the stream. It was a man on a horse.

Was there more than one? Was there a patrol near?

Baytel grabbed his clothes and slid away from the fallen trunk and crept low along its mass until he found another fallen tree and hid behind its uproots. Coming in and out of view along the brook the rider paused every so often, studying the banks and stream bottom searching for something. No others were evident, but silently Baytel criticized himself for not properly covering his tracks.

The horseman wore a hooded cloak, not a soldier's uniform. His pace was slow as he studied the bank of the brook. The rider drew near and suddenly pulled up the reins of his steed, halting at the middle of the brook. Dismounting, he touched the bank of the creek where Baytel had bathed. The horseman picked up a discarded herb and crouched to examine the tracks leading away. Then he stood up, looked directly at the uprooted tree where the prince hid. Then he threw back his hood and said, "Baytel."

It was Calidor. Relief swept through Baytel and he stepped out of hiding.

"Your tracks are not worthy of a druid," said Calidor, smiling at him and looking quite relieved. "Were my lessons in this not concise?"

Baytel walked stiffly toward the big man, putting on clothes as he approached. "I am a bit dazed from the warm family welcome. Trust me in this, Calidor, it will not happen again."

Calidor's smile faded and his expression hardened. "I am afraid from now on, Baytel, to err will be costly."

Baytel looked away, not wanting Calidor to see his distress.

Chapter 24

LORD Plet, the Pithean goblin, stood in the back of the room. His stoic expression kept the other lords and officers away, yet he did not mind. Standing at his usual attention, eyes alert and darting, he discovered intricacies and covert undercurrents at every glance. Still considered an outsider in the presence of the all the lords and high officers of the realm, Plet was usually left alone in a large gathering, which made observation quite easy for him. Where intrigue reigned and wanton desire ruled, so did treason and deliberate mischief among those seeking fortune and advancement. He wanted none of it. His only desire was to somehow regain control of his Pithean region of the West Fork and the only way to accomplish this was to keep in good standing with King Vokat and his son.

The arsenal room gathering resounded with rumors of Prince Baytel's surprising druidic strength and cunning, bringing to the forefront the king's concerns about the Citadel's reawakened powers.

A minor lord, whose back was to Plet, was conversing with an officer who was always one to relay scandal at whatever cost to his already stained reputation. The minor lord said, "I heard the traitor prince joined in with the northlanders, turned into a druid and then returned here and attempted to upsurge and kill the king, his own father!"

The young commander standing beside them was astonished, and asked, "Really? So was the power of the druids real? Do they wield magic and cast spells? Is that what Prince Baytel did?"

"Back in the old days they were evil and conspiratorial," said an old councilman, joining in the discussion. "You could not trust a one of them. As to the question of magic, I have it from the highest authority that they had in the past indeed practiced the dark art."

"Prince Ravek said they are a threat to the Southland. Could this be?" asked the commander.

"Beyond a doubt, especially if their power has returned," said the councilman.

"How many are there?" asked the lord.

"Who knows?" shrugged the commander.

Plet's mind wandered back to the battles fought during the last war against the northlanders. A druid commanded one of the northland battalions. His men, whose devotion to their leader was beyond the scope of thought, conquered an entire division with cunning stratagems, swift attacks and great strength.

Movement to his right captured Plet's attention. Chancellor Hectus sidled nonchalantly next to him. With a nod, the bulky man motioned for Plet to follow him. The two made their way through the tight crowd, bowing occasionally to an acquaintance, shaking a hand of another, until Hectus led him to a quiet nook.

A commotion at the entrance and numerous greetings were voiced as Lord Lezab entered and all in the arsenal chamber came to attention. Plet met Lezab's eye and beckoned him to join.

Lezab moved through the crowd, returning salutes and greetings, casually angling toward them. If there was intrigue within the arsenal, it immediately stopped when Lezab entered. He stood between the two, his back straight and head held high. He folded his hands behind his back and joined in their common view of the throng of officers which all seemed to back away from him, seemingly sensing his mood.

"Good evening, Commander," greeted Hectus. His eyes repeatedly scanned the room.

"Hectus. Plet." Lezab nodded to each. "Is it a good evening?"

Not one to hold back his opinion, Plet said, "I believe these stories of Prince Baytel are a little exaggerated. Though I did not know the boy in anything other than a polite conversation we had, I cannot believe him capable of attempting to murder his father. It is ridiculous to think so."

Hectus's puffed face nodded in agreement. "My thoughts exactly. Oh, but Lezab, your daughter was injured I heard. How does she fare?"

"I just left her side," said Lezab. "She took an arrow between her chest and shoulder. Luck it missed her lung. She will be fine. Thank you for asking."

Plet had not heard about Lezab's daughter and asked, "Would Prince Baytel shoot an unarmed girl?"

Lezab sighed. "Goodness no, Plet. The arrow came from one of the king's guards. She was trying to warn Prince Baytel of Vokat's death summons. The arrow came from behind her. Prince Baytel killed the guard and gave her some healing herbs to mend her wound before he escaped."

"Really? Extraordinary."

"Just so. His last words to my daughter were to tell *me* that *he meant no harm.*"

"That goes against every report I have heard, Lezab. What stories are being woven here?" Plet realized the realm had twisted the truth and was using Lezab's daughter as a pawn to further advance the reasons for war.

Hectus leaned toward them both and spoke at a whisper; his eyes showed fear and his forehead showed a sheen of perspiration. "I just came from Cyr's chambers, which he has not left since this morning. It seems Prince Baytel was not bent on revenge. He didn't return to kill his father, but to speak with him about the things he learned in his travels and at the Citadel."

Lezab raised an eyebrow. "Yes, the Citadel again? But I hadn't heard much about the rumors, being with Della."

"Yes," Hectus said. "That was the reason he left the Southland three years ago. Cyr said Baytel thought his father's realm was headed to ruin and he returned to show Vokat a better way of government. The king's guard stopped him before he could reach Vokat, and the rest is what you have been hearing."

"Vokat paints a picture of the traitor prince, his own flesh. Now that Baytel is dead, it produced a legitimate reason to advance northward—for vengeance. They will say that the northlanders captured and corrupted a Southlander, his son of all people. They will say the druids set him free to attack his own father."

Plet let Lezab's theory play itself out inside his mind. "The stage has been set perfectly by Ravek and Vokat. Why dispel a rumor when it feeds your fire?"

"Be that as it may, Plet. But whether the boy was on a mission to cure or kill, his fate in the Southland was sealed when he left," said Lezab.

"Yes, I suppose that is true."

Plet paused and then declared: "I wonder though, what Prince Baytel learned and if he could have made a difference. But alas, he is dead and we will never know."

Vokat approached the volume of commotion that carried down the corridor from the arsenal chamber. Flanked by guards and with Ravek beside him, he slowed his pace, quieting the noise of their boots on the stone passage to listen. The king could make out fragments of conversation from many groups, each speaking over the other, with the words Baytel, druid, attack, northlanders and Citadel most prominent.

So the rumors are in full swing. Good. Let them be aware that their cushy comforts and advantages may be taken away from them with this exaggerated threat.

Vokat picked up the pace and entered the chamber with a rush of energy. Immediately the congregation of lords and officers parted wide for his entourage, bowed as he passed and remained obeisant until he took his position at the head of the war table.

The king had received reports from his spies of the ranting about the circumstances involving Baytel, including the significance of him not hesitating to condemn his own son to death. Naturally, any threat on his life was fuel to further his cause, though Vokat was somewhat conflicted about the catalyst of this event. Yet the king chose to do nothing to decelerate the juggernaut of transgression his lords and officers felt about Baytel and the Citadel. It brought about a remarkable degree of loyalty and emotion that he previously judged to be merely political. The assertion that his life was threatened by anyone—friend, foe, or even family—enabled him to show his subjects that it would be met by determination and unconditional retribution until the threat was eliminated. No one could be with impunity when disloyal.

Vokat darted a glance at Ravek, smoldering with hatred for his brother, and knew nothing would have prevented Ravek from fulfilling the death summons on Baytel. Ravek would have done so without his order. Nevertheless, Baytel had condemned himself well before he reappeared. The knowledge of his druidic links lent aggravation to the council, as most of the older commanders and lords took personal exception with the Citadel and druids from past experience.

Before anyone was brave enough to offer him consolations or queries Vokat called for order and all took their seats. Setting aside his own apprehension and mourning, he said, "Lords and councilors, commanders and officers, as all of you have heard the events of the past day, I will not tire you with repeating them except to say that this act against myself and the Southland, though some exacting retribution has come to the instrument used, will not go unpunished."

The lords and commanders looked at one another in confusion. Their disappointment at not hearing an explanation seemed to anger some and bewilder others. But a few, such as Lezab, quickly perceived how the king was shaping the situation to his advantage.

"We are in our final stages of rebuilding the realm to what it once was and more. It is imperative that the momentum continue without interruption. If any of you believe this event will delay my ultimate goal, you are sorely mistaken." Vokat trained his eyes down the long table, resting them on Pikus, the lord of Azkar Rol. "What is the status of your province, Lord Pikus?"

Pikus stood slowly, without the usual subservience shown by most at council. The lords and commanders shifted uncomfortably during the long pause that followed the Azkar Rol lord, mortified for Pikus as he flaunted his arrogance.

"My province and officers are ready. My battalion is strong and the castle of Azkar Rol is impenetrable," stated Pikus with so spiteful a tone that a murmur of disquiet rounded the table.

"Thank you, Lord Pikus, for that specific account of your region." Vokat turned, ignoring Pikus's arrogance for the moment, and shifted his attention to Lezab, his most trusted commander. "And the Southland, Lord Lezab, how do we fare? Are we as battle-ready as the lord from the province of Azkar Rol so brazenly stated?"

"Your Majesty, due to the lack of an effective and organized command, I regret to report we are not ready," Lezab dutifully replied.

Vokat did not expect this, and replied, "This displeases me, Lord Lezab. It is not like the Southland to be less prepared than other regions in my realm."

Lord Lezab bowed and said, "Nor do I relish the reporting of this failure, Sire. However, had I been given adequate assistance, perhaps this report would be less troublesome."

Vokat turned to his son and asked, knowing Lezab's report, without question, was accurate. "Prince Ravek, what do you have to say to this report?"

Ravek stood quickly his eyes red with fury, and said defensively, "My command has taken another direction, Father, and I had assigned the Southland army to Lezab months ago. Ask him again why is it not ready."

Ravek sounded like a spoilt child deflecting blame toward where Vokat knew none lay. Lezab had remained standing. Lezab's very stature as the most organized and efficient commander was beyond doubt to all in the arsenal.

He responded: "Prince Ravek, you will address me as Lord Lezab. I believe that I have earned the right to be addressed in such a manner along with all its due respects. Now, as to the Southland army situation, you, Prince Ravek, are entirely culpable for the lack of readiness, and you know it. You took the most experienced officers and the best and strongest soldiers away with you to train this Pithe regiment and left me with all raw and inexperienced officers and recruits. From the beginning, I had to train officers and reorganize what you left me, most of which was in complete disarray. We have trained endlessly since. This is time-consuming, especially when outfitting an elite force as his majesty has commanded. Had you left a few experienced officers, Prince Ravek, I am sure I would be as ready as the honorable Lord Pikus."

Lord Plet interjected, "Since we are on the subject, let's speak of my Pitheans. Prince Ravek took thousands of my best soldiers two years ago and none have returned. When am I to see them back in Pithe?"

"You will not see them under your command again, Lord Plet," Ravek declared. "I am training an elite force made up of men and Pithean goblins. This force will be used to attack by stealth deep in the north. It is my personal battalion and will be under my sole command."

The discussion of the elite personal battalion and the secrecy of its existence took possession of the meeting as all present began voicing their concerns.

Vokat allowed the discussion to continue long enough to identify where loyalties and treacheries might lie. As the debate reached its crescendo he raised his hand and in a sweeping motion over the assembly, Vokat cast a spell upon them, causing all to involuntarily shut their mouths and sit back down in their chairs with such simultaneous action, the room vibrated with the movement. When the attendees realized what had occurred, they exchanged fearful glances, for they were unaccustomed to magic being performed, especially upon them, and had not truly known the depth of Vokat's power. The king registered the scent and heat of fear off their bodies as they all shifted uncomfortably in their chairs, adjusting to the after effects of his spell. And their fear energized Vokat.

With total command of their attention, the king turned to Lezab. "As things stand, Lord Lezab, what time frame do you suggest I consider when evaluating the Southland army's readiness?"

Lezab rose, showing no effects of the magical interruption. Vokat knew Lezab had a strong constitution, but he did not realize he could thwart his spell. But he reckoned it was a weak and simple spell and let it go.

Lord Lezab lifted his head proudly, fearlessly, yet with a slight bow to show his respect and loyalty, and replied, "One year from now. Next spring, Sire."

Before sitting, Lezab quickly glanced at Ravek, with an expression that showed his displeasure, which Lezab made certain was seen by all.

Vokat turned a corner of a smile, amused by the only form of disloyalty Lezab was capable of. "Lord Lezab, I appreciate your honest report. As always, you present yourself as a truthful and loyal noble of the Southland. And with your precise assessment I am able to state that one year from today, in the spring of next year, we shall go to war against the northlanders."

The cheering lasted just the correct interval of time before the usual awkward diminishment, and he raised his voice enough to silence them with one word. "However. However, before we take this initiative, there is an adversarial faction in the north that has proclaimed itself to us as a particular threat to our campaign."

Boasting and swagger over the Southland's superiority resounded across the war table. The king could hear Ravek over them all. "What could possibly be a threat to our combined greatness and power?"

Arrogance was one of many personality flaws his son possessed, and in abundance. Self-confidence is necessary, but Vokat preferred it displayed in low doses in these assemblies. According to Lezab's report, Ravek has abandoned his duties to concentrate on his secret battalion. What remained a mystery to Vokat was the kind of powers Ravek infused into this secret battalion.

What form of magic did this battalion employ and how strong was it? Has Ravek's magic grown too powerful? If so, I must be careful not to allow him any more control of the military.

Vokat turned his attention to his son. "Our self-proclaimed greatness does no one in this arsenal any good, Prince Ravek. Pontification of our superiority does not win battles. Overconfidence, habitually, is the root cause of defeat. Preparation, training and the strengthening of our soldiers and officers are essential to a successful campaign. We are well on our way and with all lords, councilors and officers diligently at their duties, I am sure we will be an exceptionally mighty force to contend with."

"What is this faction we need to deal with?" asked Ravek, his displeasure at being talked down too obvious in his blood-red face.

"Who indeed, Ravek. Lords, I speak of the Citadel and its druids. I am giving the directive to move against the Citadel and kill all their druids and all who have a connection with that body."

Astonishment and concern flooded the arsenal as their lords again flooded the room with remarks and questions. One lord shouted from the end of the table: "Was not Prince Baytel a druid of this Citadel?" initiating another outburst of questions about the previous night's attack.

The king raised his hand again and all went silent. "I will not discuss what my son had become, or who he allied with. He is dead and no longer a threat. However, the institution he supposedly attended is. Prince Ravek, having trained an elite force with stealth-like talents, I order you to hunt them down."

Ravek jumped up from his seat. "My force is not ready for such a mission."

"Then I suggest you have them at the ready soon for they will leave within the week."

Hectus, visibly agitated, rose to his feet. "Sire, I believe we are acting too precipitously. If I may, could I indulge you and those in attendance with my insight of the Citadel? It may alter your opinion."

"By all means, Hectus. Please proceed."

The chancellor smoothed his robe and stood straighter, readying himself for his oratory, though the fiddling with his wardrobe seemed endless. Merely standing, Hectus was a nervy spectacle. Yet Hectus had insight into the northlands that no other in the king's realm could claim.

Hectus cleared his throat, adjusted his robe again, and began. "The Citadel is a place of learning, not a fortress of war. People from all sects of humanity attend the Citadel to educate themselves on organizational policies of government, natural history, philosophy, the sciences, and the study of the healing arts. These druids you speak of are known to be peaceful scholars whose very existence revolves around the preservation of the land and sects of humanity. They heal the sick and tend the wounded. Realms throughout the One Land seek out their services as advisors and counselors. Their council is always against fighting your neighbor and their tendencies are to negotiate peace before conflict destroys the hope of it. This does not seem like the potential military threat some believe it to be."

Ravek guffawed and said, "Bah! You are out of touch with what the Citadel truly is, Chancellor. My brother left this castle a weak, book-minded boy. He returned with the strength to overpower four king's guards and nearly escaped while killing more. He drew with his own hand the mark of the Citadel; the same mark was seen tattooed on his body, which means he had become a druid. This proves the Citadel and its druids are a threat and must be eliminated before we set our campaign into motion."

"I agree," said Pikus of Azkar Rol, remaining casually seated. "I have seen druids commanding forces in the previous war, as I believe most of us have. I do not wish to confront such a commander again. The northlanders are fools without the druids' aid and will fall to us without their assistance. They must be eliminated."

"Prince Ravek and lords, I beseech you to listen," Hectus stated emphatically. "It is not my intention to side with these druids, nor to beg for postponement to this campaign, but to say that by attacking the Citadel you may jeopardize its success. Leave the Citadel alone. This stealth battalion, or whatever it is, may invariably alert the northlanders to our intentions. Why risk the exposure? By sitting quietly readying our armies, we maintain the element of surprise. You risk eliminating this advantage."

Lord Plet of Pithe slammed his large dark fist on the table. "I agree with Hectus. Why warn the northlanders of our growing strength? Let's attack when all our regional forces are ready."

Vokat waited a beat as the lords and commanders reignited the discussions from earlier, adding their opinions about when to attack. He raised his hand again, silencing them, and asked, "Lord Lezab, what do you have to say?"

Lezab rose and replied, "The northlanders will eventually learn of our intent. When we closed our borders this announced our isolation. Then we took control of Weyles. This was an inkling of a possible war to come. Nevertheless, I believe in what Chancellor Hectus proposed. To attack the Citadel will quite certainly alert the northlanders earlier than is necessary and for our own good. Once the north is alerted, our war campaign will last longer and cause more death and destruction. We must attack with swiftness and surprise to assure victory. I say we stay the course of training until all are ready to move at once."

"No! We attack the Citadel now!" bellowed Prince Ravek.

Pikus vigorously agreed. "Yes! Strike immediately! Do not delay the inevitable. We must confront these druids on our terms, not theirs."

Vokat noticed the gleam in Pikus's eyes. Siding with Ravek was a sham. His ambition to regain control of the Fork Mountains was blatant. Pikus viewed the campaign against the Citadel as a means to his gaining more power and authority. But Vokat knew how to curb his desires.

Ravek had been foolish in giving away control of the Southland military back to Lezab, like a child discarding a toy when tiring of its play. His powers had grown stronger and he might be vying to overthrow Vokat's throne, but he was obviously not ready for the responsibility. Vokat needed Ravek and his so-called stealth battalion to feed his fire. He needed Ravek as an ally in this war, not a skeptic. Ravek's handing off of the Southland soldiers to Lezab, the one commander he could depend on to complete the preparation of his largest army, serendipitously worked itself out for the better.

Vokat waved a hand in frustration, ending the debate. "I stand by my statement that the Citadel is dangerous, as are their arms of death and deceit. Ravek, I want the Citadel attacked and its druids, scholars and anyone else associated with that fortress hunted until none breathe again. Do it with stealth. Make sure you kill all who come into contact with your battalion. Let no one survive to warn the north of a prelude to our plans." He paused pointedly, and said, "And do not fail me."

"It will be done, Father."

Chapter 25

THE days of continuous rain swelled the lowland lakes and rivers. With the additional thawing of the East Fork, the water had no place to drain and dotted the wide meadows outside Calidor's cabin with field ponds where rafts of ducks floated at their leisure. In places where water had receded, chattering birds wild with zeal fed upon insects pushed to the surface from the abundance.

The wind blew robustly sweeping the clouds across the horizon and whipping Baytel's cloak about him as he walked the meadow. He spotted fresh green sprouts of vegetation and early buds upon bush and bough as the land came alive, transforming from hoary winter dormancy to an unspoiled verdant spectacle.

The whinny of a horse drew his attention toward the stable, where he was relieved to see Calidor departing for a hunt upon his black stallion with the zekawolf Thor leading the way. Baytel was unsure why he felt so, though he was quite certain that Calidor was relieved to depart his company too. Baytel had passed the days reticent and disoriented, mostly keeping to himself, choosing not to speak of the events other than his initial report when found. Instead he set his energy upon repairing the holding yard that had been damaged during the winter. The only emotion he felt in those days came when Thor arrived at the cabin. He greeted the big zekawolf enthusiastically, with Thor bowling him over, howling and licking his face.

Baytel abandoned the meadow for the stable yard, completed a final repair, and sat on the fencing. Internally reconstructing his near-fatal visit home and the rejection from his family once again besieged him with anger.

How could they do it? How could I have misjudged this situation so badly? Ravek said it before I left. Was I delusional in thinking I could change them? Both father and brother wanted to kill me! The Southland realm, my home, thinks me a traitor? Who weaved that fallacy? Ravek probably. Now I have no family. No home. I am truly alone.

The more he thought along these lines, the angrier he became. The harried escape was all the proof he needed, but hearing his brother's voice commanding the soldiers to cause the avalanche was the injury that pierced him most.

But there must be a purpose to all this! There must be something else that will happen to make all this make sense. But what?

Jumping off the fence, he ventured to the saturated fields, collecting early growths of herbs for healing—a custom he acquired from his studies—and storing them in the pockets of his Citadel sack.

Calidor had returned and was at the kitchen table piecing up a grouse. Baytel removed his wet cloak, hanging it by the fireplace, and stoked the fire. He laid out the herbs before the fire to dry and sat in the chair beside the hearth, poking at the fire.

Calidor was leaning against the entryway niche watching him. He asked, "Are your wounds fully healed?"

Baytel continued to fuss with the embers, wanting to ignore the question, but thought better of it. "Yes."

Thunder cracked; the rain pounded harder against the windows. Baytel moved to a window, watching the day change to look more like twilight as heavy clouds choked the sky. The lightning in the distance offered no comfort as the winds from that direction meant the harsh weather would continue unabated.

Baytel came out of his silent vigil and, pacing the room, said: "Dismayed as I am, Calidor, with no home or family to speak of, I know that something, somewhere, will show itself to me on why these things have occurred. I am not to wander the land without reason or purpose. As early as I can remember, I have felt drawn to something. The time I spent with Cyr, you, and the Citadel, learning and speaking of things to come has not been for naught."

He paused, hoping to gather his conflicting thoughts. "I have come to an understanding of not understanding what my life will become. There is more, and I feel it will be inspiring, but I cannot grasp it."

Calidor finally spoke. "You resort to melodrama, Baytel, when you should be focusing on getting on with life. It is time you end these reproaches and rationalizations and move on."

Baytel flared angrily. "To what? I do not know what to move on to!" He stepped toward the door, but Calidor grabbed him before he could reach it. Baytel tore from Calidor's grip and stomped to the opposite end of the cabin. Then he stopped. Something caught his eye as he passed the door to Calidor's bedroom. Peering inside, he focused on the portrait that hung over his sideboard. It was of a beautiful young woman. He stepped in and walked up to the painting, suddenly troubled at what he saw. He shook his head in disbelief as he realized a similar portrait hung in his father's quarters.

Baytel hastened back toward Calidor, who stood casually near the fire. "What is my mother's portrait doing in your bedroom?"

"Why shouldn't it be? Pren was my daughter."

Too shocked to speak, Baytel's mind jumped from confusion to anger, then disbelief sprouted and with it a feeling of duplicity, as if for the past three years he had been made game of.

Calidor said no more. Baytel's mind ran rapidly through the trials he had faced throughout his life. Observations filtered through his awareness as he stared across the room at Calidor. The man's physique, height, the way he stood, his mannerisms, so akin to his own that he now chided himself for not noticing them before. His jowls, eyes and even the shape of his forehead....

Baytel's perusal shifted to the plaques upon the wall, and recalled Yar's lecture about the Kings of the North and their magic sword. He looked at Calidor, and again to the plaques, and realized he was standing before the man who had handed his brother his crown; the man who led the Grey Riders; the true king of the Kings of the North!

Pren's father! My grandfather!

"Yes, Baytel. It is true."

"But...how?" Baytel asked, trying to fit pieces of tales together and relate it to all that had happened throughout his life, but it was too confusing and he could not line up the correlations correctly.

"Sit down, Baytel. Please. There are some things you must know," said Calidor, pointing to the chairs by the fire. "I have been contemplating how I was to speak with you about all this since your return. Now that this portion of the truth is unveiled, it is time that you know its complete story, for your destiny is intertwined with its many particulars."

Baytel sat across from Calidor. The crackle of the log upon the fire rose above the noise of the storm. He watched the reflections of the red flames upon his grandfather's face, seeing his own in it, and asked, "Why wasn't I told of this before?"

Calidor replied, "That was my doing. I wanted you to be yourself and achieve accolades and personal triumphs without the burden of your lineage. Being a Southlander was enough of a burden. Yet perhaps a better way of saying it is that I wanted you to find your true self before all the rest came into your head. At the Citadel, you learned of the history of the land and the ancients. From this, I am sure you have now surmised that my lineage is to this race of humanity. And being my grandson, so are you."

"So ... I assume that there are others who know of my lineage beside you and I?"

Calidor smiled. "Only those I trust."

It did not take long to figure whom. "Yar and Cyr know of my existence as your grandson."

"They do."

"And you are the king, the one who gave his crown to his brother to stay in this land and join with the Faeries and Dwarfs for the good of the land and sects." Baytel's statement came out flat, as though he was talking aloud to no one in particular except to state it clearly for his own ears.

"And you, Baytel, are my grandson; heir to the throne, true prince of the Kings of the North, and are empowered to wield the magic sword of our fathers."

Baytel looked about the cabin, but saw no special sword anywhere. Calidor lit his pipe and settled deeper into his chair. Calidor's eyes did not veer from him. The steady stare did not impose or cause any discomfort, but only communicated patience for Baytel to absorb the facts intelligently.

Baytel was on the edge of the opposite chair, too eager and full of questions to sit back. Recalling the talks in this very cabin about not interrupting when overanxious about gaining information, he forced himself to remain still to allow Calidor to supply him with whatever he chose, and at his usual deliberate pace.

Another crack of thunder shook the silence. Thor trotted past and sprawled down in front of the hearth. Baytel watched his breathing for a time; the intervals became slow and deep as the wolf fell asleep at his feet. The pause soothed his excitement and Baytel finally leaned back, prepared to hear more.

At that gesture Calidor finally broke his silence. "What I am about to disclose shall unravel your destiny, should you choose it to be."

"I will have a choice, Calidor?"

"We all have choices, Baytel. You have not survived your youth, initial escape, education and second escape without the maturity and ability to choose. By the way, those events, each and all of them, commenced with a choice. We all have pointed choices in life, Baytel. Some are thrust upon us, while others we are free to accept. It is the great man who is able to select what his destiny can be. It matters not how it originated, rather how it is accepted. Soon powers that have lain dormant within you shall be igniting. Things will alter within you that will give you astonishing abilities. These talents will empower you to new heights of awareness and ethereal talents."

His body tensed, thinking of the changes he witnessed in his brother. "Do you mean like that of Ravek or Vokat?"

"Baytel, before I explain about what is yet to develop, allow me to go back a short time in our family history so you can grasp the potential impending powers that you will inherit.

"Long ago in my youth, a waif girl child was found by the Faeries roaming alone in the wild. She was lost, afraid and very frail. She was different from any other sect of humanity found in the land. The Faeries soon discovered her frailty was not from lack of nourishment, but rather her entire being was delicate and lithe. She was gentle and quite pretty. Her hair was golden-blond. Her eyes were the blue of winter ice, and in her voice was the magical music of the land.

"Once she was healed and safe, it was discovered she was gifted with magic. Her touch and song made things come to bloom. The Tree Faeries, recognizing the similarities of both their magic, nurtured and taught her the Faerie way, for she had the magic of the land within her. They named her Olyssé, which means 'mother flower.' She grew into a beautiful, fair lady whose song touched all who heard it and the joy she sprouted everyday was infectious.

"After my return from questing, I was introduced to Olyssé. We spent many days in one another's company within the community of the Faeries and we fell in love and married. I built a small home outside a small town and we farmed the land living our days in peace and happiness. We bore a daughter during this happy time and chose the name *Pren*, after a rare meadow flower that grows in the northeast."

The story was mesmerizing as a chapter in his mother's past unknown to him opened. Baytel felt himself in the story and could barely contain his excitement.

Calidor continued. "However, Olyssé, who truly never regained her strength from her youth, passed away soon after Pren's tenth birthday. When conflicts between realms began arising, my duty as leader of the Grey Riders was calling me away from home. I proposed an agreement with the neighboring farmer to unite our farmlands, and asked him and his wife to take care of Pren. At this time in her childhood, Pren showed she possessed the same magical touch and voice as Olyssé. As the years passed by, Pren grew into a lovely young woman. She was tall, slender, and golden haired, with her mother's pointed ears and silver-blue eyes, like yours.

"While I was questing the lands, word came from the Tree Faeries that they had imprisoned one of their own for practicing the dark magic of the ancients. *Lomé* was his name. The Tree Faeries stripped him of his wings. Eventually the fallen faerie escaped from the Tree Faeries and found refuge with a small-holding feudal lord in the south. Your father. Vokat grew stronger with Lomé's assistance and learned the dark magic. Eventually, your father slew Lomé, and Lomé's evil magic infused into Vokat. That is when Vokat started his campaign of terror northward.

"As Vokat's army marched deeper into the north, he came across a small village. At the end of the cobblestone road was a field of flowers being tended by a young woman. Vokat's guards reported that the young woman was a being of magic. The prospect of another of magic possibly more powerful than him was not a notion that sat well with Vokat, but seeing her beauty, he could not kill her. Instead, he summoned the farmer, and assuming he was her father, asked for Pren to be his bride. The farmer refused. Vokat tortured him and abducted Pren. After the army departed, the farmer and his wife fled the village in search of me. Upon looking back they witnessed the burning and murder of the entire town.

"Your mother became his queen and Vokat began a war that lasted many years. Word came from the Fork Mountains that Pren had given birth to two sons. Also, word of her death at the birth bed followed."

Calidor sighed, his face ashen with hurtful memories. Baytel saw he had suffered with the losses and, even with so many years passing, the hurt had remained heavy in his heart.

She was but my age! How awful a life to lead at so young an age. To be married to a man who, with evil intent, abducted her violently and forced her into a life of misery. The sorrow she endured the last years of her life; a prisoner bride and death was her only escape.

"Well, another year had passed and the war was not going Vokat's way. We northlanders had pushed his army back to his borders. With another winter coming, the prospect of invading his lands was undesirable as both armies were worn with battle fatigue. So we devised a plan. The northland army stayed their invasion of the Fork Mountains and we allowed Vokat to capture a Tree Faerie. Cyr volunteered for the mission and became your and Ravek's tutor in the hopes you both would guide the future of Vokat's realm away from his evil reign.

"As you see, the plan partially worked. You freed yourself from the dark side of your father, but Ravek could not be swayed from the attraction of the sinister magic of Vokat and Lomé. If you are wondering whether Ravek was ever capable of escaping his destiny, let me tell you that he could not. Understand that during Pren's pregnancy, in her womb, the magic of good and evil battled. Vokat's and Pren's magic could not fuse together and this was what inevitably caused her death. Hence, you inherited the likeness and powers of your mother, while your brother inherited your father's. In the end, Pren's magic and that of Olyssé, and of the Kings of the North, infused to you, Baytel, and you alone."

Baytel's mind was reeling. Then, in a moment of clarity, he asked, "Why don't I feel her magic now?"

"It has not yet emerged," answered Calidor.

Baytel looked out the window. The rain had stopped some time in the passing hours. It was night; the clouds had dispersed and the moon shined down upon the wet plains. He walked out of the cabin into the meadow with Thor at his heels. He was bitter at what had transpired in his life without his full knowledge. Cyr, the pivotal figure in the plan, had never said a word. However, on reflection, Baytel realized that his upbringing and teachings by the Tree Faerie did not feel like a form of indoctrination or brainwashing. Piecing the events of his youth with Cyr, he recalled never once being told what to think, or what to do.

Even in the difficult years when important choices were being made, Cyr always urged him to decide for himself, saying, *"When deciding upon an act and way of handling a situation, always ask yourself, 'Is it the proper way, the fair way? Not the path of least resistance, but the intelligent, wisest way that may be more difficult. Is it for the betterment of, not only yourself, but everyone involved? It is most important to do what you feel is best. It is your life that you must lead. Your destiny is set in motion by the decisions you make for yourself today and every day hereafter."*

Baytel mused over the trials he had experienced since his first departure from his home. His desire to seek change and a better way of life was the reason he left the Southland, and now he was beginning to understand that desire's origin.

Baytel was distracted by Thor chasing a pheasant into a thatch row. The zeka-wolf, as powerful as he was, was no match for the wise old bird. No sooner had Thor approached the thatch to close in for the kill than the pheasant darted into a deeper hedge. Thor persisted with the hunt until the cock took flight, swooping low and then out of sight into the dark woods far down the meadow.

Baytel pondered his lineage to the Kings of the North, his ancestry in the magical sect of Olyssé, his mother Pren, and whatever form of magic infused at his birth. He touched his chest, feeling his heart beating, and wondered what lay hidden beneath his skin that Calidor only hinted at as being powerful and life altering.

If his father's magic could not control it, surely it was more powerful than the dark magic of the fallen faerie, *Lomé*. He lay back on the wet hillside contemplating the battle in his mother's womb. She bore into the world the future king of the Kings of the North and the Southland-and two receptacles of magic, one dark and the other, Baytel understood, as light. He owed her more than bitterness for such a sacrifice.

It was I who left my father's realm of evil and went to the Citadel. I was a student of the healer, druid and guardian of the Faerie Way. Everything I had accomplished, be it a part of a master plan or not, had been true to my heart.

He jumped up, leaving behind the sulking man he had been. He called out for Thor and returned to the cabin.

Calidor was at the kitchen table still smoking his pipe.

"Shall I call you Grandfather?"

Calidor's grin spread wide. He stood and they embraced. "Baytel, let us stay with calling me by my name."

Baytel contemplated aloud. "Calidor, I have many façades. Druid, Prince of the Southland, Prince of the Kings of the North, and a being of a magic unknown; it is a great deal to grasp."

Calidor nodded, and said, "You will be navigating a very tenuous path. You hold the magic of the land in you. The magical blood of your mother's unknown sect is deep-rooted in your soul. You have the magical blood as the Prince of the Kings of the North. Yes, you are the prince of two realms, one evil and the other of unrealized potential. You have learned of the role the Kings of the North play in the survival of the One Land and all the sects of humanity. You are a Druid of the Citadel and a descendant of the ancients. The many factions of your life are gifts from the One Land, Baytel. What comes of these gifts awaits you as your destiny unfolds."

Chapter 26

DELLA strolled along the brim of the cliff, like she had done every morning, keeping a few steps away from its fragile edge. Down the slope, the tops of poplar trees rose above the crumbled granite of the cliff that had fallen about them. She wrapped her shawl tighter around her body as she shivered at the thought of the rocks falling about her had she been beneath the avalanche. High overhead, the clouds that crowned the East Fork reflected a lustrous scarlet belly, declaring a warm day ahead.

The patter and crunch of a small red squirrel that rushed across the field brought her attention away from the cliff. Its foraging of its hidden stockpile of food from last autumn made her smile as the squirrel scampered away to its nest with its jowl full.

Della's musing was interrupted by the sweet-tempered sound of a flute, the melody so soothing even the chattering birds ceased in their morning ritual to listen. She followed the sound to its origin and there, perched upon the east battlement, was the harlequin. His presence upon that particular stone edifice was as regular as her morning walks. Seeing him there again, she felt if he had not attended to his morning music the dawn would be delayed without its reverential escort into day.

A patrol marched along the perimeter of the castle relieving the night post watch. Heightened patrol and training had escalated to a fierce level since Baytel's arrival; so much so, she hadn't seen her father for days. She followed the steady march of the soldiers as they moved underneath the harlequin without so much as a glance upward.

Returning her gaze down the steep decline to the edge of the forest below, Della thought of Baytel and wondered where the prince would next travel. Perhaps back to the Citadel where they say he had been since his departure years ago. Or he could wander the land anonymously, like a rover or wayfarer, doing his druidic duties, whatever they were? She caressed her shoulder, stretching her arm above her head. It had been only a week since Baytel had escaped and the harlequin had dressed her wound with Baytel's healing herbs. Now her arm had almost full mobility. The ointment seemed to have magically accelerated the healing process.

Della noticed the music had stopped and looking up saw that the harlequin had gone. It irritated her that she could not remember the exact moment he stopped playing his flute, so engrossed in woolgathering. The harlequin remained a mystery to her. He had showed himself to be a magical creature, a shape-shifter, and she pondered about what other talents he might possess. Even the powerful King Vokat and Prince Ravek did not know of the harlequin's powers. She had therefore stayed loyal to his request to keep his secret, even from her father, whom she never withheld anything from.

"Good morning, Della."

Started by the greeting, she turned and immediately collided with the harlequin. Gathering her composure, she replied, "Good morning, Harlequin."

The stealth he had used in coming so close to her without sound was uncanny. Standing beside him again, Della found he was taller than her by a head. His shoulder-length black hair shined in the sunlight. On his upper face he wore a different mask of feathers and jewels than before. Knowing him to be blind, she wondered if the mask itself was magical and gave him the gift of sight. If not, she would always be astounded at how well he maneuvered without sight.

"Harlequin, I never thanked you for caring after me when I was injured in the castle that fateful night. Thank you. As you see, I am quite nearly full healed," she said as she raised her arm up and down.

"The young prince helped most by offering his medicines," he said, his voice as soothing as his flute play.

The harlequin offered his arm and she took it, allowing the blind jester to lead the way along the precarious cliff top. "Even so, Harlequin, you did administer and bandage the wound as if you had full knowledge of such things. Are you a healer?"

"Yes I am," he answered.

His answer made her more curious than ever. "Why are you a jester and not healing people?"

"Jesting is a form of healing, is it not? To laugh and be merry. To feel serenity from music and song. To heedlessly cry from the recital of poems and be able to experience a deep sensation with whatever emotions that show themselves. All these heal the mind, body and soul. People can heal themselves with such revelries and simple passions."

His voice became stronger as he spoke, tenderly shedding light on his joys and abilities.

Della asked, "Your face and body, what I saw the morning you bandaged me, was that you, or another guise?"

Harlequin stopped and turned, pointing his masked face directly at her. She felt the eyes behind it boring into her own. "You are inquisitive of me?"

"Yes!"

161

"I have had many faces and identities through the many years of my life," he replied, and continued the stroll, guiding her at the cliff-side.

Della felt his loneliness and sensed the harlequin wanted to speak of himself. "How do I discover how old you are?"

"By asking," he answered with a smile.

Della returned his smile, again wondering if he actually saw it. "How old are you, Harlequin?"

"I have seen the land in its beginning. I have watched the Faeries work their magic. I am as youthful as the spring thaw and as old as the north wind," he declared with theatrical authority. His intonation flowed through her being, touching her emotions and impressing upon her the history of him. She sensed a faraway stirring to his oration, awakening in her a sense of adventure.

"You are blind yet you walk without aid. How can you get along so well?"

"Those with eyes sometimes do not see. Why are you surprised that I can see without sight?"

Della thought for a moment and then laughed. It eased the tension she carried. She looked down the cliff and asked, "Did you know the prince?"

"You speak of Prince Baytel, I presume. The one who escaped the wrath of his father and brother?"

Shocked, Della peered at the nearest post watch who sat stoically at the east gate. She whispered to the harlequin, not wanting her voice to carry. "You also know he has escaped?"

"He is in the northlands as we speak. When he discovers his true self, his family shall fall. The prince is the catalyst that will eventually destroy Vokat's reign."

Was the harlequin foretelling the destruction of the Southland? Della recalled her father's concerns about the realm, and said, "My father is Lord Lezab. He tells me things will worsen before they become better. He worries about my safety under King Vokat."

Bells! They rang from the castle tower, setting off the other towers to follow. Della turned at the cheering from the post watch and gate guards. Down the field the patrol was celebrating, howling above the clanging. She ran to the east gate and shouted to the jubilant watchman, "What is it? What has happened?"

"The Citadel, girl! Prince Ravek has waylaid it! The druids have fallen! All are destroyed!" he cried, and jumped toward her, grabbing Della's arm and dancing her for a twirl before she pulled away, disgusted at his touch and joy. She hurried back to the harlequin and away from the celebration.

"So it has begun, Della. Ravek's hated desires and Vokat's march toward war have shed their first blood. They will not turn back now and will send all into battle and to their deaths," said the harlequin, sadly.

Della felt a sudden dread from the jester's words. "What are we to do? What will become of us and our lives in the Fork Mountains?"

"Nothing will be the same here, Della."

"What do you mean?"

"Child, this war that is about to be waged—very few shall survive its tempest here in the Fork Mountains."

Della turned fearfully toward the harlequin, his masked face held high with confidence in the truth he stated. "How do you know this?"

The harlequin walked away from her without a word but Della ran after him and took the magical man's arm. Hesitant at his seemingly certain knowledge of events yet to come, yet, believing every word he uttered, she held his arm tighter and asked, "Will I die in this war?"

He placed his hand on hers, and said, "You will not survive unless you leave this land."

Della stiffened, drawing him closer. "Why do you tell me this, Harlequin?"

"Because you have shown loyalty to the young prince. He has the will of the One Land within his grasp, if he accepts the power he is destined for. Also, you have given me your trust in concealing my identity. I am in your debt, Della. So is the young prince."

"What do I do?"

The harlequin stopped walking, and said, "We will go to Lord Lezab. Your father will guide you in this matter."

Chapter 27

MINOR lords, brigade commanders, low officers and even soldiers recruits maneuvering for higher positions changed the war council into hostile engagements, with each one asserting merit over the other and all more than willing to sacrifice long friendships and family connections to gain favor. Since the attack on the king, the preparation for war had turned from an organized mutual goal to personal politics and vanity of position.

Tiring of the rhetoric, Lezab took his leave of the war room and marched down the long corridor toward the north tower, far from the raucous disputes. Lezab was bothered by what the surviving soldiers said of Prince Baytel's fighting prowess during his attempted escape, and the inconsistencies of the reasons he returned. He did not relish the idea of being the least bit confused about any aspect of the realm, knowing those beneath him would surely see it as a weakness. He needed to speak with someone and only one person came to mind.

Through the halls and across walkways he marched, saluting those he passed as a natural reflex though not truly noticing their existence at their posts. None dared stop him from entering any tower and Lezab freely bounded up the stairs to the top level of the north tower and down a short hall to the solitary door and knocked. Behind it the musical voice of Cyr offered him entrance.

He opened the door and stepped into Cyr's chambers and immediately felt mortified at invading his privacy. The Tree Faerie was standing at the window gazing out toward the northlands.

Too late to withdraw, Lezab asked, "Cyr, do you have a moment?"

Cyr turned toward him with tears streaming down his face. He had heard the reports of the Citadel. "So he has begun his war, Lord Lezab. The fabric of what the One Land has toiled at for millenniums has been torn apart at its heart in one swift stroke of Vokat's evil hand."

Lezab stood patiently, allowing Cyr to speak his mind. He felt ashamed at the cowardly attack by Ravek's battalion, but he could only ride the tide toward a war he did not want any part of.

"Do you know who they massacred at the Citadel, Lord Lezab?"

Lezab did not want to hear the answer. He could only too well imagine its brutality.

"Innocence! None of those murdered would ever have raised an angry hand against humanity. They were scholars, students, acolytes, nurturers of the mind and body. They taught those seeking knowledge of the magnificent beauty of the One Land and the life upon it."

"Vokat and Ravek ordered it sacked because it changed Prince Baytel into a warrior of supreme abilities," he answered and immediately felt embarrassed.

"Baytel's power came from a different genesis, Lezab. His mother's and other origins I cannot discuss. He learned the essentials of peace from the Citadel, not war," said Cyr.

Cyr had reinforced for him all of Hectus's reports of the Citadel and its true meaning to the sects.

The faerie moved from the window, took a deep breath of composure and gave him his full attention. "What is it you want of me, Lord Lezab?"

Lezab was immobile at the thought of what he was about to embark on with the Tree Faerie. It would be a sensitive conversation that, if discovered, would more than displease the realm. "What do you know of Ravek's secret battalion?"

"I know nothing about it," he said.

To relieve his anxiety and sense of disloyalty, Lezab paced about the large domicile, his eyes resting on all Cyr's wondrous belongings. Lit candles cast iridescent light across tapestries and trinkets beautifully adorning the walls. Inhaling deeply and distinguishing the scents of sandalwood and bergamot along with other aromas he did not recognize, Lezab felt the strain of the day drop from his mind, as the pleasing scents seemed to calm him and liberate his thoughts. He caressed the room's fine linens and pillows, their softness a basin of comfort. He sensed Cyr would not mind the gesture. Everything he beheld was beautiful and resplendent, and he pondered why anyone would want to destroy ones who could create such splendors.

He came out of his respite refreshed. "I am a military man, Cyr, but I always concern myself with the consequences of war on the innocent. What do you see happening to the people of the Forks?"

"Lezab, this war will destroy the innocent as swiftly as the deaths at the Citadel. Your concerns are a bit dilatory," said Cyr smartly.

"I could not help those whom have already perished, Cyr. My concerns are the innocent here."

Cyr nodded and said, "You worry about your daughter."

Lezab returned the nod. "Yes. I will probably not survive this war. The war Vokat and Ravek are to wage will be overwhelming. I fear for her safety. She is all I have, Cyr. What should I do? Send her away? And if I do, which way should she travel? I know keeping her here under the Southland flag of terror and deceit will only cause her pain and suffering. I cannot allow that to happen."

"Lezab, you are the Commander of the Southland forces. Your talk could be considered treasonous."

"I am not, nor will ever be, treasonous to my duty to the realm. I am too deeply entwined in Vokat's grasp. My loyalty is true, even though I despise what the Southland hierarchy has become," he answered Cyr with strength in his convictions, but knew he was a contradiction.

"I am a prisoner here, Lezab. If I say anything to you, it will condemn me," countered Cyr.

"I am a prisoner myself. What you say to me, Cyr, I shall keep silent and shall take that promise to my death. It is my daughter's life I am concerned with! I am here about nothing else." Lezab turned his palms toward Cyr, a gesture of openness and honesty. "I am open to you, Cyr. Nothing shall ever escape my lips of your connection in this matter. Della is my life!"

Cyr turned his back to Lezab, who followed Cyr's gaze out to the northlands. He could almost feel Cyr's yearning to return to his sect. He was a tortured being.

"Help me, Cyr."

Without turning, Cyr replied, "Ravek trains the secret battalion in the West Fork. Their maneuvers are only at night. If one needed to travel undiscovered and reach the northlands, there is a latent trail, established long ago, that points through the region of the West Fork. However, the latent trail should only be attempted in daylight. The high terrain is difficult, but the path is clear if one knows what to look for. That is where your daughter should travel to escape. Lord Lezab, your Della will be in constant danger in that region. But the alternative here in the shadows of Vokat and Ravek, we both know, is certain death."

Chapter 28

LEZAB climbed the eleven stories of his tower and entered his apartment, the only quarters in the tower, and immediately noticed how dreary it was compared to Cyr's quarters. A sudden feeling of shame came over him at the inadequacies he imposed on his daughter. It was a military man's residence, with no fineries or comforts a girl should have.

Calling to her, he found she was out. Concerned with what might come and agitated at everything that had happened, he paced with worried thoughts. Lezab knew Vokat would stop at nothing to rule the northlands and cared nothing for the lives he would bring to an end. His son was another concern. Ravek's magic was tainted and though Vokat was the more powerful, Ravek possessed something darker, an evil that transcended his father's. Its seed of hatred would soon fester into unbearable malevolence.

He heard footsteps and Della opened the door. He hurried to her and embraced her as his worrying consumed him.

"Father? What is it?"

He let her go and stared at her face. "I was just worried about you. Events are rapidly emerging and I feel for your safety." He stepped back and looked at his daughter and for the first time found Della to be a mature woman, no longer the frail little girl he envisioned her to be.

"I heard about the Citadel attack. Word has spread that this means war against the northlanders is a certainty. Is that true?" she asked.

"Yes, Della. It will change life upon the land and cause strife, suffering and death throughout humanity. Though I dread this in my entirety, there is nothing I can do except go along with it as Vokat's commander," the disheartened lord declared.

"I know, Father. That is why I need to speak with you," said Della.

Surprised at her candor he immediately brought his entire being to attention, seeing the concern upon her face. "What is it, Daughter?"

She took a deep breath and said, "I am torn, Father, torn in many directions. One is conflict between my loyalty to you in succeeding against an opponent which is not really our enemy. Another conflict is helping an opponent who may stop King Vokat and Prince Ravek from ruining our lives."

Della had not stammered or fidgeted as she usually did when expressing a concern. She held her head up and stood completely still, patiently waiting for his acknowledgement to continue.

So he proceeded. "What is true to your heart shall be truth in mine for you. I am old and have made choices in my life to follow my heart. I will never deny the same for you."

The tension faded from her face. "Then what I am to tell you is mind-shattering. I hesitate to say it, for it is treasonous, but I must."

Slightly offended that she was hesitant in her trust of him, he said, "Della, whatever you say, I shall keep between us. You have my word."

Her shoulders loosened. He could see her confidence build. In that moment, it seemed the transference of unease reached across the space between them and he became the anxious one.

"First, there is someone I would like you to meet, though you already know him, Father," she said, lightness returning to her voice. She stepped toward the door and waved to someone in the corridor.

"Who is it, Daughter?"

"Me."

The voice and the jingling of tiny bells came from beyond the door as Della escorted the jester in. Unguarded against his own emotions, both surprise and confusion formed in Lezab's mind, and, he knew, upon his face. "I do not understand, Daughter. Why are you with this court clown?"

"Father, the harlequin was on the walkway when I was struck by the arrow. He bandaged my wounds and since has become an acquaintance. He knows many things and I believe it is important you hear what he has to say."

The harlequin bowed and then stepped forward into the room, stopping a few steps in, standing patiently waiting for acceptance.

"What nonsense is this, Della? He is nothing but a fool. What worth would I place on anything he could say?"

"Lord Lezab, your daughter means a great deal to you, does she not?" he asked.

"Of course, fool!"

"Then if you want her to live through this war, you should listen to what I have to say."

The harlequin's voice was so untypically forceful Lezab wondered how he had so quickly accomplished it.

"Your fate is set, Lord Lezab. This cannot be changed and you know this. Nevertheless, Della's future is in jeopardy here in Vokat's land."

"Did you place my daughter in the path of danger?"

"No. Della is in no danger as of yet and what she knows will stay hidden. All the same, she must leave this land or she will perish in the crumbling ruin of this castle."

Lezab was mute listening to the harlequin's prophecy. His mind ran through the previous meeting with Cyr and he considered the possibility the harlequin had eavesdropped on the conversation. But no, he must have been with Della all morning and the faerie said nothing of the crumbling ruin of the Southland castle. "The ruin of this powerful fortress is quite doubtful. We are beyond reach of the northlanders. Furthermore, they have not the army close at hand to contend with what is to come, and soon."

The harlequin scoffed and said, "Lord Lezab, mark my words. The crumbling ruin of this castle will occur as a result of the actions you all take to war against the northlanders. As to the deaths that will coincide, would you gamble against this divination with your daughter's life?"

"And you claim yourself to be a *diviner*?"

"I am that and more," declared the harlequin.

Lezab studied the jester. The jeweled and feathered mask and colorful clothing gave him the appearance of an incidental thespian. The tiny bells placed all about the clothes jingling with his every movement were distracting.

"You claim of abilities I cannot fathom or witness. How am I to find proof of such boasts? Even if you are more than what you appear to be, the question is, why do you favor my daughter in such a way?"

"I owe Della a debt," he said.

Lezab pondered what Della had done to earn favor of him. "You help heal my daughter and you owe her something? This does not ring in truth, jester."

"It soon will."

Curiosity was winning over doubt the longer Lezab parlayed with the masked one. "How is it you have the abilities of a diviner?"

"Because the harlequin possesses magical abilities, Father," said Della, interrupting the discourse.

"Hah! Is his magic in songs and poems? Do not be fooled by those who claim magical abilities when it is trickery in their performances to entertain and please the high courts, Della, and nothing more. Whatever he has said to you is fabrication, an actor with a guise and a role to play. You have been duped by a clown."

Della stomped her feet. He quickly reacted, for he had chastised her many times over the gesture as an immature way to gain his attention. But then with one quick movement she pulled the mask off the harlequin's face, baring the blank sockets of a blind man.

"Show him, Harlequin!" ordered Della.

Her behavior toward the jester took Lezab aback, her ordering him to perform something obviously mysterious, and he wondered what her true hold was on him. A long silence stretched the limits of Lezab's patience. But Della's undeviating attention on the harlequin drew him to do the same.

Suddenly, the room wavered as if a veil passed before Lezab's eyes. Then the space between him and the harlequin tingled as if the very air snapped with an energy he had never experienced before. He became light-headed as the apartment slowly faded from his peripheral vision, replaced by the crinkling air and veil. He knew he was in the thralls of magic and the urge to flee from the phenomenon was in the background of his mind, but curiosity overpowered all his sense and he stayed his place within the veil to see the magic come to fruition.

Lezab held his breath in awe as the harlequin's features began to move on their own accord. The jester's face churned on the surface. His skin drooped and altered and eventually his face became wrinkled and old. Then his body bent forward as if needing to lean upon something for support. When the movements of his body were complete what stood before him was an old gnarled man, bent from age.

"A shape-shifter!" exclaimed Lezab.

"I shared this knowledge with Della. For her silence in this I owe her a debt. She has shown loyalty to my secret, and I trust you will do the same."

The harlequin's voice intonations had not changed, but seemed different coming from an old man's mouth. It flabbergasted Lezab to silence while the magic tingling in the air sent a shiver through his body as he realized he stood before a superior being.

"Are we of the understanding that we are aligned to one another in this, Lord Lezab?"

Lezab couldn't take his eyes off the old man, as doubts plagued his mind. He could make himself out to be anyone! Gain access to private meetings or secret councils of the hierarchy! The information he can acquire! Perhaps he already had?

"Who and what are you, Harlequin?"

"The explanation of what I am is beyond your scope of understanding, Lord Lezab. Who I am may change from time to time, and with that knowledge I offer you this understanding that may clear your sprouting doubts. I am not from the Southland. Nor do I have any loyalties to any here, in Azkar Rol, or any region of Forks, save Della here. I do not owe myself to any sect of humanity. I have no duty to those who covet power for destructive purposes, most particularly causing innocent deaths. I follow the tide of humanity. If I see a need to contravene in the events upon the land that could threaten the existence of the lives upon it, I do so."

"Do you have such powers to stop wars and deaths?" asked Lezab, wondering how long he had been in the Southland region, and at what capacity.

"No. My power is in seeing what may occur and perhaps altering the continuum of the event to give the sects of humanity a chance to thwart the incident, for their sake, and that of the One Land."

"If you have no loyalties why go through the bother?" asked Lezab, still doubtful.

"I have seen much, Lord Lezab." His tone of voice had a sharp edge to it, as if tiring from his inquisition. "To see things transpire fairly for the innocent is something I am concerned with. If it is important for you to have me claim loyalty to something, then I choose that."

Lezab felt like a child being lectured by a parent, something he had not felt for years. His doubts were fading. He could not dispute the harlequin's desires, for they were his own as well. "Harlequin? Tell me, what information does she have that puts my daughter in danger here?"

Lezab watched them exchange a glance and Della's nervous fidgeting returned and she seemed to be preparing for something extraordinary, barely able to contain her excitement. "Father, Prince Baytel is still alive."

"What?"

Excitedly, she continued, her words nearly falling over themselves. "I was at the cliff the night after the avalanche and recognized him as he walked from the rubble. He entered the forest below without detection."

"How can you be so sure, Daughter?"

"Who else could it be, Father? The way he moved was so quiet; deliberate steps, almost as if he were part of the woods," she said, the thrill of her whispered voice in step with the description of Baytel's escape. "Like a woodland animal; each step carefully placed and concealed for it not to be heard. I was truly lucky to see him."

Lezab walked to the window immersed in the knowledge that the younger son of Vokat was roaming the northlands with knowledge of their plans to invade. *Baytel is alive and a Druid of the Citadel!*

Della added, "I do not believe the things everyone is saying about Prince Baytel, Father. Remember the royal ball the king gave, the night before he departed without a word three years ago? We danced you know, and Baytel spoke to me of wanting a better form of government for the Southland, not to destroy it or his father. Why would he leave the healing herbs for my shoulder if he meant harm? Do these acts bespeak a traitor, or killer, or a wanton madman? I think not."

"Della, stop!" he shouted, which took her by surprise, as he never raised his voice to her. Lezab stepped past her and bounded down the stairs until he reached the entrance to his quarters. A soldier was marching by and he called to him. "Soldier, where are you off to?"

The soldier halted and saluted, "To the training grounds, Sir."

"Not any more. Stand guard at my door. You are to shout up the stairway if someone calls for me. Do not enter, or let another enter without my permission."

"Yes sir!"

He closed the door behind him and returned. "Della, have you mentioned this to anyone else?"

"No. Only you and Harlequin," she replied.

"Did anyone see you at the cliff that night?"

"There were two sentries on patrol far off and a watchman at the gate. But they were changing the post guard at the time."

"When you recognized the figure as Prince Baytel, did your body give any impression of discovery?"

"No, Father. I was very careful. I hid my excitement. I wanted Baytel to escape. No one saw a thing."

Lezab expelled a breath in relief. "Della, you mustn't tell another soul. If Prince Baytel's survival means that much to you, Della, bury it in your heart. To all here, Baytel is dead. King Vokat and Prince Ravek wanted him dead. So keep him buried under those rocks, for if they find out the contrary they will hunt him down. And that is the last thing Baytel would want. Not a soul, you understand?"

Lezab's compliance with their alliance seemed to please his daughter and she replied with a smile that would brighten the darkest day. The chilling prospect of war and Della's involvement in secrets that could bring Vokat's and Ravek's fury down upon them prompted his return to pacing the apartment and considering what to do next.

"What can we do, Father?"

"He can do nothing," said the harlequin.

The harlequin was entirely correct. He could do nothing but move forward with Vokat's plans. It did not take a diviner to speculate what Prince Baytel would do. The prince would most likely ally himself with the northlanders having already established connections at the Citadel. He would then gather whatever forces he could muster to disrupt Vokat's invasion plans. And Lezab could do nothing to warn his superiors, for the disclosure would lead them directly to Della.

"As you have already deduced, Lord Lezab, Della must leave this region immediately. You must send her away for her to survive," said the harlequin.

Lezab nodded, resigned to the fact that knowing all this made living in the Southland dangerous for her. "The harlequin is correct. I cannot escape from my responsibilities to the realm without jeopardizing you, Della, and if Prince Baytel is discovered alive or word comes to Vokat or Ravek, I cannot protect you. Conversely, I can contrive to save you from the tyranny of this realm. This very thing I have most recently contemplated upon."

"Do you mean I need to leave you?" She began to cry.

Lezab drew her close, wrapping his arms around her and feeling her return his embrace. She was frightened and so was he. There was nothing he wouldn't do for her and it tore at his heart knowing what he had to do. He wiped her tears and she regained her composure. She looked up into his face with such love, he almost cried himself.

Bravely, as he had taught her to be, she stepped away from him and stood straight in a pose of calm. "Where shall I go?"

Lezab took her hands in his. "To the northlands."

"But the borders are closed. How will I get out?"

"You will not travel the way of the Narrow. That would lead you through Weyles and Tridling Del, where Ravek already has influence. Nor will you follow in the direction Baytel used. His path is unknown at any rate."

For assurance he inwardly recited the escape route Cyr spoke of. It would be dangerous but knew Della could do it. "You will go by the Blue Trail, Della. It is an old, secret, unmarked path leading into the northlands across the West Fork region. On this route were planted, at widely spaced intervals, blue spruce pine trees. They were circuitously placed to avoid detection and pattern. You will not be able to see them at night so daylight travel is required. I will guide you through the first few, and then you will be on your own to find the next and so on."

"How long is the trail?"

"I do not know how long it will take. All I understand of it is its end. You will be firmly in the northlands."

Her face was downcast and she fidgeted and asked, "Is it dangerous in the West Fork?"

His heart skipped a beat at seeing her once-adorable mannerisms used in fear of something. "It is very dangerous. Ravek trains his secret battalion there. But the highland trail ends at the southern branch of the Ginhonim River, where you will be much safer and far from here."

Her fidgeting increased and he held her shoulders and looked into her eyes, calming her. She asked, "What if it is not there?"

"Cyr would not tell me of the trail if it were not a true route."

"Cyr? The Tree Faerie told you of this?"

"Yes. As it happens, I have been considering your safety here in the Southland for some time. I, Cyr, and now this harlequin, all came to the same conclusion, be it along differing paths. If you do not deviate from the Blue Trail and trust in its direction through the West Fork, you will reach the Ginhonim River."

"The Blue Trail," she said flatly, resigned to the idea.

"On the trail you must make camp in the most hidden-away places you can find before night falls, and never upon the trail itself. Use your wits, Della. I have taught you hunting and foraging skills when we camped in the wild of the Middle Fork. Use no fire whatsoever until you are deep in the Ginhonim River region and far enough away where your fire and smoke will not be detected from the West Fork. I will supply you with enough food to travel the highlands. Fish and small game are abundant when you reach the Ginhonim and the lands north."

A thought came to him. "Do you remember my teachings on how to construct a raft?"

"Yes, Father, though I recall the results of my building one could be considered suspect."

Lezab smiled at her quip as her courage showed through her nervousness. "But it floated, did it not?"

She smiled and nodded.

"The Ginhonim River has many tributaries flowing into it. Do not go ashore. Stay on the water and keep along the east shore. This will take you into its east arm. The Ginhonim narrows and bends and you will experience rapids on occasion. Let the current take you but try to stay in the center of the rapids. The river will calm soon after it straightens. Once clear of the fourth rapid, if you choose, you can travel by land. Either way, the east arm of the Ginhonim River will lead you to a hamlet called Petal Glen. Leave the river and go into the town. Keep an ear about for a band of men called the Thieves of Elangal. Find them and seek out a man named *Telek*."

Della repeated his directions exactly as he had stated them and finished by repeating the name *Telek* over and over.

Satisfied, Lezab turned to the harlequin. "What do you see, Harlequin? Can Della survive this journey?"

"I foresee more danger and certain death here in the Southland. I see her surviving. That is all I can give you. Is that not enough?"

"It has to be, jester," he said smartly, sensing the harlequin was keeping something from him, but resigned to placing his full trust in the magical blind man.

Internally, he debated the alternatives again. Perhaps he could keep her from the dangers in the Southland himself. But he hardly saw her the last week because of the duties of his command. And it will only get worse.

"Who is this man Telek?" she asked.

"Someone I can trust, Della. If he is there, he will keep you from harm until this madness ends."

"What if he is not in Petal Glen?"

"Then you will need to make your own way. Find work and survive until other things come about. He is my only acquaintance I trust in the northlands."

The single slender chance of this plan's success hung in the room's air like a wisp. But it was the only plan they had.

"Della, I wish we had time to make sure all possible variables are accounted for and your journey is without danger. But I cannot." He looked hard at the harlequin, who had quietly changed back into his jester guise and replaced his mask. "All I know is that, in the end, the harlequin says you will be alive. This and Cyr's Blue Trail are what we have committed our trust to and what we must have faith in."

As father and daughter stared at each other, their emotions in turmoil, the jester spoke up. "So it shall be, Lord Lezab. Now you will not see me again. Nor you, Della. They shall search for the Harlequin, but they shall never find him," he said as if reciting to an audience.

Lezab asked, "If you are leaving the Forks why not travel with Della? With two through the West Fork, survival is assured."

The harlequin turned and faced her. "I am not leaving the Forks. Della shall travel alone. She will survive and I shall disappear. Mind your father's teachings, girl. You shall need them all."

The harlequin bowed low and was about to leave but stopped. He removed a necklace and offered it to Della. "Wear this trinket wherever you venture."

Della took the necklace. The chain was silver, as were the three spiral shapes that encircled a precious gem of translucent violet. She turned it in her hand and as the stone passed within the firelight of a nearby candle the gemstone seemed to pulse from within and its interior bloomed with a captured light that softened the strain upon her face.

Della asked, "What is this, Harlequin? An amulet? A charm? When I look into the gemstone, it leaves me peaceful."

"It is a *triscele*. It represents the elements of the One Land. It is a humble gift to remember me by. Keep it safe and always in your possession."

The harlequin bowed once more and left. The sound of his bells receding down the stairway ended abruptly and Lezab presumed the harlequin had changed into someone else, probably a replica of himself, before walking past the soldier at his door.

Lezab took Della into his arms, kissing the top of her head. "I wish I could go with you, Della. I want to go. But if I leave, they will hunt me and kill us both. The only hope I hold for your safety is for me to remain here and hide your disappearance for as long as I can. But even though you will be discovered as gone, I do not believe they will be sending anyone to find you, so do not concern yourself too much about that. Just get through the West Fork and all should be good travel from the Ginhonim to Petal Glen."

"I know, Father," she said. Her melancholy tone brought him to tears. "Now let us both prepare me for my journey and have our time together before I depart so happy we shall remember it forever."

Cyr watched the red hawk fly swiftly to the east until he was a mere speck upon the horizon above the East Fork. He brushed away tears and turned away from the view. He picked up a piece of petrified wood from his sideboard. It had been found by Baytel when he was a young boy and Cyr recalled what the young prince said when he presented the gift to him.

"*I found it near the Narrow. It's you, Cyr. See, your body here. Your legs are crossed and you are sitting on a log. This is your head looking down, perhaps at a river below, deep in a canyon. Or maybe you are just thinking of a lesson to teach me. Turn it over. See, your wings are folded in just like when you listen to me tell you of one of my dreams.*"

More tears streamed down his face. "Baytel, how I grieve for you."

Chapter 29

CALIDOR charged out of the cabin with Thor at his heels. Baytel followed and found them scanning the cloudless blue sky, their eyes locked on a distant speck high over the East Fork. A warm breeze brushed past, caressing with the freshness of spring.

The distant speck grew into a hawk as it closed the distance toward them at a pace unmatched by any bird of prey Baytel had seen. He asked, "Why all the attention on a hawk?"

"This particular hawk is a special friend of mine," said Calidor.

"Did you find it injured and near death and nurse it back to health as you did with the zekawolf?" he asked while scratching Thor behind his ears.

"No, the story of this hawk is a tale of valor, bravery, and sacrifice," said Calidor, taking the same tone as on the previous night. "Long ago, soon after *Lomé* allied with your father, we were experiencing difficulties retrieving information from the Fork Mountains as Vokat had closed the borders and was warring in the region. Our actions against his borders were for naught and the northland army was losing ground to his forces. I decided to send a man to infiltrate his force by joining Vokat's territorial guard. My friend and fellow Grey Rider Teo volunteered for the mission. He was one of us who stayed behind with me in this land. The plan worked flawlessly as Teo became a confidant to a few of the high officers and we began receiving reports and information from Teo by way of carrier pigeon. From these reports the Tree Faeries and Ctiklat Dwarfs were able to break down the Southland's defenses.

"However, Teo was eventually discovered as an informer. He was brought before Lomé, the fallen Tree Faerie. The evil faerie tortured Teo but he never disclosed who his allies were. Lomé resorted to his magic, summoned the dark art and transformed Teo into a red hawk."

"Red hawk? I have seen this hawk before! Once while leaving the Southland three years ago and then on my way here from Balmoral!"

Calidor acknowledged this with a knowing glance. Without the slightest inkling on Baytel's part, he had kept track of him. No wonder he was able to find him in the East Fork after the avalanche. This hawk Teo was at the watch.

"Teo was kept in a cage within Lomé's chamber; his prison cell. Lomé mocked him, flaunting before him their military plans of invasion, knowing Teo was helpless to act on the information. Yet Teo was unfazed and learned all he could, for he retained his mind even in the body of a hawk.

"After your father killed Lomé he found this bird in his cage. Vokat thought the red hawk magnificent and untied his bindings to take the extraordinary hawk to hunt. He released Teo to kill his prey, but Teo flew up and away and returned to me. We tried everything to change Teo back to the man he was, but unfortunately, nothing worked. He remains in the service of the Grey Riders."

Teo's wingspan stretched wide high above their heads, flying in graceful circles on the gentle breeze. He tipped his wings and his flight spiraled into a dive until he cupped his wings and landed upon Calidor's raised arm.

"Ah, my friend, how are you this fine day?" greeted Calidor.

The red hawk jumped onto the holding yard, folding his wings at rest; his onyx eyes panned the vicinity. They came to rest on Baytel as if reading him in a detail study.

Baytel returned the perusal, studying the red hawk with the same concentration. The crimson plumage was all tipped in black, matching his eyes. His talons looked sharp and dangerous. Baytel looked for canisters attached to his legs and, finding none, asked: "He is a proud-looking hawk. How do you receive messages from him?"

"As one of the Kings of the North, Baytel, any who possesses our bloodline has the ability to understand him." He moved to face the hawk and asked, "What information do you have for me, Teo?"

Immediately, Teo began a succession of soft clicking sounds and low shrieks and the sounds became a strange language to Baytel's ears whose words, to his amazement, he entirely understood. As this phenomenon took place, any doubt Baytel had about his ancestry dissolved, sending a chill down his spine.

Teo said, *"I just departed Cyr's tower. He reported to me that Ravek has command of a dangerous battalion and they have attacked and waylaid the Citadel. The Southland claims much destruction and many deaths. Cyr is unsure if any have survived. This horde Ravek trained covertly and their powers are relatively unknown. Ravek's power grows stronger and we must assume his dark magic is infused within this horde."*

"The Citadel destroyed?" Baytel said numbly. He recalled the newly awarded druids and the acolytes who had departed in the spring like he had, and those who stayed to further their studies. Most stayed. He slammed his fist against the post of the fence, making Teo jump.

"What a fool I have been! Had I known returning to my home would be a catalyst to the destruction of the Citadel, I never would have gone back. I became the excuse they needed to start a war." *And more blood is on my hands. And for what?*

Calidor said, "Easy, Baytel. This war would have started with or without you. The concerns we have now are with the survivors and to discover the power and stealth abilities of Ravek's horde. I do not want them arriving at the gates of Kilhalen and Ctiklat without some warning and design of defense against them. Moreover, the minor fiefdoms and towns along the way could be easily overrun by such a horde."

Thinking back to Ravek and his experimentation through the dark magic in altering his own body and the creature roaming the rooftops of Balmoral, there seemed no doubt that a form of Ravek's magic was wielded by this horde.

"Druid Juliard showed me a creature who had been roaming Balmoral seeking someone. From a distance it bore a resemblance to a goblin but with deformities, and being a witness to my brother's own mutations taking form, I am certain he has altered some of the Pithean Goblins and secretly applied this dark magic."

Calidor's eyes were fixed southward over the horizon, his face stern, tight, his grimace unmoving. "Once again death is discharged from the Vokat realm begetting terror upon the land. Age after age, era upon era, the same factions control the destiny of peace upon the land. And only death marches on."

Teo clicked, *"Ravek may have unleashed a powerful force, but he would never create a force with the potential to threaten his own powers."*

Baytel nodded in agreement. "Yes, he would not make the horde too powerful. They may have some magic but not with the abilities to wield spells."

"This may be true, Baytel, but the only way to test their powers would be in battle against these creatures. We must go with the assumption that they may be able to wield his magic, until otherwise confirmed."

"The Pithean Goblins' ruler is Lord Plet. He is a proud goblin, even in defeat. He was reluctant handing over his goblins to Vokat and I do not believe he would have sanctioned the mutation of his sect."

Teo chirped. *"Lord Plet does not know the fate of his goblins. Ravek is training the Southland army with Lord Lezab. However, Ravek has abandoned the training and Cyr believes he trains these creatures somewhere either in the wilds of the Middle or West Forks."*

The faces of those at the Citadel, whose fate was still an unknown, turned in Baytel's thoughts. "Calidor, most of the druids and acolytes remained when I departed. The few who left were like me, new recipients of the Laurel. Our directives were to wander and assist where needed. They will have no knowledge of these happenings and will be caught unaware of this threat."

"How many?"

"Podius, Sezon, Areus and I were recipients. A few of the acolytes may have traveled back to their homes after the sessions ended, but I do not know for certain."

179

Calidor remained staring at the south horizon. He seemed tortured. He said, "We have worked hard at bringing peace to the One Land. The knowledge of the ancients is within the Citadel. If they get into the hands of evil all will be lost."

Calidor turned away from his southern fixation and seemed to have changed, as if the leader of the Grey Riders had found a fresh inspiration, and he said, "We must presume all are dead at the Citadel. There may be only a few of us that remain, which means we must act accordingly."

He marched to the stable and returned quickly with a side pack filled with grain for his stallion. He looked at Baytel, who nodded and followed Calidor into the cabin to pack his gear.

Calidor paused at the doorway. Before he uttered a word, Baytel knew what he was about to state. "I know, Calidor, the decision of alliances is at hand. And I have come to another crossroad."

These very thoughts Baytel had been contemplating since his escape. The time to commit to a course of action was upon him. His mindset was far from the thoughts he had when leaving the Citadel with notions of guiding his father toward a better government. His destiny was crystal clear now. Knowing all aspects of his heart as well as the truth of where his life was being led, he rejoiced in the prospect.

"Calidor, before you stands a prince of two realms; one forgotten by humanity except in myth, and the other despised. Though I am the heir apparent to both, I shall rule over neither of them for I choose my destiny to be what I have committed to long ago. I choose that which you have chosen before me. I am a Druid of the Citadel, custodian to the Faeries, and serve the One Land for the purposes of the ascension of the sects of humanity."

Calidor smiled, unsuccessfully holding back the pride in his face. "Pack only what you need, Druid Baytel, for haste is vital in reaching your destination."

Back in the storeroom, Baytel divided the supplies in two. He fixed one of Calidor's sword belts across his waist and took a sword from the armor rack at the door. He put on his cloak and draped the Citadel bag over his shoulder. It rested at his right side, freeing access to his sword at his left. He found the bag the right weight and bulk to retain even in battle. He left the storeroom and handed Calidor his share of the store. Calidor filled the saddlebags on his black stallion. He was already dressed in his travel cloak.

Teo clicked. *"The prince has the look of his mother, doesn't he, Calidor? It is good to see you alive, Young Sire. All throughout the Forks is the talk of your death. I am sure Cyr shall find the news of you alive quite heartwarming."*

"Dead? They think me dead?"

"Yes, beneath the avalanche off the cliff. This is very good. The threat of you being hunted is removed and offers you more freedom of movement. According to the information Cyr has gathered, Vokat will not invade until next spring due to setbacks in the training of his army."

Calidor pondered, "So they are not quite ready to invade, eh?"

"Not yet, though we have little enough time with this battalion of Ravek's scouring the countryside."

Calidor spoke, his voice taking on an authority Baytel had not heard before: "Tell Cyr that Baytel goes to Tridling Del and I to the Citadel. He will know what to make of it, as I am sure you already have."

Baytel walked over to Teo and ran his fingers gently against his head. "Thank you, Teo. Could you hasten back to Cyr and tell him I miss him and will be careful? Tell him I am embarking upon my duties as a druid in the service of the One Land, just as we always spoke of."

Teo jumped off the holding yard onto Calidor's arm, his talons grasping tight, apparently more excited than before. Calidor threw his arm skyward and Teo took flight, his great wings thrusting away the air. They watched until Teo disappeared over the East Fork.

Baytel turned toward Calidor, his grandfather, the only family he felt akin to, and asked, "Why do I go to Tridling Del and not to the Citadel with you?"

Calidor tightened the straps of the saddle. "Our time is short, Baytel. I go to the Citadel and look for survivors and appraise the damage. You have a separate quest. You will need to travel to the great city of Kilhalen in the north and report Vokat's designs of war. Along the way, seek out the druids that departed the Citadel when you did. They must be warned."

"Why Kilhalen?"

"It is the closest kingdom to the Southland with the largest army that has maintained a high level of training and preparations for battles. This winter in Kilhalen, specifically at the winter solstice, the Faerie Council is to convene. A few of the lords of the kingdoms and fiefdoms are suppose to be in attendance. You should be able to reach Kilhalen before they all arrive. All need to know of Ravek's death troops with their black magic and of Vokat's impending invasion plans. But before you embark on Kilhalen, you need to go to Tridling Del. When you arrive there, find the blacksmith, Make Ironwright. He is a druid like us and rode with me for many years. Tell him who you are, but tell no one else. Remember, you are dead to all you know. If discovered, you will draw out all the powers the Southland has to hunt you.

"Tridling Del is suspicious of all strangers and has been known to harbor evil factions so be careful. Tell Make Ironwright what has occurred, completely, from beginning to now, and where I have gone. I trust no other more than Make."

Tension gripped at Baytel's body. The excitement of the mission overpowered the fear of the inevitable—that he was going into battle against the evil factions of his father and brother. Again, things were happening quickly, only now a definite purpose and meaning drove him forth. The wave of events engulfed him and was carrying him toward an unknown shore, except now he was prepared for them, both physically and mentally.

Baytel surveyed the cabin and surrounding yards and meadows until resting his eyes on Calidor. Sadness set in at their separation once more. "Here we part ways again."

"We walk into danger and unknowns, so be wise and watchful with whomever you encounter. A force of insurmountable prowess and power attacked the Citadel. Be at your best guard."

"I shall," Baytel said somberly.

"The Grey Riders may be out in the wild you travel through. Do not detour from your quest to find them. If you encounter any of them, give them the same report you give Make along with any other information you happen upon. Use our ancient battle sign to identify yourself. If there is a need to leave written messages use the ancient runic language I taught you; it is our secret battle language. The Kings language."

Again Calidor paused, his brow creased with worry. "Baytel, I am sure the Grey Riders will know you before you see them. Your quest is to find your druid friends and reach Kilhalen before the winter solstice. I hope to follow soon after."

"I wish we had more time together, Calidor."

"As I, Baytel, but if all goes well, we will have time to reflect. We are family, you and I. No other in this land, and we shall be together soon."

Baytel embraced his grandfather, then stepped back, and pulled the reins of Calidor's stallion, leading him away from the cabin. "Those days I shall welcome with the hope they will be soon. Farewell, Calidor."

Calidor mounted his black, raised his hand and shouted back as he rode away with Thor at his heels, "Until Kilhalen, at the winter solstice, Druid Baytel!"

Chapter 30

A night mist shrouded the mountain range surrounding Calidor and his comrades, the black stallion and zekawolf, making it difficult to negotiate the loose ground of the slope. The darkness was oppressive. Nothing could be seen in the timberline forest, yet he was unfazed, for this was his land and his steed knew the highland terrain as well as he.

Upon reaching a flat that gradually carried him off the East Fork, he rode through a vast highland plain. A gentle breeze brushed across the open land bringing the smells of spring. The early bloom of mountain laurel seemed to glow in the moonlight as he rode, a blur of lavender pointing him the way eastward until the trace glow disappeared as he entered the lowland pine conifer forest.

Yet the beauty of the night passage through the glowing plain did nothing to brighten his mood as Calidor's thoughts constantly returned to the bleak situation. He contemplated what he would encounter at the Citadel and wondered if he would find survivors, feeling that somehow, some of those there would have found a way to escape harm. However, he knew the Citadel Druids would battle to the death to protect their home and those they love.

The first rays of morning illuminated the forest edge bright enough to be seen from far off. Unsure of the goblin horde's power or numbers, and if the enemy was near, he did not want to draw their ire, for perhaps unseen forces may have remained behind to spy. Calidor chose to be cautious rather than charge into the unknown.

He dismounted, leaving his stallion hidden deep in the woods. Standing behind a bramble of foliage on the bluff edge of the foothill he looked down at the lowlands of the eastern region. The land looked like a massive and far-reaching forest with no break except an occasional farmed clearing or a town established along the many trails that cut beneath the tall woodlands. His eyes moved farther up the horizon, beyond the woodlands, to the Northeast Territory, a province relatively untouched and unexplored since the re-creation. He scanned the vastness of the far mountains, knowing from reading the histories of the ancients that the land before him once lay below great seas. Massive bodies of water created by glacial ice movement in a time so long ago that the ancients could only guess at its era. Massive plates of ice moving at a steady pace had carved out passageways that led through once-treacherous lands into untouched wilderness. Now, the brilliant panorama of green landscape where rivers and streams ambled peacefully was inviting but still dangerous for humans.

Dawn spread its rose-tipped fingers over the treetops across the great eastern plain. Calidor could barely see the town of Balmoral far to the north and thought of riding there before the Citadel to speak with Juliard about the creatures, but decided against it. The Citadel was his destination and where that would take him only providence knew.

Satisfied with their safety Calidor made his camp inside the timberline, ate a cold meal and allowed his black stallion to roam and feed off the wild alfalfa and grasses and Thor to hunt. He rested his head against the saddle on the ground and fell to sleep, knowing his companions would warn of any predator that came near.

Later, in the dusk shadows, he rode down the bluff and disappeared into the verdant forestlands. The dark green foliage became black at night. He rode swiftly, camouflaged in darkness, and traveled this way for many nights. He kept no fire and slept in the heat of the sun, meeting the eastern landscape full of massive trees and deep valleys without seeing a soul.

Rain dropped from the night sky and continued and Calidor took advantage of its gloom by riding through the day and into the next night until high winds parted the clouds, bringing to view a star-filled moonless sky. The steady incline of the forest was his gauge that he was in the final approach to the Citadel. Dismounting, Calidor scouted the area and finding no signs of recent activity, edged to a clearing and looked up at the Citadel resting on top of the hill. The fortress was dark. Not a watch flame was lit along the battlements. Finding no movement ahead, he resumed his ride leaving the cover of the woods behind and rode up the hill to the Citadel.

The closer Calidor came, the more he noticed was not right with the fortress. There was no one moving along the battlements where sentries usually patrolled. The gatehouse above the massive doors where the Steward Stilar stood post without fail was abandoned; and as he came closer he saw the gate itself was off its hinges. His heart skipped a beat; Teo's report had been accurate.

Calidor dismounted and let the stallion roam free and told Thor to stay with the stallion. Cautiously he approached the gate, sword unsheathed and ready. The first thing he saw were the dead sentries lying across the threshold beside the broken and fired massive gate.

He entered the fortress, treading delicately through the portcullis into the outer ward. More dead sentries lay upon the ground, the dirt still stained with their blood even after the days of rain. Reading in detail the scene, he found the goblin horde had used fire as their initial assault weapon. The gatehouse and stable had been set afire. Horses that had tried to escape the flames lay in piles, burned and dead. The wall separating the outer and inner ward was in ruin; the great Pintél metal gate was bent and broken. He stepped silently into the inner ward toward the keep and he stopped.

Anger swept over him as never before. A cry of anguish escaped his lips at the horror he saw before him. Planted in the center of the ward were three wood posts. Upon them were nailed three people. They were dead. Burned at the stake were Karmen, Vernol and Roen—friends, the druid scholars, decimated by a barbarism so cruel it was hard to conceive of monsters that could do such evil. He cried out in anguish and wanted to slash out at something. He shook uncontrollably, his breathing harried. Then his mind went numb and as grief engulfed him, he dropped to his knees and wept.

Clutching his sword he pressed it against his forehead. The cool metal calmed him and slowly his control returned. His distress and anger turned then to purpose, and he whispered to the souls of the dead. "I will be your vindicator."

Calidor remained kneeling until his breathing calmed. Then, gathering himself together, he rose and commenced to read the signs about the ward. Mingled with the blood were massed carcasses in pools of black liquid, like a stain upon burned ground. They were scattered all abound the ward, unrecognizable forms of some sort. He studied them for a while, wondering what the disgusting masses were.

He walked back toward the druids looking for signs of other companions. Yar was not among them, nor was Anise. They must have found a way to escape, which was probably the reason the other druids were tortured. *Where might they have fled? Were Yar and Anise together? Had they been hunted down, killed, or were they still on the run?* Calidor left the dead behind and stalked the perimeter and found no other evidence of death. Still watchful, he entered the nearest tower and climbed to the battlement to survey the wreckage below. Destruction was at every turn in the ward but the fortress structure—walls, battlements, towers, and most gates—remained intact. Everything else was in shambles.

The battlement led to a tower turret. The door was broken and he had to shoulder his way in. He stared in dismay at the assembly room filled with more dead. Massacred bodies of students and acolytes lay beyond recognition. Around the dead acolytes were numerous black masses like those in the ward, and Calidor assumed they had to be dead goblins. *Did their bodies disintegrate when they died?*

The signs about the assembly room showed the acolytes had fought bravely and to the last against a superior power. The goblin assassins were efficient in their murderous raid, eliminating not only the druids' strength but also their future generation.

His fear for Baytel grew, now knowing he was walking into a danger much worse than they had imagined. But he pushed it aside rationalizing that Baytel was wise for his years and would become stronger once he met with Make Ironwright.

Calidor exited the turret to another battlement and stopped hearing a sound outside the walls of the Citadel. Below, outside the postern gate, a muffled cry rose. He peered down and saw a solemn scene. A gnome of early adult years was placing rocks upon a grave, crying in a soft whimper. Calidor did not speak out and left the tender moment to the young gnome, returning to the keep.

Swift, yet cautious not to raise the alarm to a possible goblin that remained behind, Calidor moved silently through the corridors of the keep, inspecting each level, eyes scanning for movement, sword at the ready to lash out. He halted on occasion to listen to the walls and feel the air, always mindful of what had murdered all the druids and acolytes. He moved on. Dead sentries and acolytes were at every turn. It was genocide and he quietly hoped he would come across a goblin to kill to expel his fury.

Before long, night had descended and as he was finally satisfied the fortress was free of intruders, Calidor raced through the keep once more until he reached a door in a darkened corridor. The door looked as though it had not been used for years. Its lock looked rusted shut and unworkable. Nearby, goblin masses littered the floor of the hall. Someone had fought hard to reach the door. It was difficult to distinguish how the goblins died, for their degeneration erased all evidence.

Calidor placed his hand upon the door and found the hidden palm lock and the door bolt clicked. He pushed the heavy door inward and stepped inside. The door instantly shut securely behind him on its own accord.

Engulfed in darkness, he felt along the walls. His hands brushed across smooth stone until they met a wall sconce, but no torch was in the holder. This disturbed him for only a druid could access the hidden corridor, and as a matter of course, they replaced used torches. Someone was still in the corridor.

He soundlessly moved forward from memory, placing his footsteps with quiet determination, until the corridor turned a corner. He stopped a few paces down the hall until he found another door and another hidden lock and opened it into a secret wing. He followed easily through the passageways that intertwined through the secret Citadel wing, avoiding passages he knew led to dead ends. The wing had been constructed so thoroughly that unless familiar with its design a person would be forever lost in the maze.

Through the multitude of passageways he came to another darkened hall. He paused, assuring himself that no one had followed or was present. Satisfied, he walked to the center of the hall and faced the wall at the end. It was like all the other passages, one more corridor that led to yet another dead end with no way to go except back.

Calidor sheathed his sword and ran his hand across the wall, searching. The stone felt coarse until his fingers met a specific inlaid stone. His eyes now accustomed to the dark could make out the brick. His fingertips sought out and found the inscription on the brick that was etched so finely it was almost impossible to identify as script. Its markings were in the ancient rune and he knew the translation by heart. *Keepers of the land . . . enter through your heart and be enlightened.*

Calidor placed his palm on the brick. Instantly a soft white glow appeared from within the stone and engulfed his hand. His senses tingled as the light coursed through his hand and up his arm. Then the glowing surged and overwhelmed his body. He did not panic for he recognized the magical light allowing it to rush through his body to identify who sought admittance and to determine whether the person was worthy.

Calidor, fully illuminated in the magic, sensed the magic searching his body and mind. He could feel the purity of the magic and it was enlightenment.

The magical light began to recede and then quickly left his body only to radiate on the wall, forming the outline of a door glowing brilliant with magic before his eyes where only stone showed before. Without hesitation, he opened the door and entered the chamber. As the door closed behind him, the light diminished, leaving Calidor in darkness. He spoke words of the Faerie and the room illuminated before him.

A quick intake of breath was all he allowed himself and he ran to the prostrated body of Anise on the stone floor. He checked her heartbeat. There was a pulse. Her breathing was shallow. Her dress was cut open across the stomach and both her arms were stained with blood. He opened her dress but found no injuries. He let out a sigh of relief; she had accessed the room in time.

No other soul was in the library. No Yar or other member of the Citadel. But clearly Anise had gained access without drawing attention to the room. She would rather have died than disclose the secret library of the ancients.

He looked into Anise's face. Her beauty was beyond measure. He pushed away the stray strands of hair from her eyes and saw them flutter and open. She smiled up at him and whispered, "Calidor, my love. I knew you would come."

Calidor smiled down at her and whispered, "I am overjoyed to find you alive, my sweet Anise. Rest now and I will make up a more comfortable bed for you."

"Good. I believe my wounds are nearly healed. I should be up and about soon."

"Quiet, Love. Shut your eyes and sleep for now. All will be well."

"Did Yar escape?" she asked, her eyes filled with hope.

Anise reached up and placed her hand on his face. Calidor covered her hand with his own and pressed it against his cheek. "Yar's body is nowhere in the fortress. I have not searched outside the fortress yet."

Anise nodded and whispered as if from a dream, "He escaped." Her eyes closed and she fell into slumber, her hand still on his cheek.

Calidor checked her wounds more closely. Not a scar, bruise or welt anywhere. Whatever wounds remained to be healed were inside her body and only she and the magic that surged through the library knew of them. He placed his pack under her head and removed his cloak, draping it over her to keep her warm. He leaned down and gently kissed her on the lips.

Calidor rose and sat on an oaken bench at a study table. The chamber rose three levels of the keep and wider than any assembly hall in the fortress. It was built with no windows; the light was created by magic that brightened and diminished when the necessity occurred, without prompting. The light over Anise was low yet where he sat it was bright enough to read. Dark wood floors, high vaulted wood ceilings and beautiful grained wood walls framed the interior. Shelves lined with books and manuscripts went from floor to ceiling containing the histories of the land and civilization before the re-creation, the treasures of knowledge saved by his ancestors from destruction at the time when the Golden Era of Mankind was collapsing. Here the mysteries of the magic of the land were sealed from unknowing and unprepared eyes. The sciences, philosophies and wisdom of the great minds of the ancients and from the beginning of time itself were carefully and covertly stored by the guarded enchantment of the Tree Faeries. The druids, Grey Riders and faeries had exclusive knowledge of its existence, faithfully adding to the histories through the years. Within the magic walls, faerie and druid had access to the insight and intelligence of the great masters of thought and learning. With this knowledge they became masters themselves. It was the druid's true power and was used with great reverence.

Anise had gained access and the library remained secret and uncompromised. The chamber was sealed with faerie magic and was infused with a magical power to maintain life—and in Anise's circumstance, to heal. A person could live forever and not age a day within the walls of the enchanted library.

Calidor began scouring through the written histories for a passage or an obscure writing about where Yar might be destined to travel in a time like this. He knew that Yar would not lead the goblin horde to the faerie lands in the west, nor would he travel toward any fiefdom or sectional border where any incident might ignite a conflict. Yar would lead them away from civilization where he could contend with the goblin horde in his own way. He would lead them far, but how far?

Manuscript after manuscript, the volumes stacked high on the desk. Occasionally he checked on Anise, still asleep under the healing influences of the faerie magic. It seemed like hours but he knew at least a day had passed within the library, and though the search for clues about Yar was in vain, the documents he read filled him with a sense of urgency. *What if I cannot find Yar and the goblin horde succeeds? Who will continue his great work?*

He was about to give up and venture outside the Citadel to search for signs of Yar when he came upon a footnote in a manuscript from the faeries' histories. It spoke of a split in the faerie tribe. One faction, which traveled throughout the newly formed lands to heal and discover, expressed interest in living outside their forest home in the west. They found a beautiful land beyond the Northeast Passage, a region rich with the youth of the re-creation. When the faerie council convened it was decided that the tribe would split, for the land and its healing were paramount.

The footnote read, *"The land they sought to live in was mountainous terrain, hence the faction that travelled to this wondrous land was named Rock Faeries. We faeries staying in the woodlands in the west were thereafter named Tree Faeries."*

Fascinated by what he read, he found the volume dated back more than two thousand years. Another entry spoke of the Rock Faerie territory where Tree Faerie elders occasionally took to a pilgrimage for silent thought and replenishment. The location was barely mentioned, stated only as an eastern trek passing between two mountains leading to a gateway to the "Valley of the Low Star." No directions were written about the exact location. The manuscript spoke only of a mountain range far beyond the Northeast Passage.

"That is where Yar is headed." Calidor spoke aloud as enthusiasm swept over him.

"What was that, Love?"

He turned to Anise, who had risen and stood behind him without him knowing. The color in her face had returned with radiance and health. He rose and kissed her full, embracing her with all his love. "You are better, I see?"

She smiled and said teasingly, "With such a kiss and embrace, what woman wouldn't be? Now show me, what have you found?"

"A footnote to where Yar may be headed. Here," he pointed to the passages, "it gives somewhat indistinct descriptions. Some landmarks and rune signs that might by now be gone or undetectable, but I will memorize them at any rate."

"You plan to follow Yar?" Concern for his safety came from her words.

Calidor nodded. "Yes. He is certainly being hunted by this goblin horde. I must follow."

"Goblins. I sensed they had some form of magic when fighting them, Calidor. It is evil and uncontrollable. Who is the source?"

"Prince Ravek. They are preparing another invasion and these monsters are the first to venture into the north."

Calidor closed the manuscript and replaced all the volumes in their proper sequences on the shelves. He took Anise's hand and relayed the information from Baytel and Teo. "Baytel is on his way to Tridling Del to meet Ironwright as we speak."

Anise smiled and said, "You must be quite proud of your grandson. As am I. During his studies the past three years, Baytel showed the promise that he was born into, a true leader and loyal friend to many acolytes and druids. He possessed gentlemanly behavior and was always proper and polite. He is a fine young man, Calidor. I am very fond of Prince Baytel."

"Druid Baytel," he corrected. "That title he holds closer to his heart than the other."

"Druid it is then, although he is my prince and I will call him Sire until corrected now that he knows his ancestry. As to Teo's report, it is most disturbing on many fronts. It seems that Ravek has grown even more evil than his father. They will fall astray of one another eventually, and an unavoidable battle between the two will surely occur. Their mutual thirsts for superiority will overpower any familial ties they harbor."

"Well before that happens, come next spring, Vokat and his massive army will begin their march into the northlands. I ordered Baytel to travel to Kilhalen to warn the Faerie Council and representatives of the kingdoms and fiefdoms. Let's hope there is a decent showing in attendance for the council at the winter solstice. My journey points to where Yar goes. Once I find him safe, I will make for Kilhalen."

"Yar is many days ahead of you."

"Yes he is, but still closer to the Citadel than where I believe he is headed. With the goblin horde resistance and Yar's gift of misdirection, I can gain time by a more direct route and hopefully arrive in the northeast before they do. And then I shall exact my vengeance on this evil horde of Ravek's."

Chapter 31

NIGHT had fallen once more. Calidor, with Anise beside him, moved warily along the upper walkway to the battlement toward the postern gate. Outside the fortress walls he could see a flickering fire. Calidor peered over the battlement and saw the same young gnome beside the fire standing vigil at a grave. He was small like most gnomes, slightly shorter than a dwarf, his black hair cropped short, and he was dressed in all green.

Calidor whispered in Anise's ear. "Let me approach this one myself."

Kissing him with her reply, she walked to the postern entrance. His eyes followed her until she disappeared in the postern stronghold, happy to see her alive and feeling well.

Seeing no present danger below, Calidor walked down the postern steps and out the gate toward the gravesite. He remained solemn as he approached the reverent scene, for he knew the one whose grave was yet unmarked. It could only be that of his friend and steward of the Citadel, Stilar.

Calidor walked into the firelight with just enough noise and at a fair distance where the gnome would not be too startled.

"Greetings and condolences, Shôrgnome," he hailed. The gnome immediately jumped up in fright. "Ease yourself, young one; I am a friend to those who reside here."

Stopping in front of the gnome Calidor looked down upon the rock grave. "This must be the grave of Stilar the Steward. It is of great regret, his loss to our world. He was a great friend."

"What are you, strange one?" asked the young gnome, still showing his fear, "and how did you know I am a Shôrgnome?"

"You have the look of the Shôr folk, and the only gnome who lived here was Stilar, who was of the Shôr. Also, the grave you have assembled is that of the Shôr folk."

The gnome nodded and withdrew back to his solemn thoughts. Calidor broke the silence again. "You look like a young Stilar, Shôrgnome. What is your name?"

"I am Cast. My uncle Stilar was my mother's brother. How do you know my uncle?"

"He rode with me many years ago as we traveled the land together. Many a fire we shared in our day." Calidor looked down at the young gnome and asked, "Do you mind sharing your fire, Cast of the Shôr?" putting a formal touch to the request with a slight bow.

"It would be a pleasure to share my fire with an unnamed friend of my uncle," replied the gnome with a return bow.

Calidor smiled inwardly at the serious Shôrgnome. Even in mourning the young of the Shôr folk had a formality that was pleasing and often, though small in size, placed one at a disadvantage. "My pardon, young sir. I am Calidor, Grey Rider and Druid of the Citadel, at your service."

"Calidor!" The gnome stared wide-eyed, his formal demeanor disarmed. The surprised expression on his face flickered comically in the firelight. "By the spirits of the River Shôr!"

"There are no spirits here, Cast. Shall we sit and talk? There are things I would like to be informed of and I am afraid you are the only one who may be of help."

He moved the gnome's pack to sit near the fire and noticed it was light as a feather. "Have you had a meal this night, Cast?"

Cast lowered his head, probably ashamed at not being able to offer a guest food at his fire. "My food supply is gone. My last meal was yesterday night and I haven't gone to forage yet."

Calidor sent a high-pitched whistle into the night. The thunder of his stallion's gallop and the panting howl of Thor forewarned their arrival. When they reached the firelight out of the darkness, the stallion cantered excitedly and the wolf jumped up and licked Calidor's face.

Cast hadn't moved; his eyes fixed on the big zekawolf. "Don't be alarmed, Cast. This is Thor, my traveling companion." He pointed to the bags on the back of the stallion. "In those saddlebags you will find cheese and bread. Bring them here to the fire and help yourself. I will join you after I take care of these two."

After tending to the stallion and wolf he sat with Cast. "You must have made a very long journey, Shôrgnome."

"It seems all for naught, Calidor," the gnome said, on the verge of tears. "I never was able to speak to my uncle. My mother and the patriarchs of the Shôr were full of stories of him, and you. I wanted to meet him and learn from him, and be part of the Citadel. When I arrived and saw those monsters and then all the dead..." He put his hands over his face, unable to hold back the tears and abandoned himself to anguish.

Calidor stayed silent while Cast grieved. Seeing death and mutilation for the first time in one's peaceful life was horrific and inconceivable to most; even to him, a seasoned veteran of death and war, it was awful.

Cast poked at the fire with a stick. The nightmare of death within the Citadel was so overwhelming to the young gnome that he had retreated into a state of numbed consciousness. Calidor had to keep him talking. "Cast, tell me how you came to the Citadel."

Jarred out of his grief, Cast took a deep breath before speaking. "I had wanted to come here since I was old enough to learn that my uncle was the steward of the mystical Citadel. So aspiring to work hand in hand with him, and magical faeries, and druids, I trained my whole life to do just that. When I came of age, and with my mother's good wishes, for she and my uncle wrote to one another, I set out. She presented me with his last letter."

He pulled out the letter, unfolded it and read aloud, "Send Cast. I have duties to share with a fine young Shôrgnome."

He paused to collect himself again. The fire cracked and a spark flew off the burning log against his boots. Cast kicked it back into the flames. "My arrival here was anything but gleeful. I neared the main gate only to see these horrible creatures depart. I laid low to the ground and hoped beyond all hope I went undiscovered. Once the creatures rounded the fortress and were out of view, I rose and quietly made it to the gate. Smoke rose high over the compound from their raid. The first of the Citadel dead I saw was my uncle at the gate he had guarded his entire life. A black gash cut deep across his chest had drawn the life from his body. All the others were butchered, burned and defiled by an evil unknown to me."

Quick sobs of anguish cut short his report until he collected himself and asked, "What are we to do?"

"First you must tell me of the creatures and where they were bound," said Calidor.

Cast answered, though doubtful and forlorn. "I saw them divide outside the west gate. Most went east with only a few headed west. They were horrible creatures with an ugly, insane look about them. What are you going to do, Calidor? Those monsters were in a host of hundreds."

He answered in a blunt manner. "What I and others shall do? Hunt them down and remove their foul lives from the land."

Cast sniffed; a gesture of disbelief. "What can one man do against hundreds?"

Calidor ignored the rebuke. "They were goblins out of Pithe from the Fork Mountains. Prince Ravek, who has aspired to practice the dark art of his father, King Vokat of the Southland, subverted and mutated them into the form you are witness to."

"The King of Blood, we call Vokat. I will call this Ravek the Prince of Blood." He spoke it like a blasphemy.

"This goblin horde's purpose is to destroy all who are a part of the Citadel— druids, scholars, students, and probably anyone who gets in their way. We believe

DRUIDS OF THE FAERIE

this is a prelude to another war against the north." He paused a moment and looked hard at Cast. "Young Shôrgnome, you are fortunate they did not see you."

Angrily, Cast exclaimed, "Calidor, we must warn the people. We must tell the great cities to prepare."

"Calm yourself, Cast. The warnings will reach the cities by another. We have our duties here."

"Duties? What duties?"

Calidor stood and called up to Anise. She answered and soon appeared at his side. "Druid Anise, this is Stilar's nephew, Cast. Cast, may I present Druid Anise of the Citadel."

Cast looked starry-eyed at her beauty and was too dumbfounded to form any words of greeting.

Anise offered her hand and he took it. "It is a pleasure meeting you, Cast. Allow me to say how sorry I am about your uncle's death. He was a good friend and companion."

Calidor turned to the gnome. "Cast, this is a most difficult time for us all, and though you are young and inexperienced, I believe you are the one that we can depend upon. We are the only representatives of the Citadel and Faerie Council present so it is my duty to call you to yours. I, Calidor, appoint to thee, Cast of the Awär Shôrgnome, the title and duties of Steward of the Citadel."

"Steward? Me? I do not know what to do. No one is alive here. There are no druids or scholars or students, no sentries." Almost in panic, he paced around the fire, mumbling, "No, I cannot do it...my uncle's station..."

"Cast! Who am I?"

Startled to fright, he said, "You are Calidor, Druid and Grey Rider."

"And who is this woman beside me?"

"She is Druid Anise."

"Yes. Therefore there are Druids of the Citadel, are there not? And as such, this is our home and you are our steward. We need your protection and stewardship."

Sheepishly, Cast replied, "My apologies, Calidor, but I assumed the Citadel would no longer be."

"It is and will continue to be for thousands of years, Cast, and one day a prince of kings shall rule from it and peace shall reign among all sects of man. But that day is far off and there is much to do before it comes. A few of us know of this disaster and more will soon learn. Your first order of business as steward is to secure this fortress from any further harm. Assemble your nearest cousins to your aid. Bury the dead along the foot of the outside walls of the fortress except at this postern gate. Find the trapvine plant and plant it upon their graves."

Calidor paced. "Druid Anise will assist you in coordinating the security of the fortress and reorganizing its functions. We will still take in those in need and will always be available to heal the sick and wounded.

"Anise will send word to Balmoral by secret courier to the Druid Juliard to summon him here to guide in the fortress repair. Do you know of the ancient rune?"

"Yes, sir. It was part of my studies," said Cast, obediently.

"Very good. Use it in all forms of communications outside the fortress. Druid Juliard will contact Make Ironwright, who is of the highest order of dwarf masons and smiths out of Ctiklat, and a druid. They both rode with your uncle and me. Tell him, in runic note, of the madness you have witnessed, but do not tell him where I am bound until he arrives here. I take no chances in case the note is intercepted by another."

"Yes sir."

"Now do you accept the appointment, Cast of the Awär Shôrgnome?" asked Calidor formally.

Anise stood beside the frightened Shôrgnome and said, "Cast, will you be my steward and manage the running of the Citadel? We need your help most desperately."

Standing straight-backed with dignity and pride, he replied, "I accept the appointment and duties of Steward of the Citadel and will hold this office with respect and guard this fortress with my life, as did my uncle before me."

"Good, Cast. Now I ride toward the goblin horde, for they have not found the master Tree Faerie Yar and hunt him as we speak."

Calidor turned to Anise. They embraced and kissed. She said, "Be careful, Love."

He jumped upon his stallion and said to Cast, "The druids shall return to the Citadel, Steward Cast, be sure of it. One druid named Baytel is among them who is the hope of the next generation. He is in search of the druids not among the dead. Hope for his success. He marches toward Kilhalen to warn the great cities and Tree Faeries on the winter solstice.

"About your other duties, Druid Anise will supply you with your uncle's duty scroll." His horse cantered beneath him, anxious to depart. "Cast, the duties of Steward of the Citadel are in your hands. I have no reservations about this, for I know it is right." He turned his stallion.

"Calidor, where are you bound?" asked the Steward of the Citadel as he ran behind.

"Northeast, Cast." He left them and rounded the fortress looking for signs left by the horde. He knew better than to look for any left by Yar. Cast had reported correctly. At the forest edge tracks leading to the west were minimal, though they left him concerned that Baytel might encounter that faction. The other signs of the horde showed as though a herd of caribou had passed through. As he had anticipated, the horde's trail aimed toward the northeast.

Chapter 32

RAIN continued to fall for the third consecutive day and night, but that did not wipe away the deep trotted tracks left by the goblin horde nor, even more blatantly clear, the evidence of their lethal destruction through the sodden forest. Sadly, Calidor found most those killed were innocent farmers and travelers, pioneers who had forged into the wild to live in peace. No one was safe when crossing paths with the murderous goblins. All the deaths were of a pattern, a black gash or stab wound that festered from a poisonous infection that spread rapidly through the body. If the wound itself did not instantly kill then surely what came of it did.

The goblins had abandoned the northeast direction and veered onto a narrow creek where they were probably on the scent of Yar. Calidor walked his stallion along the soft embankment to where the creek's clear water showed a shallow bed of multi-colored pebbles. Canopied by birch trees growing from saturated banks, the creek meandered northward through the lowland woods.

His stallion whinnied, trying to edge away from the creek. Appreciating the stallion's senses, Calidor stopped to listen and peer into the woods. Through gaps he could see deeper in the forest and noted a grove of crabapple trees that had dropped ripened apples. Calidor patted the stallion's neck and said, "No treats for you this early." And he continued guiding him up the creek.

Later, as dusk fell and the most obvious traces of the goblin horde faded away, he remained undaunted, overly convinced that Yar's direction was what he thought it to be, drawing the goblins away from civilization and into the wild. If the pattern continued, he could soon abandon their tracks altogether and head directly to the Northeast Passage where he could clandestinely plot a plan of attack.

A howl from deep in the trees disrupted the stillness of the forest. The lonely cry seemed to remain in the space about the creek, adding to the sullenness of Calidor's mood. Thor growled and the hairs on his back bristled. The steed skittered beneath him. The wail sounded again. Something moved in the brush and the stallion reared, causing Calidor to slide off the saddle beside the steed to calm him. Another howl raised more anxiety, as this time the howl came from another direction. Noting a splashing and movement from behind and to the side, he jumped back on his horse and galloped down the creek with Thor following, running along the bank.

Another wailing howl pierced the air, followed by a crash to his left as black wolves chased after them into the creek. He shifted from the open stream to the woods, slowing and scattering their pursuers, but the lead wolf caught up with them, running stride for stride beside him, its powerful jaw snapping at the stallion's hooves. Calidor drew his sword and swiped downward at the wolf. It found its flesh. Yet as quickly as it died another took its place, surprisingly larger than the last.

The steady sound of rushing water drew his attention ahead. The sound could only be of a rapidly flowing river. Calidor changed direction again, racing toward the sound, crashing through brush and leaping over fallen trees. Doubling back to the creek for a more direct route to the river brought more wolves. Downstream, a number of wolves jumped into the creek, barring his way to the river.

He reined in the stallion and was about to turn again when Thor crashed into the forward pack from the woods. Thor's jaws clamped around the throat of the largest wolf and, with a twist of his own neck, tossed him away with a hole where its neck was. The attack opened a lane and Calidor drove through, trampling two wolves as he raced for the river. He could make out a depression far ahead and knew the embankment of the creek was elevated over the river level. He charged and without hesitation rode his stallion off the embankment, plunging deep into the water.

Surfacing beside the head of the stallion, he saw the animal's nostrils flared wide and its eyes filled with fear. He kept his legs away from the rapidly pumping steed. Once the horse gained some semblance of coordinated motion of swimming, Calidor hung on to the saddle and kicked to not be so much of a burden. The current, swelled by the heavy rain and spring drainage from the thaw, was strong and carried them swiftly south, the opposite direction from the goblin trail. Rounding a bend in the river, he took a last look back and could barely make out Thor on the crown of the embankment in a vicious battle. Then the current swept the scene from sight.

Debris floated among the rapids as logs and forest vegetation hampered their headway, heedlessly bumping and grating against them. At the west shore of the river from where they came, black wolves ran parallel to them in anticipation of the river releasing their prey back ashore. Calidor grabbed the stallion's mane and guided him toward the opposite shore. Driving his legs against the power of the river, he sliced through the turbulent foam and debris, hungry for the east bank.

It was well past dusk and twilight was upon the river when suddenly the stallion settled to a stop, discovering a foothold in the riverbed. Calidor and the stallion caught their breath, resting upon the soft bed. After a moment of peace, Calidor calmly walked him to the sandy rise of the east bank. On the soggy but stable ground he checked his stallion and himself. Beaten and bruised from the barriers but with nothing broken, he guided the stallion up a minor slope to distance themselves from the river before anyone who might be in the area discovered their presence.

Beyond the shore grew brown reeds that rose up to the stallion's neck. The soft soil sucked in Calidor's feet and, as he lost his balance, he grabbed the tall grass whose razor-sharp edges sliced into his hand. The going was difficult and his legs burned with fatigue. Lighted by the crescent glow of the rising moon, he gradually met solid ground but he did not stop until he found a fog-filled hollow with adequate tree cover. There he set camp in a small dell, dark with mist and depressed so low he felt at ease to build a fire. Calidor removed the saddle and bags from his horse, fed him grains, and ate his first meal since dawn and stretched out next to the fire.

Calidor woke at midday, nudged from his slumber by the stallion. He rolled to a seated position on the ground and immediately noticed the cuts along the black's shins. The horse winced at their tenderness when touched. Finding dry wood, Calidor stoked the fire. Emptying his bag, he spread the contents out to dry. He cleansed the stallion's lacerations and made up and administered a poultice and wrapped his shins with fern leaves that were in abundance in the hollow. His own injuries he mended after assuring the stallion's bindings were secure.

Unsure of where he was and how far the river had taken him he scouted the area around the dell. Finding no sign of the goblin horde, or wolves, he foraged for food to replace what was lost in the river and returned to camp. The dell seemed to drink in the afternoon sun's warmth, drying their belongings. After a long rest, he broke camp, repacking his gear and leading the steed out of the dell as dusk arrived.

Periodically Calidor looked behind him, hoping to see Thor. It seemed like they had drifted a long ways, but he knew the zekawolf would be victorious against the wolf pack and eventually rejoin them, but first would need to find their scent once he crossed the river.

Moonlight showed an open country sparsely dotted with copses of bushes, patches of grass and an occasional magisterial and venerable willow tree. He hadn't encountered a soul although plenty of wildlife was about; mostly red squirrels, rabbits, grouse and the like, but no people. It was a region relatively untraveled, one more of the many unexplored territories of the One Land. He grabbed a handful of grass and, fingering through the soil, found it dark and rich, excellent earth and country, especially for farming.

Calidor camped under the sanctuary of the draping branches of a willow tree, built a fire to cook and redressed the stallion's bandages. Listening to the wind rustling the branches, Calidor fell asleep against the trunk of the willow.

Near dusk, he found the stallion was much healed. They set out on a walking pace as before, Calidor dismounting periodically, for although urgency was the call, so was the health of his companion. As the sun set and they left behind the open country, Calidor promised himself to speak of its richness and tranquility to others who might want to venture away from the cities. The ground rose into an oak forest where he decided to set camp.

Dusk to dawn was the routine, holding to an eastern direction, but seeing no signs of the goblin horde, he worried about finding their tracks again and contemplated heading directly to the northeast. Thunderclouds began to fill the night sky, blocking out the stars. He had counted eight days since crossing the river. With now no moon to break through the darkness, travel slowed to a snail's pace.

A crack of a twig penetrated through the quiet night and he drew the stallion to a halt. Someone or something was in the forest with him. Muffled sounds and low voices came from the woods. Calidor dismounted and left behind the steed, edging forward quiet as a deer. The only noises he produced would be taken as natural sounds of the forest. Ahead, Calidor saw the light of a fire filtering through the thickets. Moving stealthily to the edge of the light, he was outside a small clearing, where sat three large trolls around a campfire. A fourth troll lay on the ground, obviously injured.

Now Calidor understood why there were no people in the region. It was troll country. The river he had been forced into by the wolves must have been the River Cathrage, the western border to the troll lands. Even kneeling beside their fallen companion the trolls' hulking bodies were massive. Barrel-chested, with long arms and bowed legs, they had no neck to speak of and their bodies were almost square. The trolls' immense muscle structure displayed their staggering strength. Once in the grasp of a troll, you could simply and quickly be pulled apart.

Not all troll sects looked the same. In the firelight, the faces of this group looked smooth and somewhat featureless, which meant they were not mountain trolls, most of whom lived in the northwest, or gully trolls, found throughout the land, hidden away in dark hollows. These were hill trolls. They had small, round, pebble-black eyes, a short stubbed nose and a small mouth that almost looked like a dimple above a large chin. Their foreheads were low beneath their red hairline.

They hovered over the injured troll, bickering. Calidor edged closer within the confines of the trees just before the clearing, listening to their language, which likened to that of man, except they ended many words with a humming sound, as if they were contemplating the word just spoken. The trolls were discussing their patrol and coming across a large band of goblins "of some sort" and that they had clashed. Some trolls had been killed. The injured one had a deep infected wound across his face and shook with fever.

Calidor drew himself up and stepped into the firelight. The trolls jumped to their feet, baring lances. Calidor stood motionless; his sword remained sheathed, allowing his unruffled posture to show as he waited out the moment for the trolls to recognize him as meaning no harm. His stillness extended outward from his body and soon the trolls were mirroring his stillness until the tension lessened and an atmosphere of peace seemed to infiltrate the clearing. As the moment lengthened the trolls began lowering their weapons, each looking calmly at the tranquil man before them.

The largest troll stepped forward, still slightly on guard, measuring Calidor as one does an enemy. "What is your purpose'mm, wayfarer. And be cautioned, I can smell a lie'mm from as far away as the Great Sea."

Calidor replied softly, "I mean no harm and am regretful to intrude upon your camp uninvited. I seek a friend who may be in great danger and ask your kind assistance—"

The troll cut off his words. "We know of no one in great'mm danger. Move on or the one who will be in danger will be you'mm!"

Calidor ignored the troll's reply and pointedly stared at the injured troll upon the ground. "I see one of you is hurt and in need of attention. I may be of some assistance to you. Let us not quarrel." His calmness was now in full effect as the largest troll relaxed his stance. The others stayed mute and seemed almost bored.

Less harsh yet still guarded, the big troll said, "This is no country for your kind'mm. Your people never travel east of the River Cathrage unless they seek mischief'mm." He stopped and looked hard again at Calidor, measuring the man. "Who are you, wayfarer, and why would you risk'mm life to talk with us?"

The trolls in this region were known as a strong-willed, intelligent sect ruled by the same family for hundreds of years. *The Trolls of Iksut.* Although they once battled side by side with man and dwarf in the early wars and for a time attended the Council of the Faeries, the *Iksut* had since kept to themselves for many years. Nevertheless, the one thing the Iksut trolls regarded highly was the truth.

"I am Calidor."

The trolls all stepped back a pace, passing glances back and forth to one another. One grabbed an amulet hanging around his neck, as if to ward off evil. The others murmured in unintelligible tones.

Calidor dropped his calm state. "As I stated, I seek a friend who is in danger and I must find him before others cause him harm. I wish only good on your camp."

Trouble holding his fear in check, the large troll asked, "You are'mm Calidor, the Druid?"

"Yes."

"I have not heard of you'mm for many years. Our father's time has passed, as did that of our father's father. How is it you'mm are not dead?"

A moan rising from the fallen troll broke the tension.

"Well, as you can see, I am very much alive. I am also a healer. Your companion is in need of assistance. May I look to him?"

The large troll looked down at his injured companion writhing in pain, and reluctantly waved Calidor in to enter their camp.

Leaning over the fallen troll Calidor saw a black contagion had spread over the gash across the face and neck and seemed to be spreading, probably through his blood, to his upper extremities, as they looked discolored.

Calidor stood and sent a whistle toward the forest. The motion and sound startled the trolls and he said, "My horse is not far off. I must retrieve my pack and treat your friend. If this plague in his blood spreads to his heart, he will die."

The black's thunderous hooves preempted his appearance and he crashed through the bramble into camp, halting at Calidor's side. The trolls, having given the stallion a wide berth, stood mute to the side, allowing Calidor to retrieve his pack.

"I need a cup and a bowl to mix ointment and medicine." The large troll found them in their supply and handed them over. Selecting specific herbs and mixing them in hot water, Calidor cleansed the wound many times over. The process was slow as the troll writhed in pain at his touch. The poison had rooted deep and mere herbal cleansing and suturing would not entirely stop the deadly host.

Returning to his bag, Calidor withdrew a dried leaf and crushed it into the wound. He mixed some of the leaf into a hot broth and fed it to the troll. Immediately, the delirium ceased and the troll went peacefully to sleep.

Calidor drew two stones from a pocket of his tunic, clenching one in his hand and placing the other on the wound and then covering it with his hand. He had not used the ancient stones for some time and it took him a moment to recall the ancient incantation. Then, remembering, he muttered the words softly to himself and immediately, the stones beneath his hands began to glow. Soon his hands were translucent. He ignored the cries of anger and fear from the trolls, keeping his concentration on the magic he was performing. Any break would ruin the magical connection and the troll beneath him would die.

The light surged through Calidor's hands and travelled up his arms and into his body, causing the druid to be engulfed in the light. As the conduit of the magic, Calidor then transmitted the magical light into the injured troll. Glaring illumination seared through the troll, flowing deep into his body. Calidor directed the magic deep into the troll's blood vessels like fingers searching in the dark. When the search finally reached the black infection, the magic surged, overwhelming the crux of the poison.

Calidor sensed the time passing and still he remained diligent, searching and destroying the poisonous host, glowing along with the troll and illuminating the

clearing and dark woods. He stole a glance at the other trolls. They had stepped
farther away and stood unmoving outside the campfire. They had probably never
witnessed magic before, for not many had, and had they any reservations of his
identity before, all doubts were by now erased. Calidor knew the legend and stories of him had been told throughout the land, but they were so old, the trolls
probably wondered if he was indeed Calidor, or a shade, for the light that passed
through him made him appear ghostlike.

The magic light began to diminish and the troll began to respond. Only
when the light faded entirely did Calidor remove his hand to show the troll's
wound and black injection were gone. The troll opened his eyes and looked at
him and smiled. Then he closed them and he was asleep.

Calidor placed the stones back into his tunic and turned to the trolls. "He is
at rest now. Let him sleep in peace. You..." he pointed to a troll who looked so
frightened he almost laughed. "Make sure you keep this fire alive so he is kept
warm. He will be hungry when he wakes, so prepare a generous meal."

They all showed wonder and fear of him, but did what they were told, for he
had saved their companion's life. However, he still had to win over their full trust.
Calidor secured his pack and his medicines upon the stallion and led him off to
feed on the grass within the circle of light. He heard the large troll stepping
toward him and wait patiently for his attention until Calidor returned to the
campfire. Trolls were a polite folk who, because of their reclusive nature, were
unaccustomed to easy conversation with strangers.

The troll cleared his throat and said, "King Kaul of Iksut will be'mm pleased
with you for saving the life of his youngest grandson." He paused, and then said,
"I am Meetah, captain of the Fourth Line of Iksut." He raised his hand across his
chest, palm facing toward Calidor.

Calidor returned the gesture. "I am Calidor, Grey Rider and Druid of the
Citadel. I greet you, Captain Meetah of the Fourth Iksut."

Meetah lowered his arm, and said, "Calidor of the Grey, will you join me at
our fire?"

They sat across the flames from one another without speaking for some time.
Captain Meetah seemed uncomfortable with the prolonged politeness, but it was necessary, for the responsibility of the grandson's safety certainly rested in his hands.

Calidor eased into the conversation. "It was fortunate that I came along to
help when I did. The wound on the young prince was deep and the poison was
running wild."

"The Trolls of Iksut are'mm in your debt."

"It is my duty as a druid to heal those who are ailing. A willing duty. No debt
is owed," he replied, and both were silent again. Calidor had to ask about the goblin horde they had encountered but knew that the troll captain needed questions
of his own answered before surrendering any information.

Captain Meetah broke the silence and, regaining some bravado, spoke with a bite. "How did you come to our country, Druid?"

"My apologies for traveling in your lands. It was purely by accident. My stallion and I were set upon by wolves and escaped into the River Cathrage. We were carried by the current much farther south than intended."

"So you'mm travelled by the river to reach our lands?" he asked bluntly, no longer caring of politeness but rather insistence on the truth.

"I did not travel the river. I meant only to cross and was carried away by it."

Calidor knew the progression of the questions and where they were leading. The troll was suspicious of all travelers and trusted no one.

"So you were not traveling by river and wanted only to cross'mm the Cathrage. You said you did reach our land by accident." The troll paused, displaying a thin smile, thinking he had uncovered a lie. "How is it, Druid, that'mm you were going to cross the Cathrage toward troll country while not intending to travel here?"

This was a test of truth and information. The troll had gauged his questions simply but his profound sense of truth could not be avoided. Calidor was fully willing to let the conversation go the troll's deliberate way, but it was time to gain the information he needed and get on with his pursuit of the goblin horde.

Calidor told Meetah what had occurred from the Citadel to their camp making his point to the truth-seeking troll. "These creatures I have pursued of many weeks."

"Goblins, you say, Druid? How did'mm they come to the Citadel and why do'mm you follow?" he said accepting the story, wanting to hear more.

"These creatures are evil incarnates from out of the bowels of the Southland where King Vokat and Prince Ravek wield the black magic. This is a prelude to another war. I follow this horde because they are in pursuit of Yar, the master Tree Faerie. They have killed too many and must be eliminated from the land."

Meetah angrily tossed a log into the fire. "They crossed the Cathrage'mm, Druid, and attacked without warning, killing five of my troop and injuring our prince, the foul'mm beasts."

Calidor acknowledged the admission with a profound nod and asked, "Captain Meetah, how was it some of you escaped their destruction?"

The troll bowed his head solemnly and replied, holding his anger at bay. "We were'mm patrolling the border of the river. I sent six of my troop to'mm scout south of here. When we heard screams we ran back to where'mm my troop was. All were dead except for the prince. Had I known what we'mm faced, I would have—"

"It would have done no good," Calidor interrupted. "The goblin horde is more than a hundred strong and would have overwhelmed you all. Be thankful you are alive to tell Iksut of their threats to all the sects."

Thunder pealed into the quiet of the forest and lightning flashed across the sky, ending their talk. The trolls scurried to construct a shelter, tying ropes between three trees and draping a canvas cover across the expanse large enough to cover them all, including the stallion.

After they were settled under the tent cover, one of the trolls asked Calidor, "What will you'mm do if you find these goblins?"

Calidor thought for a moment, and said, "Their evil is strong as is their number. I will need all my resources." He looked at Captain Meetah. "Thank you for the comfort of your cover from the storm. I will look after the prince and then retire."

Sleep did not come, for he was tending the troll prince while the rain kept up through the night; the dull thud of raindrops was like a rhythm of drumming constantly beating, keeping him awake. Rolling thunder and lightning exploded, changing night to day instantly and often.

Calidor was grateful for cover and lodging, but would rather be on his way toward the goblin horde and Yar. His mind would not rest until Yar was safe. All he could do now was wait and watch for the troll prince to regain consciousness, making sure he was properly healed.

His thoughts darted about like a bee in a clover field. Short stops here and there to that flower and then another, with Baytel fluttering in and out of his mind, knowing the immediate dangers Baytel was walking toward. He rejected the doubt about their separating at the cabin. It was right to send him the way of Tridling Del. It is his time to confront his destiny, as it was Calidor's when he was young. Baytel would fare well.

"Your thoughts take you far, healer," the troll prince whispered, bringing Calidor back from his inducing.

"I have been far, Prince of Iksut."

The troll sat up and asked, "Is it late or'mm early?"

"Sunrise is not long off. How do you fare?"

"Hungry and a bit weak, but much'mm better thanks, I suppose, to you. Where did you learn your trade?"

"I am a druid, Prince. I am Calidor, Druid of the Citadel and Grey Rider. At your service."

The young troll swallowed and said, "Yes,'mm. You have been far. I am Kaulet, grandson of Kaul, king of Iksut. My respects, sir, and my'mm deepest thanks." He paused, looking about the surroundings. "I see you have been welcome in our camp and'mm there is probably a story behind it. If you do not mind repeating it, I will not interrupt."

"It would please me to oblige readily, for you seem in good health and I am losing precious time in my quest." He quickly told Prince Kaulet of his journey and the cause of it and also of Baytel's journey to Kilhalen, not leaving out any detail as he had done with Meetah. "This is why I must depart at once, Prince Kaulet."

The young prince stood slowly, and steadying himself with Calidor's help. "We are in your debt. What do you ask of us, Druid Calidor?"

"I ask nothing of your sect, Prince Kaulet, nothing except the relaying of what you learned of here this night and the understanding of what may come next. The Southland power is great once again. Vokat and Ravek will never stop until they have ultimate power over the sects. Let us both hope their dark arm will not reach this far, for if it does, we have failed and they will have rule over all in the land."

Calidor left the prince to his thoughts and prepared his stallion for departure. The rains had not stopped and he knew finding the goblin tracks was improbable. But with the confirmation of the goblin horde continuing to point northeast, he felt confident to proceed there. As the first light of dawn showed behind thinning clouds, he walked his stallion to the canopy edge. A thick fog had risen from the forest blotting away any clear definition of landscape.

Prince Kaulet was beside him and removed a gold badge from his coat. He handed it over and said, "Take this, Druid Calidor. It is my family crest. I cannot repay you for your kindness and healing, but if you need the assistance of the Trolls of Iksut, it shall be there. This is our bond."

Calidor took the badge and pinned it on his tunic under his cloak. He mounted his stallion, saluted the prince, arm across his chest, palm out, and rode into the fog, vanishing so quickly and completely that the prince had the sudden impression he had never been among them.

Chapter 33

THE night filled with shrieks and howls. Creatures unknown to Della sounded like they were at war all around her. She sank deeper in her sleeping bag beneath the shadowy thatch, hoping the black color of the bag and the dark overgrowth concealed her from whatever was near. She pulled the bag tighter, keeping her white face and hands in the folds.

Della could hear marching soldiers approach. They seemed as though they were coming toward her from all sides. She was not certain if they were looking for her or just on training maneuvers, and in her terrified uncertainty she shook so much that she curled up in a ball and bit down on her hand, hoping the pain would distract her from her fear and stay her trembling.

Roar of attack and the clashing of metal against metal rang out, the battle so close by she could almost feel the impact of the warrior's swords. The opposing forces battled long. Shrieks of agony and the final wails of death were all about her. She was so overwhelmed with the horrors and anguished sounds of deaths all around her that she screamed inside her bag, unnoticed in the tumult.

Finally, the shouts of triumph rang over the suffering of the injured and dying. The smell of blood was thick in the air. Soldiers and whatever creatures they allied with milled about, victors celebrating over the defeated. Then a powerful voice rose over the commotion, ordering the soldiers to another quadrant of the West Fork. Della recognized the voice and accent. It was unmistakably that of Prince Ravek.

The sounds of the troops faded and still she kept hidden and unmoving. The reek of death solidified her fearful state of mind. Only when no sounds came except the whistling of the wind did she calm herself, thankful for not being discovered by the stealthy forces of Prince Ravek.

Her father had said it was going to be dangerous and to stay hidden was to survive. He had reassured her that there was no other way out of Vokat's realm. The Blue Trail was the only way to escape unnoticed and without raising alarm. However, the many nights of frantic worry and fear of being discovered were having their effects. Evil was everywhere in the West Fork. The areas between the battles seemed heavy and abnormally dark, a blackness that seemed to be closing in upon her, edging closer every night. When she thought all hope lost, she reached for the *triscele*. Clutching the amulet, she felt it throb in her hand and immediately the sense of an ally within her confines came upon her and calmed her trepidations.

Sleep came in sporadic intervals as the horror roused her from deep dreamless slumber into a waking nightmare until, in the final hours of the night, Ravek's forces would recede once again, leaving her spent. As mornings finally rose, she got into the habit of remaining hidden until the sun climbed high. Only secure in the light of another day did she move. She avoided the battlegrounds, choosing against the urge to investigate for fear of leaving evidence of her passage behind, only wanting to hasten her journey evermore.

As another morning arrived, Della packed her gear, strapped tight her pack upon her back, and marched out of the thickets and toward the next blue spruce. Her reservation about escaping Vokat's land by way of the West Fork was a daily quandary. She would rise and look back at the smoking funnel of Azkar Rol still high in the horizon, debating whether to return or push toward another night filled with fear. Whenever thoughts like this occurred, Della would find courage in the fact that her father would never send her to a place he did not think she could successfully traverse. The Blue Trail was her objective, and beyond, the Ginhonim River and the town of Petal Glen.

Her father had taught her how to walk through the wild with soundless proficiency and Della had from the beginning of her trek adjusted her stride with what the landscape offered, bobbing, weaving, twisting her body through the bramble and brush of the trail, barely making contact with the terrain, as adaptable as the passing breeze.

She stopped often to rub the ache out of the muscles of her legs. Daylight seemed to stretch on past her physical limitations, but she always found the will to push onward to find the next blue spruce, hoping that the next one would be the last. She kept her spirits up by repeatedly reciting her father's words, her mantra to travel by. *"You are the quiet of stillness. No stick shall break, no branch shall snap. You are the drifting wind and your passage the hush of a whisper. You are the land you traverse and it will rise up to guide you to safety."*

Della made no fire and, from the beginning of the journey, rationed the foodstuffs stored in her pack and found water in the abundant natural springs of the West Fork. Moments came where she found the pleasant beauty of the West Fork amazing. It towered as high as the East Fork and Azkar Rol, and the Blue Trail meandered through valleys where wild streams had cut into rock and carved deep canyons. She hiked up rolling foothills through tall grass plains and drank in the flowering serenity of the meadows.

At times, when she lost her direction, she would find Azkar Rol and keep it over her right shoulder as a bearing point until she found the next blue tree. Occasionally, a mere blue spruce sapling marked the trail and she realized someone, an ally unknown, was maintaining the latent route.

Dusk came sooner than she wanted this day. Yet though the last night had been so horrifying, Della did long for a halt and bed. She had lost track of the days and nights; her only hope was to see the end of the trail and escape the evils Prince Ravek conjured in the West Fork.

Looking for another copse of trees as refuge for the night, Della suddenly came upon a blue spruce that grew at the edge of a cliff. She looked over the cliff and saw far below a gaping canyon where, down the slope, a river flowed. Her eyes followed the river that serpentined through the land, dividing a lush forest in half, curving around cliffs and disappearing around a bend only to reappear farther northward.

Della smiled for the first time since leaving the Southland castle. She turned back toward the south. She could no longer see Azkar Rol. She tenderly touched the blue spruce, thanking it for pointing her the way to safety. The meaning of her journey and the price of her newfound knowledge flooded her heart. Tears filled her eyes as she dwelled upon her father's sacrifices. They had both said their goodbyes knowing he would not survive.

"Damn you, Ravek! Damn you, Vokat!" she cried aloud.

Della fell to her knees and, still looking south, whispered, "Goodbye Father. I love you and shall remember you always. I shall tell of your goodness, wisdom, and strengths to our descendants! You shall never be forgotten! By the stars, Father, there shall be no stain upon your memory and your soul will dwell in peace!"

Della rose to her feet and turned to the north and began her climb down toward the Ginhonim River.

Chapter 34

AN unusual darkness enveloped the forest, casting a sinister foreboding over Baytel's excitement at finally reaching the outskirts of Tridling Del. Clouds blotted out the moon and stars, bringing cold rain to prey upon his body. But not the chill cover of the sky nor the gloom of the thick woods was the cause of the trepidation that arrested his senses like a dreaded poison. Something was in the forest exacerbating the black of the night.

He heard no sound from bird or insect, nor the scurrying animals so ordinary in forest life. It was as though they had gone into hiding, concealing themselves from the sinister atmosphere that permeated the woods. Their silence and natural ability to detect danger was too obvious to ignore and Baytel mirrored their behavior, stalking cautiously through the dark, silent and grave.

Even though his senses were alert to dangers unknown, Baytel felt an unyielding familiarity within the unnatural darkness. As he moved through the trees the feeling grew stronger and he became nauseous as though the air itself was poison. Disturbed at the unknown force that affected the woods, he stopped, sensing his next step would be fateful.

Then the woods came alive with the gallop of horses followed by the shouts of men, both from opposing directions—and both heading directly toward his location. Baytel squatted behind a moss-covered fallen tree and waited.

The darkness grew thicker as the horses approached. The dreaded sensation became stronger as though the thunder of the horses' hooves impelled the poisonous air deeper into the night. The horses and men converged and came to a halt just outside his position. It was then Baytel identified the unnatural but familiar corrupting atmosphere. There, riding through the woods on his menacing stallion and wearing his black armor, was his brother.

Ravek!

Baytel dropped lower in his secreted position, his eyes never leaving the scene ahead. *What Ravek is doing this far north I do not know. All I can do is speculate that he has power over the town and I must change my strategy of entering Tridling Del.*

Ravek and his personal guard did not dismount. The horses cantered impatiently while they waited for the congregation of men approaching from the trees to arrive. When the men entered the small clearing, one of them disengaged from the pack and approached Ravek. The man bowed and began speaking and gesturing as if agitated. Baytel cocked his head but could not hear anything of what they were saying.

Ravek then threw the man a pouch. The man quickly grasped it from the air, opened it and examined the contents. Once satisfied, the man bowed again and returned to his congregation. They retreated quickly, probably thankful to be away from Ravek's dark presence. Ravek and his guard turned to ride off when suddenly Ravek pulled back the reins of his stallion. He took a moment to look around, confusing his entourage as their horses jostled into one another.

Baytel did not move. He knew Ravek sensed something, just as he had. Since their youth they had the ability as twin brothers to feel each other's presence. However, only Baytel knew the origin of this particular sensation. Just as it was in the alcove back in the Southland castle, Ravek had no idea what was about in the forest and he sat perplexed upon his saddle. It was a hollow and sickly sensation, and had Baytel not known its origin, it would have affected him more; the nausea that the proximity to one another caused became stronger the longer Ravek lingered. Baytel felt sickness nearly overwhelm him and watched through the cover as Ravek doubled over from the same discomfort. He realized that while living together in the castle, they couldn't feel the power that drew them to each other because it was so immediate and constant. Now, because neither had been in close proximity for years and Ravek practiced the dark forms of magic, their differences both physical and magical caused more discomfort and pain.

Ravek scanned the vicinity, seeking the source of the menace that bombarded his senses. Finally, with a last look over his shoulder, he spurred his horse and rode away, but not without Baytel seeing fear upon his face, an expression his brother had never shown in his entire life. He wanted to scream at Ravek, *It's because you have changed! It is not too late to turn back!* But he stayed silent, knowing his brother had lost his true self long ago and nothing he could do could change him.

As Ravek and his entourage departed the forest, the dark veil lifted and the surroundings became alive once more. Relieved at not being discovered and feeling lucky to have been privy to the meeting in the forest and its implications, Baytel felt he remained one step ahead of Ravek and his father. However, the men in the forest were from Tridling Del and were more than likely henchmen for Ravek. He could only assume that they were commissioned to take note of any who had the look of men from the Citadel and report the identities back to the Southland. It saddened him to know his brother's and father's arm had extended so far into the northlands and it made entering Tridling Del and meeting Make Ironwright more difficult and dangerous.

Baytel recalled his studies at the Citadel of the secluded town of Tridling Del and its wealthy history. Long ago Tridling Del had been a mining town. The few who had founded the settlement to excavate for gold instead found the precious

Myrstone. The beauty of the gemstone was imposing. The cloud-like depths of the stone were streaked with the blue-green colors of the sea. When looking deep into the stone, one became calm and the mind's tensions abated.

Soon after the discovery, the small settlement became a large town as people from all walks of life flooded in, vying for a claim to mine the jewel. Decadence and unlawful behavior soon followed, as greed turned good men to bad. When the mining of the rare stone ran out, happily remaining were the farmers and shopkeepers, all rejoicing in the departure of opportunists. Nevertheless, the location of Tridling Del, within striking distance of the Southland and isolated by the mysterious Elangal Forest from the northland fiefdoms, left the townspeople in constant anxiety of occupation. In the years since the miners left, the town had not experienced many visitors and it was known they were wary of strangers.

Tridling Del had gone through many changes. It was not part of a realm, nor claimed to be a fiefdom or kingdom. It belonged to no one and was always self-governed by whomever the power rested with at that particular time in its history. The most drastic change had occurred in the present time, when Rele Ora arrived and became the magistrate of Tridling Del. Ora the Judge enforced his will without opposition and administered authority and justice through his personal police force known as the Retinue. Thus the people of Tridling Del lived in fear and distrust.

Baytel surmised that his brother must have discovered an ally in Rele Ora. Finding his own ally within Tridling Del and staying anonymous would be a chore.

The rain resumed and he took cover beneath a crowd of pine trees at the tree line. Though he needed drier shelter away from the deluge, he decided to wait upon dawn to enter town.

Chapter 35

RATTLE! *Clang! Crash!* "Oh what a noise, my gracious," the generously plump man exclaimed after dropping the pots and pans down the steps at the back door of the inn's kitchen. The flustered man turned to retrieve a pot only to send another crashing. "Clumsy, Billy. Very clumsy indeed."

He huffed and puffed as if out of breath with frustration, then reached into his apron pocket, retrieving a match. He flicked it against the coarse brick wall and lit the oil lamp that hung by the door. His pots and pans were scattered across the ground inside the lamplight. Now able to see, he stepped down the stairs, bent his stout body and grunted with every piece of cookware retrieved.

Baytel had silently moved cautiously from the woods and stood where the last pot rested. As the man reached down for it, he saw Baytel's feet.

"Oh!" Startled, the man dropped another pan. It fell on his foot and the robust man grimaced as he stared at the sudden appearance of a stranger.

Baytel reached down for the pot and handed it over to the man. "My apologies, sir, and good morning. I did not intend to frighten you."

"Well…well, ah, yes. A bit startled, yes…up a bit early this morning young man…say, you are not a guest at my inn, are you?" he asked, peering over his round spectacles.

"No, sir. I just arrived. I have been traveling throughout the day and night to reach your fair town. I happened to enter it from the woods and heard a commotion. I saw your lamp flicker and here I am. Have you a room for a tired traveler?"

"You are a polite man, I'd say, and I like politeness, oh yes I do," said the proprietor. He continued to eye Baytel over his spectacles, measuring him and smiling while doing so. "Well, you seem to be a cordial sort of pleasant fellow and you look quite weary…yes quite destroyed from journeying from afar. Of course we have a room for you, young man. Though I am not accustomed to patrons arriving so early, or by the back kitchen door, but you look as though you could use a rest and a warm meal."

He grabbed Baytel by the arm to guide him through the door. "Oh my…dear me! Young man you are as wet as a swamp toad! Come in, come in lad, and sit by the ovens."

Baytel took a stool beside the ovens, welcoming the heat they offered. The proprietor busily placed the pots in a washbasin and scurried to the cooler to retrieve something. Looking about the kitchen, Baytel saw a clean, well-organized work-station with canisters of spices and rows of knives, ladles, pots and pans neatly along the table. Two large brick ovens and a large stovetop sat across the table as all the cook needed to do was pivot from work-station to ovens.

Out from the cooler, the man said, "Welcome to The Lucky Hare. I am Billy McDuth, the owner of this fine inn along with my..." He stopped as a middle-aged woman entered the kitchen. "Well, here she is now, my better half, Mrs. McDuth, the finest cook in the northlands."

Baytel stood as Mrs. McDuth stepped into the kitchen from the back stairway. She was small, stout as Billy, and carried a smile as warm as fresh-baked bread. He offered his hand and she took it, greeting him in a sweet, matronly voice.

"Good morning, young man."

"Good morning to you, Mrs. McDuth. I am Baytel. It is a pleasure to meet you," he said, and followed his greeting with a formal bow.

"Baytel is it, a different sort of name?" Billy said. "Not from around here, anyway. Well Love, Baytel here has been traveling through the night and is most hopelessly wet, cold and quite fagged out."

Mrs. McDuth touched his arm and exclaimed, "Oh Baytel, you poor boy. Wet as a mire bunny. And now that I can see you in a better light, you look most haggardly. Sit. Sit right back down on that stool and stay warm. Are you hungry?"

"Of course he is, my dearest. Hungry and wet. Look at the steam coming off his clothes, forsooth."

Mrs. McDuth placed her hands on her hips and said, "We will have none of that language here, McDuth. I will not tolerate your bawdy tongue in my kitchen." She turned back to Baytel after her rebuke and asked, "Now Baytel, when was the last time you ate a meal?"

"It has been a while since I had a warm one."

"Say no more." Immediately, she went to the warming drawer and brought out bread, then butter and honey and spread them out atop the work-station before him. A skillet appeared in her hand from where he could not tell, and she began preparing a meal.

"Please, Mrs. McDuth, you do not have to go through all this trouble."

"Trouble? What trouble, Baytel? We are nurturing types so let us fuss over you. It pleases us to do so," said Mrs. McDuth.

Billy was watching him as he ate, seeing him savor each tender piece of venison, potatoes, pan biscuits and honey. "Is there enough for you, Baytel?"

"Yes, thank you, Mr. McDuth. A wonderful meal, Mrs. McDuth, your preparations were more than satisfying. I thank you for your kind attention," he said with a half bow, expressing his pleasure formally.

She smiled in so shy a way that he had a glimpse of the girlish prettiness of her youth when Billy was probably courting her long ago.

"Oh, how you talk, Baytel, like I am a queen or something."

"Any queen would be envious if she had a taste of your cooking," he replied, and bowing once more he took her hand and kissed it.

She turned away blushing and, kissing her husband on the cheek, stepped lightly from the kitchen saying, "I will get the room ready for Baytel, a quiet one in the back of the second floor, away from the busyness of the dining bar."

As she scurried away Billy said, "You won her heart, young man. I haven't seen her blush like that since our wedding night. Now you go right up and Mrs. McDuth will take those wet clothes and have them dry in no time. Go ahead, lad. Up the stairs and then left down the hall to the last door."

"Thank you, Mr. McDuth."

"Call me Billy. The entire town does."

Baytel started toward the stairs then stopped. "Is there something else, Baytel? You looked troubled, my boy."

"No, Billy. I am fine, but would you mind not telling anyone of my arrival? I do not know anyone in Tridling Del and like to keep to myself."

"Yes, yes, certainly, Baytel, not an unusual request at The Lucky Hare, or for that matter anywhere in Tridling Del. The way the Judge and Retinue treat people, it's a surprise anyone converses in this town. No worries. Sleep peacefully and when you awake I'm sure Mrs. McDuth will have a meal for you that a prince would love."

Arriving before the evening crowd, Baytel took a booth in a darkened corner to observe the townsfolk and learn as much as he could before venturing away from The Lucky Hare. After Billy served him a delicious and healthy portion of bison steak, aged cheese and dark bread accompanied by a full-bodied red wine, he was left alone.

As in its kitchen, the dining area of The Lucky Hare was efficiently arranged. The dining parlor was situated in the front of the inn's main floor, so patrons of the inn would have to walk through the parlor to check into their rooms and thus take in the smells and sights of the meals and drinks being served. Huge windows faced the street, inviting to any who walked or rode by. They would hitch their horse or park their carriages on the posts before the raised terrace and enter through double oak doors.

The interior was embellished with a variety of exquisite wood: Maplewood support columns rose from dark oak floors and between the beams was a light-colored wood ceiling from which oil lamps hung illuminating the salon. The tables and booths were arranged so the wait staff could negotiate the floor with the least amount of difficulty.

The dark red mahogany bar ran along the length of the back of the dining room; with its back wall entirely made of mirrors, patrons could watch the activity behind them. At one end of the bar was the swinging door that led into the kitchen. The other end led to the foyer and suspended staircase to the second floor balcony and boarding rooms.

Patrons poured into The Lucky Hare. The early ones were regular townsfolk all quite familiar with the menu, ordering *the usual* or *the special.* Some waved a greeting as they were seated, saying *you choose today, Billy. Surprise me.*

The service was fast and friendly. Customers were never rushed through a meal yet were polite enough to finish quickly to accommodate the waiting patrons. All seemed to know one another and those who came later would patiently wait at the bar, sitting on the wood stools and drinking ale or sweet mulled wine from stone flasks while previewing the meals being served to better prepare for their choices.

All the while Billy McDuth held pleasant conversations with just about everybody, telling a short tale here or a wise quote there. Occasionally Mrs. McDuth poked her head out the kitchen door and shouted above the crowd to tell her man to get back to work. His response was a jovial curse under his breath only to be scolded by Mrs. McDuth about his language. Both made sure everybody was generally having a good time, which made The Lucky Hare the most popular dining salon in Tridling Del.

The patrons were farmers, hunters and trappers from the outskirts and townsfolk and storeowners from just down the road. They all gathered at The Lucky Hare to talk of the crops, the hunt, and the gossip of the town and the news of the land. As evening progressed and nighttime arrived, Baytel found the atmosphere gradually changed as the townsfolk departed and the Retinue began to venture in. Conversation quieted, eventually subsiding to mere whispers as the laughter and merriment of the town were replaced by boisterous clamors from the Retinue.

Baytel, in the position to observe the entire dining room, found that all the Retinue were outfitted the same—black clothes and boots, a dagger and sword held in scabbards on their belts, and a red sash around their waists. Most showed little patience in waiting to be seated, yet waited nonetheless, drinking flask after flask of ale.

As the night wore on, fewer townspeople entered and the Retinue filled the inn. Their talk was mostly boasting of whom they had defeated in recent fights, or how they deserved advancement over another. Four of the Retinue caught his attention as he heard them speaking of their recent orders from their commander, who had returned from a meeting in the forest. Baytel listened in.

"Well, I don't give a pinch of snuff about that," bawled a sleazy, thin, mongrel-like man. "The Judge wouldn't say what was so if it weren't."

The others nodded in agreement and another spoke up. "And I heard the purse was the largest one ever. I would have hated being in those woods last night."

"Yea, the evil one being there'n all. All those officers, *heh, heh*," said the youngest Retinue. "All white as snow, scared right out of their wits, *heh, heh*."

"That's what they get for being officers. Bossy lot, every one," said the sleazy man.

"Now we look for the druids, eh?" said the old one, half his teeth gone. The old man scratched his bald head as if he had hair upon it that needed straightening. "Well, boys, it ain't gonna be easy killing them druids. Magic they have. Seen them in the old battles. They strike out fast and silent, like a snake, and ya never know from where. They come at ya and then disappear like they were never there, except someone's dead or hurt something awful."

The other Retinue leaned closer in to listen more intently to the old soldier. "Yes boys, that lot will be hard to kill, that's for—. Bloody death, its the Judge!"

The room resounded with the scraping of chairs against the wood floor. Most in the salon stood at attention and the table of four followed suit. Even Billy McDuth stopped speaking.

At the room's entrance a man stood looking over the crowd; his authority radiated outward, touching all at The Lucky Hare. He did not move as his eyes perused the salon and patrons, resting briefly on a table where diners were nearly finished. He stepped toward them, his movements graceful and purposeful and stared down at them until they stood and relinquished their table. Finally, he returned the soldiers' salutes and sat, being joined by two officers.

Thankful for the crowd and dark booth, Baytel was able to observe Rele Ora without notice. The Judge was a tall man, old with a hint of what used to be a fit, younger man. He wore his gray hair long and tied behind his head. His large chin, large nose and elongated forehead set off the appearance of being an intellect. It was his eyes that caught Baytel's attention most. They were deep sunk and black like a crow's, and they simmered with cunning and deceit. No wonder Ravek recruited him to do his bidding.

Billy quickly served their table ale and left without a word. The Judge leaned over to whisper to one of his officers. The officer stood and approached the table of four Retinue. He spoke to the old one, who rose and followed the officer back to the Judge's table. After a short conversation, Rele Ora dismissed the old soldier with a wave of his hand, drank up his ale and then left The Lucky Hare.

The old Retinue hurried back to the table. "Well, boys, eat up. We have something to attend to tonight."

"Whad he say?" asked the sleazy one.

"There is one in town and I know where he is. He told me himself."

"One what, old man?" asked the young Retinue with his mouth full of food. "What are ya talkin' about?"

He slapped the youth on the back of the head and growled quietly, "A druid, stupid. Whada ya think?"

"A druid? Where?"

Baytel sank back into his booth. *How had they found me out!*

"Idiot!" The old Retinue looked around the parlor. "And that's why he whispered it so ya'd yell it out for all to hear!" He struck the young man across the face.

"Whad are we gonna do?"

"Whada ya think? Now quit talkin, eat, and let's get outa here before he comes back'n sees us not followin' his orders."

Time had slipped by in The Lucky Hare. It was past midnight as Baytel emerged into the dark street. The town felt deserted, for most townsfolk avoided the late-night doings of drunken Retinue. Lamps glowed at a few storefronts offering meager illumination but a lit street was hardly needed to follow the Retinue. Their behavior would nearly wake the dead as they stomped through the middle of the main street jostling one another and shouting from drink.

As he stayed in the shadows of the buildings at a fair distance, the four Retinue were ignorant of being tailed. Heading toward the west end of town from The Lucky Hare, Baytel realized that he was not whom they searched for and was puzzled at what other druid could be in Tridling Del.

Storefronts disappeared and larger homes stood farther apart from each other as the Retinue entered a section of town where the wealthier townsfolk lived. It looked as though they were headed toward the last house in town, which rested just off the road at the end of a dark trail that led into the woods.

Leaving the town road behind, the Retinue quieted as they entered the trail. Scurrying ahead quickly, they split in two groups; two slipped deep into the woods probably to come out around the back of the home, while the other two ran up to the house's stable.

Baytel edged down the trail, keeping in the wooded side, and made the edge of the yard, staying hidden from sight of the home. He shortened the distance further, rounding toward the side of the home, when suddenly the back door to the home opened and a man walked out with a knap on his shoulder and carrying another bundle. Baytel's eyes were accustomed to the night by now but the man was too far away to recognize as he walked toward the stable and disappeared into its dark interior.

Movement from the woods outside the stable drew Baytel's attention. The Retinue pair from the woods had reached a window of the stable and the other two ran straight in.

Baytel darted from his hiding place and ran toward the stable. He heard a struggle and a scream. Suddenly, the Retinue burst from the stable, the four running into the woods in different directions.

The sudden commotion turned to silence. Baytel stood at the doors of the stable and walked quietly inside. A body lay face down, motionless upon the ground. His knap was still strapped to his shoulder and another bag was at his side. Bloodstained hay was all around the body. There were no signs of a defense. The Retinue had caught the man completely off guard. Baytel stepped closer. The man carried no sword belt. He knelt down beside the man and felt for a pulse but found none. He turned him over.

"Sezon!"

Baytel tore open Sezon's tunic and shirt to listen for a heartbeat. He was dead. Anger welled into tears and he fought the urge to cry out. He straightened the shirt and tunic and pulled Sezon's lifeless body up and embraced him. "Why you, my good friend? You who had the most talents and goodness of us all."

Baytel set him back down upon the ground gently. He found a horse blanket and covered him. "A great loss to us all and the One Land."

"Friend of yours, stranger?"

Baytel whirled and saw the filthy face of the sleazy Retinue from The Lucky Hare, a bloody sword in one hand. He stood blockading the stable door.

"Not much of a fight from that one," he said, his sinister smile showing decayed teeth. He pointed the sword at Sezon. "I thought druids would be harder to kill. This one was nothin'." The dirty man pulled a dagger from his belt with his other hand and he readied himself for a fight.

"Retinue, at times killing another is a simple task, especially as cowardly as you have done with this man."

"Shut up! I see no weapon on you, so if you want to live, don't move and we can go to the Judge. Move and you will die."

Barely able to hold back his anger, Baytel took a couple of deep breaths to calm himself. *This scum needed his arrogance checked.* "Attacking unsuspecting and weaponless people as you have, I don't believe you have the right to decide who should live or die. As it looks, I believe you incapable of killing by yourself. I suppose the killing of my friend was almost botched from the stupidity of you Retinue. From your looks, you dropped your blade and this fine man fell on it as you Retinue tripped over yourselves fighting over who was most cowardly."

The man's face flared angrily, his words he spat out with hatred. "Brave words, stranger. You said a friend? So, you are a druid also, eh?"

Baytel decided to taunt him further. "How would a coward such as you know a brave word?"

The Retinue advanced, staying positioned for battle. "Druid or not, stranger? I've no time for this."

"Yes, Retinue. Your time is surely expiring. To answer your query, yes, I am a druid. And I will avenge my friend, you murderous scum, by killing you and the other three this night." He paused and let show a menacing grin. "And I will do it with the dagger you have in your hand."

The Retinue charged, sweeping his sword at Baytel's head. Baytel jumped back and tumbled sideways, avoiding a second thrust from the dagger in the other hand. The man lunged again with a backhand thrust but Baytel sidestepped and took hold of the man's arm and broke it across his knee.

The sword fell to the ground but once more he swiped his dagger wildly at Baytel, a sure sign of a panicked man.

Baytel dodged the thrusts and bobbed sideways and backwards away from wild swipes, keeping the Retinue off balance. Then the man lunged his dagger at Baytel's face. Baytel grabbed his wrist, twisted it until he felt it crack and pried the dagger from his broken hand.

The Retinue fell to his knees, panting in pain. Both arms hung uselessly at his sides. Baytel pointed the dagger to his throat. "Now Retinue, as I promised...your dagger," and he plunged.

Chapter 36

THE Retinue scoured Tridling Del and the countryside looking for the phantom that had murdered four of their order. The people of the town silently rejoiced, yet unsure at what to make of the "funeral pyre" that burned the body of a dead wayfarer in the center of town.

When rumors spread of the wayfarer being a druid, the old tales of the Citadel's druidic magic ensued and residents suspected the dead druid's specter remained behind to haunt Tridling Del to revenge itself against those who murdered him. The Judge and Retinue were of a different opinion, and continued searching for another druid who may have mysteriously appeared the same night of the killing and avenged his fallen brother.

During the days that passed, Baytel stayed in his room at The Lucky Hare during daylight hours. Billy, almost dutifully and without reason, always found a way to reach Baytel with a warning whenever another Retinue search party appeared at The Lucky Hare and directed Baytel to a temporary hiding place in the inn.

Though everyone in Tridling Del was under suspicion, even McDuth, Billy was always there for him, never questioning Baytel's possible role in what had occurred that night, and Baytel found his loyalty a comfort equal to his stay with Juliard in Balmoral. He knew that McDuth had his reasons for protecting him and if he wanted to volunteer them, Billy would in his own good time.

When the search parties became less frequent, Baytel resumed his search for Make Ironwright. Night after night he would slip out of The Lucky Hare and make his way unseen to Ironwright's smith shop, but the shop was always quiet and unmanned. The shop was not abandoned, for someone had kept the foundry fires stoked. However, as a week of nights elapsed, even the red heat of the coals became dim.

Late one night as Baytel stalked the town to reach the shop, he had the sensation that he was being observed. It had become second-nature to him since departing Calidor's land. He sidled through the dark alleys and behind buildings peering into the darkness from hidden doorways to see who it might be. So certain he was of being observed, he found he was enjoying the act of hiding to discover, and though dangerous to think it so, it still intensified his alertness.

Whoever it was, he found his shadow as talented as he was, maybe more so, and realized the shadow chose not to interfere as yet and remained silent and hidden. To counter, Baytel decided to retreat back into the shadows to The Lucky Hare.

The next night he decided to search the perimeter of the woods. Keeping just inside the tree line, he stalked as quiet as a forest animal toward the end of town. Sure enough, he saw movement in the dark forest where it curved toward Ironwright's shop. But upon approaching the spot in the woods, he found no evidence of anyone being in the vicinity.

That morning back at The Lucky Hare he contemplated what to do next. Calidor's orders were specific. He could not leave Tridling Del without seeing Make Ironwright, nor leave without giving Calidor's friend the information about the Southland. He must wait until Make Ironwright appeared.

Baytel opened the closet and removed the bags and knaps from their hiding place, behind a fake wall in the back of the closet, and spread the contents of Sezon's personal belongings on the bed. He sorted through the healing herbs and leaves, combining them with his own. Sezon had other herbs of healing unknown to him and upon further investigation he found notes describing each cache of herbs' properties, their uses and locations the herbs could be found. Nothing in Sezon's bag offered evidence of a man of violence. *Innocence murdered by cowards. But they shall never kill again.*

Killed by his hand. He felt no remorse, reasoning his actions as a "just cause," a vengeance debt and duty owed to his brethren. Besides vengeance, it was a druid's duty that an obligation was due to the fallen brethren's life upon the land; something to symbolize their life. As he sorted through Sezon's possessions he came across another cache filled with seeds. Written upon it in rune was the symbol for apples. He smiled, recalling Sezon on a group hike, when they had come across a small apple orchard. Abandoning their duties for a short respite, they sat against the apple trees eating the offered fruit and taking in the sweet smells of the orchard. Eventually, they returned to the Citadel that evening without anyone noticing they had been missing.

Baytel tucked the seeds away in his tunic and left The Lucky Hare grabbing garden tools from the shed behind the inn. Twilight faded to night and he walked into the forest. He reached an open meadow off the road where he found the soil rich and black. He plowed the soil and planted the apple seeds in rows at wide intervals. Once done, he squatted beside the nurtured soil and said, "One day, Sezon, an orchard will grow here and their apples will feed deer, elk, and even man. Children will climb the blossoming trees and find laughter and joy here."

At the outer rim of the planted area stood a boulder. Baytel took the garden trowel in hand and chiseled in ancient rune upon it:

This apple orchard is in remembrance of Druid Sezon.
A life dedicated to healing and goodness. What was his grows and bears fruit
before you. From him, we learn life continues and prospers from our love of
duty.

Billy was pleased things were almost back to normal at The Lucky Hare as the search parties had ended. The Judge and Retinue were still suspicious of new-comers and questioned them at length, but no one could deliver the killer to them. Townspeople seemed livelier and less in fear, whereas the Retinue were not as foolhardy and looked over their shoulders more often. That was fine with Billy, the merrier the better.

He entered Baytel's room with an afternoon meal. He was accustomed to Baytel's habit of venturing out at night searching for something, or someone, then sleeping the morning away. "Good day, Baytel."

"It looks to be a fine day, Billy. How is Mrs. McDuth today?"

Billy placed the tray of food on the sideboard. "She is singing like a lark today. Just as happy as can be. Customers are happy, people are cheerful…well, we haven't seen this much joy here in years."

"That is nice to hear, Billy."

McDuth saw Baytel look away, keeping his expressions the same, a friendly, peaceful look, yet he felt there was more to the young man. Once he asked if he had had anything to do with the pyre of fire and the dead Retinue, but before Baytel could speak he stopped him. "Do not answer, Baytel. I talk so much I fear that my gibbering will cause harm. No, Baytel, say nothing and forget my inquiry." That had been all he had needed; to show Baytel he knew but he didn't want to know.

"Oh, by the stars, you know a stranger came into town early this morning. Nice sort of fellow, a smile that never left his face. Not many travelers these days with those. Well, he was no sooner settled in his room than he came down, ate breakfast, and was out walking the town. Said he had never been this far south before. Wanted a look around and would be back after midday. Well, good day to you, Baytel. I hope you enjoy the meal. The Mrs. took special care in the spices of the stew so make sure you mention it." He gave a wink and departed.

Baytel walked the town in daylight for the first time in weeks curious about the traveler from the north. Working his way behind the buildings and through the alleyways looking for the traveler, Baytel found himself behind the barracks of the Retinue. Peering in the back window he saw two large soldiers seated not far from the window. He took his dagger out and pried the window open to listen.

"Another to question," said one Retinue to the other. "When will this stop? I am tired of it."

"Me too, but what if it's another one of those druids, eh?"

"I hope not. I don't want to get mixed up with one of those," said the first one. "Magic. Some say they can turn you to stone with a stare."

"That's an old yarn from the old ones. Those druids are just like us, only mischievous. Always nosing about in others' affairs. They deserve to be wiped out. The whole lot of them. Anyhow, that's what the Judge says."

"Well, this traveler is staying at The Lucky Hare. If he is one it'll be a gold piece for the both of us."

"Right, let's go flush him out and take him to the Judge. You just let me do the talking."

Baytel backtracked to The Lucky Hare, unnoticed as he darted in and out of alleyways, and watched the pair enter The Lucky Hare. He skirted to the back door and found the Retinue had marched directly to the kitchen. He peered through the window as they began questioning Mrs. McDuth.

"Where did he go, wench?" said one, hovering over the woman.

She looked without fear at the large man, saying, "I have not seen him since this morning's meal."

"Don't lie to me. You are hiding him here. I know it. Now, which room is he staying in?"

She did not answer, which increased their hostility. Then a whistle came from the dining room and one of the Retinue went to the swinging door while the other one grabbed Mrs. McDuth, pointing his dagger against her side.

"There he is," said the big man at the door. "Call him in here, woman. Offer him a taste of this evening's meal. Do as I say or my friend here will wet his knife. And smile, wench."

Baytel watched, powerless to act, not wanting to draw more Retinue to The Lucky Hare. He hoped the traveler would handle the situation and cause no harm to Mrs. McDuth.

"Come on, wench, call him in," urged the Retinue, dragging her by the arm to the door.

She took an unsteady breath and hailed. "Oh, young man, I need a taster for this evening's meal. I want to make sure it's right for tonight."

The traveler walked through the door. "It would be an immense pleasure, Mrs. McDuth. I have always wanted—"

"Hold right there, stranger, and don't move a twitch," said the Retinue, holding his sword at the man's stomach.

As the stranger entered through the swinging door, Baytel nearly gasped in surprise. *Areus! What was he doing in Tridling Del?*

Baytel moved closer to the window to get his attention. Areus was reading the room. His eyes darted from Mrs. McDuth to the Retinue and to the pointed knife at her side. Baytel moved slightly, drawing Areus's eye to the window.

Areus's expression did not change as he saw him. Their training went far beyond just books and study.

Using a battle sign, Baytel signaled Areus to lead them into the woods. Areus acknowledged with a nod so slight the common eye could not observe it, but one trained as a druid in a place where one learned and mastered the art of survival and secrecy did.

Undauntedly, Areus quipped, "Well, gentlemen, what goes on here? Was the food not to your liking? I assure you I am not the cook."

"Keep your wit for someone else. We want to ask you some questions."

"I see you both are being a bit too antagonistic with the proprietor. Let's not harm Mrs. McDuth, for I am sure many townspeople, as well as your superiors, would be very disappointed with the prospect. After all, whoever can cook as wonderfully as she would surely be missed. Don't you think?"

Baytel left Areus and ran into the woods. No sooner had he entered the tree line than he saw Areus step out the back door with the Retinue in his wake.

Areus's pace was faster than the two and they already had to run to keep up. Baytel made his location known to Areus and ducked into hiding while Areus led them toward him. The Retinue were oblivious to his location, their eyes boring into only Areus's back as he still outpaced them.

Areus reached the place Baytel had indicated, stopped and turned to face the Retinue pair. "Now, what can I do for you?"

Panting from the brisk run, one of the Retinue asked, "Where did you come from and when did you arrive here?"

Areus answered, "I arrived late last night. I come from Kilhalen and, may I say, a stranger traveling to our city would be welcomed with kindness and not with the display of threats, especially to a harmless woman."

"Quiet, Kilhalen man. I don't care about your city. You have the look of a druid, stranger. Is that what you are?"

"Yes, I am, and I am at your service."

As Areus offered them an exaggerated, showy bow, Baytel dropped silently from the tree behind the Retinue, his dagger in hand.

"Your sword, druid, hand it to me. Hilt first," said the Retinue.

Areus pulled the sword from his sheath and as the Retinue stepped closer he drove the blunt end of the hilt into his forehead in one swift motion, knocking him unconscious.

Baytel sliced the throat of the other Retinue, and then plunged his knife into the heart of the first one.

Areus stood in shock looking at Baytel, then down at the dead soldiers slumped in a heap. "I suppose there is more to these two than just harassing strangers."

"You suppose right, my friend."

"This is a prelude to departing Tridling Del I suppose?"

"Not before we meet with Make Ironwright."

"Who is Make Ironwright and why do we seek him?"

Baytel shook off the query. Areus's presence in Tridling Del and this confrontation had further compromised the timeframe of his meeting with Ironwright. Word would surely get out of Areus's identity, if it weren't already. And he will now be a target for all Retinue. Moreover, The Lucky Hare has been placed at risk; something he has dreaded for weeks.

"Being a Druid of the Citadel has become quite hazardous, Areus. There are circumstances that you are not yet privy too that have made us an enemy in these parts. We need to distance ourselves from the McDuths so they are not considered in allegiance with us. To do this, are you willing to place yourself in a bit of danger?"

"Well, after helping kill these men, I might be willing. Let me see. I suppose I have nothing else scheduled today," he quipped. Areus never let a serious situation get in the way of a wise remark.

"Good. We must clear away any suspicions of the McDuths in this matter. You have to expose yourself to the customers at The Lucky Hare, making a point of saying your goodbyes for everyone to hear and witness. Then we will rendezvous in these woods just before dusk and seek out Ironwright. I will get my belongings and leave out the back. We must leave Tridling Del tonight."

"Good-bye to The Lucky Hare then into the woods. Sounds like a plan without much difficulty."

"Good man, Areus. Let's go."

Baytel wrapped his arms around Mrs. McDuth, consoling her fright. "Do not worry; those men will not be a bother again."

"Thank you both so much. I have never been so frightened in my life." She stepped back and looked at them both smiling. "My two favorite guests ever here at The Lucky Hare. I am glad you met each other. Why, the moment I met you, Areus, you reminded me of Baytel."

"Well, Mrs. McDuth, it surely was a coincidence we are here in Tridling Del at the same time, but we happen to know each other and are quite good friends," said Areus.

"The land is vast yet small enough to find a friend nearby," she said as she sat down on a stool. The encounter still left her trembling. "I had a feeling those two Retinue were trouble. I saw others nosing about earlier before they came in looking for you, Areus. I didn't know what to do. Then you came into the kitchen." She paused, tearing up. "Well, I somehow knew you could handle them, young man. Thank you. Thank you both."

She stood and hugged them again, when Billy entered the kitchen. "What is the matter?"

Baytel truly liked the McDuths. They made his stay feel like he had a family again. "Billy, we are leaving Tridling Del. I have overstayed my welcome and am afraid my presence will be more of a burden for you than before."

"It does not surprise me, as the town is in a bit of an uproar. There is mischief about and I believe it is not safe for any stranger here. I am sad you have to leave, Baytel, but I understand."

The McDuths gave him and Areus food for a few days of travel. Areus took his leave through the dining hall and out the front door of The Lucky Hare, saying his goodbyes loud enough for all to hear. Shortly afterward Baytel watched two customers depart behind Areus. "There they go, Billy. They will tell the Retinue that the stranger left The Lucky Hare and that will be the end of it for you and Mrs. McDuth."

"You need not have done this, Baytel. We are in good standing with the Judge and his soldiers," said Billy.

"And you will continue to be. Any further attention on Areus will be with his leaving The Lucky Hare, not staying under its roof and in your care."

The McDuths looked at each other and nodded in agreement. "So it must be. Some day visitors will be welcomed here and not harassed. I will welcome those days."

Baytel nodded and said, "Now it is time to say farewell, my good friends. Thank you for keeping me secreted away these many days and for your kindness and generosity."

"It was our pleasure, Baytel. Your time here was treasured more than you know," said Billy. "You haven't told us much of yourself, but you will always be welcome here. You are family now, Baytel. Journey safe and return to us soon."

"That I will hold close to my heart." He bowed and added, "I am Baytel, Druid of the Citadel, adopted by the McDuths and yours forever. Until my return, fare well."

Baytel stepped to the back door, turned and said, "By the way, Mrs. McDuth, the meal you sent to my room for lunch, whatever ingredient you added to the stew was absolutely marvelous."

Chapter 37

BAYTEL stopped his pacing, as it interfered with listening to the woods about him. He could not shake the feeling of being watched. No sound came other than the occasional red squirrel chattering, offended by Baytel's presence in its territory.

Areus, delayed with eluding the Retinue, finally appeared, making his way through the woods. Baytel signed to him to be cautious. His heart quickened when Areus returned the sign by saying he felt eyes upon him.

Baytel moved a few steps toward Areus when a voice out of the quiet woods broke the silence. "Hold, Druids!"

Baytel stood unmoving, listening in the direction of the voice. Areus was a few steps away and was edging toward the bushes.

"Do not move until I say," said the hidden man.

Baytel was astonished as the voice came from an entirely different direction. Wanting the man to speak again, to determine his position, he asked, "What is it you want?"

Speaking from yet another location, the man said, "I know all your tricks, young druids, so belay them and listen."

The stealth of the man was so profound it made Baytel feel more at ease, knowing any man who had mastered such a degree of silence in motion must be from the Citadel. The pitch of the man's voice was one that was not quite a whisper; enough sound that only those within a pace or two could distinguish his words. Others who might hear it farther away would discern only the sounds of the faint hoot of an owl.

The man asked, "You seek Make Ironwright? Do not answer. Be at his shop at the darkest hour, and try to be quiet. You young druids are as noisy as oxen in marsh mud."

Areus crashed into a cluster of bushes. No one was there. The man was gone.

The moon slipped behind the gathering clouds. With Areus beside him, Baytel seized the opportunity to edge quietly from the forest to the back of Make Ironwright's smith shop, attentive to the humbling criticism they had received earlier. Areus was at his side and was about to rap on the door when a voice from within said, "If you knock, you will be heard. Come in before you are seen."

They entered the shop quickly and closed the door. The room was faintly aglow from the coal embers of the foundry fire; the illumination cast dark shadows in an already dark place. Tools of the foundry trade lay about on wooden workbenches, along with scraps of bronze, brass, silver and forged metals in an order only a metallurgist could understand. Damaged lances, shields and swords leaned against the walls awaiting repair.

Beyond the foundry in the storefront, finished pieces were displayed in the front window of the finest craftsmanship Baytel had ever seen. Most of the armor collection was made of the exquisite Pintél, the most precious hard metal in the land, found only in Ctiklat Mountain. Baytel's eyes widened at seeing on the wall the same cast plaques as those in Calidor's cabin and the Citadel.

A dwarf stepped out from behind the wall; his beard was long but not fully gray. He was of medium height, four and half feet, the height of all mature dwarfs. He had a muscular build, large sad eyes and short thick hair. He wore a green leather tunic with metal clasps all woven with precision, brown pants, a shirt and heavy field boots. At his side hanging from his belt were a short sword and what seemed like a type of axe. His gaze was cold yet searching.

"Make Ironwright, I presume," said Baytel, seeing a slight nod from the dwarf. "It is a pleasure seeing you finally. I have been trying to find you for days."

"Yes, I know. I have seen you from a distance. You have good habits, young druid."

His studied stare left him and moved toward Areus. "You must be the Kilhalen man everyone is looking for."

"Yes, I am Areus of Kilhalen, at your—"

"You are not Areus of Kilhalen anymore." His voice was stern yet unpretentious. "You are Areus, Druid of the Citadel. Your sole claim is that and only if necessary."

"I stand corrected." Areus bowed slightly. "How did you know we are druids?"

"I have observed both of you. You used the ancient battle sign taught only at the Citadel and your mannerisms display other Citadel teachings. Such behavior is distinctive, which can be admirable, or a flaw in certain situations."

Baytel drank in the sight of the dwarf, observing him in a much different light than Areus did. Make Ironwright, along with Calidor and the Grey Riders, had cleansed the land of evildoers in the Quest of Champions. He was a Druid of the Citadel, an Elder of the Highest Order of the Dwarfs of Ctiklat, and a friend and confidant of Calidor.

"Make Ironwright, I was instructed to seek you out by a friend of yours. I have information for you regarding the plight of the land. He told me you would know what to do and did not elaborate upon those instructions."

Baytel waited patiently for the dwarf's response, as did Areus, who had learned a few particulars from Baytel while waiting in the forest.

"Well, young druid, did this friend of mine have a name and do you have one, or did they escape your memory?"

The stately dwarf walked toward him to get a better look. He stopped short and Ironwright's study of Baytel took on a more detailed peruse, nodding during the viewing as if acknowledging something to himself. He tipped his head looking congruently at Baytel's ears, and then to his face.

Uncomfortable under this examination and almost forgetting the question, he replied, "My name is Baytel and I was sent to you by Calidor." He paused, awaiting a response, but none came. Make just continued to stare at him, reading every detail of him. "Calidor, Druid of the Citadel, Grey Rider—"

The dwarf finally replied. "I know his exploits, boy." The dwarf approached closer and stopped only a step away from Baytel. "Young Baytel of the Citadel, do you know his exploits?"

"Yes, I know them," he said formally.

"And are you entirely familiar with his ancestry?"

"Calidor's ancestry was one of the lectures at the Citadel."

"Yes, I suppose it had to be in this instance. And your ancestry, Baytel? Did Calidor inform you of your lineage?"

Areus glanced curiously at the dwarf and then to Baytel but Baytel ignored him.

"Yes sir, he told me everything."

Make Ironwright nodded in recognition. He smiled for the first time and though the smile showed some glee, it seemed to Baytel there was a hidden sadness behind it.

"Baytel, you have your mother's face and your grandfather's strength, from the looks of you." He paused, and then continued formally, "I am Make Ironwright, Druid of the Citadel and Grey Rider. Welcome, young druids, and come sit. We have much to speak of."

"You knew my mother?"

"I did. Pren was most beautiful and as pleasant as the warmth of the sun."

"What is this about your ancestry, Baytel?" asked Areus.

Make said, "Let us both hear. Please begin at the beginning. Start with your first remembrances."

They sat around the foundry embers in the amber light while Baytel told the story of his young life, his running away for the Citadel, meeting his savior Calidor, and what had occurred after he departed Areus's company after earning their Laurels.

Baytel concluded with the telling of Rele Ora meeting Ravek in the forest outside Tridling Del and his directive to hunt down and kill all who were a part of the Citadel. He spoke of the Retinue's murder of Sezon, his vengeance, the pyre of fire and the planting of the orchard.

Make humbly said, "His orchard shall be tended with care and reverence."

"Astonishing! I had no idea," said Areus. He started to ask Baytel several questions but was silenced by Make's interrogation:

"Areus, why are you in Tridling Del?"

"I came south and was to pass through Tridling Del to the Southland to visit Baytel. Had I known that things in the Southland were such, I would not have traveled here."

"It was a foolish risk even without the knowledge," said Make. The dwarf, having absorbed Baytel's life story, now spoke volubly, still in a commanding tone. "Areus, know this. Your life has drastically changed since leaving the Citadel. You now walk the land for a purpose. You learned this at the Citadel. Baytel knows this for it was forced upon him. He is cautious and you both now must heed the ways of your training every moment of your life.

"Evil is trying to gain control and destroy what the Tree Faeries have created. As druids, you are trained and educated to uphold a higher order. This responsibility did not begin with you, but you now hold the full weight of it, for there are only a few of us left. Ten days ago a Citadel courier arrived at my door. It was not the regular courier and it took some time for me to believe his report. As Baytel noted, the Citadel has been waylaid. The dead number most of those in attendance. The report came to me from a gnome courier and it had the mark of a steward, but not Stilar's."

"Stilar is dead?" asked Areus.

"All are dead there except Druid Anise. Yar, who was not found among the dead, is most likely being hunted by the grotesque creatures you mentioned. Calidor is determined to find him and is in pursuit."

A rap at the door froze them in place. Ironwright peered around to the front of the shop where two Retinue soldiers stood on the porch. The dwarf moved toward the door and whispered, "Hide as best you can and move not until I say."

Hidden among broken shields and armor Baytel listened to the question and answer exchange about a traveler from Kilhalen about the town. Make Ironwright deflected their inquiries deftly and without alarm and bid the Retinue a respectful goodnight, agreeing to report any stranger who visited his shop.

"The Retinue has stepped up their search for you, Areus. You both must leave town as soon as possible." He turned and asked, "What are your plans, Baytel?"

Ironwright's serious tone reminded him of Calidor when posing a question of vital importance. Baytel's mind flooded with a vision of the land in peril and the race to war and death already spreading from his homeland while northlanders were unaware it was at their door.

"I will travel north to Kilhalen and hope to reach it by the winter solstice. Along the way I will attempt to find the remaining druids to warn them of the forces that bloodied the Citadel and get word to the other sects of the Southland's taste for war."

Make asked Areus the same question.

"I will travel with Baytel and do what I can to help."

Make sat and pondered, with one hand to his chin and his index finger raised along the side of his head. An ember hissed. After a deep breath, he rose and walked to a sideboard. He opened the lower compartment and removed a wooden trunk. He opened it and took out two bundles. "These garments were sewn with magic by the Tree Faeries and are worn by Grey Riders. Put them on. They will blend in with the land about you and keep you warm or cool, depending on the weather."

As the two young men dressed in the garments—a cloak, pants, shirt, tunic, all of which somehow formed perfectly to their bodies—Make began removing some floorboards and pulled out a large wooden box and placed it upon a work bench. He rested his hands on the box reverently and seemed to drift off in thought.

Areus asked, "What will happen now that the Citadel is no more?"

As if jarred from his thoughts, Make replied, "The Citadel shall always be there, Druid Areus. Already, Druid Anise, Druid Juliard and Cast, this new steward, are hard at work. We shall rebuild its strength and revive its purpose. As to what will unfold from the attack, only the events of the present and where our paths lead will determine the answer to that question."

Make was staring at Baytel while he spoke. He had not removed his hands from the box on the bench.

"Areus," he said, addressing the young man but keeping his eyes on Baytel. "Let you be a witness to history. You are a descendent of the kings of Kilhalen, so you will understand. I see before me two young druids with strength of mind and muscle, strong character, will and honor."

Baytel once more became uncomfortable under Make's stare. He stood unmoving and poised, sensing a powerful significance to what Make was about to say.

The dwarf continued, "Baytel, in your body runs the fiber of your grandfather and the blood of the Kings of the North, the ancestor of the ancients, wielders of ancient powers and rulers of the glorious past unknown to man today. Also within your body runs the blood of your mother who belonged to a sect unknown to us all, a mysterious and beautiful people who have the gifts of magic from the One Land and possess powers yet to be revealed."

Baytel looked down as Make opened the box. Inside, upon brushed leather, a cloth of fine white silk covered an object. He swallowed, his body rigid with anxiety at what lay beneath the cloth.

"Baytel, your grandfather, Calidor, was king of the Great Race of the North. The Kings departed this land many years ago without their talisman of power.

Calidor's father fought to his death alongside the king of the Dwarfs of Minion in the First Age of the One Land. Calidor succeeded, yet relinquished his rightful place on the throne, giving his brother his crown. Hence the Kings returned to their lands over the Great Sea and Calidor remained here, in this land, to stay among us and assist in setting the sects on the proper course with the One Land.

"Calidor found the talisman of his father. It was placed in my care until a time should come when one of his blood was ready to take it and use it for the good of the land." His voice lowered to a softer tone. "Calidor sent you here for this."

Make removed the silk and revealed a sheathed sword. It was deeply inlaid in its scabbard in the leather case; barely a shine projected off the dull steel. In all the time Baytel spent with Calidor after the Citadel, he never saw the sword and assumed Calidor kept it hidden from him. Looking down upon the sheathed blade, he was seized with hesitancy. Here was the sword of unparalleled power and history, an instrument of unbounded magical powers. And here was he, Baytel, barely more than a youth, untested in full battle, leader of no one but himself.

Make turned the box, pointing the hilt at him. "Yes, Baytel, it is the Sword of the Kings, forged by the ancients when the land and man were in accord with all things. The sword was given to the Kings of the North to wield on behalf of the land. You, Baytel, shall wield it. You are the heir to the ancients and shall lead, as did Calidor before you, without state and without reward, until the time comes when the mantle of the Kings of the North is restored to its rightful place on the precious land we walk."

Baytel's entire being was drawn into a suspended state. He stared at what lay in the box. It seemed to be calling to his soul, amplifying the same calling he had been hearing since his youth. He reached and gripped the hilt of the sword in his hand and the small act suddenly removed all uncertainty. Baytel felt the sword touch something within him and he became wholly aware of his place in time, holding the sheathed talisman.

And he recalled Calidor's words before they had separated. *Make will know what to do. Understand and accept what he offers, for you will see the purpose of why you were sent.*

Baytel pulled back his cloak and attached the scabbard to his belt. Then, with purpose, he unsheathed the sword. The sword glowed in his hand as if the sun had been imprisoned within it and finally freed. A surge of power from the sword coursed through his body like lightning. He clutched it tighter, feeling the need to show it his own strength. Then the sword ignited something within him, deep in the core of his being, and at that moment he knew that Calidor's and Make's words of his ancestry were true. He was the Prince of the Kings of the North.

So did Make and Areus, for the moment he unsheathed the weapon they both fell to one knee, seeing his touch ignite the magic of the sword of the Kings. They said in unison and with reverence, "Sire."

A revelation brushed across his consciousness. He was different than they. He knew henceforth there would be a separation and he did not want it to be.

"Rise and do not bow to me again. Nor call me sire or anything but Baytel. I am a Druid of the Citadel and that is my only claim. This sword will someday lead the land and be held by a king. Until that time, we have much to do."

As they rose, he fixed his stare at Areus and asked, "Areus, will you journey with me not as a subject but as a friend, as you have been? Will you journey with me as a companion with a common cause? As equals? I will have it no other way with you."

"I shall, Baytel. My sword shall be at your side, now and forever."

"As friend and equal?"

Areus smiled and patted Baytel on the shoulder. "As the best of friends and equal in all things, Baytel."

"Then promise me, Areus. Do not tell a soul of my ancestry. It must be kept from all."

"You have my word, Baytel."

Baytel looked at the sword. Its glow had disappeared. Yet the sword's finish seemed to pulse with majesty. No diamond-crested hilt or jewel-embossed flagrancy was upon it. Anyone seeing the sword would know it was no commonplace object. It was simply pure strength.

Baytel turned to Make, seeing a look of melancholy upon his face. "What is it, Make Ironwright?"

"You both remind me of the companionships of the early years, so fresh then, though all of which remain to this day."

Make Ironwright walked to the back door, peering out to see if it was clear of Retinue. "It is time for you to leave. Go by way of Elangal Forest and then through Konart Pass. Once out of the pass, reach the Awär River and follow it to Kilhalen. No one will pursue you from Tridling Del into the Elangal Forest for the Retinue believe it filled with mysticism and untold dangers."

Areus threw his bag over his shoulder. Taking that as his readiness to begin, Baytel sheathed his sword, gathered his bag and stepped out the back door into the dark night.

Chapter 38

BAYTEL had never thought in his wildest imagination that he would be the source of so many deaths, but at the same time he felt no remorse over the dead who lay in his wake. From the moment he and Areus departed Make Ironwright's shop and entered the clearing before the forest, the Retinue were on them. The ensuing bloody skirmish and resulting casualties of the Retinue would immediately be reported to the Southland. It was not so much the fact that many Retinue perished. Rather it was the way they died. The Retinue had attacked on horseback and with superior numbers, yet were completely defeated by only two men who were on foot. Nothing other than that could be reported for too many Tridling Del townsfolk had witnessed the engagement. No reasonable defense would arise to hide the fact that two men, one a known Citadel Druid, had caused the Retinue's demise.

Make Ironwright had been correct in his assessment that the Retinue would not pursue them into Elangal. Nevertheless, Baytel knew their sanctuary would be fleeting, as another contingent, one more formidable than the Retinue, would begin pursuit.

Baytel stopped to rest, exhausted from the fast pace he had set once entering Elangal Forest. Areus followed suit and both leaned heavily against an enormous greenwood tree. Remaining cognizant to any movement or sound in the quiet of Elangal Forest, Baytel opened the pack Billy McDuth had given them and served out a small meal of dried venison and biscuits.

Areus's relaxed disposition was like an elixir to Baytel. His friend had no knowledge of the events taking place upon the land and had volunteered immediately to the quest at hand with no hesitation. Forcibly awakened to his druidic duties by Make Ironwright's lecture, Areus went from a carefree traveler to a hunted man and met the circumstances with a smile.

"How long before they follow us into Elangal?" Areus asked through a mouth full of dry biscuit.

"The Judge will be able to reach Ravek in a few days, unless one of Ravek's spies has already sent word ahead. Then the hunt will begin. Now that they know you are of the Citadel, I suspect Ravek will send a more dangerous force, especially after our sport before entering here."

Areus nodded solemnly and said, "With the Citadel out of commission, the Southland will become more daring and sent their hunting parties deeper north."

Guilt at being the catalyst to the deaths of Sezon and those in the Citadel weighed heavily upon Baytel. The enemy will come and there was nothing he could do but warn the north and hopefully intercept whatever factions Ravek and Vokat sent to kill the remaining druids and acolytes.

"Yes, Areus. You are correct. Vokat and Ravek will extend their influence farther north. They already have control of Weyles and, as we witnessed, a foothold in Tridling Del. They will have no qualms about crossing into the north when ready."

Baytel thought of Tira cut off in the occupied city of Weyles. He assumed that word of his supposed death had already reached her and she did not know of his survival. The thought of Tira not being a part of his life lay heavy upon his heart. The pureness of the joy he felt in everything he had experienced with her was overwhelming him; a lump formed in his throat. Just being in her presence, the way she always touched him while speaking, made him feel as if there was no one in the world except the two of them. Each slight contact seemed to convey her entire spirit directly into his heart. Then, recalling when they left one another at the castle—the embrace and the passionate kiss they shared—he knew there would be no other woman in his life. Being dead to her left his heart with a void where Tira should be.

And Della? That tender, kind and thoughtful girl. No. Woman, for she had sprouted into a graceful beauty who, as Baytel realized, seemed to be constantly on his mind. What was to become of her under the yoke of the Southland?

Taking a deep breath, Baytel forced himself to store the emotions, affections and hopes for now and quickly refocused on the task at hand, which needed his full and immediate concentration. Reaching the other druids and Kilhalen was all that mattered and, to do that, they had to navigate Elangal Forest.

Traveling from dawn to dusk, Baytel kept their routine concise. Alternating the night watch every four hours left enough time for sleep. Though they went without fires, the clothes sewn by the Tree Faeries somehow kept them warm. The food they carried ran out shortly after the fourth day of travel and they foraged as they hiked, collecting berries and seeds, wild mushrooms and edible plants, all of which were in abundance in the bountiful forest. They passed on wild game, for cooking the game meant fire and fire led to unwelcome eyes.

From high above where eagles brushed the treetops to the ground where forest animals roamed, everywhere in Elangal Forest was green. Ferns and grass, moss and bush blanketed the ground while hearty greenwood trees towered above all, their branches so densely canopied they concealed most of the sky. Dark ivy grew upward upon the hulking trees, its overgrowth draped down from their limbs, further enclosing the forest and giving Baytel the feeling of being cramped even though he was outdoors. Even noise did not travel easily. Hailing each other from afar was nearly impossible as the sound was swallowed up by the heavy foliage and thick air.

Wild boar, red deer, bear and majestic elk shared life within Elangal Forest. Hawks, eagles, osprey and numerous ravens combed the high boughs. Squirrels, rabbits, grouse and pheasant were ever-present, as were signs of the territorial and vicious zekawolves and gray wolf packs.

The environs were difficult to figure. They felt neither cold nor warm, dry nor wet, but the air of the forest seemed a bit thicker and it took more of an effort to inhale a full breath. The forest seemed to stay a stable temperature even as the days turned toward summer. Baytel's Citadel studies of Elangal Forest accounted for nothing of what he had so far encountered. However, he kept a wary eye, recalling the forest was known to be a haven for thieves and villains. Concealment was easily accessible and rogues were known to wait for unsuspecting travelers to assault with no warning or mercy. These assaults occurred so frequently that Elangal Forest became mystical and folks resorted to travel many days around the forest rather than fall into its clutches.

The sparse rays of light that penetrated so desperately through the dense canopy showed, by their persistence, that summer had arrived upon the land. A continuous breeze whistled through Elangal, making its way around the green-woods and elm trees, setting off a constant rustle of leaves and swaying of the ivy vines. The forest had serenity to it, yet the feeling of being hunted occupied Baytel's thoughts. Wild menace felt inevitable. Both young men remained guarded against the comforts and beauty of Elangal.

The thick foliage left no clear paths to follow and keeping on point was difficult. At times, they were relegated to cutting through wild growth simply to gain open ground. When forcing through one thick drapery of ivy, Baytel saw Areus stumbled over something. As he rose from the fall, another head popped up from beneath the ferns.

"What? Who?"

Baytel saw a young man, rubbing his eyes from a slumber, and then realizing that the one who woke him was a stranger. The young man immediately jumped up and drew his sword. Baytel studied the young man, who looked like he had just departed adolescence. The frightened youth was on the verge of panic, pointed his sword back and forth between he and Areus, frantically alternating.

Areus opened the dialogue. "My pardon, young man. I did not intend to step on you."

The young man said nothing, keeping the point of his sword before them. Everything about him showed fear rather than fortitude. Baytel felt the situation could turn bad if the youth did not come to a calmer state, and said, "Friend, we are traveling through Elangal Forest and mean no one harm. Perhaps you could lower your sword so we can talk? Do you live here in the woods?"

The youth remained tight-lipped. Baytel tried once more. "My name is Baytel and this here is Areus. We are here in Elangal Forest with the most peaceful of intentions." Baytel extended his hand in greeting. "Let us confer…"

The youth grabbed the horn that hung about his neck, brought it to his lips and blew. The deep tone resonated through the foliage, a feat Baytel though impossible. The young man blew repeatedly and retreated to the opposite end of the fern-covered clearing.

Then the hail of numerous men came. They must not have been far off and soon came crashing through the ivy into the fern patch with drawn swords. All the woodsmen came to a stop in a protective cover position in front of the young man, and all quite ready to do battle.

Baytel counted twenty men, each dressed in irregularly stitched green and brown swatched pants and shirts that blended perfectly with the surroundings. Some carried short swords and others held lances, while the larger men had filled their hands with broadswords and knives. With a slight hand movement, the woodsmen quickly moved and suddenly Baytel and Areus were surrounded.

The slight hand signal Baytel recognized immediately, but he kept it to himself and offered Areus their battle sign for them to practice patience and to keep their swords sheathed.

"What gives here, Malin?" asked one of the woodsmen.

The youth was still nervous, but had gained confidence with the arrival of his friends. He replied, "These drifters attacked me while I was on patrol. I think they are here to cause trouble."

"What are you doing in our woods?" demanded the woodsman.

Areus politely responded. "Sir. We did not attack the young man. See, our swords, they have never left our sheaths. The young man was asleep under the ferns and I stumbled upon him. He jumped up with drawn sword and that is all. We are passing through Elangal Forest on the way to my home in Kilhalen."

The youth they called Malin, roused from embarrassment, shouted, "He lies! They attacked me!"

The woodsman was curt. "Drop your sword belts, strangers. There are others who you must answer to."

Baytel stepped a few paces away from Areus in the event the misunderstanding turned ugly. He drew the attention of all in the clearing by the movement.

"Where are you going to, stranger? Drop your belts!"

Baytel replied calmly. "I do not think that disarming ourselves will be necessary, sir. We will gladly go with you to whoever has questions for us, but not without possession of our weapons."

A tall woodsman stepped forward, "You will do as we say or feel cold steel. Now drop them, or die."

Baytel signed to Areus for no deaths, and addressed the woodsmen once more. "We do not seek death or anyone's blood. We can accomplish all you desire without battle and we will go with you in peace, but we will keep our weapons."

"Then you will die, wayfarers!"

The foolish youth, Malin, attacked. Baytel unsheathed his sword, meeting Malin's charge, and with a twist of his sword Malin became the first casualty, down unconscious with a sword gash to the arm and the blunt end of Baytel's hilt against the back of his head.

Areus moved farther away, creating two fronts of defense. With no leader directing their attack, the woodsmen momentarily became a disordered group crossing positions with each other and unable to take the offensive.

When gripping his sword Baytel immediately felt its power. With the rush of energy something sparked to life within him. He detected an awareness of himself he had never experienced before, like an awakening to his place among the beings of magic. Then, as the woodsmen charged, the sensation did not leave him and with this new cognizance, he met the attacker with a sense of wholeness, as though a part of him filled an internal gap he did not know he had. The woodsmen stabbed, slashed and charged in wild fashion and Baytel countered blocking, deflecting, and maneuvering so naturally he felt as if it were a dance. He and Areus traded glances every now and then during the skirmish, each synchronizing the fight with the other as if they could read one another's mind, just as they had when sparring at the Citadel.

Five woodsmen were on the ground and out of the battle with injuries. None would die yet all would have a memento from the fight. Slashed leg or arm, knocked unconscious or dizzy, these men were unknowingly fortunate, for Baytel was not certain if these woodsmen would turn out to be an ally or remain an enemy. Their aggression continued but at each renewed attack Baytel and Areus induced the same result, with another of them down and out of the fight.

The men of the forest withdrew to regain their wind and then quickly refocused and charged in full company. But their efforts Baytel and Areus thwarted with ease, leaving only more injured. As the battle waged on like this, the enthusiasm of the woodsmen dwindled and each foray became weaker. Only four woodsmen remained on their feet, and they circled. Baytel, who stood back to back with Areus, remained unfazed.

From out of the woods, an arrow sailed by Baytel's head, sticking in the greenwood beside him. Another arrow flew by, sticking next to the first. Three horsemen rode into the fern clearing and the four woodsmen gave way to them, happily able to rest. One horseman pranced forward to survey the wounded. The other two Baytel assumed were the man's guards. They sat upon their mounts behind him, one holding a long bow with knotted arrow and the other an unsheathed broadsword.

The leader sat upon a chestnut mare perusing his fallen men. He was a proud-looking man and tall in his saddle. He had dark hair, a sleekly manicured mustache and predatory green eyes. His garb was like the other woodsmen's except it seemed to fit him more precisely, as if the uniform of an officer. The other two horsemen sat straight-backed and carried themselves in the same proud attitude as their comrade. Baytel sensed these men had some form of military training.

The mustached man asked the four woodsmen, "Where are the others?"

Panting with exhaustion, the four woodsmen looked at one another, confused. Then one answered, "Others, sir?"

Annoyed, the man rephrased the question: "The other men who waylaid you. Where are they?"

The woodsmen looked abashed. "There are just these two, sir. No one else."

He turned his attention toward Baytel and then Areus. Looking at them from head to foot, he raised an eyebrow, appearing to notice that neither was hurt.

Baytel met his eyes and for an instant, the contact seemed to cause the horseman to hesitate. Then he used a hand signal to his guards.

Baytel recognized the sign, a simple abbreviated version used by hunters throughout the land when stalking game. Before the guards moved, Baytel said, "There is no need for your men to maneuver behind us. We meant no harm and would like an audience."

Surprised and annoyed at Baytel's knowledge of their private hand signage, the leader replied, "Your actions here do not deserve an audience."

"Our actions, however regrettable, merit it. Our reason for travelling through Elangal Forest was out of necessity and with only peaceful intentions. Our affairs are in Kilhalen, not here. We did not attack these men. We only wish to move on without further incident."

The horseman with the broadsword cantered up. He was the oldest looking of the woodsmen and gave Baytel pause; there was something familiar about him. Could he have met this man before? He could not put a name to the face.

The old soldier said, "One does not journey through Elangal as if it were a common town road."

The leader added, "Beside the fact that you are trespassing in my forest, you have drawn the blood of kinsmen. Justice must be served even in the deep forests of the land. So, strangers, it may be a long time for you to have the freedom of travel to your destination through Elangal."

Baytel studied the leader while formulating a reply. He sat confidently and at ease upon his mare, but Baytel could see in his eyes that the leader was unsure of what events unfolded in the clearing.

Then Areus remarked, "You dole out judgment without hearing the facts? What form of justice is that?"

The leader offered the slightest half-smile and said, "It is the only justice you will be accorded in my woods."

Baytel jumped into the discussion. "As to rights of passage and its enforcement, your men seem inadequate to the task. However, had we been properly dealt with from the beginning instead of attacked without regard or reason, we would not be in this situation."

"Let's kill them and be off, sir. We have no need of them," shouted a woodsman.

Another called out, "That's right!"

The fallen shouted for blood, reigniting their bravado. The leader raised his hand, silencing them.

He looked directly at Baytel and said, "You speak bravely, stranger. Or is it foolishly?"

"We did not enter Elangal Forest to prove our bravery or our foolishness. We entered to reach our destination faster. Time is of the essence and swift travel is imperative. We are on a quest of great importance. This fight was forced upon us after we volunteered to be taken to you. You may not have noticed, but none of your men are dead or maimed. We purposely showed restraint."

"I'll show you restraint, fool." A man they thought wounded lunged, aiming his lance at Baytel's chest. Baytel spun to one side, avoiding the jab, and in the same motion brought down his sword on the outstretched lance, shattering it to pieces. Then swinging the man's body to face him, Baytel rammed the hilt of his sword against the attacker's forehead and drove his heel into his chest, propelling him backward to tumble unconscious over his fallen companions.

The four unharmed woodsmen attacked, but Areus jumped forward and cut off their charge, guiding the four toward the edge of the clearing. The old horseman galloped toward Baytel and he rolled away from the horses' hooves, bounding to his feet only to avoid an arrow that stuck in the ground where his body had just stood.

With one down, three woodsmen retreated from Areus's position and ducked behind the old horseman while the leader attempted to gain position behind Areus. Areus caught the maneuver and charged the three, dodging the old horseman and engaging the three, felling one with a leg wound. Once again, Baytel and Areus were back to back.

Bleeding and unconscious men were strewn about the battlefield. Broken weapons and blood smeared the beauty of the green ferns of the clearing. The injured renewed their shouts for blood and hatred, and tensions mounted as the woodsmen continued to circle, waiting for either Baytel or Areus to make a mistake.

Just as their anger could not go further without blood, the leader lazily cantered into the circle and called for his men to stop. He looked down at Baytel, his uncertainty mingled with the evident anger behind his green eyes. Baytel returned his stare with one just as perceptible. The forest went deadly quiet except for the groans of the injured woodsmen. Then the leader sheathed his sword and broke the silence. "What are you called?"

Baytel studied the man a moment longer. Still seated proudly on his mare, his eyes changed from anger to something that looked like admiration.

"I am Baytel. Who are you?"

"I am Adetin Gar, leader of the men of Elangal Forest."

"Adetin Gar. Again I state, my companion Areus and I entered Elangal en route from Tridling Del to Kilhalen. We did not seek this battle, nor to injure—"

"Why did you not disarm yourselves when asked?" said one of the woodsmen.

Baytel did not answer immediately. Instead, he put before the woodsmen the attitude and posture of one who should be addressed in a more formal manner. Then, ignoring where the inquiry came from, he answered to Adetin Gar. "We gave quarter. That should have been sufficient. However, the need of weapons for our quest is great. We did not want to part with them."

"Sir, if I may," said Areus, stepping from behind Baytel. "Do you not think that if we planned to attack your land and waylay your band of men that we would have come with a contingent of men capable of completing the campaign? We are on an urgent quest. We could not risk the time it would take to travel around your forest. As to our weapons, we need them to overcome a dangerous adversary who may be in pursuit. To cast them aside to strangers, unfriendly at that, with no way of knowing whether they would be returned, and not knowing whether your band of men were friend or foe, was a chance we could not take."

"And here we are weapons in hand and blood drawn unnecessarily. Let us end this foray with no deaths, mend our wounds and embark on a truce to discuss the matters in a composed atmosphere," Baytel concluded, hoping to distill some sense of calm to the situation and feeling this Gar was a careful man, suspicious and doubtful of all strangers.

"Eloquent speeches. I am almost certain I know whence you came to command that aptitude," said Adetin Gar, surveying the fallen men again. "The same place you learned your swordsmanship, no doubt."

Adetin Gar turned to a standing woodsman. "Who attacked first?"

The woodsman's eyes darted from his leader to his fallen comrades. "Well sir, we heard Malin's horn and came to the clearing and saw—"

"No details. Who initiated the conflict?" spat Gar, already irritated at the question not being immediately answered.

241

"Malin, sir. He attacked them while we were engaged in discussion," he said soberly.

"And was this discussion the same this man reported?" Gar asked, angrily.

"It was as he stated. They asked to be taken to you without disarming themselves, but in peace," said the woodsman, looking down, then added, "Their swords were still sheathed, sir."

Adetin Gar shook his head. "Sheath your weapons, men; hold back your taste for blood. Enough has been shed this day." Gar turned and called toward the woods. "Kalti, look after the wounded. First see to Malin."

The man Kalti rode into the fern patch from the dense greenwoods where he had been hidden, his bow and quiver now strapped on his back. In one fluid motion he slid from his saddle-less horse and began giving orders to the men to help with the wounded. Kalti found Malin. The young man was still unconscious. After rousing him, he nodded to Adetin Gar.

Gar declared to Baytel and Areus: "You are safe now; or should I say we are safe, eh? These hostilities are over. We have much to speak of. If you have any wounds, Kalti will tend to you at camp." He turned his stallion and, with the old soldier's company, galloped out of the clearing and disappeared in the dense foliage of Elangal.

Chapter 39

FIRES dotted the campground, waxing the vine-curtained enclosure and massive trunks of greenwood trees in ominous flickering illumination and shadow. Tents were staked in military fashion, every other facing in an opposite direction, eliminating surprise attacks from front and rear. Sentries kept at watch along the camp perimeter, with guards rotating every hour.

Left alone and in their own tent, Baytel and Areus felt comfortably safe from any mischief from the woodsmen. Adetin Gar had proved to be their uncontested leader and his word would not be crossed.

Areus was putting the finishing touches on Baytel's wounds; each had addressed the other's minor cuts and abrasions from the supplies in their bags. "From what I have gathered," said Areus, "from the sprinkling of conversation I picked up, these woodsmen are a band of thieves who live here in Elangal. They do not care for life in towns, nor want anything to do with farming. They have come together seeking adventure and fortunes the easiest way possible, through the dishonest trade of thieving. I gathered they also offer their fighting talents to whoever pays the most in gold and jewels, or promises of treasures from plunder."

Baytel nodded. "Well, we have no such objects of desire to share and no time for any more nonsense. The sooner we can speak with this Gar, the better."

The need to reach Kilhalen was paramount for Baytel, knowing his brother already had a foothold as far north as Tridling Del. *If they gained a firm base in the north and with their vast army loosened upon the northlanders, defeat of the Southland forces would be impossible.*

The tent flap opened and Baytel was able to see that a guard had been posted outside their tent. His presence was surely more for listening than protection, but that was to be expected. From the open flap, the man Kalti entered carrying a bag. He knelt beside them and began removing items from a packet—bandages, sutures and needles.

Kalti was a fair-skinned man and Baytel was surprised to see that he had pointed ears like his own. Kalti's dark blue eyes and shoulder-length blond hair gave him a pristine look, as if from a sect unknown. He was not a tall man, but his physical structure was lithe and muscular. Kalti was looking about the interior of the tent, studying it and their possessions. His eyes rested briefly on their swords that lay beside them. Then he looked to their wounds.

"It seems I am not needed here. You dressed your own wounds. Are you healers?" His voice was almost music-like, not high, not low, a perfect pitch of sound and clarity.

"You are the one they call Kalti. Good evening to you. I am Baytel and this is Areus. Yes, our teachings were in the art of healing."

Baytel couldn't help but notice the comical expression on Areus's face as he kept looking back and forth between Baytel and Kalti. Ignoring him, Baytel asked, "Are you a healer, Kalti?"

"No. I just mend wounds when the need arises. I have been tending our wounded since this morning. It may be that you could look over my work on the more serious wounds, in case of infection."

Areus had not taken his eyes off Kalti and Baytel, making both uncomfortable. Baytel gave him a questioning look. All he did in return was smile.

"Of course we will look at your men. It would be our pleasure to see through your work."

"Excuse me," Areus broke in. "Kalti is it?"

"Yes."

"May I ask where your land is? I mean, where you originated? I am from Kilhalen."

Kalti's uneasiness increased. "I was found by Adetin Gar and Telek deep in a forest far to the northeast. I understand that I was a very young boy barely out of infancy, from what they say. No others of my kind were about. I do not know what land I came from or to what sect of humanity I belong. Neither do Adetin Gar or Telek." He stood and was about to leave, then said, "Another will come to summon you."

Kalti took one last look at Baytel and then left the tent.

"Areus, what is the matter with you?"

"Didn't you see it, Baytel?"

"See what?"

"His resemblance to you is uncanny. Same facial features, pointed ears, even his body is the same as yours, except perhaps thinner. You could be brothers, Baytel."

Baytel said nothing, hearing the reason for Areus's ridiculous smirking and Kalti's staring. Yet now that he thought of it, the similarities were uncanny and he wondered if Kalti was from the land and sect of his mother. He disengaged himself from those thoughts. The urgent need was to get away from these thieves and back on their quest.

"We must talk to Adetin Gar of our quest, Areus. I believe this is the only way to approach this situation and continue on. My first inclination is to trust him. I feel there is more to him than just a leader of thieves and fortune hunters."

"What of his men? Once you do battle against someone, it is difficult to gain their trust," said Areus.

He contemplated the battle and how it ended. "Adetin Gar is their leader. Whatever he says is law in Elangal. His men will obey whatever his orders may be."

They heard heavy footsteps outside, then whispering. The tent flap was pulled back and a man entered. It was the older warrior who rode away with Adetin Gar. His skin was weathered but body strong, as sturdy as an oak. He stood rigid as if at attention but with a slight lean to one side. His eyes showed a glimmer like that of a man smiling yet no smile was present. His broadsword and long dagger were both sheathed at his side. The hilts had the look of many battles, as did the man.

"Good evening," said Areus, breaking the silence.

"The sun has set upon the forest.

"Its green the black of ravens.

"The whisper now rules the night.

"We succumb to its silence and stealth."

Completing his recitation, the old soldier said, "You will follow me, wayfarers."

Baytel asked as he rose, "Where do we go?"

"You go in my footsteps," said the soldier, flatly.

"And may I ask who you are, sir?" Areus asked politely.

A whimsical expression creased his face. "I am he who shall lead you to end your queries."

They followed the old soldier to Adetin Gar, who sat at a fire in the center of camp far from his men. Joining him were Kalti and the old soldier. Gar did not rise to greet them so Baytel sat upon the fallen tree and Areus followed his example. The old soldier remained standing as though on guard and prepared for any irregularity that emerged from the meeting.

Adetin Gar spoke right off. "Your story holds true. Malin attacked first. He is young and still learning our trade. He is somewhat misguided. My sister's son. What can one do?" He spoke as if to establish a friendly atmosphere.

"We were not sure whether your band was friend or foe. That is why we did not take anyone's life," said Baytel.

"You still don't know," said Gar, smiling cunningly. "Now why are you traveling through my forest and in such haste?"

Though Baytel sensed Adetin Gar was not a man he would voluntarily collaborate with, he held nothing back, speaking of the Citadel, the Southland's taste for war, the force from the Southland hunting Citadel druids, and their need to reach Kilhalen before the winter solstice. "The arms of the Southland are already deep in the northlands as we speak."

"How do you know they hunt druids?" asked the young Kalti.

"Beside the fact that we are druids and aside from learning of it in Tridling Del, the information reached us by secret courier from the Citadel. Areus and I barely escaped Tridling Del, where the Southland already holds some authority."

"So here you are in my forest, under guard in my camp. You are druids and are being hunted by the Southland. Well, what a prize you both would be to the Southland and a treasure for us."

"Treasure? I assure you we are no prizes to be valued. The Southland will begin war against the north and soon. Killing us or delivering us to them will not make you richer in gold and gems. It will only further entrench their power in the north and enjoin you in their evil influences."

Gar had listened without interruption. He then stood as if the audience was over. Both Kalti and the old soldier followed his lead. "At the winter solstice in Kilhalen, what happens?"

"The heads of the great cities will be in attendance and we will relay to them these events," said Areus. His statement had overtures of his princely mannerism.

"Not all the heads will be in Kilhalen," said the old soldier.

Areus replied quickly, and with the same high airs of princely gentility. "Correct, but those that are will hear of the plight of the land. According to Baytel, and I have no reason to doubt his word, the Southland army has grown strong in number as well as powers."

Gar's eyebrow rose at the last statement and he asked, "What powers do you speak of?"

Earlier, Baytel had thought hard about the subject of magic and evil that was interwoven in his life, from its origins in his newly confirmed ancestry to his immediate family's practices. Should he venture into the subject of Vokat's and Ravek's true powers, they would surely raise more questions and eventually more open talk of his own powers. If he withheld anything, they would undoubtedly negate the legitimacy of his statements. He had to proceed with truthfulness.

"King Vokat and Prince Ravek wield the dark magic of the ancients."

"What?" asked Gar. "What magic you say?"

"He said the magic of the ancients. The dark art. They control these shadowy abilities and when they move north, they will be employing these talents to destroy and rule," said Areus.

Gar pulled on his earlobe, contemplating this. The leader of the thieves was not to be trifled with and even though Baytel thought the conversation was going positively, he still was uncertain of Gar's character.

Gar asked, "How do you know this?"

The time had come to shed his identity, but not all. Baytel looked to Areus for assurance, though he knew he had none to offer.

"Before I speak more of this subject, I must be at ease with what you intend for us. As you now understand, our quest is for all the sects of humanity to be free from tyranny."

Adetin Gar gave a half smile. "In order to decide your fate, I must know more. However, you should know that bargaining with the Southland is not a desirable option."

Unsettled at the prospect of trusting a band of thieves, but realizing there was no alternative Baytel again looked to Areus, who acknowledged his silent reservations with a nod.

"Very well then, Adetin Gar, we must trust you and accept the consequences of that trust."

Gar chuckled and replied, "I see it no other way."

Baytel acknowledged his reply with a slight bow of his head. "As you know, my name is Baytel, and I am a Druid of the Citadel. However, before I rose to such a privileged station, my home was in the Southland," he paused and took a deep breath. "I am Prince Baytel, son of King Vokat, and brother of Prince Ravek—"

"The dark prince? Vokat's son?" shouted the old soldier.

A veil of guarded reserve suddenly closed over the campfire. Baytel felt immediately isolated. The full extent of the hatred of his family was evident on the soldier's face. It was like the malevolence Baytel had experienced in the presence of the acolyte Ekar, back at the Citadel.

Adetin Gar was unmoved, showing no reaction to the information. After an uncomfortable period of time, Gar finally spoke. "So your father and brother think you are a traitor and rightfully so if you travel to Kilhalen to stop them from spreading warnings of war and evil to the northlands. Are you being hunted by them as we speak?"

"No. They believe me dead beneath an avalanche rock in the Southland. They think they have succeeded in killing me, Adetin Gar, but they hunt all who are associated with the Citadel."

"Such as you, Areus."

Areus took offense to Gar's sharp reply. "That is correct, Adetin Gar. They are particularly hunting for me and the few other druids that still live. Now your decision is at hand as to what you will do with us. I hope for the sake of all humanity, it is the right one."

"I advise you not to take that tone, Druid, or you will see your tongue cut from your mouth," warned the old soldier.

"Easy, Telek, no reason for threats." Gar stepped away from their circle, indicating an end to their discussion. "Sleep what little you can this night, gentlemen. Dawn is not far off and we must move in the morning. I must think further of this."

Baytel watched their backs until they disappeared into their respective tents. He threw another log upon the campfire, irritating the embers to ignite the dry stump. He was unsure what Gar would do, but was relatively certain turning them in to his father and brother was not going to happen. He contemplated their next move.

Areus reiterated the options out loud. "Gar really has only two choices. We know they do not align themselves with Vokat, which was quite evident by the reaction from this henchman Telek. The Thieves of Elangal are a small band of men, so most of their contacts are probably smaller fiefdoms looking for an advantage in battle. I doubt handing us over to one of these fiefdoms is a possibility because they have might have taken sides with too many different factions and the trust factor is thin. Also, being hidden away in Elangal Forest and way-laying passersby certainly has not endeared them with many nearby towns, so I see them either letting us go our way, or possibly escorting us through Elangal to figure some other move, keeping time on their side."

"Perhaps, but let's not rule out the possibility of them handing us over to someone who deals with the Southland where they are not directly negotiating with my father or brother. If you recall our lessons at the Citadel, there are ten score of goblin sects and other wild factions all about the land that will gladly attempt to mediate between Adetin Gar and Vokat. And there are always the possibilities that they will make contact with Tridling Del or Weyles."

Areus interjected, "I cannot see Gar doing that. He seems a complex sort of man, but I do not see him as sinister."

"The man he called Telek. Did you see the look on his face when I mentioned my father and brother? No, they do not like the Southland. Not at all. But complex or not, we must wait till morning so let's get some sleep. Gar was right. Morning is not far off."

They walked toward their tent, feeling the day's exertions when Baytel slowed. Something was not right. A feeling of something unfamiliar invaded the periphery of his awareness.

Areus had stopped, seeing his discomfort. "What is it?"

"I don't know. A sensation deep within me." He shook his head and walked toward their tent.

As they neared it, Baytel saw that the guard was lying down at their tent entrance asleep. "It looks as though our sentry guard decided to ease at his post."

They laughed at the soldier of fortune. Then for reasons unknown, Baytel's hand went to the hilt of his sword. He grabbed it as if needing to feel its place upon his side. A tingling sensation from the hilt made his hand grip it tighter. Suddenly, a surge of energy from the sword ran up his arm and traveled through his body. The sensation made him stop in his tracks.

He looked at Areus, who immediately noticed the change in him.

"What is wrong, Baytel?"

"Something is happening to me."

Concentration was difficult. His vision blurred. Baytel momentarily lost track of where he was. Then remembered he was walking toward their tent. Vision returned and he recognized his surroundings again and focused on the sleeping soldier at his feet. His body was lying oddly; his arm was across his back in a bizarre position. Baytel's study stopped at a wet mass that pooled beneath the soldier.

"Areus, this man is dead."

A scream came from the tent and something lunged from the flap, knocking him over. Baytel rolled away and came to his feet, unsheathing his sword. An explosion of light filled the campsite, nearly blinding him. He staggered backward, surprised and unsure where the light's source was. He continued to retreat from whatever monster that had burst from the tent when he realized that the light was emitting from his sword.

Baytel waved it curiously before him, testing its weight as if he had never held it before. It was like holding a shaft of fire. Then he felt its power surge through him like a bolt of lightning. It overwhelmed his senses as his entire body seemed to be meshing with whatever magic emitted from the sword. Time suddenly slowed and the world around him felt suspended in place. He and the magic of the sword were caught in the center of the timelessness.

Baytel ventured a glance toward Areus, whose shocked expression was frozen on his face. Then he saw the monster that had emerged from the tent. It was immobilized in motion. The quick glance gave Baytel the impression it was a goblin of some sort. Baytel's mind recessed from the scene before him and melted into the phenomenon coursing throughout his body and mind. It accelerated within the everlasting timelessness and he realized that it was magic that was infusing itself within him.

Baytel followed it as it streamed on, able to plot its journey through his body and he sensed its route had a purpose. Yet even with the uncontrolled invasion of magic, he was able to have a sense of self and stay in check and still be aware of the surrounding situation, for in the blink of an eye the timelessness vanished and the horrid creature was rushing at Areus.

Now into the split-second reality, Baytel stepped in front of Areus and blocked the creature's sword just in time. He pushed the slow-reacting Areus away and placed himself between his friend and the monster. More screaming came from the woods and two other monsters jumped into camp. Areus finally reacted, unsheathing his sword and joining in the fight. Still more monsters sprang from the tent and Areus maneuvered a few away, ducking between and around the tents to keep the monsters at bay.

Baytel faced four and contrived to lead them to the center campfire for a broader area to battle. His sword blazed white as he clashed its steel against the monsters'; the tones rang out like music. Again he felt the power surge through him and it brought a feeling of invincibility. Smiting one monster down he met the next charge with a thrust into the chest of another and swiveled around ready for the next assault.

Five monsters circled him. It gave him the opportunity to study their appearance in the firelight. They were horrid creatures; misshapen muscular frames with a mad look upon their dark faces. Their hands seemed claw-like with fingernails long and sharp. Their teeth were fanged and they bared them like wild animals to prey. They were certainly goblin-like, but terribly altered.

Out of the corner of his eye he saw Areus kill his first and wound the second when suddenly more monsters charged from the woods. It was maddening. The creatures shouted horrific screams, enraged and incensed with killing. They thrust and retreated, attacked and fell back. Their fighting prowess was nothing more than wild combat without thought or uniformity, to kill no matter the cost.

Other shouts surrounded the battle, for now the camp was fully awake and witnessing the fight. But Gar's men did not join in and Baytel understood, as they were awestruck by witnessing his magic and unsure what the beasts were.

The sword's power never ceased its flow and streamed through him, intensifying, quickening his physical abilities to a level he never knew he had. He thrust, stabbed, blocked, and sliced his way to killing one after another, moving onto the next with so fluid a movement, and so naturally, it felt effortless. On and on he fought. The sword with its brilliant blade was an extension of him, willing to do his bidding, yet testing him to reach deeper into himself. It brought him to the verge of uncontrolled chaos only to allow him to gain balance again, and then it would plunge him back toward chaos and propel him to reach deeper for control.

His body was wet with sweat, his muscles strained tight as he reacted with blinding swiftness to the many attackers. It was two battles in one, fighting the beasts of death and the magic surging within him.

An arrow flew by his head and struck the neck of a monster before him. Then another arrow flew past and imbedded into the head of another. He stole a glance and saw Kalti at the outer ring of the battle fitting another arrow. Yet the thieves remained back, awaiting the end of a battle that touched into the realm of the unreal.

As the magic continued to flow through his bloodstream, he sensed it entering every nerve, intertwining all to become one under its influence. The power of the magic commanded every fiber of his person, and he gave his all, for he had never felt this whole and conscious in all his life. Noble and high was the purpose the magic rushed toward, and in the midst of the magical infusion his ancestors were awoken and unfolding onto him the histories of the Kings of the North and their noble charge leaving no doubt who he was and where he was in the chronology of them all.

In that instant, the magic came completely under his control and found the mutual true footing within him. At that moment the magic of the Kings ignited another magic within him. It was the magic of his mother's unknown ancestry and he felt the power and beauty of her sect—he glimpsed the virtues and decency of the people—and a foundation was laid as the magic of both noble races joined in perfect harmony.

With a final rush, he met Areus at the campfire. Upon killing the remaining monsters together, Baytel fell into a trance-like state, unable to move. All he could sense was that he stood in the center of camp, panting and near exhaustion. Someone was speaking to him but he could not respond. The magic within him was all that mattered. It had continued to move through him, opening corners of his mind and body, searching and learning its new conduit, clearing away the confusion within him, and introducing him to the magic of the Kings and the magic of Pren.

Finally, Baytel felt the magic recede deep within him, yet he sensed it was ready to emerge at his command. Then the sword dulled to its usual silver steel. Turning to Areus, who stood beside him in shocked silence, Baytel heard him take a sharp intake of breath. He felt Areus's hands on his face and the sound of Areus's voice broke the spell and he came out of the trance. "Baytel! Your eyes! They glow with the white flame of the sword."

Baytel gently removed Areus's hands from his face. He did not see fear in Areus and was thankful, though he showed the signs of exhaustion also and clearly had fought well. Looking past Areus's shoulder he saw that the thieves still held their place outside the campfire battleground. Leaning toward Areus to speak privately, Baytel said, "It's the magic of my ancestors, the Kings of the North and that of the sect of my mother. Whatever doubts I have had of my lineage, I can put aside. I have seen the ancestors within and I have no doubts. I am who I am."

"Whatever doubts I had have also vanished. As I stated in the presence of Make Ironwright, my sword is at your side. Always."

Areus was about to kneel but Baytel but stopped him with a look. "No, Areus. Remember, no one needs to know of this."

He nodded and patted his shoulder. "Friends and companions for life, Baytel. As promised."

As the magic faded deeper, Areus said Baytel's eyes looked back to normal. He wiped the black blood of the dead off the sword and sheathed it, finally letting go the hilt from his grip. They took an account of the battle area. Eighteen of the creatures lay dead at their feet.

The thieves began gathering around some of the dead monsters that lay scattered and bleeding around the camp. The goblin blood flowed black; their bodies deformed in ways inhuman. Twisted and grotesque facial features with pronounced teeth, misshapen legs and arms, clawed feet and torsos of oversized muscle. They were the same creatures he had seen with Juliard in Balmoral.

Baytel thought about the battle and found something familiar in their techniques. The way they held their swords and how they stood; these were routine drills and practices taught by the officers under the command of the Southland. They fought bravely but stupidly. Seeing them resting in death, he noticed similarities in their physiques that matched those changes that occurred in his brother's body.

He whispered to Areus, "They are Pithean Goblins transformed by my brother. He has used the dark magic on them, altered then and sent them out to do his bidding. He is the mastermind behind this."

Baytel cringed as each of the creatures began to disintegrate, their blood acting as an acid to their shell. The evil behind such a creation was beyond anything he could fathom Ravek capable of. Yet here before him was evidence of his brother's sinister magic. To create beings that, once dead, eliminated their existence was so deeply rooted into the darkness it saddened him. The Goblins of Pithe were a proud sect. Ravek reduced them to horrid monsters of death.

"Baytel, we fight against an immoral enemy. This goblin horde makes my blood run cold. It is sad to see any sect tainted by evil."

In a guarded voice, Baytel said, "Whatever we do, Areus, let us not forget that these creatures are no longer of Pithe. They are our enemy. They are an arm of the Southland and death is their only intention."

"Baytel, I am just saddened that there is an evil in our land capable of this. My compassion is for what they were, not what they are, and it intensifies me to continue." He paused for a moment and added, "Remember, this assault was not directed toward both of us. They were hunting me."

The gravity of Areus's statement made him feel guilty. He was the cause of these aggressive acts. He wondered if he could have stopped Ravek before he ventured so deeply into black magic. But he may have been too late, even before leaving his home for the Citadel. All he knew was what he witnessed of his brother the night he left. Ravek was too far gone by then and he was certain his father was also. The only thing to do now was fight against them.

Baytel touched his sword for reassurance and recalled the goblins' reaction to it; it was like poison to them. He killed many. However, so did Areus and Kalti and they without the aid of magic.

From the first time he drew the sword and during all the times battling against the Retinue and the thieves, it stayed dull. It was only when battling the goblins that the magic emitted from it. Magic against magic. Good against evil.

Areus broke into his thoughts. "They will send more after us once they learn of their defeat. They will hunt us down one by one. Others will be caught unaware and unable to defend themselves against so many. I have been fortunate to find you to have your help. Warning our brethren is more important than ever. I suggest we go separate ways in order to reach more of our brethren before they fall prey to these monsters."

Kalti, Adetin Gar and Telek appeared from out of the woods and approached. Kalti said, "Baytel, one escaped. It bolted into the forest after being injured. I followed but it sped off and then his tracks disappeared.

"In which direction did it go, Kalti?"

"South."

Baytel could see the thieves clenching amulets to ward off whatever misfortune they believed would occur. Superstitions were strong in Elangal.

Gar saw it too and shouted to his men, "Enough of that! You men, get back to your tents. We break camp at first light."

Telek began herding the thieves toward their tents. "Move it, boys. Get your rest. You will need it."

Once their men were back either at postwatch or slumber, Gar, Telek and Kalti returned to the campfire.

"What goes on here, druids?" asked Telek.

"It is as we stated earlier. Ravek and Vokat hunt us out to eliminate our existence from the land," said Areus, a bit more aggressively than was necessary. He was still wound up from the fight.

Adetin Gar's hard stare never left Baytel and he pointed at him accusingly. "You are one with magic, Baytel. It seems there is more to you than what was said earlier this night."

Baytel decided to answer the unspoken question *Who are you?* without hesitation. "Adetin Gar, Telek, Kalti. This is the sword of Calidor, patriarch of the Kings of the North. He is also the leader of the Grey Riders and a Citadel Druid. He gave me this sword for our quest. It was forged in the beginning of time to be wielded by the king of the Great Race of Man, and until that time, it will be my burden to carry."

"Burden to bear a magical sword of a mythical powerful sect of man?" asked Gar, contemptuously. "Baytel, are you the prince of the Southland, or something else entirely?"

Baytel sensed he was loosing the thief's trust. "Adetin, my life is complex. You see what forces we fight against. It is something far more complicated than merely man against man. It is good against evil battling against a dark and inhumane magic that, in the histories, caused the destruction of the ancients. It is upon us now and before it becomes too strong we must stop it. The survival of the sects of humanity and the land we live on are at risk. If these creatures are able to freely roam the land, what other evils will we encounter? I ask you now, Adetin Gar, will you help us by letting us continue on our quest?"

253

Baytel watched the emotions run through Adetin Gar's face. He knew he was confused about what to do. In a short time since their first encounter, Gar had been witness to druids, monsters, stories of mythical kings and the power of magic. All this seemed beyond belief. Insane.

Yet Adetin Gar had witnessed it and Baytel felt it troubled him. Hidden away in Elangal for so long, Gar had lost touch with the fiefdoms, kingdoms, the power and political struggles of them. Gar looked lost, yet Baytel could see that he was not entirely devoid of the need to do battle against such a foe. Deep beneath his hard exterior, Gar was a warrior and what better reason to wage battle than against evil.

"I need time to figure things out. We will talk again in the morning," and Gar stomped off with Telek at his side and Kalti hesitantly following.

As they left, Baytel said, "All we can hope for is that Gar will come to a decision as soon as dawn, which is not far off."

"I should go along a different path than you, Baytel. I can misdirect those that follow and not hinder your ability to reach Kilhalen safely."

Spoken like a true friend, and it was not without some degree of logic. He could get there faster without the burden of being hunted. "No, Areus. These creatures cannot be confronted alone. It is better we travel as we have been, but more cautiously. We slackened our routine of caution when we met this band of thieves. We cannot let it happen again.

"Ravek will indeed send more goblin assassins for each of us. I keep wondering how Ravek knows how many of us there are out in the wild? It is as though someone is feeding Ravek information known only to one of us from the Citadel. But who could it be?"

Chapter 40

COMPROMISING the security of the Southland castle should have been suicidal. At nearly every stage of his infiltration, Ekar drew attention to himself. Dressed in a stolen Southland army uniform, he stumbled across post watch patrol changes, collided with soldiers as he hurried through the many yards and wards of the castle, lost his bearings in the passageways, opened doors to rooms occupied by officers in heated discussions-it was all almost comical had it not been for his fear of discovery. Yet with the lack of discipline and poor organization throughout the Southland castle, his inexperience in infiltration and bundled clandestine activities were essentially ignored.

Once fully inside, he took on the simple disguise of a kitchen servant and, with this garb, was able to gain access to private officer meetings—without fumbling, he noted to himself—which offered him a wealth of information about the activities within the realm. And this information was everything to him if he was to succeed with his own plans.

Ekar laughed to himself at the ease of accessing these meetings with the mere act of piling a cart or tray full of food and drink, and he was welcomed with enthusiasm. No one questioned his presence or asked who ordered their feasts. Disdain toward a lowly servant placed him at a position in the meeting rooms of being ignored. The officers' confidence of their positions and safety within the castle walls meant they held nothing back in his presence, speaking of war plans, strategies, military might and their hopes of higher positions when the war with the northlanders was won and the regions were divided up among the victors. The Southlanders believed victory was a preordained fact and all they had to do was advance their massive army north and the various northlanders would surrender from fear of it.

The first utterance about Baytel came to him in the past tense-the dead traitor prince. Soon after, Ekar discovered that Baytel had somehow secreted into the castle and attacked his father, was pursued and then was killed, buried beneath an avalanche of rock while attempting to escape.

Good riddance. Ekar knew there was something about Baytel that had escaped everyone at the Citadel and he was obsessed on discovering what it was, which was why he was in the Southland. Ekar hated Baytel from the moment he met him for being a Southlander. That he was in actuality King Vokat's son was the secret Baytel had kept from them all. It was a surprise to Ekar also. Whatever Fate had plotted for Baytel was deserved. The Tree Faeries must be all agog with anger, realizing Baytel was dead. The stupidity in Baytel's attempt to kill his father was beyond belief. Baytel must have taken to the teachings of the Citadel so deeply that he found no alternative except to turn against his own father.

Now with Baytel dead, the reasons for infiltrating the Southland eliminated, Ekar set his sights on another objective. With no title or lands, he desired a region of his own to rule over, just like the officers he spied on dreamed of. The only way for this to happen was to somehow ally himself with the Red King.

Through the many days of clandestine activities, Ekar learned all he needed of their strategies and found the common thread to weave himself into their confidence. Hearing that the Citadel had been sacked and its entire community killed, except a few who roamed the land, he felt no sense of loss, no remorse or grief for those that he had shared part of his life with at the fortress. He had detached himself some time ago from any such friendships or relationships with the acolytes and druids. Then he was passed over, not being awarded with the Laurel, a designation he deserved more than some who received it.

The Acolyte Sezon was undeserving! He was a weakling and should have never been awarded the Laurel. Baytel has since proven his true worth to all, for had he not returned to kill his father, the Citadel would still exist, with all there alive. Then there is Podius and the arrogant Areus, both nuisances!

His hatred of them all caused him to be somewhat elated at the deaths of those in the Citadel. Then when information came from Southland scouts in the northlands that a deadly force in the wild regions had proved to be a mighty adversary, killing an advance troop dispatched by Prince Ravek, Ekar knew the time had come to initiate his plan. It was a druid that had countered Ravek's factions in Tridling Del and in Elangal Forest, and Ekar knew who remained of the druids and acolytes who had departed the Citadel. This bit of information was his opportunity to an invitation into the brain trust of the Red King's high council; his portal into their world and the fulfillment of his desires.

Hearing of the announcement of a full assembly of officers, councilors and retainers, Ekar knew the moment of his disclosure was at hand.

Hidden away in an unused room in the armory, Ekar could barely contain his excitement as he commenced collecting and attaching weapons. He then draped his serving robe over his clothes and took to the kitchen, piling food and drink upon a serving cart. Ekar made his way up the winding interior ramp of the tower toward the assembly chamber, preparing for battle along the way.

Chapter 41

THE tension at the war council could be cut with a knife. Vokat would have it no other way. The only intrusion to the stillness in the entire assembly was the rustle of Chancellor Hectus's clothing from his constant fidgeting. At times, the chancellor's nervous antics were comic relief; now they were annoying.

Vokat had learned the news from a chambermaid. *A chambermaid, forsooth! Everyone seated at the war table had prior knowledge of these reports and none informed me! Am I not king here? Two confrontations Ravek's forces had against the northlanders and both times we came away looking incompetent and entirely defeated.*

Vokat purposely kept his anger in check. Such displays were not his way, but those present would soon know his mood with perfect clarity. Actually, it was none of their responsibilities to report these events. That rested on no one else but Ravek.

Ravek's very presence made all assembled uncomfortable, as he no longer kept the changes he had made to himself hidden, but now vainly flaunted his wickedness before all. At each war council of recent weeks, Ravek looked darker. Vokat sensed his son's powers had reached depths that would soon command his attention for he realized Ravek had become proficient in some form of a forbidden magic; a magic, in his opinion, better left unpracticed.

Vokat stole a glance along the side balcony where low-ranked officers and retainers sat. It would be their first war assembly and all seemed elated at being allowed the privilege of inclusion. He had called the meeting to gather all together to set in motion his plans for the final stages of war preparations. Pithe, Azkar Rol and Southland armies were training independently. It was not his intent to have three factions within his realm, but to have one unified force so powerful the northlanders would be more apt to surrender than fight. Either way, he wanted his force to be unified.

Unexpected sounds from the hall outside the assembly chamber broke the silence—the clanging of an upended service cart along with trays and utensils crashing onto the stone floor. As the commotion continued, the sounds took on a different pitch. Mumbled voices and shouting and then running footsteps extended beyond the fallen cart. Then a clash of metal against metal, a sound that could only be perceived as sword against sword. A battle was being waged in the hallway. Screams filtered through the doors followed by the thump of falling bodies. Agonizing cries were cut short and replaced by the moans of the dying. No one could ignore the disorder. Most in the assembly were on their feet and moving toward the commotion.

Then the doors flung open, slamming against the interior walls and nearly coming unhinged. Castle guards spilled into the room in retreat. Vokat could not see over the heads of the defenders to make out who the aggressors were.

Then a flurry of action unfolded and only four guards remained fighting, and the antagonist entered the room. It was a lone man. Not tall, a bulky physique dressed in all green. He held a broadsword in one hand and a short sword in the other. Blood was splashed across his clothes and face. Behind him the dead and injured lay scattered upon the corridor floor. The man moved with the fluidity of a mountain cat and re-engaged the remaining guards. Within four quick strides and as many maneuvers, the guards were down and the man calmly strode deeper into the assembly toward the war table.

Officers jumped from the balcony, intercepting his advance and they met his sword with their own. The warrior dispatched them one by one with ease and still he advanced. More joined the fray but were ineffectual as the man effortlessly parted them of their lives.

Vokat was captivated by the display of swordsmanship. The lords and higher officers were of the same mind, all awestruck and rapt in the warrior's movements. It wasn't until Lord Lezab stepped to Vokat's side that the captivation was broken.

Lezab spoke low for him alone to hear. "Sire, his fighting style is nothing we teach anywhere in the Fork Mountains."

Vokat smiled. "Yes, he seems to have certain skills that our men are having difficulty with."

"He has killed off many of our elite guards and now a few of our officers. Sire, I must intervene."

Lezab began to step toward the foray when Vokat caught his arm. "Lord Lezab, you choose not to test your officers against a superior opponent?"

Lezab replied, "How can they be tested without the proper teachings? They can observe and learn, instead of plunging in and dying. In any case, it is becoming a slaughter."

He smiled at his friend and said, "Always the teacher, Lezab?"

Lezab smiled back. "I believe my example sets the tone of loyalty to you, Sire."

Lezab walked toward the man with only his sword in hand and stood alone before him. The warrior attacked and Lord Lezab met each tactic he employed blow for blow. Officers and lords drew closer, forming a circle defining the battleground within the assembly room and shouting their support of their leader and champion.

Vokat watched from the war table. To his surprise, Lezab was actually verbalizing the fight to the crowd, offering them insight into the warrior's maneuvers and the defense of them. The fight slowed as each warrior tried difficult maneuvers to create a flaw in the other's style and gain an advantage. Neither gave ground and, as the fight wore on, their strikes weakened and it became evident the battle was to be a draw.

Vokat edged his way into the circle and the shouting ceased. The fighters backed away from one another, holding their ground a comfortable distance apart.

Vokat motioned the officers to stay in their place, seeing a few advancing into the circle with swords drawn. Archers had entered the assembly and were positioned in the balcony awaiting his order to let fly, and arrows would fall upon the man like rain, but he was intrigued.

Lord Lezab stepped toward Vokat, breathing heavily, and bowed. Vokat could see he was near exhaustion, but Lezab hid the knowledge well. No one but Vokat could see he had reached his physical limit. He gave Lezab time to catch his breath and offered his goblet of wine, though he knew Lezab would decline the offering, as he never consumed any spirits.

"Quite a display, Lord Lezab."

"An extraordinary opponent, Sire."

The faint smile on Lezab's face showed Vokat that the commander had further analysis of the stranger. "What is it you see, my friend?"

"His training could have come from only one source, Sire."

The king nodded in agreement. "Yes, his style looks quite distinctive. It is something I have not seen practiced in many years."

"As I, Sire. Not in almost twenty years. That man is Citadel trained. I have no doubt."

"The Citadel again, eh? The place has been unspoken of for twenty years and now it is on everyone's lips. Do you think he is a druid?"

The commander turned to study the man further, as did Vokat. The intruder remained standing at battle-ready position, his breathing steady and even; his eyes darted between Vokat's and Lezab's.

Lezab offered his opinion, saying, "It's his eyes that give him away. I would be able to recognize a druid from their eyes. Their abilities, knowledge and formidable wisdom are evident in them. They take in all at one glance and have a calming effect in all situations. This one here is a bundle of nerves. No, Sire, he had not reached that level of achievement. Perhaps he is a failed acolyte?"

Vokat was surprised at his knowledge. "You know much about their order, Lord Lezab."

"One must know his enemies to judge their strengths and weaknesses in order to evaluate any threats that they may impose upon your realm. This is what I do to keep you safe, Sire."

"And this is why you are my most trusted commander, Lord Lezab. Thank you for your assessment. Please dismiss everyone from the chamber. Tell them to take the dead away and the injured to the infirmary. Then bring this stranger to the table. I want to speak with him."

Lezab hesitated before asking, "And Prince Ravek, Sire?"

"He must stay, of course, as well as you."

With the dead and injured gone and the assembly hall otherwise empty, Lezab escorted the warrior to the table. The man sat without offering the usual stately protocols to Vokat.

The king ignored the slight, and asked, "What do you call yourself?"

"Ekar."

"Ekar. Strange name. Your skills of swordsmanship are extraordinary. I always have said the Citadel instructors are the finest to teach that art."

"You know of me?"

"No. I recognize your style of swordsmanship. I have fought against it before."

"Against your son Baytel, perhaps?"

Ravek reached across the table but Ekar was fast to react and spun away with his sword out in a flash.

Vokat held up his hand and said, "Prince Ravek, we are here to talk, not fight. The Druid Ekar must be given an audience without the threat of violence against him." The king motioned him to retake his seat, and as he did asked, "It is Druid Ekar, is it not?"

His face broke out in blotches of red as though he had been slapped. He did not answer.

"I see. Perhaps not, then."

Ekar blurted out, "I should be, but others were against it. I have completed all the training and schooling but did not receive the Laurel, if that is what you want to hear."

"What I want to hear is not the point to this discussion, Ekar. But since we are on the subject of druids and you mentioned my son's name, how did you know Prince Baytel?"

"Prince? You still claim him as your son and prince? Did he not try to kill you?"

"Is that not what your Citadel trained him to do?" Ravek interjected accusingly.

"I heard of no such plan," Ekar responded. "The strategies and devices Baytel employed were his own affair. Personally, I found him weak in the matters of battle and not worthy of receiving the Laurel and Druid status. He was too willing to please and play nice."

"And you do not play nice, Ekar?" asked Lord Lezab.

Ekar cocked his head from the question and replied, "Let's just say I prefer a more aggressive approach to matters of interest. Not everyone has to be friendly acquaintances. I choose to fend for myself."

"Hence your dramatic arrival to my assembly?"

Ekar laughed, causing Ravek to nearly jump from his seat again.

"Son, please. Allow Ekar the privilege of uninhibited behavior. After all, are we not being open with one another in this private session?" Vokat smiled at Ekar, but the expression would never be mistaken as friendly.

Vokat continued, "You take chances, Ekar. Do you play me for a fool?"

"No, King Vokat, you are not a fool. Nor am I making game of you. You see, I have been in your castle and among your subjects for weeks."

Vokat contemplated the statement. Weeks of clandestine study and activity in an isolated realm with no one but his own abilities to rely upon was brave by any measure. It was also reckless, unless the reward far exceeded the risk. The question was what reward would suffice to inspire Ekar into such an undertaking? And why the dramatic display of strength and talent? Ekar had a plan and a desire that far overstretched common sense. He was a wild being, a juggernaut of mayhem, which, Vokat presumed, was one of many reasons the Citadel decided to deny him druid status.

Lezab asked, "And you chose this moment to introduce yourself? Why?"

An arrogant smile crossed Ekar's face. "I chose this moment having discovered a simple fact that you are not yet aware of."

Vokat's curiosity was piqued by this arrogant man's boast. "And what is that?"

"That you are approaching the invasion of the northlands overconfident; that unless you align yourself with an ally that has been out of this isolated region, your campaign will surely fail."

Ravek slammed his fist on the table, his anger simmering over. "Fail? You fool of a man. We are thousands strong and trained beyond that of any army ever conceived upon the land! We are invincible!"

Vokat's eyes never left Ekar and he watched the young man nod knowingly, witnessing Ravek's outburst as confirming his assessment of their overconfidence.

Ekar simply replied, "No one is invincible."

Ravek could not keep his mouth shut, and boasted, "I am invincible."

Ekar tilted his head as if in scrutiny of Ravek's claim. "I am certain your declaration of invincibility is sound, Prince Ravek. I sense your power and believe it may be incredible. However, you have no notion of the powers beyond these mountains you have been sequestered behind for so long."

"What makes you the expert in what powers are beyond our reach, Ekar?" asked Ravek, calming after the slight compliment.

"With what I have learned, I can offer only conjecture at their potential."

Lezab asked, "You spoke of us needing an ally. I presume the ally you speak of is you?"

"That is the reason I risk so much. You need what I have to offer."

Vokat said, "Your fighting skills are exemplary, Ekar, but we already have fighters. You have not offered anything but inferences and opinions."

Ekar waved his hand in the air as if disregarding Vokat entirely, and said, "Heralding your greatness is a weak boast and a waste of good breath."

Ravek rose to his feet and unsheathed his sword. "Take that manner with the king again and you will feel my steel pierce your body!"

Ekar shrugged at the threat.

Vokat raised his hand again and addressed his son. "Ravek, if you interfere with this conversation again, I will have to ask you to leave."

"He insults you and diminishes our accomplishments as if you and they are nothing!"

"Perhaps they are nothing. However, until we hear the entire explanation of this man's claims, we cannot judge them to be anything more. Now sit down or leave."

He sat and Vokat studied Ekar further. He did not have the look of a gentleman of culture or show any refinement of manners other than what he might have learned at the Citadel. He obviously took to their training in every way, seated straight in the chair, not against the backing, almost as if he were at battle stance while seated, much like Lord Lezab. Disciplined. His eyes still darted to and fro, as if caged and seeking a way out. But his face showed fierceness and intelligence. *What does he really want?*

"What makes you think our destruction of the Citadel was so inconsequential?"

"Surely you cannot be under the illusion that you destroyed all the druids in your sacking of the fortress?"

No one spoke. Vokat fumed silently as he had assumed exactly that. Ravek and the rumors confirmed it. The pause in the chamber was cut by the sound of thunder as a rainstorm arrived. Vokat looked to Ravek who had readjusted his seat numerous times in the seconds that passed, his discomfort reinforcing the truth in Ekar's statement.

Ekar added, "I see the prince knows I speak the truth."

Lezab asked, "Prince Ravek, do you believe there to be more druids out in the wild?"

Ravek did not answer and Ekar continued, "All you did was ruin a fortress and kill insignificant acolytes and a handful of druid teachers. The druids and advanced acolytes had already departed the Citadel before you attacked. Once word spreads of the sacking of the Citadel, these disciples will assemble and retribution will be their call. The consequences of this will be calamitous to your plans."

"How many are there, Ekar?" asked Lezab.

Ekar raised both arms in a noncommittal motion. "I believe this is where we open a negotiation of alliances and rewards."

"And the price you place on your information?" asked Vokat, wanting to speed up.

Ekar's eyes darted faster, his mind running at high speed. "Sire, my price is as follows: mutual loyalty with you and all in your realm. The title of Lord and a realm in the northlands of my own, and of my choosing after the war. And of course the riches that come from plunder."

Vokat laughed loudly. "That is all?"

Ekar's face flushed red again. The man did not like being the object of jest. He was an angry man and men like that were wild and unpredictable. Trusting him to be loyal was the easy part of the alliance. Making him a lord of the realm without being of royal blood was not an optimal situation, though not unheard of, and Vokat wanted his information. "I need more convincing. Give me something that will convince me you can earn my loyalty."

"Easy enough." Ekar paused, allowing the sense of anticipation to build. "Let's see, since the Citadel fell you have killed one druid. He was the Druid Sezon, the weakest member, by far, of the new Laurel recipients. An easy prey."

Ravek nodded, confirming the kill. Vokat wondered why he had kept this information from him but said nothing.

Ekar continued, his confidence building as he went. "On the other hand, there is another druid who, like Baytel, earned his Laurel with high marks, even exceeding the skills of his teachers. This druid is from the largest kingdom in the land except for your realm and that of the Ctiklat Dwarfs. He is Druid Areus and he is the first prince of Kilhalen."

"Areus!" Ravek nearly shouted it.

"Yes, I have heard of your forces' defeats at Druid Areus's hands in Tridling Del, and again just recently in Elangal Forest. Areus is quite resourceful and is only one of a few who now roam the land. I know when all of them departed the Citadel and where they are headed. I know how they think. Without my aid, they will rally the kingdoms and fiefdoms against you. So goes any possibility of surprise."

Lezab asked, "So this Druid Areus was the cause of these two defeats?"

Ekar answered: "Yes."

Vokat turned to his son and asked, "Ravek, is this true?"

Reluctantly, the prince replied, "Yes, if this druid is Areus as this man states, he was the one who escaped our men at Tridling Del and our attack in Elangal."

Vokat asked, "Ekar, how many of these druids remain?"

Ekar replied, "Are we allied with one another, Sire?"

Vokat was tiring of the banter, wanting to be done with this arrogant man. However, it seemed the realm needed him. "I agree to your terms. Now you must agree to mine. Your total loyalty to my realm and me is unconditional. You deviate at any stage from this arrangement and, I can assure you, the consequences will be long and painful."

Ekar stood and bowed to him, "Sire, you have my unyielding loyalty. Now we must act quickly for the Druid Areus will still be travelling through Elangal Forest and the other druids and acolytes are not far from there."

Vokat turned to Ravek. "Prince Ravek, you will take *Lord* Ekar with you and do what you must to find these Citadel Druids. Kill them all. I will have nothing interfering with my invasion plans. I am depending on you both to eliminate this threat. Do not fail me."

Chapter 42

ADETIN Gar remained in his tent all morning. He felt uncomfortable, as his usual routine was disrupted because of the two druids his band of thieves had happened upon. The sudden disjointed atmosphere that seemed to infiltrate his entire being from the Druid Baytel's words resounded over and over in his mind. Gar had been isolated from the politics and powers of the great kingdoms for so long he had lost touch with what mattered outside Elangal Forest and was thrown off balance. He had, at times, felt like a sovereign ruler within the boundaries of Elangal Forest, but Gar now realized, after the events of last night, how inconsequential he and his thieves were to all but themselves.

The trade of thieving had slowed to a crawl as caravans were choosing to travel the eastern route, adding weeks to delivery of their goods, rather than risk Elangal. Hence, boredom had crept into the daily life of his band of thieves. Many abandoned thieving altogether to return to the towns and cities for honest work. Though most that departed were not loyal men, it still stung his pride, not being able to retain these superior soldiers of chance. But that was the way of the fortune-seeking purloiner.

Then Baytel and Areus had arrived, both with gifted fighting skills and loftier culture. He had thought there was an opportunity to expand his trade to wealthier targets. However, that possibility was shattered after the battle that introduced his thieves to the realm of nightmare. Now Adetin Gar was embroiled in an unbridled torrent of events that he had trouble turning his back on.

Had they not encountered the two druids, would this probable conflict have touched Elangal, causing him to pick sides either way? Or would he and his thieves go untouched by it all, holed up and separated from the ills of the land deep in Elangal? *I should have killed them and taken their possessions immediately and been done with them! Instead, I am debating with myself!*

The tent flap slapped open and Telek entered. "Are you going to stay in here all day? Camp is packed and the men are milling about with nothing to do, and you know that is particularly vexing to me."

Gar ignored his report and asked, "Telek, what do you think about these two men?"

Telek snapped to attention in regimental fashion. Before venturing into thieving, Gar and Telek were rover soldiers, volunteering to fight for causes and campaigns with whomever needed their swords. Telek never tired of the military way of life and continued to play the role, which set a fine example and kept the company of thieves in line, though he was many years removed from its formality.

Telek answered, "They are young and probably somewhat inexperienced. Nevertheless, I cannot disregard that if they are Citadel Druids, their knowledge must be far-reaching."

"That we have seen." Gar suddenly became irritated with his old comrade standing at attention. "Will you relax!"

Finally seated in a canvas chair, though straight-backed, Telek continued his evaluation. "I do not know anything about their education; however, their fighting skills are second to none. The way they battled those monsters last night was outstanding. The maneuvers they utilized, exploiting the monsters' weaknesses, playing off one another's strengths until victorious—all this was far beyond anything I have seen in battle. Their movements were so fluid they seemed to drift outward as if pre-arranged, never wasting time and energy with hesitations or uncertainties. It was like a dance, but death was the waltz's end. It was exquisite."

Gar had never heard Telek praise anyone like that, and all he could do was concur. "Do you believe their story of the Southland's taste for another war?"

"I've been thinking on this all day. Those monsters were created to destroy, or if maimed or killed, destroy themselves. The magic capable of this surely is dark and evil. If they say these monsters were from the Southland, then Vokat and Ravek must be the source of such an evil incarnation. It cannot be interpreted any other way."

Gar paced back and forth. He remained uneasy with what to do and what to believe about the druids. Magic and monsters were not a part of life in his Elangal Forest and he felt ensnared by the circumstances the druids brought to his door.

"He carries a magic sword, Telek. I know little about such things, but I can surmise that in order for the magic to work, the person engaging the magic must have it himself. Baytel says the sword belongs to Calidor of the Kings of the North. I think he tells us a portion of what is truth. Baytel is more than he claims to be, my friend. If he wields magic, and admittedly being Vokat's son, he may be one who helped create these monsters."

Telek shook his head. "He may be Vokat's son, but I cannot believe he was part of the creation of the monsters. Not the way he reacted toward that goblin horde. He was genuinely repulsed by them and showed sorrow of their existence. He may be more than he claims, but he is not evil. I do not sense that in him."

"Then what do we do? Their being here has caused the death of one of our men! I should be doing something about that!" Without realizing it, Gar was shouting. The events had caused a total dishevelment of his life and he did not like it. "They personally have injured nearly all our men. We should have killed them for this! Why is it I cannot decide what to do with them?"

Telek rose slowly from the chair and stood at attention once more. "I believe there is more at stake here and you are afraid to accept it, Adetin. Baytel and Areus are on a quest for the land and sects of humanity, the gravity of which we witnessed last night. We are unaccustomed to meeting anyone remotely like these men. It is like they are from the past where heroes reigned and chivalry was abundant. We have been fortune hunters and thieves for so long, we forget what it is like to crusade for a cause. Baytel has thrown down his gauntlet at you. Subliminally, yes, but a challenge to you it was. Do we assist them, or let them continue their quest without us?" Telek paused, and then declared, "I say we help."

Adetin Gar stopped pacing. He did not yearn for soldiering again. The monotony of regimental discipline was intolerable. But so was the boredom he was experiencing thieving. Guiding Baytel and Areus through Elangal Forest on their way to Kilhalen could be the panacea to break up the tedium. He turned to Telek, and said, "Assemble the men."

"They are assembled," he said and threw the tent flap open, holding it back for him.

As Gar approached the men, they jumped into line and stood at attention. The entire camp was packed and the horses were tethered behind the men. He glanced at Baytel and Areus who stood separately from the thieves. All they carried was their swords on their belts and bags across their shoulders of the same design.

With Telek at his side, Gar addressed the men. "At times it is our duty as fighters to offer our services to causes that happen to cross our paths. These men, Baytel and Areus, are Druids of the Citadel. As you all witnessed last night, they fight an evil that has emerged from out of the Southland. Some of you are old enough to remember the war with the Southland, but for those who do not, these events may be a prelude to another war, and against an enemy of greater power. These druids must reach Kilhalen. It is our duty to escort them safely through Elangal Forest. Telek will relay patrol schedules and orders. Let's move, men."

With Telek in charge, the days that followed came easier. During their trek, the druids treated the men with the more serious wounds and they healed rapidly, which diminished the men's residual anger and resentment toward them for causing their injuries. By the fifth day out from camp, with all entirely healed, the thieves fell into a solid routine of scouting. Patrols were dispatched ahead and to the rear in intervals at dawn, dusk and after the midnight hour. Gar was even proud that his band of thieves, turned escorts, fell so naturally into the military style of patrol and cautious travel.

Gar avoided contact with the druids, who had joined in on patrol duties, taking orders from Telek and Kalti. On occasion, when at night as his men sat around the campfire, he listened from afar as Baytel and Areus spoke of the Citadel, the One Land, sects of humanity and their plights to survive. They talked of the Tree Faerie folk and their magical existence and importance to the land—how they healed and created new things with the magic bestowed upon them by the One Land. It annoyed him that his men listened with such heightened intensity, but most were young and marveled at things unknown.

Areus was discussing what he had learned at the mystical Citadel when the serene night was jarred by a shout for help. Adetin Gar rushed from the outer perimeter of the campfire toward the wail and almost stumbled over one of his men. Trun had crawled back to camp. He was bleeding profusely from a black gash across his chest. Trun's breath came in short gasps.

Supporting his head in his lap, Gar asked, "What happened, Trun?"

"Monsters…same as before…all of patrol dead." He extended his arm and pointed back toward where he had been, and then Trun expelled his last breath.

Gar laid Trun's head down and looked upon his wounds. They were already festering. Gar saw Trun had something clenched his hand. It was a leather satchel he must have taken from one of the goblins. Prying Trun's fingers from the bag, he dumped its contents on the ground. Tools to make fire and strange looking food fell out along with a small scroll. Gar unwound the scroll. Towns and fiefdoms were written down one column and beside them were names. He read down the column and came across Kilhalen and the name "Areus" jumped off the paper as if it shouted from it.

He looked for the druids, and saw them exiting their tent, their packs and sword belts attached.

"Where are you going?" spat Gar, angrily.

"To find these monsters before they cause more death," said Baytel. "I am sorry for your losses, Adetin. I am truly sorry, but we must go." He turned to Areus and asked, "Ready?"

"Let's go," said Areus.

"Stop!" yelled Gar, standing above his fallen soldier. "Before you go, look at this."

He handed over the scroll and watched as both their eyes turned from curiosity to anger. "Where did you get this?"

Gar pointed down at the satchel. "Trun must have pulled it away from one of them. Why is your name on this, Areus?"

"These are the names of the druids and acolytes who were not present when the Citadel was attacked. I am one of them."

"Why are you not on this list, Baytel?"

"They think I am dead. Areus, this note confirms that one of us has turned traitor and is assisting Vokat and Ravek. It was our worse fear."

With a dead companion at his feet, Gar wanted to strike out at something. Yet the situation called for a calmer mind. He could do nothing about the deaths except allow the druids to pursue the goblins, Gar decided. "Trun's patrol was to the west. On the list is written the town of Petal Glen. The goblin horde was most likely traveling toward Konart Pass. It is a passageway that cuts through the Lumithien Mountain Range. That is the fastest way to reach that town. Kalti, go with them. We will regroup at the Ginhomin River just south of Petal Glen."

Gar and Telek walked the trio toward where Trun's blood trail led. "Kalti, keep a keen eye and your arrows true. You druids get these monsters out of my forest!"

"Farewell, Gar. Keep a strong watch," said Areus.

Adetin Gar stormed off without a response.

Chapter 43

BAYTEL picked up the tracks of the goblin horde a short distance from camp. Their path was easy to see, as the horde had marched recklessly through the forest. It was a larger group than the one that raided the camp. The three men pursued them without stopping through the night and into the next day and night. When the following morning lit the forest, Baytel found that the horde's tracks had split. One pointed toward the northwest, which Kalti confirmed was the direction to Konart Pass. The other, larger, group headed back along the route that they just travelled, back toward the thieves' camp.

Baytel stood at the divided tracks; a sense of dread nearly overwhelmed him. He bent down, analyzing the goblins' footprints. They were not fresh tracks. "They are still far ahead of us."

"We should not have divided ourselves. We should have stayed with camp," said Areus.

"The small group that is headed to Konart and then to Petal Glen is to find one man. These others are on a murder raid back for our camp," Kalti said, touching the prints. Kalti had proven himself to be an extraordinary tracker and good travel companion. "They are a half day's march ahead of us. We will not be able to intercept the goblin horde before they reach Adetin Gar. They will have no warning of an attack unless they continue to patrol. But if they do not…"

Kalti's statement seemed to linger in the air as Baytel brought to mind the battle at the camp when the goblin horde first appeared. The thieves would be annihilated.

"How many of these evil hordes do you think the Southland sent out, Baytel? Do you have any inkling about the size of this army?" Areus asked. Exhaustion was evident in his voice. It was on all their faces.

"All I know is that before I first journeyed away from the Southland, Ravek was organizing a powerful army, a force of personally trained men under his supervision. These creatures we have seen may be that force—an elite horde of assassins subverted by his magic."

"The larger group that travels toward Adetin," said Kalti. "They do not suspect anyone to be following. If we cannot warn Adetin, or intercept the goblin horde, we must do what we can to make sure these demons do not go unpunished."

Areus declared. "The goblins traveling toward Konart Pass are not just after one man, Kalti. There are many other names identified on that list."

Both Areus and Kalti turned toward Baytel. They said nothing more. He held their gaze as they waited, and he felt a change in their companionship in the quest. He had become their leader, and final decisions were now his to make.

Shaking off the feeling of change, he said, "We must set aside the list for now. We go after the larger group. Kalti. Take the point."

Eating cold meals on the run, Kalti kept the pace pressing to gain on the larger goblin group. Twilight came quickly and exhaustion was close at hand. Baytel was about to call for a halt when, deep in a grove of large greenwoods, Kalti raised his hand in warning and all dropped to a knee.

Up ahead, coming in and out of view between the massive greenwood trees was the goblin horde. Kalti signed their company numbered twelve. They marched without care and with no apparent orderliness. Kalti signed again saying that he was separating and he crawled away before Baytel could stop him.

Lightning flashed an incredible bolt illuminating the sky and thunder roared immediately overhead as a storm had suddenly come to Elangal. Baytel touched the hilt of his sword and felt its magic surge through him, awakening the magic within him.

Baytel looked at Areus and said, "Stay close."

Chapter 44

ADETIN Gar counted the remaining men at camp. After Kalti departed with the druids and the deaths of the patrolmen and sentry, his thieves now numbered forty. At one time not so long ago, Gar thought his band of thieves mighty and their hidden sanctuary impervious to the forces and influences of the realms and their petty disagreements. Now the aura of commanding fear from any who passed through Elangal Forest seemed to be a distant memory as his thieves were experiencing uncertainties of their strengths and considerable confusion about continuing to work their trade. Their brash ways and carefree bravura had been supplanted by outright fear for their own lives. Adetin Gar did not exclude himself from these consternations.

Gar altered the patrol routine to shorter intervals while he and Telek aimed their travel in the same direction that Kalti, Baytel and Areus had gone in. He found the men scouted more earnestly since Trun's death, altogether attentive that negligent security could mean death with the goblin horde in the forest. Additional watches were posted around camp and Gar received immediate reports from the returning patrols.

Adetin Gar returned from a short ride of the perimeter of the main body of his men and was in the back of the elongated position when he heard a horse approach. He turned, seeing Telek, and reined in and waited while the men continued their march. It had been four days since the druids and Kalti had separated and Gar was somewhat relieved but also troubled about the fact that they had not come across any sign of the goblin horde. Either they had skirted the area the horde traveled, or something was amiss.

As Telek rode up, Gar noted his frown. "Adetin, the afternoon patrol has not reported back and it is getting late. Do we send the dusk patrol out or wait for their to return?"

Displeased at the routine's interruption, Gar could see Telek was more so. Telek had been a soldier during the Southland war and, unable to bear the idea of farm life afterward, never returned home and they had been riding together since. Through the years Gar found his council wise, his strength and bravery second to none and his loyalty beyond question. Telek always knew the correct order for whatever situation arose, but kept to the chain of command and always waited for Gar to give the command.

Gar replied, "Patrols have been late before. Give them time but keep the other patrols here for now."

Telek was about to say something but held his tongue.

"What is it?" Gar asked with an edge to his voice that he had been finding difficulty holding back. He was still upset at himself for allowing Baytel any consideration and placing his men in so dangerous a situation.

"It is Malin's patrol, Adetin."

"Malin! Cannot he keep to his orders? My sister's ways of raising her children escape all reason!" Cursing until he exhausted every possible profanity, Gar, finally calmer, said, "Give him a little more time, but not too long. We are approaching the area of Belwas Swamp so tell the men to keep sharp. If he is not back soon you and I will take the next patrol."

He watched Telek ride back toward the point. Telek slowed to personally inform the men that Belwas was near so they must keep on the trail. As he warned the men, in his bellowing voice he began singing, which always was a welcome intrusion.

"A maiden in waitin' dressed right for the evenin', with skirts of white-lily, just as proper as can be.
A tall man in fine coat donned with cape came a callin', for attention and purpose and a hand full of charm.
A huntsman come enter, barrel chest and built slender, offered words to the maiden, and in a blush she obliged.
Fancied man came a courtin' till he saw her a floatin' in the arms of the huntsman, lily-white skirts risin' high.
The two men went a tanglin', left the maiden in shambles, till an old handsome thief stole her away for his own."

After some laughter and with their captured attention, Telek said, "Ah! Belwas Swamp, the living swamp nestled in the center of Elangal Forest. No one with any sense would enter that place willingly, men. Yet some men do. Those who have braved into Belwas Swamp are lost forever, save for a few who escaped with no mind, crazed and babbling nonsense, so heed what I say, and stay clear of the mist."

"Have you been in Belwas Swamp, Telek?" asked one of the young woodsmen.

"Lad, do you know what it is like in there? I quake with fear of the deadly bog. What darkness awaits in a swamp where there is no soil. Where the trees of the swamp grow out of crevasses, their gnarled roots intertwining between and under rocks like fingers groping for a possession of earth, grasping onto the only life-nurturing hold they can find in a desperate haste to existence. They defend these claims, you see, with such viciousness that no man or beast is safe. To survive in Belwas Swamp, the sponge-like mosses and fungus have warped into growths the likes of which will haunt your dreams. The air is sodden, heavy, penetrating; it's like breathing in cotton. But worse than that is to lose your sense of direction, which leads to wandering aimlessly into many other perils. Oh, yes, men, Belwas Swamp is alive, just as alive as you and I."

"What other perils could there be?" asked the young thief, already fearing the swamp.

"If being lost and blind in its mist does not drive you to madness, then surely the engulfing mud bogs, trapvine plants that eat flesh and poisonous needle lily bushes will. Deadly snakes and enormous insects live among the heavy foliage and strike with lightning quickness. Yet the worst of all undesirable ways to die in Belwas Swamp is being at the mercy of the great swamp cats. They are larger than man and devour all that dare enters their territory. But men, let us not worry for none of these dangers live outside the swamp. So stay focused, men. We are safe outside the mist or the goblins will be the least of our problems."

Adetin Gar listened to Telek relaying the details of the deadly swamp. His ability to orate the threat without panicking the men seemed to somehow lighten their sprits and ease their hearts even at danger's doorstep.

Afternoon came and Malin's patrol had not returned. Gar was about to send another patrol when he heard someone hailing from behind. Turning, he could see one of the men running toward him from the back of the column.

"Hold up, men. Telek, who is that?"

Telek shook his head and replied irritably, "He is one of Malin's patrol men."

They galloped to the man and stopped as the scout bent over to catch his breath.

Gar demanded, "Where is the rest of the patrol?"

"Malin sent me back," he said, still panting from the run.

"What for?" asked Gar.

The scout hesitated.

Telek barked, "Come on man, out with it!"

"Malin was patrolling recklessly and I told him so. Sir, he was not taking special care, hurrying through thickets, causing too much noise for the patrol to serve its purpose. I spoke up and Malin got angry and dismissed me."

Gar asked, "How long ago?"

"It was late in the afternoon. It took me about an hour to reach you here."

"Where was your last position together?" asked Telek.

"Near the basin where the wild corn grows. Malin was convinced that was where goblins were probably headed. To stock up on food," he answered.

"Why did he not stay in the ordered pattern?"

The soldier shrugged. "He said his way was best. He wanted to be the one to waylay the goblins."

"What is in his head, rocks?" shouted Gar. "These beasts are meat eaters! What does he expect them to do, sit down and peel corn for a picnic? Dolt! Damn and blast!"

Gar dismounted, took his pack and strung it on his back. With his sword secured at his hip, he said, "Telek, let's leave our horses with the men. No sense in announcing our presence while looking for my fool of a nephew. Soldier, take my horse. You are point now. Keep the men moving west toward Konart Pass. Belwas Swamp is a little ways north of here, so keep your eyes and ears open. Scout only our perimeter. Do not send any more patrols outbound until we return. Let's go, Telek."

"Should you and I split up? We can search more ground that way," asked Telek.

"No. We stay together."

The forest was darkening and still with no sign of Malin's patrol, Adetin Gar's state of mind went from frustration to concern, and toward fear at the prospect of not finding Malin before nightfall. Finding the wild corn basin, and searching around its edge, Gar saw movement in the corner of his eye. There, entering the corn, Gar saw a dwarf at the same moment the dwarf saw him. Both stopped. Neither held any advantage over the other as the dwarf stood entirely still on the opposite side of the corn, his feet solidly planted and his weapon, a delve-axe from what Gar could make out, hung casually in his hand.

Telek leaned toward Gar. "A dwarf in these parts?"

Gar nodded. "Curious. Isn't it?"

Gar hailed, "Dwarf, what is your business in Elangal Forest?"

"Minding my own business. What is yours?" the dwarf responded.

Gar smirked, amused by the typical dwarf response. Not wanting to cross a dwarf, he hailed, cheerfully, "Well, let us approach one another and talk. We have no quarrel with any dwarf."

The dwarf did not respond but strode toward them. He had the look of all dwarfs, sturdy and strong, stocky build, and the eyes and face of wisdom. He seemed young for a dwarf to be traveling alone, but Gar experienced that most dwarfs were older than they appeared. Perhaps this one was allowed to leave their sect to prove his worth to the elders. The dwarf had sad brown eyes, a pudgy nose and a large chin where a paltry thin beard grew. He was dressed in green and brown pants and shirt and a black tunic and carried a leather backpack.

"Greetings, men of Elangal," said the dwarf.

"Greetings to you, friend dwarf," said Telek.

"Good day, dwarf. I am Adetin Gar and this is Telek. Have you lost your way?" asked Gar. Dwarfs were not fond of disclosing any information about their comings and goings so Gar decided to ease into the conversation.

"No. I know exactly where I am, thank you."

"Well then, how can I be of assistance in my forest?" Gar said, insinuating gently that the dwarf was on his land.

"I need no assistance. I am a short distance from my destination. And to save time and further inquiries: I am traveling through Elangal Forest from Tridling Del," he said.

"A fine day for a stroll, dwarf. I hope you have enjoyed our forest," said Telek.

"Indeed I have," he replied.

"Well if I cannot be of help to you, perhaps you can be of assistance to me?"

"It would be my pleasure to offer you any aid possible," the dwarf said with a bow.

Gar liked the dwarf already. "We are looking for a small patrol of my men. Have you seen men dressed like us in your recent travel?"

"I have seen many things," the dwarf replied. "I have observed a couple of men pass me by most recently; walked by me a couple of paces away without noticing me in the least. A very ineffective patrol if you pardon my saying. Other things crossed my way; strange things."

"What things, friend?"

"As I had remained hidden from view, I noticed shadows pass overhead, high in the tree branches. They were not eagles, nor osprey. Much larger than any bird of prey I have seen before. I couldn't tell what they were. The shadows circled a few times then moved on. Searching for something, I gathered. I sensed danger so I stayed low until they were out of sight."

"Were they searching in the direction of my patrol?" asked Gar urgently.

"If the men I saw was your patrol, yes. The shadows were headed that way," said the dwarf.

"We would be in your debt, friend dwarf, if you could lead us to where you last saw the patrol. It is imperative we find them." Gar spoke with the knowledge that living in the debt of a dwarf is a solemn charge to carry. The memory of a dwarf is long.

The dwarf pondered, with one hand to his chin and his index finger raised along the side of his head, contemplating the offer, and finally replied, "I accept your obligation. Follow me." The dwarf led them to the place he hid and pointed to the tracks of Malin's patrol.

"Telek, follow the tracks ahead. We will watch our backs." No sooner than taking a few strides up the path, Telek hailed them. Gar and the dwarf ran forward, finding Telek bent over the tracks.

"Goblin tracks are mixed together with the patrol. They are fresh."

Without a word, Gar bolted up the trail at a run with Telek leaving the dwarf behind. Ahead, a clearing came into view. As they reached the outer edge of the clearing, a cry of anguish escaped Gar's throat.

Upon the trees that defined the perimeter of the clearing, spiked and hanging above the ground, were Malin and his patrol. They were dead; their stomachs cut open and insides pulled out of their midsections. Anger swept Gar to immobility; he fell to his knees. In all the wars and battles he was involved in, he had never witnessed such inhuman brutality.

Telek and the dwarf began carefully removing the bodies from the trees, placing them upon the ground with gentle solemnity.

The dwarf stood amid the bodies, shaking his head in disgust and disbelief. "What are these creatures who would perform such an act of viciousness?"

Solemnly, Telek answered, "They are from the Southland. An evil power created these monsters and released them against the Citadel Druids, and anyone else that stands in their way. We encountered them for the first time some days ago. They were goblins, but were transformed by a dark magic the Southland now wields."

Gar finally rose to his feet and spoke through his grief. "You said earlier that you saw things flying above. What did they look like?"

Scanning the high branches to recollect his memory, the dwarf said, "Smaller than man, larger than dwarf. The were cruel looking, even from afar, and their wings black and spread wide." The dwarf suddenly pointed through the boughs. "There is smoke to the east."

Gar looked in dismay at the rising smoke. "The men! The goblins are attacking us!"

Without a word to the dwarf, he and Telek bounded heedlessly toward the smoke. All Gar could hope for was his men to hold off the goblin horde long enough for them to help, but he knew it was wishful thinking. He slowed, seeing in the distance a darkened stain between the green of the forest. An eerie feeling came over Gar as he led Telek and the dwarf, who had followed, toward the stain.

Dusk had crept into the forest and an uncomfortable quiet inhabited the area. The greenwoods looked as if lightning had struck and burned a wound into the forest. Logs lay smoldering upon the ground, the smoke curling off the charred bark in wisps. As Gar stepped into the clearing, he felt Telek grab his arm. He looked at the old soldier and saw tears well up in his eyes. Then Gar looked again upon the charred patch, realizing what he now saw, his own tears blurring his vision. What he had thought logs were the remains of his men; decimated, unrecognizable, and burned dead. He fell to his knees in shock with Telek in wide-eyed anger at the horror. The dwarf had stayed at the perimeter, barely visible through the smoke rising off the men.

"It is madness, senseless murder. All our men…dead." Gar felt his strength drain away as despair set in. All he could do was hold onto Telek, who returned his hold equally; both a small comfort to one another.

A loud crack resonated as one of the burning greenwood trees fell across the charred clearing, snapping Adetin Gar out of his anguish. He looked skyward to see if any goblins flew but all he saw were the rolling gray clouds of a coming storm. Thunder sounded in the distance and lightning flashed the sky. He looked down upon his band of thieves, remembering the laughter and merriment he shared with them, and his despair turned to anger, and thoughts of revenge.

The dwarf was at the base of the clearing, inspecting the grounds. In an attempt to take his mind off the death of all his men, Gar asked, "What are you called, dwarf, and where is your country?"

Still not taking his eyes off the ground, the dwarf said, "I am Dirk Ironwright of Ctiklat Mountain."

"Ctiklat Mountain, eh?" said Telek. "A ways from your home, dwarf."

Gar was pleased that the dwarf did not hold back as strangers usually do. "What are you doing in Elangal?"

Finally looking up, Dirk Ironwright replied, "I am looking for a man who is believed to be traveling through these woods."

"Why do you seek this man? Do you seek revenge of some sort?" asked Gar, for if any man wronged a dwarf, the dwarf's soul could not rest in the hereafter until the wrong was righted by death or deed. Some dwarfs spent entire lifetimes seeking vengeance or deeds to pave the trail of their afterlife unburdened.

"No. Revenge is not the purpose of finding this man. I seek him out to join with him as a fighter and companion."

Adetin Gar stepped nearer to the dwarf, eyeing him suspiciously. "Ctiklat Dwarfs do not volunteer themselves as companions to others. They stay among their own kind or by themselves on personal quests. You are an oddity, Dirk Ironwright."

Ignoring the declaration, Ironwright pointed away from the charred clearing into the woods. "I believe the monsters are marching northwest. From the signs here at the perimeter, your men must have wounded a few of them. Here, you see spots of black blood leading away."

Gar disregarded the dwarf's changing the subject, and not wanting to press the young dwarf about his quest, answered, "Their blood turns to an acid and burns their own flesh."

"Adetin, my guess is they are traveling to find the druids," said Telek, pointing up the trail. "They head toward Baytel, Areus, and Kalti."

"Baytel!" The dwarf spat out the name excitedly. "You said, 'toward Baytel'!"

Gar approached the dwarf and asked, "What do you know of Baytel?"

"I know nothing about him except that I was told to seek him out and journey with him," answered Ironwright.

"Who sent you?" Gar's annoyance rekindled.

The dwarf held up his hands and said, "Put your minds to ease, gentlemen. I do not seek Baytel to cause him harm, but to accompany him in his quest. My uncle spoke to me of him on my last visit. He said my deeds of life could be fulfilled if I travel in his company. So I seek him out for that purpose."

Gar was shocked to curious silence. The circumstance of meeting up with a Ctiklat Dwarf who was directed to seek out this Citadel Druid to quest with him was, at that moment amid the events taking place, baffling. He wondered what other bewildering happenings were to come.

The dwarf was looking up the trail. "Adetin Gar, if what you say is true, that these demons head toward Baytel, we must stop them. We must overtake them or warn him. We must leave now. We waste time here."

"Hold now, Dirk of the Ctiklat. Before we move we want to know who this uncle is, and how he knew of Baytel, and then we will decide our next move, and if it includes your company," said Telek.

The dwarf nodded at the logic and said, "My uncle is Make Ironwright of the Ctiklat Dwarfs. He was one of a company who quested alongside many brave men against evil long ago. He said Baytel came to him in Tridling Del by way of an old friend and riding companion but did not mention his name."

Telek asked, "The blacksmith in Tridling Del? That Make Ironwright?"

"He is my uncle."

Gar's eyes met Telek's, and their thoughts went back to the story Baytel and Areus told of the beginning of their quest. Baytel's words and this dwarf's rang true.

"Well, Dirk, we met up with Druid Baytel and his companion Druid Areus a few weeks back. One of our companions travels with them. But before we relay the story of our meeting and the events that have taken place since, you are right, we need to move."

"Do you know where he is?" asked Dirk Ironwright.

"No," said Gar, "but if we follow this murderous goblin horde, we should find him soon enough, for Baytel and Areus are who they hunt."

With one last look at the dead, he and Telek and the dwarf Dirk Ironwright set upon the trail of the goblin horde.

Chapter 45

THUNDEROUS rain pounded down. The storm clouds eclipsed the twilight as the deep green woodland turned black. Brilliant flashes of lightning streaked the forest allowing Baytel, crouched low beside Areus, to distinguish the goblins marching through the thickets.

"I do not know what Kalti is up to but if we are to fight, I want to attack first. The element of surprise is our only advantage," Baytel whispered with care.

"Right. They will surely panic and run away." Areus's sarcasm was his way of relieving tension, and heartened Baytel.

As the goblins came close and the lightning shattered the darkness, Baytel could see their features clearly. Their misshapen forms showed strength and power, yet they seemed awkward, as if unaccustomed to their own bodies.

"I like what I see, Baytel. They are not marching in an orderly fashion. Overconfidence will be their undoing," whispered Areus, through the low ferns beside him.

Areus's words sounded distant to Baytel, for once he gripped his sword, he was overcome by magic surging through his body. It pulsated with life searching in the darkness of his being until finding its base only to flow deeper. As it came under his control, his entire being was revitalized and he readied for battle.

The goblins entered an opening in the woods. Their steps arrogant, defined, uncaring of anything but themselves. Or was it just lack of the obvious carefulness they were used to. "Overconfident may be a stretch, Areus. They are just sloppy." The goblins shoved each other when one crossed another's path, unconcerned with any dangers that might exist within the surrounds. It reminded Baytel of the Retinue in Tridling Del.

They came within yards of him, and Baytel could feel their presence and he sensed his magic was alerting him of another being of magic in the vicinity. Baytel wondered about the magic the goblins might possess, its power, their ability to wield it, and knowing its origin came from his brother, he thought of whether Ravek's magic was superior to the one so recently discovered in himself.

The answers, he knew, would come, and soon. Baytel leaned toward Areus to signal to attack when the sound of an arrow in flight gave him pause. The next instant, the lead goblin dropped almost at his feet with an arrow protruding from his forehead. The goblins changed direction and charged toward where the arrow had come. Another arrow flew, and from a different location, piercing the chest of another goblin. Kalti, with only two arrows, wrought enough confusion to allow the druids to attack as Baytel charged from the recesses, sword unsheathed and brilliant, illuminating the fern clearing as he and Areus struck fast and furious.

Baytel downed the nearest goblin and Areus drove another goblin back against the trunk of a tree swinging his broadsword and slicing across its underbelly bringing the goblin to the ground in a shrieking rage.

The goblins reacted fast and redirected their attack rushing toward them both. Baytel maneuvered away from Areus and engaged a hulking beast of a goblin that held a heavy saber in one hand and spear in the other. The beast was twice his size and it glowered with maniacal eyes. The monster charged, his saber whooshing violently past Baytel's. Baytel spun, sidestepped a spear thrust and brought his sword down, severing the goblin's sword hand from its arm.

Baytel raised his sword to kill the one-handed goblin, when a horrific scream came from high in the trees. He looked up to see what it was but a rush of air whirled around him and something slammed him to the ground.

Stunned from the blow, but aware enough to tumble away from whatever hit him, Baytel rolled until coming to a stop against a fallen tree. Rising awkwardly to his knees, head spinning and vision blurred, Baytel looked across at the creature rising from the ferns reaching its feet. Its leather-like wings fully spread, exposing the horror of this brother's making. The winged goblin brandished only a sword. The beast strode with uncertain steps toward him. At the same time, the one-armed goblin staggered toward him. Then it stopped seeing something in the ferns. It was then Baytel realized he had lost his sword.

The one-arm dropped his spear and was reaching for Baytel's sword that lay a few feet away. The goblin gripped its hilt and began to raise it when fire erupted from the steel of the sword and sprang up the goblin's arm. The goblin screamed in horror and, dropping the sword, fell to the ground engulfed in flames.

Baytel regained his wits and, retrieving the sword, plunged it into the neck of the burning goblin, and in the same motion turned and faced the flying goblin's penetrating stare.

"Prince Baytel, is it? Yes! Yes it is! The Southland traitor! We Pitheans all thought you dead! But here you are before me!"

Astonished at being recognized by name, but finally able to lay to rest any doubt of the goblin's origin being Pithean, Baytel kept his sword pointed at the creature and maneuvered for better battle position. The goblin's unbridled loathing was written across its horrible face. Its leer was filled with a hatred begotten from some deeply ingrained wickedness. Being so near, he felt the goblin's evil magic as if it was a perceptible plague. The goblin opened and closed his black wings, flaunting himself, showing him to be an incarnation of his creator Ravek.

"How does it feel, Prince Baytel, to be the spark that caused what you see before you?"

The goblin's declaration shocked him. "Yes, boy, had you not come back to your home and revealed how powerful you had become, your precious Citadel and loyal druids would be alive today to interfere as usual. Now they lie dead in a pool of their blood in a ruined fortress."

Bile rose from his stomach catching in his throat, its bitter taste equal to the revulsion that stood in front of him. Disgust and anger flashed through Baytel. He looked away for an instant, noting Areus keeping several goblins at bay.

The winged goblin struck out at Baytel and their swords clashed. Baytel stepped away from the enemy blade, allowing it to pass, and maneuvered to face the goblin's next assault.

The goblin seemed set upon talking while he fought; his first mistake. "What a fool you were to return. Had you expected a warmer welcome back into the bosom of your family, Prince?"

They clashed swords again, but Baytel met his blows with ease. The winged goblin was a foolish fighter and showed flaws with every attempted incursion. The claw-like stumps that once were his feet were slow and announced every movement that followed. But Baytel stayed cautious.

The goblin ranted on. "They condemned you the day you first abandoned the realm, you know. Your father and brother hunted for you, not to welcome you back. No, they wanted you back to set an example of what happens to a traitor to the realm. Your execution before all would have shown that disloyalty to King Vokat and Prince Ravek would not go unpunished, no matter who you are. But that does not matter. Soon my blade will drip with your blood and all the South-land will rejoice in your death."

Baytel, tired of the prattle, swiped his sword toward the goblin's head. The goblin met his sword, turned, and countered raining strike after strike as fast as he could. Then the goblin backed away, and verbally accosted him with another droll remark. "I will personally give your head to Prince Ravek. Oh traitor prince, my reward will be great. I will be promoted to commander of a winged legion and shall rain terror over the northlanders. The Southland storm is coming, Prince Baytel, and you can do nothing about it."

The goblin charged and, just as he came within striking distance, flew up, slashing down at him. Baytel deflected the sword away and stabbed upward but missing as the winged goblin flew higher. Baytel darted to take a position between the trees keeping the goblin from a direct line of attacking from the air. But with the maneuver the monster was momentarily hidden in the canopy. Also, Baytel realized his shimmering sword was a disadvantage, as the goblin could easily locate him. He waited in his own brilliance knowing the assault would come quick. Then he saw the goblin diving toward him.

Baytel rolled and sprang to his feet bringing his sword up for protection and as their swords clashed, they rang out. The goblin flew high again, retreating into the boughs. Baytel bolted deeper into the hardwoods for concealment. A glance in Areus's direction showed Areus battling three goblins at once using the same tactic. Areus dueled, drawing the goblins in and striking fast from concealment, only to disappear and pounce once more from an entirely different place.

Patience was the strategy he and Areus employed, and while the battle was prolonged arrows flew from Kalti's hidden bow. Baytel and Areus engaged goblin after goblin, striking without mercy as one by one they fell dead.

The winged goblin dove again, then suddenly halted in midflight, hovering above Baytel, his hideous wings beating wildly to keep in place. The creature maneuvered sideways and back, always within sword reach as he stabbed and swept, exchanging blow after blow with Baytel. Yet, Baytel read each shift and strike, as if the goblin had announced them before hand. In a way, Baytel was toying with the creature, which would eventually expose a fatal flaw. It did not take long before Baytel recognized an opportunity, and as the goblin reared back to arch his sword, Baytel sliced across both his legs. The goblin screeched in pain and withdrew into the treetops.

Another large goblin charged from the woods. Baytel blocked each blow the brute delivered but it was powerful and had backed him against a tree. Baytel ducked to avoid his head being taken off and its sword struck the greenwood and stuck. Without hesitation, Baytel plunged his sword deep.

Baytel heard the crash of branches from above and knew the winged goblin was diving at him. He tried to free his sword but it was stuck in the large goblin. He let go and pulled out his dagger and turned to face the diving goblin. The goblin seemed to falter in midflight and then a terrible scream ripped from his throat as he plummeted hard to the ground at his feet. Baytel looked down at the goblin, its body and wings twisted and broke from the impact. Using the toe of his boot, Baytel turned the winged monster over and saw an arrow deeply embedded in the goblin's head. Kalti's marksmanship was beyond compare.

The battle versus the goblin horde continued to progress but in a methodical and slow manner as the surviving monsters had caught on to the druids' tactics. The horde kept their distance and then attacked in groups while others in their troop crept through the trees, attempting to surround Baytel and Areus, but again, Kalti's arrows thwarted their strategy.

A lightning bolt struck a huge greenwood outside the clearing sending a charge into the forest. Then the rain increased tenfold. Baytel found Areus and pulled him toward the deep woods to find a point where they could hold off the goblins, but wherever they went, the goblins were already there. It was to no avail as Baytel's retreat maneuver backfired, creating an opening for the goblins that cut off any possible escape, and the fighting intensified. Soon the two druids were fighting back-to-back, surrounded and fending off assault after assault.

A shout from the thickets was followed by two of Kalti's arrows finding two goblins, and suddenly from out of the brush appeared Adetin Gar with Telek at his side and a dwarf swinging a strange sort of axe, striking the front line of goblins with extraordinary skill.

Gar shouted in Baytel's ear, "Fall back and follow Kalti!"

Too stunned to question, he grabbed Areus by the cloak and swung him toward the fleeing archer.

The fight turned to a footrace as Kalti led them away. Baytel did not know what was happening, only that the moment was being dictated to him and all he could do was follow. He shouted to Kalti, "Where are you leading us?"

Kalti turned as he ran, not missing a step. "Belwas Swamp. Follow closely. Stay on my trail."

Baytel sheathed his sword on the run and quickly glanced back at the pursuing horde and saw one take flight. "Another winged goblin! Keep a watch above yourselves." Abruptly, the air became difficult to breath. A cold dampness settled around them and the surroundings turned gray. Then, in the next few steps, as sudden as a flash, all was still. The blowing and howling wind had disappeared and Baytel was immediately enveloped in a dark mist. The rain stopped; at least it stopped dropping from the sky as the raindrops now seemed to hang in the humid air, as if unsure in which direction to fall. The hard forest soil had turned into a sodden, sponge-like cushion and Baytel found his boots pressed deep into the soggy earth making traction difficult.

Kalti slowed their pace while leading them through the dense mist. Gar hailed from just ahead of him for Kalti to halt. Baytel was so disoriented that he thought Gar had been behind him the entire time. He was handed a rope from ahead but did not see who it was.

He heard Gar say, "Secure the rope to the one behind and in front of you so we do not lose track of ourselves. Stay close and do not strain the rope. Keep in the footprints of the one in front of you and listen to Kalti's instructions. Do not deviate."

Baytel tied himself to who he found to be Gar and then to the dwarf behind him. He wondered where the dwarf had come from but questions and introductions would have to wait. An unseen Kalti began to move and all followed, advancing deeper into the tangle of wetness and mist of Belwas Swamp, certain the goblin horde would not be far behind.

Passage was at a snail's pace, and being blind to the surroundings caused anxious steps and unease of what might jump out at them. Kalti, with his keen eyesight, communicated their trail ahead, carefully relaying exact placements of footsteps and locations of potential dangers of the swamp.

Baytel, toward the back of the group, could barely discern Kalti's warnings and direction, as his voice reached Baytel like a whisper from a spirit within the mist.

"Stay on my tracks."

"Watch for the needle lily bush on the left after the exposed tree root."

"Keep to the center of the trail, away from the right. There is a deep mud bog."

The deathtraps of the swamp were numerous and Kalti's commands became a haven signal of safety. So attuned to the voice from the mist and the hazards along the trail, Baytel lost all sense of time, and it seemed as though an eternity passed while abiding to each command. Day and night were undistinguishable in the swamp. The strain of the entire trek without rest or food was having an adverse effect on Baytel. Even though they were tied to one another, a feeling of isolation and abandonment crept into his mind. Occasionally, he would tug on the rope that led to Gar in front of him and the dwarf behind. Both tugs always drew an immediate response, which was an indicator that they all were feeling the same discomforts. The mist of Belwas Swamp seemed to be penetrating more than their clothing.

Confirmation came to his ear from behind of the steadfast pursuit by the goblin horde. The guttural commands as they called to each other were muffled in the thick swamp air but still offered him enough to detect that their position was close and their pursuit to kill resolute.

When Kalti finally stopped for a rest, they all bunched together and Baytel spoke out. "How many goblins did you see take flight, Adetin?"

"I saw only one. I believe four entered on foot close behind. But I could be mistaken," he answered.

Kalti's voice whispered back to Baytel. "On their trail back in the forest where we saw they divided their force, the trail to our men showed twelve sets of footprints. Had I known they could take flight, I would have taken better care at reading their tracks. They may have a few more in their company that flew in and out of their patrol. But I cannot be certain."

"Belwas will take care of these creatures before long. One misstep here or there, and the goblin horde will be no more," said Telek with assured confidence.

Telek's confidence was comforting, but Baytel knew that they too could fall to the same fate and vowed to continue adhering to Kalti's directions until clear of the dangers as they continued on.

The trail turned and he had to crouch low to keep below an entirely different kind of foliage. The landscape plants became thick meaty leaves of enormous sizes. Now on his knees and sinking into the spongy ground, Baytel felt the rope connected to the dwarf was as taut as a bowstring. He seemed to be dragging the dwarf forward. He tried to hail Gar to slow the progress but his voice died in the thickness of the landscape.

Emerging from the heavy foliage was not the relief Baytel had hoped for. Belwas Swamp had become deadly quiet, as if something dark and sinister lay waiting somewhere in the mist. A sense of foreboding came to Baytel that they were lost and there was no end to their blind trek and no forgiveness from the swamp. The flight from the goblin horde into the swamp tested his will. He recalled the resolve Calidor exhibited during the snowstorm back at his cabin and found the strength to pull himself together and keep his mind away from failure and fright, and on the path at his feet and Kalti's instructions. Yet no matter how confident and in control Baytel was, he had no control of the others, and was ultimately dependent upon each one on the rope to survive. His rope attached to Gar and the dwarf. Who was behind the dwarf, and who was ahead of Gar?

Adetin Gar, Telek and the dwarf had come to their rescue when surrounded by the goblins and it brought to mind the thieves. *Where were the other thieves?*

From behind a loud twang of a snapping vine was followed by a blood-wrenching scream that filled the misty stillness. A second scream came from the gray darkness and slowly faded until all was silent once more.

"What happened?" asked the dwarf, seeking an answer but more likely needing to remind everyone he was still among them.

Baytel heard Gar reply. "Vine trap, Dirk. The vine snaps and tightens around its prey until dead, then feeds off their flesh. It sounded like two of them were caught in the vine."

One mystery solved. I now know the name of the dwarf. Dirk.

The troop moved on able to stand once more. Then the ground began to rise and Baytel found they were hiking up a steep slope. Yet the ground remained sponge-like, and they made halting process, spending more strength on compromised footing and the steep angle of ascent. Nevertheless, the steepness of the terrain proved they were traversing up a foothill, or what seemed to him to be a small mountain. Occasionally, the slope leveled and they traveled a short distance on flat ground only to meet with the slope again. Baytel was on such a flat when he stopped in his tracks hearing the sound of something stumbling ahead of him. He did not feel a tug on the rope and quickly, Kalti called for a stoppage. Baytel listened intently to what seemed like something struggling forward of their position. A rushed intake of breath came out of the mist followed by a frightened shriek. The goblin's breath came in quick gasps until a hard swallowing gulp and nothing more was heard.

Telek spoke up. "Murk bog. Death is what the creature sought and death is what it found. The land bestows equally to what one offers and the righteous shall reap the glories of life. We tender good will and we are embraced by the good of the land; even here in the drudges of Belwas Swamp."

Baytel smiled at Telek's huge repertoire of quotes and statements, always recited with profound poetic eloquence and wondered if the old soldier was ever a member of a traveling thespian group that roamed from town to town.

The soil hardened at the next ledge and though footing was still steep and hard to climb, the ground was firm rock. Baytel could finally distinguish a trail and wondered briefly whether it was man or beast that had blazed it. The thought passed because at the moment he did not care who or what had formed it, only that it felt solid.

Snap!

"Drop to the ground!" yelled Kalti.

Baytel fell flat as the sound of many arrows whisked by in the still air and then the multiple thuds telling of the end of their flight sounded. A creature began to suffocate, its labored suffering finally calmed as it exhaled in death. The arrows had found their mark in another goblin.

"Needle lilies," said Kalti. "Another is dead."

No one spoke, withdrawn as Baytel was, all wondering what device of the swamp would cause their demise. His own private thoughts moved from realizing their good fortune to have survived the swamp so far, to no longer concerned with the goblin horde, to fearing Belwas Swamp itself.

The mountain slope steepened and the air was easier to breathe. A gentle wind wafted through the swamp but the mist stayed thick and damp. His body was tiring. His muscles were tasked to their limits. Foliage through the mountainous swamp still brushed against him on the path, unpleasant, dangerously uninhabitable. With complete exhaustion nearing and no open ground to camp anywhere in sight, their only course was to plod ahead, unsure where the trail led and if at its end they would find their survival or their deaths.

A blood-chilling scream sounded from the darkness above, and Baytel recognized the attack cry of a flying goblin. Before he could get a bearing and draw his sword, the goblin rammed into him. The last thing he saw was a sword slicing through the air cutting the rope attached to Adetin Gar. Forced off the trail by the collision, Baytel lost his footing and crashed through the foliage. Then the bottom fell out and he dropped over a ledge, falling in a weightless downward plunge.

Chapter 46

ADETIN Gar heard the screech, but before he could react, he was pulled backward by Baytel's line and dragged off the trail. Gar slipped over an unseen ledge and fell until the slack from above went taut and jarred him to an abrupt stop. His back was wrenched, the rope digging into his waist as he dangled in mid-air. Unable to see more than a few feet in the gray mist, he lost sight of the ledge. The line attached to Baytel bore no weight. Feeling around for it, Gar pulled it up and found it was severed clean away.

"Baytel! Dirk! Are you near?" His voice sounded dead in the thick air. Hailing repeatedly but hearing no response from the two that were attached to one end of the line, he called upward to those of the other end still on the trail. "Areus, pull me up!"

No response. Suspended horizontal with the land; the rope gripped about his waist held all his weight and was arching his strained back uncomfortably. Grabbing high on the rope he straightened to a vertical position and reached for the slope. His hand made contact with a plant and snatched it for a purchase. Gar hauled at it when suddenly the plant, on its own accord, fastened on to his arm.

"Trapvine! Blast and damn!"

The vine continued to crawl up his arm, tightening its clench along the way. Determination edged its way into his actions and with his other hand Gar drew his dagger and hacked wildly at the trapvine. The trapvine finally released its grip and he swung free. He kept his dagger at the ready as the rope swung back and forth in the mist, coming precariously close to the cliff and a glimpse of the deadly trapvine plant.

Gar climbed higher on the rope and resumed hailing when he finally heard a return hail, recognized Telek's baritone voice. "Adetin! Baytel! Dirk! Can you hear me?"

Gar shouted up the slope. "I am here. Pull me up fast. There is trapvine on the slope." The line dropped a few feet and, after a short hesitation, he was heaved upward and flew over the ledge and landed against Telek as both fell to the ground.

Relief swept over him being back on the trail, the same trail he feared a few moments ago. Huddled around him were Areus, Kalti and Telek.

Areus asked, "Where are Baytel and the dwarf?"

Gar showed him the cut line. "They must have fallen to the bottom of that ravine. I hailed for them, but got nothing."

"I have a longer rope. We can lower someone farther enough down to hopefully raise them," said Telek.

"I'll go," said Areus.

Gar replied. "No. If they cannot be found, your survival is essential to whatever plans you druids are at. Tie the rope to me. Kalti, find an area off the trail that is free of this trapvine plant. It took hold of me and wouldn't let go until I cut myself free."

Telek tied the long rope to him and secured the other end onto he and Areus. Kalti led them to the place where no trapvine grew.

"When I slap the line three times, that is the signal to pull me up quickly and be ready to cut any trapvine off me."

Gar gripped the rope. "Now, down we go. Keep an open eye for more flying goblins." He looked back at Telek, saying, "Hold on tight."

Areus smiled back at him and said, "Don't worry about a thing. We won't let go. But if we lose our footing, we'll see you at the bottom."

"Comforting." Gar edged toward the opening in the foliage off the trail. "Here I go."

Gar slipped over the side and dangled, twisting as they lowered him into the unknown. Unable to see past his outstretched arm, he stopped the mid-air twisting by reversing the perpetual motion, and soon steadied the descent.

Hailing frequently through the gray, cotton-like air, he still heard nothing from the druid or dwarf. His foot inadvertently touched the slope and trapvine immediately clung to it and advanced quickly up his leg. He took out his dagger, cutting away the attacking trapvine, when another creeper seized his knife hand. Struggling to free his sword with his other hand, he let go of the rope. The trapvine moved too quickly. With one arm immobile, he ignored the impulse to attack the vine with his sword and slapped the line once, twice, and was about to slap for the third when the vine caught his other hand and trapped it, paralyzing him to the rope.

Gar felt the trapvine creep across his body, tightening with great force as it advanced upward. More of the creeping plant joined in the attack, increasing the constricting pressure. Breathing became difficult. He hailed, "Pull me..." and then the vine was around his mouth and throat. The seconds passed like hours as he involuntarily held his breath. The trapvine constriction became unbearable. His vision began to blur. He became disoriented. Flashes of tiny starlights dotted his sight and he knew oblivion was not far off.

At the moment he sensed the darkness of death, he felt the vine loosen about his mouth and chest. Gar filled his lungs. A flash of a sword crossed before his blurred vision. He felt the motion of the rope once more and realized he was floating away from the creepers.

A knife was cutting the vines that had crept across his body. It was Areus slicing them away. But the trapvine, though cut from the slope, still attacked. Gar gasped, "Cut my right arm free!"

Areus did and Gar was able to help cut the remaining vine from the slope. Areus slapped the rope three times and they were hauled up.

Safely upon the trail once more, Gar could see the trapvine pursue, creeping across the trail toward him. He unsheathed his sword and cut at it until it receded.

"Bloody trapvine."

Gar turned to Areus, and said, "Thanks. I was lost down there."

"Did you hear anything from below?" Areus asked.

"Nothing. I cannot imagine those two surviving the fall, let alone the dangerous plant life along the way."

"I'll try this time," said Areus.

"No. It is too dangerous," said Gar.

"We cannot walk away from them! We can find them!"

"Areus, there is no way down and we will die in the attempt. There is nothing we can do," said Gar, with finality in his voice.

"There is something I can do."

The voice came from out of the mist. As they all turned toward the voice, they saw the mist part, revealing an old man. He was short and walked casually toward them from up the path. Coming from the mist and gliding silently at his side was a black swamp cat, nearly the height of the old man on all four paws.

The old man addressed them again. "Your friends fell into a ravine. The angle of the slope would have deflected their fall. Also, the trapvine does not grow that far down the slope. They should be able to climb up avoiding the deadly plants, if they find the right path. I am certain they will be fine."

Adetin studied the old man, who wore a black robe and dark boots. His gray beard hung down to his chest and his hair drifted wildly out of a pointy black hat. The old man somehow held back the mist around him, as if something about him recoiled the mist. Gar wondered how.

Gar asked, "How do you know they will be alright?"

"This is my home. I know my swamp as well as you know Elangal Forest."

Surprised by the old man's declaration, Gar asked, "How do you know I am from Elangal?"

The old man held up a hand for silence and Gar somehow felt compelled to obey. "You three are the thieves who ride through Elangal. And this fellow I presume is from Kilhalen, eh boy?"

Areus, stupefied, muttered, "Yes, but...?"

As if losing patience, the old man cut off any further questions. "Never mind. Never mind all this, and that, and thus, and such, Kilhalen man with the druid bag. Now is the time to get you all to safety. That I can do."

"What about our friends below?" asked Gar, feeling the old man had something else for them in mind.

"My cat, Azul, will help your friends. He will guide them to where we are bound."

The old man began walking up the path, taking the clear air with him. He stopped and spoke over his shoulder. "By seeing me walking away and taking clear vision with me, an intelligent fellow would presumably fall in step. Do I have to offer sanctuary twice to you obviously lost souls? Come on, stay within my presence. We are not far off."

Gar shrugged. "And you are certain our friends are safe?"

Still walking away, the old man replied, "I am realizing reiteration is necessary when conversing with you all. So yes, they will be fine."

Gar turned to the men and then took the lead in following the clear air surrounding the old man up the trail.

Chapter 47

TWISTED together during the tumble, the dwarf jarred against Baytel's ribcage upon every impact with the slope of the ravine. Each brunt blow bounced him rotating in the air until the next, stealing the wind from his lungs. Then Baytel hit bottom, and he and the dwarf were abruptly slammed against the solid ground finally at a halt.

Baytel rolled away from the base of the cliff taking the dwarf with him while escaping the shower of loosened dirt and rock. When the debris cascade ceased and all was silent, he unraveled the rope from the dwarf and checked his body for injury. Surprisingly, there were only scrapes and what he knew would be deep bruises, but no broken bones and everything else seemed to still work.

The mist remained thick but he could see the dwarf was covered in the rubble at the end of his rope. The dwarf stood, shaking out the dirt from his tunic, grumbling something under his breath. Baytel thought he heard a few curses upon someone's family and those connected thereto.

Baytel asked, "Are you injured?"

"I am alright," he said, gruff yet uninhibited.

A scream came through the mist and this time, Baytel drew his sword. Its glow parted the gray mist and he could see the approaching flight of a winged goblin. Baytel met the diving monster just as it was about to strike and, with a swift upward swipe, cut the monster in two. The last he heard of the goblin was its death screech.

The dwarf had moved, placing his back at the cliff. He stared wide-eyed at the sword. "By the jewels of Minion! What magic you wield! As ancient as thought!"

Baytel looked upon his sword again, still alive with light. He quickly scanned the area where they stood and then up the cliff, studying the terrain before the illumination of the sword receded. The sword kept the mist away for a few more moments and then faded, and the mist engulfed them once more.

During the short altercation with the goblin, Baytel felt the magic ingrain itself to more of him. He realized that each time he used the sword, its magic surged through his body, discovering channels for the magic to develop and identifying for him his powers that were being prepared for use when needed. Baytel wondered: If he did not have the sword in hand, would the magic come to him in another form, and be at his command?

Baytel sensed his magic was still in its infant stages; he could feel its growth. He also felt its unpredictability, and was learning to gain control of the essence of the magic, but it was difficult for there were so many unknowns and the deeper he went with the magic, the more overwhelmed he felt. Nevertheless, he recognized the magic was true and good, and he decided he would use that as a base to control it. And as Baytel pondered these thoughts, the magic within seemed to acknowledge his recognition, and the edginess he felt within the magic eased.

Finally, the magic receded and he focused through the mist on the dwarf still attached to him by the rope. "I saw where we fell from, rather, the path of our fall. We must climb to reach the trail again. Do you have climbing experience?"

"All dwarfs of Ctiklat are trained climbers," he said.

"I could hope for no less. Follow my lead. Call out when you cannot find a proper hold. We should be able to reach the path, but let's be wary of the evils of this swamp."

The dwarf scoffed and replied, "Swamp evil and whatever else that flies our way."

Baytel nodded, though the dwarf would not be able to see the acknowledgment. He asked, "Ready?"

"I am your servant, sir. Lead the way."

Baytel found the peculiar way the dwarf spoke was typical of their kind. Dwarfs were not the easiest people to communicate with. The few he came across at the Citadel were rather stoic and private. But all were a determined lot and he felt confident the dwarf would not be a hindrance.

The cliff was not as steep as he had first thought. From his short perusal with the aid of the sword, the slope looked relatively easy for climbing. However, once on the cliff face he discovered its frailties. Holds were suspect; every few feet, he or the dwarf lost a secure grip and, being tied together, both slid, losing ground.

The ascent was delicate. One foot above the other, arms extended and fingers searching for holds, he pulled straight up from where they had fallen, trying not to deviate from the path of their abrupt descent. At times, no rock was exposed and Baytel had to dig into the dirt of the slope in order to find a secure purchase. Although unfamiliar with one another, Baytel and the dwarf worked the slope and the rocks with careful and exacting proficiency and the dwarf proved to be an excellent line partner. They advanced up the slope without straining each other, outside the occasional slip, and communicated the precise direction to one another effectively. Baytel was reminded of the lessons Druid Roen taught him on the escarpment near the Citadel. The memory of his dead instructor saddened him.

Baytel hailed to their companions on the trail as they climbed, but the mist deadened his voice. Finally, his hand reached above the brim of the ravine and he pulled himself up along with the dwarf and found the trail, but could not see or hear the others.

"How long were we down in the ravine?" the dwarf asked. "Do you think they came after us from up here on the…"?

Thud!

It sounded like a thick branch dropped from above against a rock, cutting off the dwarf's question. Baytel drew his sword and, as it swept the mist away, he found himself before two of the largest goblins he had ever seen. At their feet was the dwarf, unconscious and bleeding from a gash on his forehead.

The smaller of the two hulking creatures drew a quick breath and exclaimed, "Those fools back in the Southland should have searched for your body in that rubble, Prince Baytel."

Baytel stayed mute, studying the grotesquely misshapen winged figures. Dark bulbous eyes that bulged beneath a ridged brow dominated their faces. Their wide mouths revealed sharp, pointed fangs and their disfigured muscular physique was quite disturbing. Seeing the monsters before him, he recalled the sight of his brother writhing in pain in his quarters while his newly formed wings hatched from his back. Both goblins held broadswords and both leered hatefully. Death was all he saw in their eyes.

"You are not who we were after. We couldn't tell which of you was the druid," the smaller one sneered, looking down at the dwarf. "But this is much better, you, Prince Baytel the druid, standing here, and wielding a magic sword no less."

The larger goblin spoke. "A good offering it will be to Prince Ravek. Our reward will be great returning with such a prize, eh?"

Baytel had read them long enough and, unthwarted by their bravado and contempt, replied, "A shallow hope and a reward you shall never see. Look at you both; a sorry existence compared to the proud Pitheans. If Lord Plet knew what my brother created, he would—"

"Lord Plet is an old fool and you are a young one. But you will see the end of your fool's life soon enough," said the smaller goblin. "You are alone. Your friends have long gone up the trail and this dwarf will be no trouble. So the reward is practically in our hands…as will be your head."

The goblin sprang at Baytel, its broadsword missing by inches. Baytel bore down and away to avoid another thrust and on the rise rammed the hilt of his sword down upon the goblin's shoulder and, bringing his knee up into its jaw, sent it stunned to the ground.

Baytel cut the rope still attached to the dwarf and caught the larger goblin's weapon in time before the sword-point pierced his chest. Pushing himself off their entangled swords, Baytel fell back to better position himself for the fight and parried every assault, strike for strike, from the bigger goblin.

The smaller goblin had regained its feet and joined the fight and all Baytel could do was maneuver on the narrow trail fending off blows. The goblin's fighting skills were good; he detected Ravek's style of swordsmanship in both. They fought viciously, attacking with expert maneuvering, playing off one another's tactics to break Baytel's defenses down, but Baytel thwarted each strike deftly for his training far exceeded anything Ravek could have taught. Baytel timed and measured each turn in the battle, balancing his defense with maneuvers that exasperated his opponents, and, all the while, he waited patiently for his chance to kill.

As the fight persisted, the magic of the sword was kindling the fire that grew within him and Baytel was propelled to a higher plane as more recesses of his mind and body opened to the magic, and more of the magical unknowns were revealed to him. It elevated his fighting abilities, and he was glad to have it for the monsters were strong and he had to reach deep within himself to keep them at bay.

They sparred relentlessly yet with intemperate recklessness. Their hate of him took possession of them, but he also sensed their admiration of his sword and an obsession to possess the magic in it.

Backed to the side of the trail, he felt movement behind him and saw a trapvine crawling toward him. He pivoted and slashed at the vine and rolled away up the trail. The maneuver led the smaller goblin to lunge at him and miss. The result was that he and the goblin had switched places and the vine seized the goblin's leg.

The goblin shrieked, slashing at the vine. That created the opening Baytel sought and he sliced the goblin across the arm, nearly cutting it off. The goblin's cry was deafening in the mist as it dropped to the ground in pain. The other goblin charged placing himself in front of the injured goblin and attacked.

They fought strength for strength, blow for blow. The large goblin pounding Baytel with tremendous sweeping blows of fury. The close proximity with the evil sparked something in his magic and he sensed it searching out the powers that drove the goblin. In that instant, Baytel's magic identified the evil source and its dark foundation, but not before Baytel's magic revealed its own origins and showed Baytel its ancient superiority and confirmed that his power was superior to the magic Ravek and his father wielded. With such knowledge, he embraced the magic and allowed the magic to flow free. Now it was no longer the magic of the sword that drove him but his own awakened magic, and its power was entirely his to control. It was exhilarating and magnificent.

Baytel thrust at the goblin and it countered. Baytel blocked its strike, then stabbed at the goblin and moved again to counter another strike. Baytel rolled away, tumbling, avoiding the broadsword swipe and was back to his feet with such quickness he had trouble fathoming his own abilities. Readying for the next strike, he noticed a change had come over the large goblin. For the first time, he saw fear in its eyes.

At the perimeter of his vision the smaller goblin had regained its verve. It unfolded its black wings to take flight. Just as it rose, a roar emerged from deep in the foliage, shattering the stillness of the swamp. A great swamp cat leaped into the battle and caught the lunging goblin's leg in its powerful jaws. With a swipe of a clawed paw, it ripped the goblin's neck open, nearly tearing its head off.

The sudden appearance of the swamp cat startled the larger goblin and, with a swift strike, Baytel plunged his sword deep into the large goblin's chest. Exhausted, he pulled out his sword from the crumpled body and dropped to his knees. Although fatigued, he felt exhilarated, for his magic continued to pulse through him.

He looked up the trail and saw the swamp cat watching him. It was a mammoth cat, with stark black fur and emerald green eyes. The only part not black on the huge animal was one white paw. The cat sat there, staring at Baytel, as if waiting for something. It did not seem remotely interested in attacking him.

A moan from down the trail brought Baytel's attention back to the injured dwarf, who lay motionless. Without a second glance at the cat, he returned to the dwarf and felt for a pulse. He found it weak; the dwarf had lost much blood.

Retrieving the Citadel bag he had discarded during the battle, he quickly treated the head wound as best he could. The swamp cat gave a small roar and he quickly turned, bringing up his sword. The cat just turned and made his way up the trail. It stopped and looked back, giving Baytel another soft growl as if to say, "follow."

After another purr, Baytel said aloud, "I have seen enough to know a friend when one was needed, whatever form it may be in."

He draped Dirk over his shoulder, sheathed his sword and followed the swamp cat closely up the trail as the gray mist enveloped him once more.

Baytel was on the brink of collapse but the constant encouraging growl of his new companion urged him on with the near-dead dwarf draped across his shoulders. When he felt he could no longer go on, a stirring within him confirmed the magic was contributing to his strength. It was a gentle reminder that he could call upon this wild seed within him if needed.

Hiking up the trail gave Baytel time to contemplate the powers he possessed. He had previously grasped that he was not a creature of magic like the goblin horde, rather a catalyst to it, able to channel and wield the power toward a purpose he chose. With this realization, a comfort in a mutual existence with the powers progressed. He perceived that the magic had always been a part of him, latent and waiting to mature, as natural as any other physical changes he experienced from adolescence to adulthood. Even though the magic was new to him, now that he was aware of it, he felt it had been his forever and looked upon the sword as the igniter of the magic that was in all those who possess the blood of the Kings of the North.

The trail became less arduous and the mist began to thin, making breathing easier. The swamp forest on both sides of the trail could be clearly distinguished;

its many hues of green growth. The trap-vines, needle lilies and other death traps looked and remained devious and uninviting. He worried about the others and whether they had succumbed to these perils, but hoped that perhaps the cat had something to do with their survival and it was taking Baytel to them.

The swamp cat continued up the slope, peering back at him through emerald eyes, making sure he still followed. As the slope gradually flattened he was able to narrow the distance between them. Then in a blink of an eye the mist cleared and the heavy foliage of the swamp ended. He found it replaced by the rocky terrain of a mountain.

Stars flickered in the night sky and a crescent moon smiled down. The trail ended at the foot of hewn stone steps that curved around large boulders. The black swamp cat bounded ahead and was quickly out of sight. He followed the hewed steps until they led into a low tunnel carved in the mountainside. Bending, the weight of the dwarf straining his back, he followed the passageway until it emptied onto a plateau.

The sky was filled with brilliant stars. The ground was soft, covered with cut grass. Standing stones were intermixed in random order upon the plateau and around the perimeter of the plateau grew massive pine trees, presumably planted so that a distant observer looking at the top of another precipice would only be able to see some rock outcroppings and tall trees, and not the plateau itself.

At the end of the clearing stood a cabin and what looked like a stable that seemed weathered and worn. Plantings lined the rocks and ivy had grown upon the façade of the cabin, making it nearly impossible to discern as a building. At the opposite end of the clearing, sitting around a campfire, were Adetin Gar, Kalti, Telek and Areus. He was too tired to smile though he was overjoyed to see they were safe. Among them was the swamp cat, and beside the huge cat sat an old man. They all turned at the same time and immediately jumped from the campfire and ran toward him.

The men took the dwarf from his shoulders and carried him to the fire. Baytel said, "I need water to wash his wound. Areus, get your bag and bring your medicines here."

The old man sent Kalti to the cabin and he returned with water and cloth. Areus prepared an ointment while Baytel cleaned the dwarf's wound. The gash was not as deep as he had thought. During the cleansing and sewing of the sutures to close the wound, the old man hovered over Baytel's shoulder whispering to himself. It was annoying Baytel and he nearly told him to back away until he began to listen to what he was saying. It was as though the old man was reading from the Citadel's lesson book of the procedure, reciting in his quiet voice what medicines to apply and the style of stitching he was employing in the suturing and so on.

When Baytel finished, the old man snickered under his breath and mumbled, "Very good. It will heal in no time. The dwarf will be quite happy with the results. Not too much of a scar."

Kalti and Telek carried the dwarf off to the cabin and Gar tapped Baytel on the shoulder. "Baytel, are you injured?"

"I'm bruised and tired, but am alright. How long have you been here, and where is here?" he asked, hearing exhaustion in his voice.

"Do not fret about all that right now, young man," said the old man. "It is time to mend your fatigue with food and rest. Come to the cabin where there is venison and bread, and I have a hearty wine to warm your blood."

The moment Baytel heard the word food, hunger pangs raced through his stomach, but he was also suddenly too weak to rise. Gar and Areus each took an arm and practically carried him to the cabin. He was seated at a wooden table and Areus fed him a hot soup and black bread. After he drained a goblet of red wine, he was led to a bed and without a word he collapsed asleep.

Chapter 48

BAYTEL perceived it to be late afternoon as he hid his eyes behind the blanket from the glaring sunlight coming through the windows of the cabin. As if anticipating the exact moment he woke, Areus entered the cabin carrying a tray of food.

"Good afternoon, my friend. I have for you that venison stew the old man spoke of last night along with black bread, honey and a mug of tea," said Areus, setting the tray on the end table by the bed. "Compliments of the house."

Hunger pains resurfaced again and Baytel rose out of bed only to find that his clothes were missing. "My clothes, Areus? Sword?"

Areus pointed to the bureau standing against the wall. "The sword is there beside the tallboy. The clothes are being washed."

Baytel sat at the table by the window with a blanket wrapped around him and was immediately consumed in the meal.

Areus pulled up a chair and sat across from him. He was not often without a smile on his face and the one he flaunted now seemed overly amusing. Curious, Baytel asked, "What is it?"

"Knowing you as well as I do, Baytel, I chose the dusk patrol so I could give you my splendid company this afternoon to answer the questions you undoubtedly have."

With a mouthful of food, he asked, "Are there any other goblin tracks about?"

"No. You and the Belwas mire disposed of those that pursued us."

Baytel slowed his chewing and thought back to the events that had brought them all here. "I was surprised about the sudden appearance of Adetin, Telek and the dwarf back in Elangal when we were fighting the goblins? What happened that brought them to our aid?"

Areus paused a moment and cleared his throat. "According to Telek's report, the band of thieves was attacked by the goblin horde. Adetin, Telek and Kalti are the only remaining members of their company."

Baytel pushed the tray away. The report took his appetite away. "What happened to them?"

Areus told the story of Adetin Gar and Telek searching for Malin's late patrol and finding them dead and then returning to camp only to discover the massacre.

Baytel hung his head in despair. "We should have escaped from Gar's camp the day we arrived. They all would still be alive today if we had."

"Escape was never an option as you well know. They were not going to let us go so our only avenue was for a parlay. We cannot take responsibility for all that has happened in Elangal. Each man in that forest had a duty to perform, and just because they crossed our path, or we crossed theirs, fate or destiny had their hands in all that occurred. These monsters did not turn back to kill us. They were out to kill anything and anyone that they came across. The thieves would have been stumbled across by the goblin horde whether we meet the thieves or not. The goblins kill all they encounter and do it to keep the element of surprise terror to their advantage throughout their travels."

"But they would have never been in Elangal had it not been for me, Areus!"

Areus waved his hand at him, disregarding his statement. "You had no choice. Providence dictated our travel through Elangal Forest. To think otherwise is absurd. It was the only choice, for our duty to this quest lies to the north, as you well know better than I. Just the same, we could not alter our course around Elangal Forest or more deaths would have happened."

"And still may happen!"

"Yes," Areus agreed soberly. "Yes, they may."

So many were dead and still they had not reached the unwarned druids, fiefdoms and kingdoms with word of the threat. How far the goblins had penetrated into the northlands I still do not know. How many of them are there? They are hunting us as opposed to us hunting them. We must turn the tables soon, or all will be for naught.

"Well," said Areus, pulling Baytel from his thoughts. "As to the dwarf, he came by Tridling Del looking for you when he came across Adetin Gar and Telek. A very serious young dwarf."

"Looking for me? Why was he looking for me?"

"His uncle told him to find you."

"Dwarfs do not lend themselves out for others to lead. They tend to keep to themselves." Baytel recalled the climb of the cliff and the dwarf's injury. "Is he feeling better? He seemed a good sort. Good climber. We scaled that cliff off the trail together. Wait...you said his uncle sent him to find me? What is his uncle's name?"

"Ironwright."

"Make Ironwright?"

"The very one, and I will let him enlighten you in the telling personally. For now, let me tell you what has happened since the attack in Belwas."

Areus adjusted his chair. "The moment we entered Belwas Swamp all time was lost. From what I have recollected, we trudged through that swamp for two days before the encounter with the winged goblin. That monster attacked through the mist and cut the rope between you and Adetin but took Gar along with you over the ledge. Immediately upon stepping off the trail you all were lost from sight and sound. We hauled Adetin back up to the trail and experimented with rappelling down the ravine but the trapvine was too dangerous. Then the old man appeared, parting the mist before him up the trail, accompanied by his pet, the same you made acquaintance with. The old man told us to follow him to safety and assured us that his cat would find you and not to worry. We arrived here, replenished ourselves with food and drink and the old man sent out the swamp cat to look for you. The next night you arrived carrying Dirk." Areus paused, giving him a knowing look, and whispered, "Baytel, I believe the old man is a druid."

Baytel said nothing and waited for an explanation.

Areus fumbled along to clarify. "It…it's something odd…he has the ways of a druid, but he is so old. His mind is sound though and he is…well, he seemingly knows everything that occurs in the swamp and on this plateau. Anyway, the way he speaks and his mannerisms are telling, and I believe he is from the Citadel. I am almost sure of it."

Baytel turned toward the door that was kicked open, admitting Adetin Gar carrying his clothes. "I am not accustomed to delivering laundry, Baytel." He threw the clothes on the bed. "When you are ready, come out to the stable and tell us what happened. Dirk told us of the fight at the bottom of the ravine and of the climb. I am sure you can add to his story, although his telling will probably be much more entertaining." Gar offered a half smirk, turned and walked out.

Baytel followed his back until the door closed and turned, giving Areus a quizzical look.

Sheepishly, Areus said, "Baytel, I told them a thing or two."

"A thing or two what?"

"Baytel, it was two days you were gone and they had questions about us I could not ignore," Areus replied quietly. "So I told them of Tridling Del."

Baytel angered. Areus had a promise not to disclose anything about him. "What about Tridling Del, Areus?"

"I told of Calidor and he being your grandfather and of your grandmother and mother being from an unknown magical sect. And that you are the prince of the Kings of the North, the rightful heir to the Sword of the Kings. Be it wrong or right Baytel, these men have gone through so much in our cause, I believed they deserved to know all."

Baytel nodded accepting the wisdom of it. "I will not admonish you for breaking our oath, Areus. Actually, I am glad they know. Knowing the circumstances as I do now, had I been there with you, I would have told them myself."

Baytel watched as the relief of his acceptance eased the tension from Areus's expression. "You are a good friend, Areus. I need you for things like this. You are a reminder to me of what my true self is. The changes occurring in me are complex. It is the magic. It challenges me. Using the sword with such frequency has ignited something within me, blending with whatever magic I possess, unknowingly, that had lain waiting to be awakened, and it has made me a more complete being. The magic launches me in stages of learning that I can only describe as chaotic. However, something I was born with controls the surge of power, allowing me to absorb the enormous intricacies of each stage. It frightens me, Areus, yet in the same breath, I can say it also exhilarates me!"

"Is it the same magic your brother wields, Baytel?"

"No, it is not the evil art Ravek has acquired; nor is it the magic of Vokat. In my blood is the union of two powerful magical beings, Areus. The magic of the Kings of the North has merged with that of the unknown sect of my mother. This magical bond created within me is a glorious, extraordinary power that I am still trying to decipher."

Baytel wanted Areus to understand how his destiny had come to being. "Areus, do you remember the oath we spoke at Make's shop? Well, without my knowledge, all the stages of my life until meeting Make Ironwright were planned with particular care. The Tree Faerie Cyr tutored me, Calidor advanced my education by training me. Cyr and Calidor both planted the seeds of the teaching of the Citadel in me to the point that it was expected I run away from home and seek it out. All this was done to prepare me to use this sword and control a magic both knew lay hidden within me. Calidor, Cyr and even Yar knew my destiny lay in the path of the magic and had prepared me to be able to control it and embrace it."

Areus's expression changed from awe to sorrow and Baytel knew Areus had realized at that moment that he was different. Baytel said, "It is in my blood; so do not feel sorrow for me. I am still and always shall be the man you met at the Citadel, Areus. And we have a quest to finish."

Baytel knew Areus was saddened and remembered back to the first days at the Citadel, when both were young and full of enthusiasm, and he said, "It has become quite a quest from our beginnings as acolytes, eh Areus?"

Areus nodded and said, "Yes it has, Baytel. But you must understand something…something that I think you do not fully realize, being the solitary, private and lonesome fellow you are. This quest is not yours alone. We are druids, Baytel, and quest for the One Land. We began as friends, became like brothers and now are companions in deed and quest. I am proud of this quest and my inclusion in the battle for it. And I am honored to be able to call you my friend and brother and journey at your side." Areus paused to spread a wide grin across his face and said, "so long as we take time at a town along the way to meet a lady or two."

The jest was a tension reliever and Baytel felt fortunate to have a friend like Areus. "Now, Areus, to the thieves. Adetin does not look like a man who recently lost all his fighting men and way of life."

Areus continued with his interrupted report. "We were all exhausted that night we reached this plateau. The old man fed us and poured wine while we relayed how we came to Belwas Swamp. Adetin, Kalti and Telek spoke of their losses and when they finished with their tale of sorrow, the old man began singing. The song was strange. The words in an ancient tongue I have never heard before. It was soothing and then I woke and we all found we had slept through the night and were in better spirits. Baytel, this old man has a powerful magic. He came to us in our dreams."

Baytel sat at the end of the bed finally finished dressing, and gave Areus his full attention. "What do you mean he came to your dreams?"

"We all had the same dream, my friend. The old man came to us and showed each of us small glimpses of visions of events to come. In the dream he spoke of the higher order of justice we could strive for and to trust in our destiny for the One Land had chosen this to be our lot in life."

Baytel remembered the old man hovering over his shoulder when he treated Dirk Ironwright's wound. "Areus, the old man said all that in your dream and this healed the hearts of the thieves? Hard to believe."

"Yes, as hard as your explanation of your magic. Nevertheless the pain of death, anguish and loss they felt has disappeared."

"What is the old man's name?"

"Well…I do not know. He never said."

Curious and fully apprised, Baytel stood, attached his sword to his belt, and they left the cabin for the stables with the sense that everything they all were experiencing was guided by the magical winds of fortune and destiny.

The grass was a soft blue-green shade and stretched across the plateau until reaching the tree line. The afternoon sun showed brightly; its warm rays bejeweled the high glade. A light breeze flowed through the trees gently swaying the branches with a sound like rolling surf breaking against the sands of a beach, and it all brought peace to his mind. He smelled the air finding the sweet scent of honeysuckle and the perfume of wild roses drift past. Scanning the plateau he saw flowering bushes and plantings everywhere. Rock outcroppings jutting up out of the pristine grass had the appearance of monuments from an ancient civilization. The old standing stones were chaotically arranged except along the northern part of the meadow. These had been set in a circular pattern with some stones across the tops of other. Most stones stood alone; hallowed sentries of blue-gray granite partly covered in ivy budding white flowers. Every part of the high glade was beautifully manicured; the grass, flowers, standing stones and plantings a serene display of harmonious beauty.

Telek's booming voice rolled across the meadow. "When I was your age, after a battle, I would be up from my slumber to meet the dawn. Ah, Adetin, the youth these days…soft to the core."

The men stood before a rundown old stable. Gar, Telek and Kalti were smiling at him as they approached and Baytel replied, "It's just like you old-timers to leave when the real fighting was at hand."

"Well, if you hadn't been off running about with goblins we would not have had a couple nights' rest, so thanks for falling off the trail," said Gar.

They laughed again as they converged, greeting him with handshakes and firm backslaps. It was a joyous reunion but Baytel still felt deep remorse for their losses. "Areus told me of your men, Adetin. I am sorry for them and you all. These are the times that I wish our journey had not come through Elangal. If I could turn back time to erase all that has happened, I would."

Gar was nodding, as was Telek and Kalti. After a brief pause, Adetin Gar replied, "Baytel. We have had time to think and had a few visions to set our minds at ease. As we see it, there is a higher purpose in our survival and the losses and bereavement that go along with the sacrifices we all make will occur. But know this, Baytel; vengeance is still strong with us, and we now have more of a reason to help you in your quest. And if it defines purpose to our lives, then so be it. In the meantime, we *thieves* will be hard to reckon with."

Telek added, "By traveling into Elangal Forest, you awakened a spirit inside us that had lain dormant behind greed and selfishness for too long. Plundering and pillaging had little purpose for us anymore. You came to us with a cause that, no matter how we were introduced to it, has appealed to us. So I say rejoice in the path you chose through Elangal. As young Dirk Ironwright of Ctiklat put it, "My life is to quest beside the Druid Baytel whose sovereignty to all runs in his veins. I follow to be fulfilled."

Baytel looked into their eyes seeing their strength and hearing their commitment. They had made their choice, the same choice he had many years before.

Areus offered his hand to him. Then Adetin Gar placed his hand upon theirs followed by Telek, the passionate soldier of fortune, and by the quiet, resourceful Kalti, whose bloodline may be that of his own. As they held this commitment and each met the others' eyes, quietly the dwarf walked up and placed his hand upon theirs.

Dirk Ironwright said, "We journey through life with a bond of friendship and duty. Let no man or myth break its trust."

Baytel choked back his emotions and said, "I have pledged my life to the One Land and its sects of humanity long ago. My age and experience are young. My teachings are from a Tree Faerie tutor, from my grandfather Calidor whose deeds go uncounted, and from the scholars of the Citadel. Together we unite strengths of an immeasurable magnitude. Not just the might of the body, but the potency of our minds and souls, the power of which is unlimited in every man. You say the quest of life runs in my veins. I say that no man could be as fortunate and privileged as I to have such men to companion beside."

Baytel unsheathed his sword; its magic surged with white light before him and he extended it into the center of the circle of companions. "I pledge by the magic of the One Land, our duty to one another as companions, to ensure the safety of the land and the sects of humanity. Wherever we go, be it together or apart, our commitment is to each other's trust, to the righteous path of humanity, and to the care of the land."

They all took hold of the magic blade and, as they held it, they recited their pledge in unison.

Baytel glanced over their heads, seeing the old man sitting against a standing stone. The black swamp cat lay beside him on the grass, shaded from the heat of the setting sun. He scratched the cat behind its ears and it gave his master a deep growl that he could hear across the glade. From afar, Baytel met the old man's eyes and could see the gleam. The peculiar old man gave him a nod that seemed to reveal his approval, and then he leaned his head against the stone and closed his eyes with a satisfied grin.

Chapter 49

DUSK brought a serenade of crickets to the mountain; their lulling *crip-crip* followed Baytel as he took a stroll in the glade. Since the gathering at the stable, it was the first chance he had to be alone on the small plateau.

The flawlessness of the flat terrain amazed him. It was surely magic of the One Land at work and he felt its enchantment all about him. Reaching down he broke off a blade of grass. It immediately repaired itself back to its original form, just as it had back in the tall grass of the clearing outside the Citadel. Yet, he remained perplexed about the mountain, the swamp and the old man. Baytel had walked past the old man earlier and the man gave him a wink and nodded, pointing to the stable as if to say *good work*. The private gesture of affirmation reminded him of Calidor.

At the northern end of the plateau Baytel sat against a standing stone that bordered the cliffside. He looked down at the shroud of mist covering Belwas Swamp and watched as the setting sun coated the cloudy mire in red-orange and had renewed relief wash over him at escaping its dangers. When the sun sank behind a far-off mountain range, the hues disappeared as if someone had smothered a colored glass lantern, leaving darkness below and the fiery glowing outline of the distant mountain.

Baytel pondered the next leg of their journey and where it would take him both physically and magically. Charged with magic and still retaining his self, he understood more challenges were in store, and he was ready for the tasks they commanded of him. He turned hearing footsteps and saw Dirk Ironwright approach.

The dwarf said, "I hope I am not disturbing you, Baytel."

"No, Dirk. My mind was wandering. Actually, I am glad you are here. I had not the chance to speak with you earlier. Since the attack at Elangal and then our trek through Belwas, I have been preoccupied."

"Yes. We have been mixing it up," the dwarf said.

Baytel smiled at what was high-spirits for a dwarf. He looked better since the morning meeting. "How is your head? You took a heavy blow from that monster."

"Healing rather quickly and it no longer hurts. It serves me right not paying attention atop that ravine. I learn as I go, and, surviving, will be better because of it; with a generous scar as a reminder."

He found Ironwright's common sense refreshing. But all his companions looked at peace and seemingly without regrets. *Why then do I feel that something is missing within me? Like a burden I cannot shake. Where is my serenity? My peace?* The uncertainties had surfaced repeatedly since the stables.

Overwhelmed and flattered that the men chose him to lead their now-shared quest, Baytel worried about the great risks they volunteered for. Risks that increased now that he held in his hands the responsibility of their lives. He leaned against the cool bluish monolith and shut his eyes to clear his mind from the doubts that seeped inward.

"You are disturbed, Baytel. I can read it on your face," said Ironwright, who had remained standing patiently beside the stone.

"Yes Dirk, I am. I fear what happened to the band of thieves will reoccur wherever I travel. There are many more of these goblins in the wild and what drives them is an evil that we might not be able to conquer. There seems to be no escaping them. We have only experienced small samples of their capabilities and I am certain that when Ravek hears of their failures, he will send a larger, stronger contingent of goblins after us. I do not fear for myself, but for all your lives."

The dwarf sat beside him. "Fear is evident in everything we do. In every act, however brave or ordinary, fear is present. It is the silent thief that sidles in the night and steals away part of our confidence and plants caution into our minds. But this is good, Baytel, for it balances the rashness of vaulting aspirations. It creates reason, and from reasoning comes wisdom and with wisdom one makes courageous decisions. This is what separates a leader of men from a tyrant."

The dwarf's words hit their mark and the disquiet Baytel was feeling faded. Watching the moon slowly rise over the pine trees, the glow cast the plateau in a soft woolly light. Baytel looked at Dirk Ironwright and saw a younger version of his uncle, Make Ironwright. "You remind me of your uncle."

"It was he who sent me to find you. Uncle Make told me that a young man, whose character and strength surpassed all he had seen, set out from his foundry on a quest; that the quest was not for individual glory or accolades, but for all sects of humanity. He said that to travel with one of such conviction would fulfill my life with peace and make the land a better place. I sought you out to find the truth in his words." He looked away as if embarrassed by the statement and after a silent moment, Ironwright continued, "I am not certain of the truth in what he said, but I see before me an unselfish man who talks of peace, and the sects living harmoniously upon the One Land, so I say to myself that this alone is a worthy enough quest and whatever truth that comes from it, will come. That is why I took the oath with you."

"Fair enough, Dirk. Whatever happens during this quest, be assured it is not for personal gain. I have no need of accolades."

"Then you shall have my delve-axe at your side, Baytel. But I know there is more at work here that just this quest. You are one from the ancestors of old. I have seen the Grey Riders and know their workings upon the land. The legends of the great race are on the lips of many, but none suspect the Grey Riders as them. You are one of the Kings of the North."

Dirk deserved to know his lineage as the others were told it by Areus. "My grandfather is Calidor. He was once monarch of the Kings of the North. He gave his throne to his brother to stay in this land. I did not know this until this spring. Also, on my mother's side, I am descendant to an unknown sect of magical being."

"I have heard you are also Vokat's son?" he asked.

"I am."

"So you are the prince of two kingdoms and the grandson of legends."

Was the dwarf provoking me?

Ironwright held up his hands and said, "Do not be angry with me, Baytel. I know the importance of this. I too am of the old ancestry, a descendent of King Minion. My uncle quested with Calidor and I shall quest with his grandson. So this shall be our bond."

Ironwright extended his arm and he gripped forearms. Baytel stood, lifting the dwarf off the ground to stand with him. "I carry no flag, Dirk Ironwright. The prince of both kingdoms, I am afraid, shall be destined to never to claim either throne. The duty to which I swore to is to the Citadel. My only claim is that of a Citadel Druid, and only as the man you see before you; Druid Baytel."

"Then the words of my uncle are becoming truth."

Baytel laughed, not knowing what prompted it. It was good to laugh, and his lingering worries faded away.

Their stay with the old man lasted four more days. While they rested and healed, they captured the serenity of the mountain in their hearts. Seeing the stable in such poor condition, Baytel and the men took on the task of its repair as a consideration for the old man's generosity. With the repair completed, Baytel called for the men to pack their gear for a morning departure.

Spirits were high and all looked forward to the quest. After a fine meal of grouse, wild mushrooms, greens and whole-grain bread, all prepared by Ironwright, who turned out to be an accomplished cook, they took their ease in the cabin. With long weed pipes supplied by the old man, both Telek and the old man smoked a fragrant leaf, blowing smoke rings at objects in the cabin while Baytel and the rest judged each ring, its sustenance, shape and perfection as it rolled to the object aimed at.

All were engrossed in the competition when the old man suddenly stood up and moved to the rocking chair by the hearth. He stared at each one in turn, lingering longer on Baytel in a way that seemed more of a study, reminiscent of an artist reading the shapes of a piece of marble yet to be sculpted.

The old man addressed them with a comfortable tone, gently rocking back and forth. "Well, gentlemen. Your stay with me has been very enjoyable and I appreciate the work you have done on my stable. Now that you are prepared for the next stage of your journey, you should know that the way down the mountain is as difficult as the way up, except this time, Azul and I will guide you out. So rest this night while you can for the trail will tax you."

The old man turned to Baytel and asked, "So Baytel, where do you journey next?"

"Through Konart Pass and then north to Petal Glen. Another of our brethren of the Citadel is from those parts. Eventually we need to reach Kilhalen before the winter solstice."

The old man continued rocking back and forth, pulling at his bearded chin while deep in thought. He was a comical figure, but Baytel could feel the old man's power, though it was a sophisticated, veiled sort of magic, not one to fear, rather one whose significance to the One Land Baytel could only speculate at.

"Konart Pass, eh?" the old man pondered aloud. "Huh? Yes. Well...I guess that would be one way to reach Petal Glen...that is without returning the way you came circling the mountain range in the east." He stopped rocking as if distracted by something. He stooped to stoke the fire and threw another log upon the embers, and then continued, "Yes, that is one way. Very dangerous country. Most travelers avoid Konart altogether. Yes...terrible things have happened there for many years now. Far too many. The land from Elangal Forest to Konart Pass is *Trog* country now. They settled there some years ago. Not many willing to venture into their land. No, definitely not deliberately."

"Konart is our destination, old one. Unless there is something you can share about the pass we may not know of?" Baytel asked, not necessarily to take his advice.

The old man looked at Baytel and then to the rest of the companions, one by one, as if contemplating their verve. "Konart Pass is a narrow path through the high spires of the Lumithien Mountains," he said speaking to all, but his eyes on only Baytel. "High elevations, snow-capped peaks and ice make scaling the mountain range impossible. As I recall, the path was founded long ago by a man named Joseph Konart, hence the name of the pass. Nonetheless, when his discovery spread both dwarf and man took it upon themselves to cleave the narrow passage wider for travel ease. They cut deep into the heart of Lumithien without care or concern at the destruction they inflicted upon the mountain. Evidently, the mountain took exception and grew angry.

"It lashed out vengefully against dwarf and man, causing the wind to blow with horrific force, its wail driving those who cut into its heart mad, and to their doom. Ever since that time, when man or dwarf travel through the pass the *Siren of Lumithien* wails its song of woe and calls down the rocks and winds of retribution. Those who survive the tempest vow never to challenge its wrath again."

Baytel saw Dirk Ironwright fidget uncomfortably and sensed the dwarf was familiar with the story and was all too aware of its implications. Baytel said, "Before we concern ourselves with Konart Pass, I am certain we will not be a welcome sight traveling through the land of the Trogs."

"That's right," said Telek, standing to pour himself a flask of honey-mead. "Danger lurks in every shadow once we leave Elangal Forest and travel west to Konart. Though the Trogs live in the caves south of Lumithien, they do patrol and will attack anyone who ventures into their land. Trogs are known to be a vicious, cunning sect."

"I have never heard of this sect. What are Trogs?" asked Areus. They were not taught of the Trog sect at the Citadel and Baytel was silently thankful Areus asked the question.

Telek replied, "In the histories, Trogs were trolls at one time, but evil befell them when a brutish sect of goblins attacked and killed off all the male trolls. They seized possession of their women and their descendants are what exist today."

Baytel found too many unknowns in their quest and it disturbed him. "You have had dealings with these Trogs, Telek?"

Telek gulped down the honey-mead and replied, "Only from a distance, Baytel. We share the border that runs along the western section of Elangal."

So the thieves have never fully interacted with the Trogs. Perhaps the Trogs are not what they are reported to be. All the same, careful travel was the order and Baytel would surely not want to cause more delays. "Detouring around Lumithien will put us back another month and we will miss the winter solstice in Kilhalen, so that is not an option."

Areus added, "Let's not forget the goblin horde had split and is headed toward Konart and undoubtedly to Petal Glen."

Baytel declared, "With that being said, we leave at dawn. Old man, you say there are those who have survived the tempest wrath of Lumithien?"

"Yes, there are many who have survived. How else do we hear its stories, eh?"

That made perfect sense, and Baytel replied, "Our task is urgent and we are well rested, so let's get a good night's sleep and start fresh at dawn."

"Right," the old man jumped up. "Until dawn then. Good night all." The old man stepped to the side room with Azul at his heels, stopped at his door, turned to them, waved and closed the door.

The curious gestures of the old man were always amusing. His quirky temperament and oddities were endearing and would be missed in the coming days of travel.

No matter his position on the cot, Baytel could not sleep and he lay restlessly atop his coverlet. It was well past midnight, and the sound of peaceful slumber from his companions reverberated through the cabin, especially Telek, whose snore sounded like the wind gusts in a maelstrom.

Thoughts of the coming trek kept comfort at bay, especially the idea of traveling through Konart Pass. Movement brought his attention toward the open door to the old man's room. The old man was tiptoeing past the sleeping men and out the cabin door with Azul. Curious, Baytel followed them out and found both by the standing stone they had rested at in days past.

The man was leaning over in whispered conversation with Azul. The next moment, the black cat sprang off and disappeared into the swamp with a speed he found difficult to comprehend. When he looked back, he saw the old man waving him over to the stone.

Stopping beside the seated man, Baytel saw him just staring up at the heavens, stargazing. Baytel followed his gaze upward and was met with a tapestry of starlight. The vastness of the star-filled night filled him with an absurd sensation that they were looking down at him in judgment. Then the old man had started humming an odd piece of music that seemed to have neither beginning nor end. Baytel felt his head swaying to the melody and he became weary as the sleep that evaded him finally set its roots. He sat against the standing stone and drifted into a dream.

Snow was falling so heavily he could distinguish only the silhouette of his guide before him. Where was he leading him? His legs burned with fatigue from plodding through the drifts. The wind blew ferociously, scourging his exposed face with slivers of ice. The burden of the heavy pack on his back weighed him down as each step became more onerous than the last.

Puffs of snow exploded on each side of him from the high drifts. Then he realized falling rocks were tumbling down onto the trail from the two granite sheers they traveled between.

His guide shouted, "Quickly! Back to the high valley!"

The guide reversed field and ran past him back toward where they had come from. Following blindly, avoiding falling rocks, he tried to keep in step with the guide, but he was fast and soon fell farther behind. A deep rumble sounded from above and he knew from experience that it was the first stages of an avalanche. Rocks were falling and he was just able to keep ahead of the deadly projectiles, each falling rock brought insistent dread as the thunder of the avalanche was gaining on him.

Reaching the mouth of the pass and upon entering the high valley, he came to an abrupt stop slamming into this guide. He looked up from the deep snow and was met by a host of the most hideous spirits and waifs he had ever seen. His guide did not move. Looking behind them, he found the pass was barred from the avalanche, and before them, frightful demons stood cutting off their other escape route. He drew his sword, expecting a flash of light but it remained dull steel. He began to panic. He looked beside him to ask his guide what to do, but he was gone.

Then he heard over the shrieking demons and the blasting wind his guide's voice. "Follow me! There is another way!"

He sprang toward him just avoiding the demons' charge. Evading spears and arrows in pursuit of his guide, who was far ahead in the valley, his legs driving through the deep snow, he gained ground on the creatures behind, but not on the guide as the guide had shot forward with such speed he was sure to lose sight of him. The valley sloped downward toward a cliff sheer, the east face of the mountain and he ran laboriously through the drifts toward the fading guide. The weight of his pack was becoming heavier and he was about to leave it behind but something was telling him if he dropped it, all his efforts through the days of travel would be for naught and failure would be at hand. With the demons on his tail and the only evidence of his guide being footprints in the snow, he felt lost.

Then his guide came into view, standing upon a ridge on the sheer. As he reached the guide, the man turned toward the rock wall, raised his arms and, in a booming voice, shouted at the wall words in the ancient tongue. The sheer rumbled back as if in reply. Again the guide shouted in the same ancient tongue. Suddenly, the rock wall moved and a door appeared and opened before them.

He glanced past the guide looking into a cavernous expanse. He grabbed the guide and turned him to see his face. It was the old man of Belwas Swamp!

The old man shouted over the wailing wind and the charging cries of the demons. "Young druid, enter the hall. It is the only other way to escape!"

He was confused and replied, "What hall? All I see is a cave!"

"Heed my words, Druid. This cave leads to Old Warriors' Court, the hall of the dead soldiers!"

The old man seemed to have grown stronger. A wind gust knocked his grip from the man and he fell to the snow on the ledge. The old man leaned down looking at him with eyes brilliant with life. "Old Warriors' Court shall lead you to the other side of the Lumithien! Do not fall into battle with the spirits of the court. Keep your weapons sheathed and restrain your thirst for battle, for if you sustain a wound by a spirit, you will become an apparition doomed to battle in the hall of the dead for all eternity."

The demons were almost at the sheer. He wanted to ask the old man more, but when turning back, he found the old man had disappeared. He panicked and shouted, "Where are you old man?"

Then a voice from the oblivion of the snow came to him. "Be wary of the voices of the past. Your inner strength must restrain your desire to fight."

"Wait!" he shouted. "Don't leave me!"

"Remember, Druid; heed not the spirits of the ancients! Hold true to yourself and you will reach the sun once more."

Fear was replaced by anger and he crawled to the gaping cavity. Then he felt something being placed in his palm and the old man's voice was in his head again, barely penetrating the howling storm.

"Use it when there is no escape. Speak the tongue of the sect silent within you, yet very much alive upon the One Land." Then the old man said a word to him so beautiful, it removed the veil clouding his mind and cloaking his heart, and amid the chaos of the storm and the approaching demons, calmness stayed his soul.

As he entered the cave, he asked, "Old man, who are you?"

The echo of his voice rolled over and over in the empty chasm. As it faded, he heard laughter, like he had heard numerous times on the plateau.

"Why don't you know, Druid?" another chuckle, and the voice said, "I am Belwas!"

The cave door slammed closed leaving him in total darkness with the sound of a chuckling old man in his head.

Baytel woke with a start expecting darkness but seeing dawn had crept above the eastern pines illuminating the dew-laden plateau. The air was still compared to the dream, no biting wind or cold, just the quiet warmth of the glade. Alone at the standing stone, he felt something in his hand. Opening his fist he found a smooth dark blue stone that fit perfectly in his palm. Then he recalled the wondrous word whispered to him in his dream and it gave him a warm feeling deep within him. He placed the blue stone in his tunic pocket with reverence.

Baytel stretched the scanty sleep away and went looking for the old man. He entered the cabin to find Adetin Gar waking the men, but no old man. Disturbed, he left the cabin and ran to the stable, but found no sign of him or his cat. Standing at the gates of the stable he thought about last night's dream and decided to keep it to himself for now and turned his attention to getting off the plateau and through Belwas Swamp. Returning to the cabin he found everyone ready to move.

Areus asked, "Is there something troubling you Baytel? You look as though you lost something."

"We did lose something. The old man is gone. So is Azul. I saw them leave the cabin last night and followed them to the standing stone. Azul darted into the woods and I fell asleep before the old man left. I do not know where they have gone, or if they were ever here. The whole night is a puzzle."

"So again we are on our own," said Adetin Gar. "Let's make good time of it. We are packed and dressed. As soon as you do the same, we will be off. The old man helped us and we helped him. Our accounts square. That is good and all are left better from it."

The men seemed in concord with the situation and they looked at Baytel awaiting his order. Baytel's thoughts returned to their oaths, and that these fine men had volunteered to take arms with him. Areus's words from the other night came back to him. *"Leaders are chosen. Those who aspire to lead do not make the best commanders. It is those who rise to leadership that exemplify what a good commander can be. One who shows bravery, courage and responsibility to the command shall lead and have the respect of his men."*

Baytel shrugged his self-doubts away as well as the confusion of his dream and gave his first order. "Kalti, scout the area at the base of the clearing for any signs of where the old man and cat departed. If you find none, search for a trail out of Belwas pointing toward the north end of Elangal Forest. Telek, Dirk and Adetin, secure the windows and doors of the cabin and stable in case the old man does not return. Areus, upon conferring with Kalti, leave a note in the ancient tongue as to the direction we are headed. And we should make sure we all find a bite to eat before our departure. There will be no stopping for a meal in that swamp. I will be out momentarily."

Baytel joined everyone at the far end of the glade tying the familiar rope to one another and was about to enter Belwas Swamp when Azul appeared out of the mist and pranced to the lead position. The black swamp cat glistened from the mire. The cat looked at Baytel, gave a soft roar, and walked into the mist.

Baytel nodded and followed Azul into the mist. Just before the swamp engulfed them, he heard Adetin say, "It's too bad the animal doesn't speak. That would add to the strangeness of this visit perfectly."

Chapter 50

DELLA floated naked and half submerged in the Ginhonim River. Her pack with all her gear and clothing was secured high upon her back. Balanced upon the end of a log she floated with the current of the river longer toward sunset than she would have liked. The many bends of the river and the unseen boulders jutting up from below the surface created white water and rapids that kept her kicking vigorously to avoid being driven against the granite bank and smashing her and her log to pieces.

With darkness descending, she dreaded being caught without finding an accessible shore to beach her log or any other relief from the raging Ginhonim, but this stretch of the river was harsh sheer granite walls and no bank was in sight. Della felt she would soon lose what little strength she still possessed and would not be able to steer the log from the many dangers of the rapids.

Nevertheless, she felt she could go farther and her backpack remained dry and once she found relief, she would be able to rest and sleep dry for the nights were cool and she needed to warm her body before jumping back into the turbulent rapids of the Ginhonim River.

The towering granite cliffs that bordered the river rose to such a height they blocked out the sky except for the narrow opening the river cut through. The only wildlife seen were the magnificent white-headed eagles soaring over the river hunting for fish. The rapturous birds would dive with legs outstretched and talons flared and, with only a subtle splash upon the surface of the river, clutch their prey and carry it high overhead to feed.

Through the dusk-light, Della urgently steered the log away from the strong rapids in the center of the Ginhonim kicking toward calmer waters. Each boost of her legs was painful. She was hungry and tired but still able to sustain the fight against the current. She clung onto the log appreciatively as it had carried her from dawn to dusk, and with no burrs or splinters she had been able to lie with her body half on the smooth surface of wood without scraping her skin.

The Ginhonim River cut a canyon by the passage of time, beautiful and awe-inspiring. Green granite with shining gold specks glittered and reflected awesome light. Alas, Della had found the wondrous Ginhonim region difficult to travel through. She had been unable to find enough wood to build a raft to sail the river, as the trees at the Ginhonim's birth waters were too mature and the river was lined at each side by granite sheers with only a rare stony bank to rest upon. Throughout the days of travel, she depended upon floating branches, always hoping the next bend would expose a dry resting place where she could warm herself by a fire. But none had appeared for days and so she remained on the long smooth log letting the Ginhonim be her guide.

Ahead, just before the turn onto another bend of the Ginhonim, Della noticed a crease in an otherwise flat façade. As she neared, the crease turned out to be a crevasse in the cliff wall. She steered toward the breach in the rock and was able to ease toward it, for the current diminished slight enough for Della to entered a calm pool. With rapid kicking, Della angled the front end of the log at the crevasse and, as she placed all her weight on her end of the log, elevating the opposite end above the surface, the log slammed into the crack. The impact almost thrust her off but the log stuck at an angle above the surface.

Testing the firmness of the hold, she found it solidly jammed deep in the crevasse. With the current sweeping beneath her, she climbed up the log until reaching the impaled end and rested with her back against the cliff face, dripping slightly above the surface of the river.

"Blast! I'll never be able to free this log. Well, I'll have to watch for another log to pass my way tomorrow."

Della did not feel strange talking to herself. She had begun doing so once she left the West Fork region. She would imagine speaking with her father when making a critical decision on the river and it helped. Sometimes she would reflect upon the Harlequin and wonder what forces drove him to do whatever he claimed to be doing and the power of magic he seemed to possess in abundance.

Della's hand drifted down and grabbed the *triscele* the Harlequin gave her. As she held the amulet, she felt the now familiar strange sensation emitting from the stone, as though it were alive and could read her emotions. The warmth seeped from the stone and, as always, imbued a sense of peace and calm to her mind and worked as a barricade against fear and trepidation, leaving her convinced she was safe from harm. In a way, she felt the Harlequin within the stone, making certain she would reach Petal Glen.

Della skinned off her pack, examining it, and was pleased to find it dry. She unpacked her clothes and dressed while delicately balanced upon the log. Once warm, she removed a small container of fishing tackle and a portion of fish meat she had saved from the night before. Della had fashioned a fishhook with the plume of a feather she found floating by earlier, and tied some of the fledging to the hook and tying it to the line, she set it afloat.

Immediately, a fish took her bait. Della pulled hard, sinking the hook and drawing the captured fish toward her. The fish resisted gallantly. The line cut into her hand as the fish flapped and fought until she could reach it, grab it by its lip and lay it on the log, holding it down with her feet. She pulled out her knife, cut off its head, sliced its underbelly, extracted its intestines and filleted two thick pieces of fish meat, discarding the remains into the river.

Della leaned back against the cliff, happy as she could be biting into the raw fish. She recalled her father's lessons and her first taste of raw fish when she was eight years old. They were camped beside a high lake in the Middle Fork. *He said, "When there is water and no means or conditions for a fire, raw fish is as nourishing as cooked. And it does not taste that bad once you become accustomed to it."*

She turned her nose up at the first tasting of uncooked fish, and her father said, "Della, try not to be such a girl about it. Anyway, it is less disgusting than it looks, isn't it? And it is for your survival I show you these things. One never knows what the future shall bring. These are good things to know."

With her stomach full, Della smiled at the memory of him and how she missed him. She longed for him to be at her side with the love, support and comfort he always gave, but knew it would never again be.

Della washed away the fish from her hands and pulled out her sleeping bag. She crawled in and immediately felt her fatigue. She rubbed her hands together, feeling her wrinkled fingers that had been constantly soaked and wondered how much farther until the granite banks would open to a traversable shore and a way less wet to Petal Glen.

She sighed at the thought of floating through another day with a heavy wet pack on her back until finding another log, but shook the negative thought from her mind and said, "Let's you and I worry about that tomorrow, Father. Goodnight." And she closed her eyes and fell asleep smiling.

Chapter 51

THE trek out of Belwas Swamp was uneventful compared to the journey in. The black swamp cat had been an efficient guide, not venturing too far ahead, so Baytel and his companions could navigate through the swamp unscathed. When reaching the end of Belwas Swamp, Azul gave a playful rub along Baytel's leg, nearly knocking him over, roared loudly at the men and sprang back into the swamp.

Free of the misty mire and standing in the deep green of Elangal Forest once again, Baytel should have been relieved, but he remained disturbed by the disappearance of the old man, Belwas, and the lingering thoughts about the dream.

Adetin Gar extracted him from his troubled thoughts: "Baytel, we are farther south than I anticipated. We need to travel northwest to reach the Trog hill country. We are some ways off."

"Alright then. Kalti, take the point. Telek, you have the rear. We will travel until dark and eat our meals on the march. Let's go."

Elangal Forest's northern country was much dryer with sturdy walnut, maple and oak trees spaced out where their branches stretched toward one another, towering romantics reaching close enough to caress, only to be drawn away moments before they touch by the passing breezes.

The farther the men traveled north the cooler the days became as the first hint of autumn unfurled upon the land. Their passage would have been quieter had it been earlier in the summer where acorns were not so abundant and crunching beneath their boots. Baytel found it a pleasant passage and welcomed sunlight that filled the space between the trees, walking into its warm rays and the taking in of the change of season, for Elangal was cascading yellow, orange, and red, transforming the landscape into a mural of color that swayed and glimmered its radiance and touched them all with its magnificence.

Baytel kept the men on a fast pace covering many miles, calling only short halts for rest and food, never discontinuing their patrol routines, knowing not to repeat the mistakes of the past as goblin attacks were a constant in their minds.

The days passed quickly and without trouble. While they traveled the conversation changed from the initial polite talks of acquaintances to friendly banter among genuine companions. Their spirits were high. They talked often of their pledge to one another, the good of it, and as friendships flourished their bond to one another welded true. Baytel felt genuinely fortunate and thankful for their commitment and friendship. Though pain and suffering had caused them to join forces, it was real companionship.

One evening, Kalti waved Baytel forward and he found they had come to the border of Elangal Forest. It was dusk and Baytel watched the sun set over a horizon showing glimpses of a beautiful country of tall amber grass upon rolling hills. Above the horizon, clouds accumulated from the north, filling the sky with scarlet and yellow. But quickly the sun disappeared as though someone had stolen it from the sky, and the vast hill-plain disappeared.

"Dirk, Adetin, and Telek, set camp. Kalti and I will scout the hills and return before the second watch."

Areus, already lying at the edge of the warm grass rested his head against this bag and said, "Do not trouble yourself with hurrying back, Baytel. I need my beauty sleep."

Warily, Baytel crept from hill to hill, keeping within sight of Kalti who patrolled a little way to the north. The small hills were short distances from each other and rolled across the open plain with each valley at varying depths. Warned of the hill country being the home of Trogs, he was extra careful, especially at night, understanding from the thieves that the Trogs were nocturnal in nature.

The undulating terrain made judging distance difficult. Without the aid of moonlight he signed to Kalti to patrol closer. Without seeing or hearing anything disturbing, Baytel was about to turn back when Kalti raised a hand for halt.

Baytel lay flat to the ground and crawled to Kalti's position. "What is it?"

He pointed to the north. "Trog patrol."

Appearing in and out of view was a small troop of Trogs marching up and down hills toward them. Baytel counted fifteen. They were dressed in full battle gear. They marched in no specific pattern and were careless of the noise they were making; comfortable in their land. And two were hauling a body on a carryall.

Baytel took advantage and, with Kalti, keeping low, stalked forward until in audible range. They paralleled the Trogs' position, eavesdropping on the slow-moving troop. The Trog accent was thick, but the language was the common tongue most spoke throughout the land.

"This stinks, carrying Dolog all this way. For what? He'll die soon anyhow," one of them said in a twanging voice like an injured crow would sound. "I say we drop him off here."

"What do you say, Captain?" asked another Trog. "If he is lucky, the wolf pack will finish him before he wakes."

"Shut up! You are as lazy as you are dumb. We carry him to the caves and they will patch him up. He fought strong back at the pass and without him the both of you would be dead."

"Better off dead than go back to the caves and tell of our defeat," crow-voice said. "What were those things? They were uglier than we are with their burning blood and all."

Baytel whispered, "So, the goblin horde has reached Konart Pass. I wonder how long ago? And how far we are behind them?"

The Trog leader continued, "They killed twenty of us before we killed one. Surprised us...in our own land!"

"We killed ten but I bet fifty or more made it to the pass," a small Trog said from behind, hindered carrying an extra pack and walking with a limp.

"Well let that demon pass kill them off," muttered the leader.

The crow-voice dropped his end of the carryall, causing the wounded Trog to tumble off onto the ground with a moan. "Someone else carry this thing. I can't do it anymore."

"All right, let's make camp here. It's been a long march after that battle."

The Trogs congregated at the top of the hill dropping their packs. Baytel pulled Kalti back and returned to camp, finding Telek at watch.

"Keep a sharp eye, Telek. A troop of Trogs is camped to the northeast. How long have you been on watch?"

"I've slept enough. I relieved Adetin," said Telek.

"Wake us before dawn. We start before the sun."

The men made almost no sound, staying low in the dark valleys while Baytel and Kalti patrolled from the hills. The wind blew steadily from the northeast, so any sound of the Trogs would reach their ears before their noise, however minor, could be heard. Dawn revealed the tops of the hills and amber/green grass of the open land. Careful not to create long shadows Baytel kept low, skirting crowns, and rejoined the men in the valleys.

As the sun rose higher, he sighted smoke in the distance and sent Kalti to investigate while he kept a stationary watch from a hilltop.

Kalti returned faster than expected and reported that the Trog troop had abandoned their injured comrade. "I was close enough to see he was still alive but unconscious. All other signs point to the troop's departure south. His fire had died down to smoke with little heat from the embers."

"Can we approach his camp without resistance?"

"Yes. I doubt the Trog is strong enough to raise himself off the ground let alone resist unwanted visitors. No one else is in sight. The troop is long gone."

Baytel stood and waved the others up from the valley. "Maybe the Trog is not beyond our help."

They approached the Trog camp and found it just as Kalti reported; the lone Trog asleep and the fire low. At the crest of the hill Baytel looked down upon the fallen Trog and saw he had sword wounds across his legs, arms, and chest. The deep gash across his ribs and hip still bled. He and Areus knelt beside the injured Trog and gave him a light shake, but could not rouse him. "Dirk, stoke this fire and get some water boiling. Areus, what do you think?"

Areus removed the meager bandages and studied the wounds. "They are filled with dirt. Let's cleanse them, starting with the deepest here along his chest, and then work our way down to the lesser wounds. Once cleansed, let's apply that herbal mixture you took from Sezon's bag. Make a poultice out of it. It is a strong curative."

The length of the gash ran across the Trog's chest and around the rib cage. The skin was discolored along the sides of the wound. Baytel said, "We better hurry. The infection has already spread."

The fire stoked and the water boiled, they immediately cleaned the wounds, extracting the poison from the flesh, applied the healing poultice, and bandaged the Trog. The activity briefly stirred the Trog as he opened his eyes but fell back asleep.

Baytel looked up from his attention on the Trog, seeing the men hovering about, and said, "Adetin, you and Telek patrol the vicinity. Let's make sure the Trog troop moved out of the area and then set Dirk on watch on that high hill to the south. Kalti, set our camp in the valley below. I do not want us exposed up here in the open."

Baytel brewed tea and Areus raised the Trog's head and fed him the drink. Though he did not wake, he gulped it down without losing a drop.

"I think we stopped the infection in time, Baytel."

"I agree. Let's hope he comes around soon. We need to know what he knows of the goblin horde."

Dolog felt the hot liquid on his lips again. He opened his mouth wider, letting the fluid flow into the back of his throat, and he swallowed. The warmth of the drink coursed through his body, awakening his blood, and immediately the pain of his injuries returned.

One of his arms he could not move. He raised his free arm, touching his chest and finding it freshly bandaged. He opened his eyes and saw two men returning his gaze. They were smiling at him. He did not return the smile. He turned his head and scanned the surrounding camp. His troop was gone. "Am I the only one you spared?"

"No," said the young blue-eyed man. "Your companions departed before dawn. They left you here to die, but that will not happen. We tended to your wounds and you will fully heal."

Dolog looked warily at both men. They were dressed the same. They both had the same look in their eyes, strong, confident and purposeful. He did not like that.

"Why do you do this? I do not know you. Your kind never helps my kind."

"We are men of the Citadel. Our work is for the land and its sects of human-ity," said the dark-haired one. "To leave you unattended is against our oath and commitment."

There was more to it than what the dark-haired one stated. "And?"

They exchanged glances. Dolog was right. They had other intentions.

"And...we need to ask you a few questions. I believe you can be of assis-tance."

"When answered, then to be disposed of? Keep the Trog alive another day...then reward his assistance with death?"

He began to rise but the pain was too great. The other man, fair-eyed and with peculiar ears, had not said a word. The man had a studied appearance to him. Dolog touched his bandages again, this time with intricacy, and realized these men truly had the healing art. Had he been conscious when they arrived, he would have never accepted treatment and would probably be dead. This alone infuriated him more than being left for dead by his troop.

He shut his eyes to center his mind. *Things need to be resolved before death takes me, such as returning to the caves and taking revenge upon the weak-minded leader and troop for abandoning me! Perhaps my survival will gain me a more prominent title and stature in the tribe? Especially after how bravely I fought against those monsters.* The more he thought, the more tired he became and all went black.

The sun rose majestically, blazing warmth across the amber hills. The blan-ket of dew shimmered golden crystals, bringing Dirk Ironwright's voice from the campsite below.

"If only it was real gold! Adetin, can you imagine mining such a vast trea-sure?"

Gar replied, "It would be more like collecting, as if we were bees to pollen."

"Collecting or digging for gold, either way I am game for."

The fanatical desire the Ctiklat Dwarfs had for gold was unmatched. Baytel left the conversation with Dirk mumbling about lost treasures of their ancestors and the gold bullion Ctiklat Mountain had yielded in the past, and walked back to the sleeping Trog. Sitting at his side in the quiet dawn, Baytel waited for him to wake. The Trog had slept restfully since the afternoon the previous day. Areus had stayed with him throughout the night, had changed the bandages once and reported the positive response to the poultice.

The Trog stirred as the sun reached their hilltop, alighting them all in a glow of orange. He opened his eyes, beholding the rising sun. The Trog's serene expression showed an appreciation that unfolded a new perception to Baytel: Perhaps these Trogs were not a sect of violence alone. If they could recognize beauty and savor it, as it seemed this Trog did, perhaps the reputation of the Trogs was misleading.

The Trog turned and they met eyes. "I have seen the sun rise and set over our hills for fifty years and never do I tire of the sight."

"It is beautiful country," Baytel replied. The Trog pulled himself up to sit. His face crinkled in pain as he struggled. Baytel reached out to help but the Trog pushed him away. Sitting at eye level was the Trog's subtle way of saying that the ordeal was over and he would accept no further assistance.

The Trog steadied himself and Baytel allowed him time to accept his pain and find whatever comfort from the position he could.

After deep breaths, the Trog stated formally, "I am Dolog, of the Trog."

"Good morning and how do you feel?" asked Baytel, looking at the wrappings to see if his wounds had opened from his maneuverings.

"I am fit enough. You and your companion have the healing art."

The Trog was studying him. He sensed the Trog was a deeply reserved fellow and intelligent. "I am Baytel, Druid of the Citadel, as is the other man who helped you. His name is Areus. We are healers."

"Why are you in our land?" he asked, his tone gruff.

"We were patrolling your country night before last to find safe passage without encountering your sect when we came upon your troop. We kept hidden while your troop set camp. Our quest points through your country out of urgency. If we had more time, we would have avoided your hills entirely. Our destination is the city of Kilhalen."

"You have others besides this Areus?" asked Dolog.

"Including myself we are six."

"All druids?" asked Dolog.

"No, just Areus and I are of the Citadel. There is Adetin Gar, Telek and Kalti of Elangal Forest and Dirk Ironwright of the Ctiklat Dwarfs."

"Where are they?" he asked.

"Camped separately in the valley below."

"Druids, thieves and dwarfs? This makes no sense. You must all be thieves. Is this your urgent matter in our land? For if it is, you will only find death!"

Dolog was trying to rise but stopped and grabbed his side. Baytel held him down, and said, "You tear those wrappings and you will surely die. We seek no fortune or treasure. Our mission is for the One Land and its sects of humanity. We came upon your troop and overheard them speaking of monsters. They are a goblin horde sent out from the Southland where the black art is upon the land." And Baytel, sensing without knowing why that he could trust the Trog, spoke quickly of their quest.

Dolog starring blankly into the fire; the memory of pain passed on his face. "Surprise attack defeated our troop, and the advantage of their numbers. We Trogs lost many that day."

"We have fought those monsters also. We have been hunted by them and now are the hunters. We need information about where they have gone."

Dolog raised an eyebrow. "I hear truth in your voice, yet you travel with men of Elangal, the Forest Thieves. You say you battled this *goblin horde* as you call them, but you look unscathed. Many questions must be answered before I can give any assistance. It may be you are looking to raid our caves. But probably not, for you could have followed the troop." Dolog paused and then said, "I need time to think on these things you speak. I am tired and will rest."

Baytel understood. Trogs have endured years of torment from outsiders. Their existence was not created by the One Land, but was a product of war. They could not erase the atrocities their ancestors committed, but they are here, wanting only to live as any other sect would.

Yet there was so little time. Knowing how long ago the horde entered Konart Pass and how many goblins remained was so important.

Baytel rose when Areus arrived from camp. "Is there anything to be concerned about, Areus?"

"Adetin reported no signs of Trog movement other than the tracks of the troop departure south. A few wolf tracks to the northwest but they were old. He suggests keeping our fires low and out of sight of the hilltops."

Dolog had fallen asleep again. Areus kneeled down and began re-wrapping his bandages.

"We must break this camp and use only the valley site. I'll get Telek to help you move Dolog below."

A sliver of a falcate moon hung over the hills like a dim smiling lantern, barely illuminating enough to see clearly, but not blotting out the lights of the star-filled sky.

Dolog sat up with difficulty and scanned the others about the small campfire in the valley. He saw the dwarf asleep at his watch. *How easy it would be to kill them all as they slept.*

He could return to the caves and tell of the invaders he had slain in their land after being left behind for dead, gaining even higher stature in his tribe. But those thoughts were fleeting as one of the thieves stirred, the older one whose night noises would wake the dead. He recognized all three of the thieves.

No, he would not kill them. Dolog found truth in the words of the druid Baytel. He seemed their leader and was patient not to force his concern upon him. *Uncommon for so much wisdom to run in the veins of one so young.*

Dolog rose to his knees. His head immediately began to spin. Rising to his feet with a grunt, he walked to the fire where a pot of food remained. He had not eaten since the night of his abandonment. Finding a spoon he ate what remained and his thoughts drifted back to the other druid, Areus.

They had talked while the others were on patrol. Areus spoke of the Citadel and meeting Baytel, and detailing the events from Tridling Del, and Dolog heard the pain behind his words. That was when he decided to assist these Citadel men. Whatever the reasons, they all wanted a common enemy destroyed. The goblins that had attacked his troop would return without fear. They must be eliminated.

He finished his meal and threw the pot down on a rock. The noise quickly woke the men from their slumber, and at once they were on their feet, swords drawn and readied.

"Ha!"

"Hold!" yelled Baytel.

"What was that?" hailed the dwarf from above.

"Your wake-up call, Dwarf," said Dolog.

"You play games with us, Trog?" said Telek.

"No games, Thief. I was awakened by the noise thundering from your sleeping mouth. Lucky I woke you or every Trog in the land would have heard you."

The Druid Baytel gave the old thief a nudge, smiling, and they all sheathed their swords. He said, "Well, it seems you are feeling better."

"I am fit enough for travel. We Trogs heal rapidly. I was hungry and helped myself to your food. Now, I am ready to repay my debt to you. What is it you wish of me?"

"You are indebted to no one, Dolog. If you leave our camp now to your home you will get no resistance from anyone here," said Baytel.

"My people distrust all wanderers who invade our land. Many years have passed since men had free will in our hills. Always when men enter our land, bloodshed and despair remain after they leave. We are a simple-minded people, but know the truth of things. You saved my life and I owe you a debt of life. I know not how a Trog will be able to fulfill this debt to druids, so for now, I will answer your questions as best I can."

"Your assistance will be remembered always and will be reported to the Faerie Council. My report will point to you being the representative of your sect," said Baytel.

Dolog shrugged, not understanding his offer and not caring much about it either. He focused on the matter at hand: "The black art of the Southland must be very powerful to create such monsters as we fought outside Konart Pass. They entered it five days ago. Is that one answer to a question?"

"Yes," said Baytel. "How far is it to Konart Pass? And will we meet any resistance along the way?"

"To tell you the distance in time I can answer. As to any resistance, it may come from many ways and in different forms. I do not know how many goblins we fought. Many more than you all can handle. The land is wild and until you gain the high ground of Lumithien, you will be vulnerable."

"How many days to the high ground?" asked Gar.

"You are the leader of the thieves. I recognize your name from the many years of sharing the borderlands. I heard of your losses. It is unfortunate to lose so many. We lost many at the foot of the high valley that leads to the pass. It is three days' march west and north. You will find the terrain rises steadily at the end of the second day and a birch forest upon the ascent into Lumithien. Keep the birch trees to the south and follow them to the high ground."

"Are there Trog troops near Konart Pass?" asked Areus.

Baytel said, "Yes, this would be a situation we want to avoid. With you assisting us through your land, it would be inhospitable for us to—"

"Bite the hand that feeds us," voiced Telek, smiling.

"You will find no patrols northwest for four days so do not delay in your departure." He was displeased with the sharing of information on their patrols, but he was alive and must trust them.

"This goblin horde is now five days ahead of you. I hope you can overtake them, though with only six, it is certain death you march toward."

"Break camp. Dirk, keep watch until we depart." Baytel turned and said, "Thank you, Dolog, you have freely given service to the One Land and it will be stated by me at the Faerie Council at Kilhalen. This I promise you as a man of the Citadel, and as a friend."

Dolog stared down at the hand the druid extended and grasped it at the forearm. "I accept your friendship, though whatever you said about faeries and councils I care nothing for. I bid you safe journey, man of the Citadel. I speak for my people that you are welcome at our caves when you venture into our lands again."

Dolog grasped Areus's arm in friendship and then walked to the top of the hill to watch the druids and their companions march away.

Chapter 52

ENTERING the Lumithien region had brought the towering precipices closer. For two days since leaving the Trog hills behind, the group steadily rose until they realized they were on the foothills of the Lumithien. The highland was dotted with aspen trees and open pastures that, if known and accessible, would be perfect for the grazing of livestock.

At dawn the third day out, a heavy fog blanketed the ground, reaching up to Baytel's chest. The higher he led, the thicker the fog. Soon only their heads stayed above the fog. He heard laughter and he turned, seeing Dirk Ironwright's hat on top of his delve-axe bobbing in and out of view above the fog line. Baytel called a halt and told Dirk to tie himself to Kalti and Adetin Gar behind. "Let's not lose anyone in this fog and cause any further delays. I want to enter Konart Pass in the light of day."

Afternoon brought the row of birch trees Dolog had mentioned, appearing ghost-like in the thick mist. Baytel slowed the pace, unable to see beyond the haunting birch trees. The foothill steepened and through the fog a lonely cry of a wolf confirmed what he was thinking: They were in a canyon. Baytel sent Gar to scout ahead, unsure of what environment was before them.

But soon, at a bend in the canyon, the fog dissipated. Moving out of the foggy canyon and into the light of afternoon sun, he found the towering peaks of the Lumithien Mountain Range surrounding the entire bowl of a beautiful highland valley. Dark green clover budded lavender across the valley floor. Mountain laurel glowing lighter green speckled the landscape. The change of season was progressing faster in the high elevation as the aspen trees had already changed to yellow, a stark contrast against the ashen rock of the haughty cliffs. Pine trees grew along the base of the high rock, and though towering in their own right, were minuscule to the spectacular height of Lumithien.

The wind swept across the basin and whistled as it escaped through unseen crevasses. Baytel lifted his eyes to the jagged rock facade until they met the snow-capped summits of the numerous peaks, all too dangerous to attempt climbing. Eagles sailed high above, hovering and banking on the wind swirls, hunting for prey.

Adetin Gar, far ahead in the valley, hailed and pointed toward a notch between two peaks. He had located Konart Pass. Then Baytel saw Gar hesitate as if studying a patch of terrain at his feet. He signaled more urgently and waved them forward.

Arriving, Baytel looked down at the blackened earth where broken swords and lances lay, the only objects that remained from the battle the Trogs had waged with the goblins. No other evidence of carnage remained for the blood of the goblins had burned everything away.

Areus knelt, investigating the remains. "We are farther behind them than I thought."

"The blood of these goblins even burned away the Trogs too," said Ironwright, shaking his head in disgust.

"We shall sweep clean the land of this malicious incarnate," said Telek.

Baytel turned from the scene. "Let's go men. We waste time here." A howl echoed off the rock walls.

Gar had moved ahead and shouted back, "There are fresh wolf tracks everywhere."

At a second howl, Baytel looked back from where they came, seeing a wolf standing resolute as if on post watch.

Telek was at his side. "It's a gray wolf, Baytel. They hunt in packs. Their dens number thirty or forty wolves. They are relentless hunters."

A howl ahead stopped Baytel. Then more howls from behind as three more wolves appeared.

Gar had returned to join them. "Gray wolf pack at the entrance of Konart. I counted twenty. Maybe more."

"Look," cried Ironwright and they saw more wolves congregate behind the one at the canyon opening.

"We are cut off," said Kalti.

Baytel watched both wolf packs gather, the ever-fiercer howling bouncing off the rock. The packs paced, impatiently waiting for a signal from their leader. He looked across at the wolf pack blockading the entrance to Konart Pass, their numbers doubling before his eyes. No one spoke as they all unsheathed their weapons.

Then Baytel remembered the dream—the guide and snow-filled valley. *But was this the valley of my dream?* He scanned the valley and saw it dip toward a distant cliff. *It must be!*

Gar calmly said, "Stay close, men. We will fight the pack with our backs to one another."

"No!" Baytel looked at the far end of the valley. Then back to the wolves. He decided. "Follow me! This way!" and he ran toward the cliff.

Baytel turned to check on the men and saw they hesitated. "Come on! Hurry!"

They caught up with him.

"Where are you going?" yelled Ironwright.

Baytel sensed the dream he had was much more than a fantasy. The old man, Belwas, his magic was powerful and Baytel felt he sent him the dream to show him an alternative through Lumithien. He was certain of it.

So he ran and the men followed and the gray wolf pack chased and gained at every step. "We must get to the east end of the valley. Quick men!"

The valley sloped down and the grass ended. His feet met rock and gravel nearing the east cliff.

"Baytel. Where are you taking us?" yelled Areus on his heels.

"We are almost there! Keep up!" He glanced back seeing the lead wolf gaining on the dwarf. "Dirk! Behind you!"

On the run, Dirk swung his delve ax and it found its mark. The wolf broke off the attack, bleeding where he fell.

Seeing blood, the lead wolves stopped and began a frenzied meal preying upon their own, but others in the pack took up the chase again.

Baytel reached the façade of the cliff and ran along its base. "Where is it?"

"Where is what?" yelled Telek, as the men reached the cliff, all looking for something, yet not knowing what to find.

Baytel climbed up a boulder and jumped onto the face of the cliff, clinging to a small hold. He studied the façade from the ground up and finally found what he sought. "There! There it is! The ledge!"

He jumped down and ran to a protrusion of rock well off ground level. He climbed up the façade and stood on the ledge. "Climb, men, up to this ledge! Quick now!"

They followed him up and stood upon the ledge as the salivating wolf pack gathered below.

Gar said, "We are not food yet."

"Silence!" he shouted. He needed it to concentrate on the dream and what the old man recited at the cliff.

Turning, Baytel faced the cliff wall. He slowed his breathing and focused inward, searching his memory. Then the ancient words came to him and he pressed his forehead upon the cold stone, whispering them for reassurance and pronunciation.

Satisfied, he raised his arms and hands toward the cliff and spoke the ancient words of Belwas aloud.

Nothing happened.

Baytel looked down at the wolves below. They were clambering up the stone face, one over the other, trying to reach them. However, as they attained the top, they met Dirk's delve-axe.

Baytel refocused and called upon his own magic for assistance. He spoke the ancient words to himself and his magic was stirred. A gradual swelling sensation rose within him and empowered him to meet the challenge of the ancient magic.

Then his magic released itself to him, reaching another level of control. Now, he realized he could command it. He was his magic's sole possessor.

Baytel shouted the ancient words with a force he had not known before and the facade began to crumble before him. Rocks fell from above and the ledge rumbled beneath his feet. He gauged his tone and spoke the words again as if he knew his words would strike the cliff like a hammer to rock. Then the cliff face yielded to his magic and a flash of light seared out from the rock, revealing a door. Baytel commanded the words once more and the door opened.

"Inside! Quickly!"

They all scrambled in. As the last of the men entered, the door slammed shut on its own, engulfing them in total darkness and silence.

Chapter 53

BAYTEL crouched low against the wall of the cave, holding his legs to his chest, trying to gain control of his magic that rushed through him. He could see nothing in the cave and the only sound audible was the breathing of the men in the darkness. Someone was fumbling about in a pack. Then a flint was struck. The short flash of light was enough to see a torch on the wall. Another strike and he saw Kalti's face in the glow from the torch flame.

The firelight partially illuminated the surroundings but Baytel still had difficulty seeing through the veil of his magic that clouded his sight while it sprinted through him, taking him to another level of its power. It was surging rapidly within him and he was on the verge of being overwhelmed by it. *I must gain a mastery of it before I lose control.*

Baytel receded deep within himself, pursuing the current of the magic that had infiltrated every cell of his body. Catching hold of the tail of the phenomenon, Baytel joined the flow and aligned his mind and body with the magic. From that fixed position, he seized the magic at its roots and slowly, carefully, began taking control, adjusting to its ebbs and flows. Baytel then commenced to guide it and soon established dominance over the magical current until it became wholly a part of him, like his heart, his limbs, or any other part of him. Then, with confidence, he commanded the magic to advance and then to withdraw, and it obeyed him without hesitancy. With that knowledge Baytel knew, from that moment, he could call upon it to do his bidding at any time, and it gave him pause.

As the magic veil receded and his sight returned, Baytel found the men's expressions full of wonder. They too had also realized he had used his magic without the aid of his sword!

Areus asked, "Baytel, are you alright?"

Baytel looked at each man, all silent and waiting for an explanation. He knew he owed them one. They deserved the truth of what he was becoming. *I am different than them.* And he felt deeply saddened by the fact. "Yes, I am alright. I cannot explain what has happened to me except to say that the sword has awakened a magical power within me. As it progresses I am charged to absorb the power while learning to control it. Through the months we have traveled together, it has

331

developed within me, and now the power is mine to wield, though to what extent I still do not know."

They all nodded and did not question, as if it were a matter of course. Yet the separation was apparent and no matter what they encountered together it would be thus. Nevertheless, they had previously accepted him as a man of ancient hierarchy and magic but also as a companion and friend; the latter suited him best, and this fact remained.

Telek cleared his throat, the usual preemptive gesture toward a quote. "As all know of the inevitable end, so it is that we witness a beginning."

Baytel took in the surroundings. They were in a cave-like vestibule. It was dark and dry. The rough-hewed wall had no visible writings or markings. Cobwebs hung like ivy off the low ceiling, some briefly catching fire from the small flame of the torch. Dust lay thick on the floor, evidence of it being undisturbed for a long time. The vestibule had one exit, into the heart of the mountain through a dark tunnel.

Gar asked, "How did you know of the ledge and this cave? And how did you know what to say to open it?"

"I did not bring it up before, thinking it was not important. The night before we left Belwas Swamp, I sat with the old man and he placed a sort of spell on me and I fell asleep and I had a dream. I believe the old man sent the dream to me pointing to an alternate route, other than the Konart Pass. In the dream the valley was full with snow. At first, I looked for the entrance at ground level, not compensating for snow accumulation. I climbed up the face, found the ledge and his words came to me. I do not know how he did it, but here we are."

Telek said, "It's a good thing you have the magic. We'd be wolf food had you not, Baytel."

They all nodded again, acquiescing to his powers that went beyond their own. "Telek, save your accolades until I finish this story. You may soon wish to be facing the gray wolves again"

Telek replied, "Continue, Baytel. We do not need sugar with this meal."

"Men, this is no ordinary cave. I am sorry to say that I have led you into the entryway to Old Warriors' Court."

"The hall of the dead soldiers!" exclaimed Ironwright, his voice already quivering with fear.

"Yes, Dirk."

"Out of the frying pan and into the fire," said Telek. They all turned toward him questioningly. "An ancient saying…it fits."

Areus asked, "Where does this hall lead?"

"Through Lumithien."

"What of the dead?" asked the dwarf.

"Surely, Dirk, you don't believe those old yarns," said Areus.

Baytel was quick to dispel Areus's statement. "Believe you must, for it is truth. Belwas, that is the old man's name, said the apparitions might appear. They have a power here stronger than any of us can imagine. He said once they appear, the spirits will attempt to draw us into a fight. It is emphatic we resist any temptation to do battle against them, for the spirits' purpose of drawing you into a fight is for them to take your life. It is their only chance at renewing their own lives again and gaining freedom from the hall of the dead. Our resolve must be strong to resist fighting the dead, for when you commence a battle against a spirit and sustain a wound, you become one of them, a spectre, and are doomed to the hall forever. We must keep our weapons sheathed and stay composed, or all will be lost to us."

"...and be transformed into a soldier of ghostly form, destined to fight within the Hall of the Dead for all eternity," quoted Telek. "It is from the written legend of the saga of Old Warriors' Court."

Baytel took the torch from Kalti. "Let's stay close to each other."

After a short distance, the tunnel turned and spiraled deeper into the bowels of the mountain. The ceiling remained low; all except Ironwright had to walk with bended knees and back. Studying the walls of the tunnel, Baytel noticed the construction had a familiar design. Columns and cornices were sculpted into the stone of the passage. An artisan's talented hands must have chiseled them but he could not put an origin to them. Baytel asked, "What are these etchings of?"

Ironwright answered immediately. "They have the looks of the older dwarf structures, but whose hand carved them so artistically I do not know."

The tunnel stretched downward, ending at an oaken ironclad door. The wrought iron hinges were stuck and it took Telek, Areus and Gar together to move the door. They entered another passageway. It rested level and extended a long way. The ceiling was higher and the walls were adorned with architectural crowns of an artistry Ironwright reaffirmed as being "most definitely that of the ancient dwarfs. They have the appearances of artwork of the Minion Dwarfs."

Baytel looked back to make sure everyone was still together and noticed Ironwright had stopped to study one of the cornices. "Get up here, Dirk."

The floor turned from stone to plank wood and, after a long stretch, it ended at a wide stairway that led upward. Baytel stood at the bottom of the stairs and saw light above.

"We are here. Keep the torch alive, Kalti. Remember, men. Keep your weapons sheathed against the dead."

Baytel led them up the creaking stairs. At each step, he cringed from the sound. Reaching the top, he saw the landing opened directly into a grand hall. The room was so large he could barely see the opposite end. Massive stone pillars supported the high dome ceiling. Along the walls and pillars burned torches that lit the chamber in a pallid red hue. A large wooden table sat in the center of the hall with nearly one hundred chairs around it. Place settings were strewn across the table. Broken lances, swords and shields lay about the hall. Armor and mail sat in corners and against the walls, discarded, bent and worn from battle use.

"Let's go, men. Quiet and easy."

Baytel felt an eeriness linger at the edge of his awareness. He felt as if eyes were upon him, but he saw no one. He led them farther into the hall, stepping carefully to avoid discarded weapons and armor, not wanting to disturb the quiet reverence that seemed to seep from the grand hall.

Telek, just behind him, edged close and whispered, "Baytel, something is near. I can feel it."

A moment later, Telek whispered again, "Baytel, I can hear it now. A familiar voice but I cannot put my mind to who's."

Baytel heard Telek's fear and sensed the old soldier had moved even closer behind. "Easy, Telek, whatever it is, it's not real. Keep calm and poised."

Baytel stepped so softly not even the floor dust stirred. He looked back at his men and found Ironwright had fallen back again. He watched as Dirk seemed to be gesturing with his hands, looking like he was speaking to himself. He stopped to allow Ironwright to bring up the rear and tighten their line when he heard Telek's intake of breath.

Telek's voice rose in a panic. "It draws near me!"

A wall torch suddenly extinguished and then Kalti's torch went out. Another torch followed, then another, sending the hall deeper into shadow. A foul dusty breeze swept through the hall, leaving only a few torches lit.

All were huddled close and Baytel took a count as the darkness descended. "Areus?"

"I am beside you."

"Adetin?"

"Here next to Kalti."

"Telek?"

No answer. "Telek?"

A faint whisper, "I am here next to Areus."

"Dirk?"

He did not respond. "Ironwright?"

Nothing. Then he saw a spirit appear, floating past the dim light of a torch. It moved slowly until reaching Ironwright, and then halted hovering above him and the dwarf dropped to his knees.

Dirk kneeled obediently below the wavering spirit, wide-eyed with fear. Never before had he seen so noble a dwarf as that which appeared above him. He sank humbly, bowing his head in tribute. Then looking up at the apparition he noticed a frosty smile upon the ghost's lips, but it disappeared quickly, replaced by an expression of sorrow.

The spirit spoke with a voice sad with regret and lost hope. "Rise, distant nephew. Rise and be my equal."

"King Minion, I am yours to command," Dirk Ironwright mumbled, frightened beyond understanding of the most renowned ancestor in Dwarf history.

"Dirk!" They shouted his name repeatedly but Ironwright was so captivated by the spirit he was oblivious to all around him.

Seeing the apparition mouthing words silent to his ears, Baytel asked, "What is it saying? Can anyone hear?"

"Ironwright!" yelled Gar. "Dirk!" But it was no use. The spirit was in control of Dirk.

"Brodin!"

Baytel turned and saw Telek facing another ghost. "Telek! No!" he shouted but it was too late. Telek and the ghostly soldier clashed swords.

"I killed you once, annihilator of innocence!" Telek bawled over the ringing blades. "One death is not enough for you, bastard of demons!"

"Fall back, Telek!" shouted Kalti.

"Telek! Stop! You mustn't," cried Baytel.

"Wrong, Baytel! I must! It is Brodin! The evil ravager, murderer of innocent women and children!"

Baytel watched as Telek battled the spirit he called Brodin crashing across chairs and broken armor. He looked back and found the dwarf spirit was leading Ironwright back toward the stairs.

"Dirk! Come back!" Areus yelled.

Baytel shouted, "Adetin! Grab him!"

"Aaahh!"

Telek was down on the floor with the evil spirit Brodin hovering over him. Telek was wounded, cut across the arm and chest, but the wound did not bleed.

Telek looked at his arm and chest. With the realization of what the injury meant and the terror of his own mortality, a great scream of fear burst from his lungs.

Dirk Ironwright fell to the floor whimpering in fear, wanting to escape from the spirit, knowing all the while that to follow was wrong, that to follow was to die, but the will of King Minion was too strong. It was luring him into the spirit world, into the realm of the dead, and he couldn't stop.

"I am old, young Ironwright. I must pass my mantle to one who is my blood. You are my chosen, Nephew," the ghost pleaded. "You are of my bloodline and must follow in the path of the kings of Minion."

"I…I…" Dirk couldn't form words. *How can I speak? This is King Minion, the patriarch of all Ctiklat Dwarfs before me!*

He heard someone shouting his name. The voice seemed familiar, yet he was not sure where it came from. He was so enveloped in the nightmare spirit world that the world of the living was now the unreal dream.

Dirk tore his eyes away from King Minion and, for the first time, saw the ranks of ghostly soldiers in the hall and wondered from where they had come. Then he looked back at Minion and followed, its voice leading him down the hall.

"I have riches beyond belief, young Dirk. They can be yours. When we deserted Minion Mountain, I hid my treasures and vowed to return."

The talk of treasure brought him back to the present and his fear was replaced by greed. "The famed jewels of Minion?"

"Yes! Yes, Ironwright, and they are yours! Come! Come to me. Take my hand and be one of us and you will be rich beyond your dreams."

"They are there? In Minion?" he asked forgetting what was happening to him.

"Yes. The treasure awaits you. It can all be yours," prodded King Minion.

Dirk hesitated, hearing his name again at the border of his consciousness, but it was not enough to tear him away from his desires and the possibility of riches that now consumed him. "Where? Where in Minion Mountain are they?"

"In Minion Mountain, the window to the stars will lead you to them. Come, take my hand and I will guide you there. Come!"

Dirk slowly walked toward the specter and reached out to take its hand, lost in his greed for treasure and riches and the spell of King Minion. Their hands were about to touch when the apparition changed before him. The sorrowful face of Minion turned hateful and death showed in its eyes.

Dirk screamed in terror as Minion's hand was filled with a dagger and rose to strike. Dirk countered to defend and pulled out his delve ax. Before he could swing it to kill the spirit he was grabbed from behind.

"No, Dirk!"

He was pinned to the floor, flailing about trying to reach past the one who held him, only seeing the hovering spirit baring the dagger.

"Dirk, it's me, Adetin!" he shouted. "Dirk! Dirk Ironwright of the Ctiklat Dwarves!"

At the word *Ctiklat* the nightmare faded and Dirk returned to the realm of the living. He felt a heavy weight upon his chest and realized Adetin Gar was sitting on his chest, bellowing his name, shaking him.

Dirk shut his eyes, frightened of seeing the ghost again. "Adetin! Is it gone? Is King Minion gone?"

Gar looked about. The ghost had disappeared. "Yes, Dirk, it is gone. But you stay with me from here on. Do not leave my side!"

Dirk clung to Adetin's arm as if it were the last hold before dropping into a chasm. He was pulled to his feet, and said, "No power on earth will persuade me from doing just that, Adetin Gar!"

The shade of the murderer Brodin laughed hideously as it toyed with the powerless Telek, brandishing its sword mockingly over his prostrate body. An insane cruelty seeped from its translucent form and although an apparition, its body seemed to be altering as new-found mass became apparent on the spirit.

As Brodin raised its sword to complete the destruction of Telek, Areus jumped in front of the ghost, blocking its attack. Then Kalti joined in placing himself over the prostrate body of Telek, drawing his sword. The apparition rose, confused, and then it attacked Kalti, who ducked from the sword thrust and dashed down the hall, drawing the ghost away.

"Areus, take Telek's other arm." They pulled him off the floor and held him up. He could not stand on his own, weak from the wound that did not bleed. Adetin and Dirk joined them. Dirk's face was wrenched with fright.

Baytel asked, "What was it?"

Dirk stayed mute, numb with fear, his hand tightly around Adetin's arm. Adetin answered for him, "The most renown patriarch of his race, King Minion."

"Keep him close, Adetin."

"Depend on it."

Baytel led down the grand hall toward the far doorway, and Baytel looked over his shoulder at Kalti who was skirting around fallen chairs and weaponry, jumping over the long table with the shade at his heels. "Kalti! Strike up that torch and run for the door at the far end of the hall!" shouted Baytel.

With Telek between him and Areus, they ran, stumbling over discarded armor and chairs. He lost his grip on Telek and fell, bringing Telek and Areus with him. Instantly, other spirits appeared all about them with malice and death in their eyes, for they became aware of the fortune that had come their way—living beings in the midst of their dead world and the possibility of becoming flesh once again.

By the frenzied commotion of the specters in the hall, it must have been hundreds of years since any living being had set foot in Old Warriors' Court. The ghosts followed them down the hall, stalking just beyond the torchlight, haunting from the shadows and inching closer. Panic had moved into the forefront of Baytel's mind but before it took hold he reasoned that Belwas would not have sent him into Old Warriors' Court unless there truly was a way out.

Snubbing his trepidations, he needed to calm the men, who were at wit's end amid the magically frightening nightmare. The phenomenon of Old Warriors' Court was astounding, terrifying and lethal. The ghouls spoke from the darkness, enticing with promises of extraordinary desires achieved only with their aid. They were relentless. Baytel needed to thwart them from fogging the minds of the men. He had to do something extraordinary for them to escape.

Areus was beside him, saying, "We must get out of here. Telek will not last. He is changing into one of them, becoming lighter by the moment, and Dirk is useless to us."

Baytel looked out at the apparitions waving before them like banners in the wind. All sects of humanity were accounted for—goblins, men, trolls, dwarfs, pixies, gnomes and some he could not identify, all were warriors at one time in the history of the One Land and all died in battle. Heroes and villains of war, enemies and allies, as one in their haunting lair, eager to fall upon any who dared enter their realm.

Dirk was whimpering with fright and Telek was moaning in pain. Areus and Kalti held Telek while Adetin had a hold on Dirk; all seemed powerless against the ghastly hosts closing in from all directions.

Areus leaned toward him and said, "We are surrounded, Baytel. Draw your sword."

Baytel hesitated. "Belwas said not to engage the spirits."

"Draw it, Baytel. Let's see what they do. We are closed off."

The penetrating horror of the spirits and the terror in the eyes of the men were demoralizing. Drawing the sword was their only option. However, would his magic come to life in the Hall of the Dead?

"I do not know if it will work, Areus."

"We need a diversion to reach the far door. Do it, Baytel. Use your magic."

The dead soldiers edged closer, readying to attack. He stole a glance at the men; Telek wounded, clinging desperately to Kalti, and Dirk lost to his fear, clinging to Adetin.

Baytel closed his eyes, blocking off the surrounding frightfulness and withdrew. He called upon his magic and it instantly came forth like a torrential internal wind and his entire being was charged with the wild seeds of magic empowerment.

He drew the sword. The flash of light from its exposed presence flooded the hall with surprising velocity. The spirits fell back, stunned with shock and in fear of the magical light.

Then one of the spirits shouted over the commotion. "A magic sword!"

Other apparitions' voices raised up, "It's the sword of the Kings!"

The clamor rose to a feverous pitch and some spirits fell to their knees.

"It is the future king!"

"Grab it!" said one ghost, but a kneeling spirit rose and blocked the way.

"No! It is Man's!" the ghost soldier yelled.

"Take it!" said another.

Another spirit jumped forward. "Keep back! It will guide the land!"

"Step aside, fool. It can be ours to free us all from this hall!"

"Yield, I say! It is Man's!"

The clash of their swords echoed throughout the vast hall as the ghosts took arms against one another. It was a melee of fright as grunts and shouts of battle were all about them. More joined the battle, and though they were all dead and no one could die again, they fought with renewed passion for they were still proud soldiers now doing battle once more for a cause.

"To the end of the hall! Kalti and Areus, you have Telek! Adetin, you have Dirk. Run!"

Baytel dashed down the hall after the men, defending their retreat. The haunted battle followed them as ally and foe clashed to keep his sword in sight. A particular phantom caught his eye, hovering above the fighting spirits. The ghost wore unadorned armor its mail woven into a leather coat, and about its waist was a sword belt with an empty sheath. Each time Baytel stole a glance, he found the spirit grinning as if amused. The spirit had a familiar look about it. Then it struck him; it looked like Calidor.

No, it was not Calidor, but the spirit carried a regal air and Baytel realized he was looking at the ghostly form of his great-grandfather. The specter had the look of a man who commanded armies, a leader who sent both young and old into battle with the promise of honor and glory and probably made certain they received both in life as well as death.

Baytel's companions reached the door at last and fled the hall. Baytel stopped and turned toward the ghost of his great-grandfather, raising his sword to salute the patriarch of the Kings of the North. The great man returned the salute with a gesture that sent him on his way.

Baytel bounded down the steps, catching up with the men as they descended into the bowels of Lumithien. The clamor of pursuing spirits echoed in the passage and he kept to the rear defense position. The going was slow but they were gaining distance on the spirits, as their noise seemed to lessen.

Areus was carrying Telek alone. The big man must be a great weight to take alone and Baytel asked, "How are you and Telek holding up?"

"Not good, Baytel. I am fine but Telek has become much lighter. Look, he is becoming transparent."

"We must reach the outside before he becomes one of them. Be quick, men. Pick up the pace."

The passage narrowed and the ceiling height lowered. They ran in single file. Kalti had the lead followed by Dirk on Adetin Gar's back and Areus carrying Telek over his shoulder, balancing him with one arm like a sack of cabbage. The passageway curved to a corridor and to another stairway. It plunged deeper, and the farther they went, the darker it became and Baytel did not notice until they were far down the stairwell that the noise of the pursuing host was gone.

A door at the base of the stairwell blocked the way. They shouldered the door open and Baytel found they were in a dark cavern. The glow of his sword was dulled to a soft glimmer, the steel hardly the brilliance it had displayed in the Hall of the Dead moments ago, illuminating only a small area around them. Before taking another step he allowed his eyes to adjust to the dark. It was a small cave. The walls and ceiling had been chiseled by primitive hands with no artful designs anywhere. The floor was layered with dirt and broken rock, not the polished stone of the hall. The paltry light cast angry shadows.

Baytel's magic tingled his senses and he took the forewarning to heart and said, "Let's continue cautiously, men. I do not like the feel of this cave."

A heavy wariness seemed to be seeping into his body from the still air. The cave felt evil and his magic shouted from within him that danger was at hand. The traces of dread pervaded his senses and he knew that the ghosts back in the assembly room were not the only things haunting Lumithien.

The door slammed shut behind them. The darkness became blacker as even the floor was now undistinguishable. A wisp of foul air flowed past. Baytel felt eyes upon him once again and heard the shuffling of many feet. Suddenly, dim light was born from the walls and out of the darkness ghosts appeared. They were not the proud soldiers of the Old Warriors' Court but fell souls, dark, horrific beings, who had committed atrocities and caused unspeakable horrors to humanity when alive. Here they haunted, their pasts manifested in the afterlife.

Baytel held his sword outward as the ghouls' faces appeared. Revolting goblins of death, ogres, horrific sprites and foul dryads edged closer. The wretched creatures of death and destruction that fought and died at evil's side haunted the cave, unwelcome even in Old Warriors' Court.

Baytel looked past the horrors at the opposite end, seeing what looked like an opening to a tunnel. "Gather close, men. We walk together to the next door."

Baytel moved forward, using the sword as shield to keep the evil ones back, but halfway to the tunnel, he could go no farther, blocked by the unyielding ghouls.

The men huddled together, their faces so close to one another he could smell their fear and desperation. Baytel called upon his magic, but it seemed unfamiliar with the magic that lived within the cave. Baytel examined their position. Telek was more transparent than human. Dirk was struggling to get away from Gar, who kept a brave front as the shade of King Minion had reappeared in the cave and was urging Ironwright to come with him. Baytel's sword glow, still dull but alive, showed his magic had not abandoned him; it was piecing together a defense against the power in the cave. And once more, it was up to him to free his men from the horrors before them. The dream he received from the old man had been clear about Old Warriors' Court, but what about this cave? There seemed to be no escape.

The ghouls became more aggressive, advancing into their space, pulling at their clothing, their hair, jabbing them with spear and sword not necessarily to draw blood, but to provoke a battle that would cause a sequence of deaths so the ghouls could be free of the spirit world. The ghouls would charge at them and stop within inches of their faces, and the men shied away in horrific fright.

Kalti was beside Baytel, his eyes shut blocking away the horribleness. Baytel studied Kalti's face. His resemblance to his own, as noted by Areus upon first encounter, was unmistakable. Baytel had no doubt Kalti was of the same unknown sect as his mother. Then it came to him. A forgotten moment in the dream.

The blue stone!

Baytel reached into his tunic, retrieving the smooth blue stone. It was cool against his palm. Simply holding the stone for a brief moment was enough for him to feel its power. In the midst of the haunting cave, the stone had a calming effect upon him.

Baytel found Kalti's hand and placed the blue stone in his palm and closed his fingers about it. Baytel leaned to Kalti's ear and said, "Kalti, listen to me. This stone was given to me by Belwas. It has magic properties whose origins are from our ancestry."

Baytel watched the play of several questions run across Kalti's face, showing he, too, must have recognized their similarities. Baytel continued, "Yes, Kalti, I have no doubt we are of the same secular blood."

Baytel watched him nod. "Now Kalti, hold the stone tight. Do you feel its power?"

Kalti did not answer him, but the elation on his face showed he could.

"You must speak a word to the blue stone. I do not know what will happen but it is my belief it is a word so beautiful and true that it will bring forth joy and lead us to freedom. Take the men to that far tunnel access and I will follow, guarding our backs," he paused, arching his sword, keeping the spirits back.

Then Baytel whispered into Kalti's ear the word spoken to him by Belwas in his dream. Hearing the word, tears rolled down Kalti's face.

Kalti pulled his gaze away from the frightening ghouls and looked directly into Baytel's eyes and said, "Cousin."

Kalti smiled as though a veil that had obscured his soul had been swept away, leaving him with an exaltation of peace and hope. Then Kalti turned and faced the ghouls. Gone was his fright and in its place was joy, confidence, and wanton elation. He lifted his fist above his head and spoke in a clear, commanding voice the word.

"Eästarîl!"

A deep blue light exploded from the stone. The dazzling brilliance was like poison and fire to the ghouls. Smote by waves of the blue stone's power, cowering in pain and fear of the magic, the ghouls shrank away in complete agony.

Baytel saw an opening and shouted, "Let's go, Kalti. Gather up Telek, Areus! Adetin, you have Dirk!"

They ran from the cave into the start of a tunnel that sloped downward until they reached another cave and a dead end.

Areus asked, "What do we do now?"

Baytel's sword had sprung back to life, illuminating the cave. "Search for another door!"

"Here!" shouted Areus. "Baytel, rune markings! They are in the tongue of the faerie."

Baytel ran to the markings to illuminate the deeply cut etchings. Behind, he could hear the spirits advancing down the tunnel. He had no time to read the rune and turned away from the wall, sword raised and ready.

"Areus, read the rune aloud to me!"

Areus dashed behind him and shouted the language as the first ghosts arrived. He switched places with Areus and sheathed his sword. The tunnel went black. He brought his hands up and placed them on the wall of the cave. His magic surged from his palms into the wall and he spoke the faerie rune aloud.

The wall began to shake beneath Baytel's hands and a thin sliver of light bore through from the outside. He blocked out the commotion of the spirits from his mind and again spoke the faerie rune with authority. The words reverberated off the walls of the cave stilling the tumult of the ghostly mob. In a flash, the cave wall illuminated a door and it swept open, emitting brilliant daylight into the cave.

"Freedom!" yelled the ghosts. "The outside!"

The ghosts rushed the open door to escape but as soon as they met daylight they shrank away, as it was fire to their transparent skin.

Baytel and Areus grabbed Telek and threw him out into the daylight. "Areus, Kalti, get clear!"

Baytel turned to retrieve Dirk and Adetin but they were nowhere to be found.

"Adetin! Where are you? Where is Dirk?"

Adetin Gar shouted, "Here! I see Dirk! He is walking back up the tunnel toward the spirit of Minion!"

"Adetin! Get him out of here!"

Gar yanked Dirk away from King Minion who had nearly took him beyond the cave back into the tunnel. Baytel caught up with them and, grabbing Iron-wright's other arm, he and Gar dragged the dwarf into the sunlight. Then the doors slammed, shutting out the raging screams of King Minion's spirit and the ghosts within.

Chapter 54

SO caught up with his private thoughts of what had occurred in Old Warriors' Court and the caves, Baytel came out of his all-consuming retreat away from the base of the Lumithien to find it was late in the afternoon.

The autumn season had settled in the northland forest region. The dense woods they left behind were filled with color and an open country of matted grasslands lay bare before them. Small poplars grew along-side larger elms; their dead brown leaves blew across the landscape on the soft breeze. Maple trees also found the rich soil of the country nourishing; their branches spread wide, and leaves of red-gold lay upon the ground around them, blanketing the land in brilliant color.

Unknowingly, Baytel had put a fair amount of distance between him and the other men. Each one of them had been deeply affected by their experiences in the Old Warriors' Court, and he was concerned for them. All had been silent throughout the day since their escape, trudging along in the unfamiliar land, probably as insensible as he had been, deep in their personal contemplations. Every one of them, including himself, were touched in different ways by the ordeal, and he was afraid that doubts of what they volunteered for would sprout and he thought some might walk away from the quest.

For now, Baytel stayed on course and allowed the space between them to remain, wanting to give the men time and freedom to work out whatever apprehensions they might be experiencing.

Areus was looking at Baytel far ahead entering a sunlit meadow.

"Extraordinary magical powers were at work in that mountain and we would be among the dead had it not been for Baytel."

"We would not have been in Old Warriors' had it not been for him, either," said Telek, limping and quite exhausted from the ordeal.

"And what did you think you enlisted for, Telek? A quiet walk in the woods?" countered Areus, sarcastically. "This entire quest is about magic and the alignment of power and rule. The duty you volunteered for is to battle against such aggression. Baytel held nothing back when he spoke of the trials that lay ahead. I for one will hold true to this duty no matter what the cost. It is more important than anything I previously held as significant in my life, and nothing will cause me to deviate from this quest. Not ghosts, goblins or anything else."

Gar chimed in from behind, his voice carrying in the open land. "Areus is right. We are championing for the freedom of humanity itself. We are the warning shout before the mouths of evil spew their foul breath upon the innocent. I am with this quest to its end."

Telek flared red with anger. "Who said I was quitting this quest? Those words did not escape my lips nor did the thought enter my mind! So shut your gap about it!"

Baytel heard the loud exchange and he smiled to himself. No one could ask for better or more loyal men. Hearing their commitment he called to them and ordered them to commence with their patrol routine, calling for Areus to take point for he knew the region best. Dirk Ironwright immediately responded to duty, taking the more arduous rover position whereby his route would circle theirs.

Ironwright had not spoken to anyone since departing Old Warriors' Court. As the day wore on and when his patrol route wound back, he continued on without pause or glance except to report from afar that all was well.

Areus hailed that he had come across a meandering creek. Feeling they had traveled enough that day, Baytel ordered a halt; they set camp creek side. His mind constantly returned to the mountain and he recalled the moment, after the cave closed, sealing off the specters, when Kalti returned the blue stone to him and again called him *cousin*. Kalti continuously smiled wherever they went. Upon his return from patrol, Baytel said, "Perhaps you and I can search for our ancestors when this quest is complete."

"I would like that, Baytel, more than anything."

He watched Kalti walk off with an uplifting stride, seeing at least one of his men was affected positively by the experience of Old Warriors' Court.

Telek had fallen behind and was nowhere in sight after Baytel set camp. Baytel backtracked and found he was not as far back as thought. Telek's stride had improved from earlier and he was recovering quickly since being thrown from the cave. The wound and transparency from the ghost of Brodin had disappeared the instant Telek was thrown clear of the cave entrance. However, he commented about a deep coldness that remained where he sustained the wound.

"You seem much better, Telek."

"Sluggish and the wound remains cold as winter, but the farther we travel from Lumithien, the less I feel it."

"Good, my friend. We need the return of your old whimsical self."

They reached the roaring warmth of the campfire. The sun was still above the horizon and they had daylight for a while longer. Baytel noticed Ironwright had not returned from patrol. "Adetin, go find Dirk. I want all of us back at camp to rest and we need a warm meal."

"I saw good cover for grouse while on my patrol. I'll fetch Dirk and a couple of birds for our meal tonight."

Adetin Gar followed Ironwright's trail for a while, chasing down a few grouse along the way. Dusk was near and just as soon as he started to think perhaps Ironwright might be lost, he saw him not far from camp turning to start another rotation.

"Dirk! Dirk! Hold on!"

Gar caught up with him and noted Ironwright did not look up; his eyes were downcast and his shoulders slumped. "Baytel set camp, Dirk. He wants us all back before nightfall. It's not far off. I have some fine grouse here for the meal."

"I'm not hungry," Ironwright said sharply, and he kept on walking away.

"Hold it, Dirk. You are exhausted and you need rest."

Ironwright stiffened, and then dropped his head. "I need nothing but to resign from the pact I made with you all. I am so ashamed of how I behaved in Old Warriors' Court, I cannot breathe."

He heard the pain in the dwarf's voice, and asked, "What do you feel shame for?"

Angrily, Ironwright turned to face him. "You were witness to what I became, Adetin! We were in grave danger and all I could do was cower away in fear."

"You went through quite an ordeal, Dirk. That ghost almost possessed you and you fought it off."

"No. I shrank away from my duties and wept like a child in fear. This is not fighting!"

"Dirk, we did not know what we were to encounter when we entered Old Warriors'. None of us had ever witnessed anything from the shadowed realm. We were all frightened, each and every last one of us."

"I didn't see you or anyone else fail in our duty. I had to be carried out, powerless to leave and powerless to stay! Disgraceful!"

"You did not see because you were spellbound to that spirit, Dirk. Telek had troubles, also. He almost did not make it out. I did not think any of us would make it out alive. The magic of the Court and the specters we encountered and the power they wielded played upon our weaknesses. We all have fears we react to differently. I recognized who it was you encountered. It was King Minion, wasn't it?"

Ironwright shut his eyes at the memory. "Yes."

"I am no dwarf, but if the father of my people came to me in spirit form, believe me Dirk, I would have reacted the same as you."

Ironwright's head rose up. Gar continued, "When Baytel uses his magic, what do you think he goes through? Every time he uses it, he fears. Yet he learns and has created a mastery over it. We all learn from our fears, for it humbles us and chastises us when no one would dare—and we learn from the fear and persevere with that knowledge, for when it is time to confront the fear again, we recognize it and will be able to guide ourselves through it with commanding strength. You know this, probably more than any of us."

"Adetin, for me, seeing and speaking with King Minion…" he paused, shaking his head, "we became the Ctiklat Dwarfs because of his vision and leadership. What you see as Ctiklat Dwarfs originated in King Minion's dreams. Dwarfs were not thought of in the ancient histories as we are now. We are not scorned, looked upon as inferior, or laughed at anymore. We are proud, strong and intelligent. Ctiklat Dwarfs' counsel is sought after by all sects of humanity."

"Surely Dirk, your King Minion was an inspiration then and his legacy lives on with your people, but he is dead. That was his spirit in Old Warriors' Court and all King Minion wanted from his blood relative was to kill you and live once more. Do you understand that?"

Ironwright nodded in resignation.

"Good. Now, let's put this behind us. Your feeling sorry for yourself is tiresome. You are a necessary part of our troop and it is time we go back. There is much more to be done on this quest, especially when there is a meal to be made." He again held up the grouse, grinning mischievously.

Ironwright finally smiled and said, "So that's it. You came to me only to find a cook!"

"Well, after all, I did the hunting. The least you could do is—" Gar stopped talking and held a hand up for quiet. He heard a loud, wheezing noise approaching through the darkness. He dropped the birds and unsheathed his sword. "Stand ready, Dirk."

Suddenly out of the dark grass a figure charged screaming and brandishing a sword and shield. It was a monster goblin.

Ironwright's delve axe was the first to meet the charge and he swung it wide, striking through the goblin's shield and imbedding the axe into its arm. The force of the blow staggered the goblin, but it quickly regained its wits. Its scream was deafening. Tossing its shield clear, it threw Ironwright and the attached delve-axe aside.

Gar attacked and they clashed swords. Blow after blow, the goblin countered every move he made. Stealing glances toward Ironwright, Gar could see him trying to free his delve-axe from the goblin's shield.

Trying to buy time, Gar skillfully guided the powerful goblin into the tall grass to slow its assault. He ducked behind trees and was about to run toward camp when he heard a heavy thud. The eyes of the goblin turned blank and the creature fell face first to the ground. Ironwright's axe had found its mark in the back of the goblin's head. The goblin's blood was already at work decomposing its body until all that remained was a black stain upon the ground.

"Well, Dirk," said Gar, panting from the excursion, "nothing to be ashamed of here. You certainly came to the forefront of this battle."

Gar turned at the sound of the others crashing through the grass and the rest of the men arrived.

"We heard screams," said Areus, and then he looked at the sullied earth. "One of the horde?"

"Yes. We happened upon each other. I was fortunate to have Dirk with me. I was having difficulty handling this monster," said Gar.

"Which direction did it come from?" asked Baytel.

Gar pointed and Baytel dispatched Kalti.

"Did you see any others?" asked Telek, panting heavily.

"No," Ironwright spoke up. "It must have been traveling alone. If there were others, they would have shown themselves by now. That scream was as loud as thunder."

"Only one, with no other companions? Goblins never travel or fight alone," said Baytel.

"They are not goblins any longer, Baytel," said Areus.

"No, Areus. They are. Their minds are still goblin. They showed me that in Belwas Swamp, when I was recognized. No, there is something else with this one," said Baytel.

"Here! Up this trail!" hailed Kalti and all followed. "There is black blood here and up that way. The goblin must have been injured before it attacked. The blood trail comes from the north."

"Adetin, you and Dirk go back and break camp. We will follow the blood trail as long as we can before sunset. Make haste. Kalti, take the lead and be careful. There may be more goblins ahead. Let's go, men. Keep a close watch."

Baytel called a halt when the dusk light faded. "I think it is safe to say that it was a lone goblin, so let's set camp here."

Gar pulled from his game sack three grouse and Ironwright dropped his pack and retrieved his cookware. "We'll get to cooking these."

"A small fire, Adetin. Only enough for cooking."

Baytel looked over to Ironwright and asked, "How do you fare, Dirk?"

"Just right, Baytel. No worries here."

He glanced at Gar, who returned his unasked question with a nod, affirming that the dwarf was good.

Telek dropped to the ground before the unlit kindling, winded and exhausted. "Yes. Let's eat and rest. We haven't had a hot meal in a while."

Baytel asked, "I would be more at ease if I knew where we are."

Telek said, matter-of-factly, "The village of Petal Glen is not far off. We won't attract anyone to our presence this far south of town."

"How far off is this Petal Glen?"

"If I can get a few winks of sleep so as not to slow everyone down, we should reach it by tomorrow evening," said Telek, his sleeping bag unwrapped and him already horizontal.

Baytel nodded and said, "My turn to patrol. Eat and get some sleep, men. I will take my meal when I return. Then we will be off before dawn."

Petal Glen seemed lively enough as seen from the forest. People moved in and out of storefronts and cottages that spilled onto the cobbled road that cut through the center of town.

The blood trail had disappeared on the outskirts of town. No other signs of goblins were present. Being a stranger in the northlands, Baytel had to depend on the men to guide their next moves while he stayed hidden in the woods.

Telek spoke up. "We will look very suspicious entering town from the forest. Petal men are hard folk not given to welcoming strangers, let alone ones from the dark recesses outside of town."

"Something is amiss," said Gar. "Look over by that yellow building. That man is relieving the other man. Petal Glen is on a scheduled watch. That is not normal here."

"Let's retreat back into the woods and come out on the other side of town," said Areus. "The dock road from the Ginhonim River leads into Petal Glen. We keep to the woods until farther up the road and enter from there."

"Sounds right, but not all of us. Now, Adetin, Kalti and Telek have been here. How recently?" Baytel asked.

Gar smiled. "If you are asking if our faces will be recognized in Petal Glen, the answer is yes."

"Well if that is the case you three can enter from here. Areus, Dirk and I will go by the dock road and enter Petal Glen that way. And we stay separated through our stay. We can reconnoiter later, but where do we go from here?"

"The Red Antler!" said Telek quickly. "It's small, dark, always full."

Gar laughed beneath his breath, and said, "And it has the best ale in the northlands."

Telek shrugged and said, "Oh, right. So it has. I was about to mention that."

"All right, The Red Antler at midnight. Try to be inconspicuous," said Baytel.

Baytel watched the smile form on Telek's face and said, "That grin could light up the Hall of the Dead."

Telek replied, "Ha ha! I'll do my best to blend in with the drinkers of the establishment."

They all laughed and parted ways with Telek reiterating, "It truly is the best ale I have ever tasted."

No sooner had they entered The Red Antler than Baytel found the uninhibited, talkative patrons of the tavern speaking of a dead man and the hideous beast that had killed him. Seated in a booth, Baytel kept his eye on Adetin Gar and Kalti at a table nearby where they were engaged in conversation with a tracker that had the same look as the thieves, clandestine and suspicious of all about him. Meanwhile, Telek stood at the brawny bar where a crowd had gathered around him made up of huntsmen, townsfolk and a lady of dubious repute, as he told tales, slapped backs and flirted with the blushing woman. The louder Telek spoke the louder his new acquaintances talked until most at The Red Antler could hear.

"Telek is a master," said Dirk. "Look at him. It's as though he had lived here forever and known these folks all his life."

Baytel nodded and said, "I have to admit, as I can see by your empty goblet, Dirk—this is exceptional ale."

Dirk nodded, wiping the froth off his upper lip. "I have never tasted better in all my travels. What is Adetin saying, Baytel? I cannot see him."

Baytel's eyes never left Gar's hand signing as they secretly conversed across the tavern. "Adetin is saying that no one knows the identity of the dead man. A number of monsters entered town late last night, grabbed him and killed him before making their escape."

"Did he say where they were headed? Their tracks were not on the road," said Dirk.

Ironwright touched Baytel's arm and directed him to look to the opposite corner. "The man in that booth."

Without being obvious, Baytel found the man in question seated in the dark recesses in the far corner booth. "What about him, Dirk?"

"Look at his clothes. Aren't they like those you wear?"

Baytel turned his head to get a better view. As if preordained the man did the same, quickly exposing his face from the shadows only to retreat just as fast. "They certainly are."

"Baytel, did you see the color of his eyes? They have your color. Is he one of them?"

"I am not sure. He could be a Grey Rider. Let's find out." He shifted slightly in the booth and signed to the man in the ancient tongue taught to him by Calidor; Baytel used the sign for *friend.*

In one swift motion, the man stood and walked toward the door. He was tall and his steps purposeful and strong. His hand dropped to his side and he immediately commenced a reply.

"Friend. Meet me at the edge of town. North off the road in the cedar clearing."

Baytel's heart skipped a beat with excitement and he leaned forward and whispered, "Grey Rider! Let's drink up and leave. Slowly, and without drawing suspicion."

"No one saw the exchange, Baytel. He was very good," said Dirk.

"Be sure of it." Baytel signed to Adetin Gar while speaking his direction to Dirk Ironwright. "We will leave first. Telek will follow and then you and Kalti. Make sure we are not followed." He stopped signing and asked Dirk, "Where is Areus?"

Dirk grumbled his reply, "Look to the back wall where the congregation of almost every pretty woman in The Red Antler is. Where else would he be?"

Baytel sighed, "Again? Well, get his attention and tell him what is happening. Tell him from me that this is no time for frolicking with lovely maidens, and have him follow Gar out."

Chapter 55

CEDAR trees exuded their sweet scent all about the clearing. Baytel eyed the man curiously. He was as tall and had a look that mirrored Calidor's—hard, steel-blue eyes, a chiseled jaw and chin, and a lean, muscled body. He wore the clothing of the faerie folk and rode a magnificent dark gray steed the size of Calidor's black stallion. Saddle, horse and man blended into the surrounding forest so perfectly he was barely visible until they came within hailing distance. Surely he was a Grey Rider.

"Greetings, Friend. I am Baytel and these are my companions, Areus, Adetin Gar, Dirk Ironwright, Telek, and Kalti."

"Baytel?" The Grey Rider hesitated. He looked down from his mount in careful study. Then his eyes caught sight of the hilt of Baytel's sword and he gave a quick intake of breath.

"Sire!" He jumped from his mount and bowed. "I am Duncor, Grey Rider and Druid of the Citadel."

"You know me, Duncor?"

"All of us who ride with your grandfather know of you. It gives me much joy to see you in the flesh."

"Why?" interjected Gar.

The Grey Rider flashed a hard look at Gar that could have halted a charging boar. "My travels take me far, Thief. I hear many things." He turned back to Baytel and continued. "It has been told that you perished in the lands of your father. I am glad to see it not true."

"How do you know I am who I say?"

Duncor smiled. "You have the build of Calidor and the features of your mother, Pren, and your grandmother, Olyssé. I have no doubt who you are and I am honored to be at your command."

Duncor was the first King of the North he had met besides Calidor and Juliard, and Baytel wanted to ask him many questions, but other needs prevailed. "It is a great pleasure and honor meeting one of the Grey Riders."

"I couldn't help but observe your companions at the Red Antler. From their sign, you seek answers about the slain man in Petal Glen?"

"Were we that obvious?" asked Areus.

"No, Kilhalen man," he said with an irritated edge in his voice. "Unless you sought to find signs none could possibly notice. Of course no one could have understood our ancient sign, anyway."

Baytel was fascinated that Duncor already knew the origins of their small troop, calling Adetin *thief* and Areus *Kilhalen man*. Duncor had that ageless quality about him that Calidor possessed, yet the eyes showed the wisdom of years uncounted.

"Yes, Duncor, we still seek answers."

Duncor looked at him apologetically. "Sire, there was a raid in the village at a boarding house two nights ago. According to the locals, a swarm of monsters attacked and killed a man. No one knew the wayfarer but they said he put up a strong fight, killing four of the beasts. They buried the man not far from here. I inquired of the man at the magistrate's and was given his possessions."

Duncor opened his saddlebag and removed another bag and handed it to Areus. "It is the bag of a Citadel Druid, but the name is unfamiliar to me."

Areus opened the bag and then said sadly, "Yes. We knew him. Podius, Baytel. Another of us dead."

"What goes on here, Sire?"

"Death, Duncor. Death, ancient evils and another war drawing closer. Let me appraise you of the events that brought us here."

As he did, anger flushed across Duncor's face. "The Citadel attacked?"

"Yes, almost all were killed. Yar has escaped and is being hunted by goblins from the Southland, like the ones that killed Podius. Calidor is in pursuit of Yar and the goblins that follow in the east."

"You say these goblins wield the dark magic of the ancients?" asked Duncor, skeptically.

Baytel nodded. "Yes, altered by Ravek. They have infiltrated deep into the northlands and hunt the surviving druids. Once that is accomplished, my father will begin the invasion of the northlands."

Areus added, "We have encountered a few of these goblins along the way. The evil spell Ravek holds over them overpowers their minds, making them relentless in battle."

The gravity of the report seemed to settle heavily on the Grey Rider and he fell silent.

Baytel finished, saying, "They have succeeded in killing most of us outside the Citadel. We are always one step behind them, and the atrocities of my father and Ravek accumulate."

Duncor asked, "What are you doing this far north?"

"Calidor has instructed me to reach Kilhalen by the winter solstice to speak before the Faerie Council of what has transpired and hope to find the heads of the kingdoms and fiefdoms there to come up with a plan to thwart the Southland invasion."

Duncor returned to his quiet deliberation. It was a sobering report and Baytel saw the pain of loss upon his face.

"This is most dreadful news. I have just come from the faeries lands and the Tree Faeries will not be traveling to Kilhalen. Even if they were to attend and convene the council, Kilhalen alone will not be able to stop a Southland invasion."

"Duncor, the Southland army is vast and well-equipped; ten-fold the size of their force in the first war. And with Azkar Rol and Pithe as allies, it will be massive and overwhelming. That is why we must reach the northland kingdoms and fiefdoms to warn them, or all is lost."

"Sire, you said Calidor is in the east?"

"The last report from him to Make Ironwright was that he was in the east following Yar, who is being pursued by goblin horde."

"We must reach him. We will need him to persuade the great kingdoms to march toward the Southland. If their army reaches the open countries of the northlanders, they will be unstoppable," said Duncor.

"How do we get word to him?" asked Dirk. "Are there any Grey Riders in the east?"

"No. We are few and have been west for most of the year. I must return to the faerie lands and speak of these events. They will without question travel to Kilhalen once they hear of this. Are any of you familiar with the eastern lands?"

Kalti stepped forward. "I am familiar with the troll lands, but not beyond their borders."

Duncor stared at Dirk Ironwright and said, "We must warn Ctiklat also. They must attend this faerie council. Dwarf, you are of the Ctiklat Mountains, are you not?"

"Yes," Ironwright answered quickly, surprised.

"You." Duncor pointed to Kalti, "I know not of your origin, though I can surmise it by your familiar look," he said looking back and forth between Baytel and Kalti. "How are your abilities as a tracker?"

"He is the best tracker I have ever seen and could stalk up to a deer without its ear even flicking," said Gar. "We trained him in the old art and he has surpassed us by a good measure."

"Are you able to find tracks that may be old and worn by weather, for that is what I ask of you?" queried Duncor.

"I can find Calidor, if he is alive," Kalti said confidently.

"Oh, he will be alive," said Duncor, amused by the quiet confidence of Kalti. "And he may find you before you find him."

Baytel knew where the Grey Rider was leading, and said, "Dirk, write a note to your king telling of our plight and our request to march as much of a force as he is willing southward to reach Kilhalen by the winter solstice. Give the note to Kalti. Also, ask for his assistance to expedite Kalti on his way east. If all goes well and Kalti finds Calidor within a month's time, you and Calidor will be able to join us in Kilhalen."

Duncor jumped atop his gray steed. In the ancient tongue Duncor said to Baytel, "You may not be welcome in Kilhalen. You are a Southlander and a druid. Calidor and the Grey Riders are a distant memory to them now, as are the Kings of the North. Only to the Tree Faerie and Ctiklat are we known."

Baytel looked at Areus, who nodded in understanding. Baytel saw Duncor acknowledged the exchange.

Still in the ancient tongue, he said, "Areus, you are a druid also? Sire, it is good that you will have an ally at Kilhalen. Prejudice is strong there, as you shall see."

Telek cleared his throat, breaking the secret conversation, and asked, "Do you know where the goblins that killed this Podius were headed?"

"They departed by land the night before last in the direction of the fiefdom of Tiginset," he said, and then looked at Baytel. "Sire, I beg your leave. Until Kilhalen."

He watched the Grey Rider disappear into the forest like a dream forgotten when waking. "Areus, give Dirk something to write his note on. Keep it simple yet concise. One note for entrance into Ctiklat, the other to your king. Be sure the note introduces Kalti properly and convey the importance of this quest and his hasty departure from Ctiklat to find Calidor. Make certain you mention the Grey Rider Duncor and his intentions in the note. Kalti, you will have to purchase a horse, so you will have to wait until dawn."

Telek, Gar, and Kalti began to laugh. "Kalti can depart as soon as now. We have other ways of acquiring what we need," said the thief, giving Baytel a wink.

"Very well, Kalti. As soon as Dirk completes the notes, be off and be careful. We depend greatly upon your reaching Ctiklat and Calidor."

Ironwright read the notes aloud and, satisfied with their contents, sealed them in wax and pressed the Ctiklat seal from his signet ring onto the soft wax, one addressed to his uncle, the king, and the other to the gate steward.

Kalti was about to leave when Gar stopped him and said, "Kalti, you take care. Do your duty without too many risks. You come back to us, you hear?"

Telek added: "Do not get caught up in being a hero without support around. Don't talk to strangers along the way. Directly to Ctiklat, you hear, and without pause. Like Adetin said, do your duty and return unscathed, if possible. I would abhor having to break in another to get used to my ways."

With letters in hand, Kalti said his farewells and was off to town to requisition a horse.

Baytel gathered the men around and asked, "Now, why Tiginset? What is in Tiginset that would bring the goblin horde to their doorstep?"

Areus answered, "Another student acolyte from the Citadel is a young prince from Tiginset. He arrived late in the winter. I recall him being a very quick learner. He came to the Citadel to study castle defense and troop deployment to assist his aging father's realm. I believe his name is Nopel; a fine young man with promise."

Baytel's face hardened. "By all that is magical, this one will not die."

They found the goblin horde trail not far from the road near the Ginhonim River dock. Their footprints meandered inside the tree line along the shore. As Baytel led, he found more tracks join onto the main trail and followed until the ground was so trampled down, it looked as though hundreds of soldiers had passed, all headed toward Tiginset.

Ironwright and Gar returned from patrol and reported, "The goblin horde is camped ahead. And they are constructing rafts. Hundreds, if not thousands are in their force. Tiginset is a small fiefdom. They cannot defend against so many. They will be slaughtered."

"Can they reach Tiginset before we do?" asked Baytel.

"Not from that part of the river. They need to travel south, past the fortress atop the opposite side of the river high on the cliff, and then they need to find a place to launch up-river. There is no other way for them to reach Tiginset," said Gar.

Baytel replied, "But we can. Goblins cannot swim. That is why they are building rafts. Not all may be winged like the ones we fought."

"Where is the quickest place to cross?" asked Dirk.

"Without being seen, back at the dock. The river is narrowest at that point," replied Gar.

Baytel looked down at Areus, who was placing items from Druid Podius's bag in his and Baytel's bag. He handed Baytel's bag to him and asked, "Ready?"

Baytel nodded and said, "Let's go, men. We can reach the dock, cross the Ginhonim River and make Tiginset as fast as we can. Let's hope the goblin invaders will not be there before then."

Chapter 56

PRINCESS Delphinade peered through the thinning leaves on a high-reaching limb of the fallen tree, making sure her patrol was on the route she instructed them to be. Though her father, the king, did not trust her with authority to lead a patrol, she secretly ignored him, not only leading patrols but restructuring patrol routes and frequencies outside the castle town of Tiginset.

Since her initiatives commenced, Delphinade had intercepted four gray-goblin raiding parties, prevented livestock theft from the local farmers, and stopped numerous crimes against the homesteaders who lived outside the walls of Tiginset castle. Her reputation as a strong-willed warrior princess preceded her as the men in her patrol held her in the highest esteem, respecting her leadership and successes, which she was unable to take credit for.

The early morning was quiet. The first frost of the season was upon the ground. She was chilled, but did not mind for she had long ago tired of the summer warmth and lazy autumn weather.

Delphinade heard movement ahead and identified a soldier in her patrol moving into position. She noticed every sound, every movement from the scampering red squirrel bounding haphazardly upon the leaf-covered ground to the quiet steps of whitetail deer. A couple of chickadees jumped from perch to perch, as if they were playing a winged hopscotch game upon the limbs, chirping their progress to each other.

She turned as an obtrusive sound came to her from far off. A crunch of a footfall followed and Delphinade located the sounds as coming from the north. She leaned over to her companion, and whispered, "Something is out there, Eale. I want you to move to the east a ways for a better view. Go quietly and keep sharp."

"Yes, Princess Delphinade," he answered.

Observing his progress, she nodded, pleased by his silent passage as he took position thirty paces away. A few moments passed without a sound and suddenly three figures appeared out of nowhere about fifty paces to the north. The two men and a dwarf unabashedly continued to walk straight toward her position.

Delphinade carefully looked about the area, seeing no others about. The patrolman in the west held up three fingers, acknowledging only three intruders, and signed, asking what to do. Delphinade replied, fingers flying conveying her orders for him to circle around and behind the strangers. He acknowledged and she watched him sign to the others in sight as she had trained him to do. All in her patrol knew what was expected of them.

She felt she had complete control of the situation. Just before the intruders walked beneath her perch, Delphinade jumped from her hidden blind and landed before them with her sword unsheathed.

"Hold, you three! Do not move another step!" Delphinade immediately felt awkward, as their reaction to her demands seemed too calm. She sensed something was wrong. "You are surrounded so keep your weapons sheathed."

A tall steely-eyed young man spoke, his voice tranquil and unthreatening. "We mean no harm. We are looking for the fiefdom of Tiginset."

Four of her patrol showed themselves with swords in hand behind the three strangers. Eale stayed hidden. The tall man had seen them approach and she saw him making some kind of hand sign she did not recognize. His two companions seemed to relax even further.

Delphinade asked, "Why do you seek Tiginset?"

"We seek a friend, and would like an audience with the reigning lord," said the man.

"What business do you have to warrant an audience with our king?"

"You are from Tiginset, then?" asked the dwarf.

Delphinade glared irritably at the dwarf while silently rebuking herself for the slip. Then, suddenly, her men broke rank and attacked the three intruders. One patrolman grabbed for the dwarf's weapon while the other three patrolmen lunged for the other two men.

The tall one ducked, clenched the arm of one soldier and threw him into another. The dwarf did the same as the other man kicked the sword out of another patrolman's hand, and within a blink of an eye all of her patrolmen were down upon the frosted ground without their swords, moaning in pain.

Panicky, she pointed her sword back and forth at the strangers, unsure what to do and hoping Eale would come to her aid. The tall man held his hands out and she observed that none of them had brandished their weapons. They had disarmed and disabled patrolmen with only their hands.

Delphinade heard someone shout from the area where Eale was stationed. "Baytel, I have the other one." And then she saw an older man leading Eale at sword-point.

"Please drop your sword, lady."

She jumped, startled at the suddenness of the declaration behind her. She felt the point of a sword in her back. With her men incapacitated and captured, she could only do what was asked, but not without some satisfying act. She dropped her sword, pivoted quickly and slammed her fist into the face of the one behind her.

The man dropped his sword and grabbed her by the arms, holding them behind her back. His body was so close Delphinade could feel his heart beat against her breasts. He was tall like the other one. His smile showed a mouth full of white teeth. Then Delphinade met his eyes and her heart skipped a beat, as their blueness seemed to look into her soul. As he continued to hold her close, she felt a sudden, intense warmth, a sensation she had never experienced before.

The man holding her said, "Please do not fight. We are friends of a young man in Tiginset."

"Let her go, Areus," said the first tall man.

The handsome man released her and Delphinade stepped unsteadily toward her men, attempting to regain a sense of command. She tried to keep the color from flushing to her face though feeling heat race through her body, so enraptured by the beautiful smile and strength of the man the other called Areus.

"You waylaid a Tiginset patrol and you laid your hands upon the king's daughter!" shouted a patrolman.

"Then you must be Nopel's sister!" said Areus.

Delphinade paused, as did her men. She studied the five strangers, wondering how they could know her brother. "Who are you?"

"Allow me to introduce myself and my companions. I am Baytel; next to you is Areus, and here are Telek, Adetin Gar, and Dirk Ironwright. We are friends of Nopel. We have come a long way to warn him of dangers to him and your fiefdom."

"What kind of dangers, and how do you know Nopel?" her suspicions were still high.

The steely-eyed man continued. "We are on an urgent mission, my lady, and it is imperative we meet with your father and brother. Can you take us to them?"

"Your name is Baytel?"

"Yes."

"Well, Baytel, if the situation warrants it, I will escort you to Nopel and the king, but you still did not answer my questions."

The man bowed as an apology and said, "Princess, we are from the Citadel and the information we possess is of incalculable concern that should not be spoken of here in the woods."

Her curiosity about the strangers increased. Men of the Citadel had not visited their fiefdom since she was a child, but she remembered them to be very secretive and dark. They would arrive in the middle of the night and her father would immediately convene the king's council. Then the Citadel men would leave the castle so quietly most did not know they were even in Tiginset.

"How do I know you are from the Citadel?" she asked, hesitant to trust the strangers.

Then Baytel and the beautiful Areus lifted the sleeves of their cloaks, exposing their tattooed forearms.

Druids!

The fiery young princess was silent most of the walk through the forest to Tiginset castle. Baytel tried to engage her in conversation, but received only curt replies.

They emerged from the forest and met the setting sun behind the castle. The structure was smaller than the Citadel but looked to be a stronghold of majestic impenetrability, able to withstand siege towers, mortar mechanisms and well-supplied enemy armies.

Entering through the main gate, Princess Delphinade led them through the ward directly into the main tower that Baytel assumed was the king's keep. Up a wide and winding staircase and at the top of five levels of stairs, the princess was met by a maidservant who assisted the princess with removing her coat. As she removed her cap, her dark hair cascaded down her back. Baytel noticed her steal a glance at Areus and, seeing Areus's eyes widen, she turned with a pleasing beam on her face.

"Follow me. It is not far off."

What *it* was Baytel would see soon enough and he fell in step behind her. The princess strode the long hallway with her hair shining black in the dim lamplight, bouncing and swaying to her movements. Baytel recognized trained muscles beneath her patrol garb as well as a shapely body. However strong and determined she looked, she could not hide the beauty of her femininity, which had enraptured the attention of all his men, as evidenced by the low whistle from Areus walking at his side.

Delphinade marched with purpose and her every movement displayed her strength. Occasionally she would look back to see if they were keeping up. Her violet-blue eyes seemed to rest on Areus longest, and he never lost the opportunity to meet her stare with his usual brilliant smile, causing her to turn away quickly and speed up her already hasty pace.

Baytel turned toward Areus, seeing his raised eyebrows and flushed face, and gave his bewitched friend a warning stare to keep his emotions in check.

Up another level of stairs they came upon a vestibule where a sentry snapped to attention, seeing Princess Delphinade.

"I am here to see my father. These men seek an audience with him. Let us pass."

The sentry opened the vestibule door and they followed Delphinade down another long empty corridor. At its end, the princess stopped at a set of massive doors where a pair of guards were stationed. She turned and said in a demanding tone, "Wait here," and she withdrew behind the doors with the sentries.

Areus whispered, "I'll never tire of looking at her."

"Take care, Areus. We are here for other reasons. Let's hope she can gain us admittance, or fetch Nopel."

Faster than anticipated, the doors opened and the two guards waved them into what looked to be Tiginset's royal assembly chamber. Baytel quickly took in as many details of the chamber as he could before stepping in. The chamber was cathedral-like, the ceilings raised three levels with arched wooden rafters supported by hewed stone columns at equal intervals across the stone floor to the raised platform where Delphinade stood beside a man seated on a throne. On the lower level of the platform were others, probably his advisors.

Baytel walked slightly ahead of the other men, subtly announcing he was their leader. As he approached the raised platform, he could not help but notice that Delphinade's face was scarlet and anger seeped from her eyes. Baytel shifted his attention to the man on the throne and immediately recognized the family resemblance to the acolyte Nopel. The man was equally angry, as something had transpired between him and his daughter.

Baytel stopped before the throne and bowed formally, as did his men.

Delphinade stepped forward, saying in a curt tone, "May I present King Forel, reigning lord and master of the Fiefdom of Tiginset. Introduce yourselves."

King Forel looked at his daughter and Baytel recognized by the weary roll of his eyes that the king had lost patience with her behavior, including her curt introduction. The king had a thick head of gray hair, his aged skin cut deep into his face. Dressed in formal royal green and gold, he looked down, firmly surveying the small troop.

"Sire, I am Baytel, Druid of the Citadel. Here beside me is Areus, also Druid."

Baytel introduced all in his company, each bowing in turn to the king. "On behalf of us all, I thank you for accepting our attendance."

"My daughter reported your desire for a meeting and warns me to be careful of you all for I am to understand you waylaid a Tiginset patrol without brandishing your weapons?"

"Our intentions were not to gain your favor by force or threat. However, we saw fit to disarm the patrol for they had become inhospitable. Nevertheless, no blood was shed and we are thankful for your ear," said Baytel, bowing again.

A door along the wall to the side of the platform slammed closed and a young man walked casually up the steps to the king's level. He stopped as his eyes rested on Baytel, and then Areus.

"Druid Baytel! Druid Areus!" exclaimed Acolyte Nopel.

The young man bounded down the steps to greet them. "Sirs, what brings you here to our castle?"

"Acolyte Nopel, you look well," said Baytel, glad that the formalities of explaining their mutual acquaintance were now eliminated.

"And you, also. Druid Areus, how have you been? I had not seen you since the Laurel ceremony."

"It was a fine ceremony, was it not, Acolyte Nopel."

"It was beautiful. I am surprised to see you both visit."

"Unfortunately, Acolyte Nopel, the reasons for our visit are not social. An urgent matter has arisen that has to do with your survival and that of your father's fiefdom. I was about to discuss this when you arrived. If your father would allow me to speak of our quest and the calamity upon the land which we strive to prevent, it will be clear to you in all of its gravity."

Baytel looked to the king and waited for permission to continue.

King Forel adjusted his robe and said, "If Nopel attests to your disposition, you may proceed."

"I most certainly do, Father."

Baytel's oration was concise, spoken with clarity and at times in powerful detail, and those in attendance gasped at the horrors of his testimony. "This goblin horde now masses a short distance from here, King Forel. There is no time to waste, for their destruction will be swift and brutal."

The king leaned forward with a questioning gaze. "They mass an army to kill one man because he attended the Citadel? This seems highly improbable. Nonetheless, we here at Tiginset can take care of ourselves. We have been doing so for hundreds of years."

Baytel offered the king a slight bow of respect and answered, "We understand it is difficult to fathom the situation at hand and appreciate your belief that whatever force that may attack, your kingdom can withstand, but these goblins are not what you believe goblins to be."

"Father, let me send a small patrol to see if these men tell the truth," said Delphinade.

"Child, be still!" spat the king. "Should you not be someplace else?"

Delphinade's face broke out red with embarrassment. She stomped her foot and stood directly in front of the king, her hands in tight fists at her sides. "Like with the women? To serve at the pleasure of a man? Bear and nurse their children? I am not like that!"

"Delphinade, not now, not at this time," said Nopel.

She turned angrily at her younger brother. "Father should have sent me to the Citadel, Nopel. He didn't, but do not ever direct a word to me in that condescending tone again. I am more than your equal in all aspects of Tiginset's administration and military and have been trained by the best warriors in the realm. So Brother, let's not pretend, shall we?"

"Delphinade, if you continue on this discourse, I shall have to dismiss you," growled the king. "At any event, the Citadel does not admit women."

Areus stepped forward with a formal bow and said, "With your pardon, sire. One of our most respected druids is a woman. Her name is Anise. She is beautiful and powerful and is healing her wounds as we speak, wounds inflicted by these goblins we have been pursuing and battling from Tridling Del to here. Everywhere they go, they leave death in their wake."

"And how is it you are all alive to tell of them?" asked the king smartly.

The king looked old and tired. In his studies at the Citadel, Baytel recalled the reports on Forel's rule and his small kingdom Tiginset. The king had been a turbulent monarch compared with his father who died long ago. King Forel had been young when taking over Tiginset, but wise to the ways and comings and goings of the land and the sects. Now, as death was moving steadily to his door, he had sent Nopel to the Citadel, for through the years the Citadel Druids had offered him good counsel on many occasions.

Baytel replied, "We survived by not underestimating their strength, cunning, and power."

"Well, let me enlighten you druids. Through the years most every sect has attempted to conquer this fiefdom. My father built this magnificent castle, assisted by the Ctiklat dwarfs," he nodded to Ironwright respectfully. "This fortress has protected the lives of our subjects, withstanding all attacks, and will do so without interference from the Citadel."

"Father, please, I know these men. They would not fabricate such a tale," said Nopel.

"You are young, Nopel and not as travel wise as most," said King Forel.

"You sent me to the Citadel to study and learn because you believed in the truth they profess and their wisdom and strength. Why do you not believe them now?" asked Nopel.

The king said nothing and leaned back on his throne, tired of the banter.

Becoming frustrated by the king's stubborn, even arrogant, confidence in Tiginset's defenses, Baytel's voice rose in passion. "Sire, the goblins are on a mission of death and will stop at nothing to complete it, and its completion ends in the death of your son." He pointed at Nopel, dramatizing the threat. "They have already sacked the Citadel and have hunted and killed two other druids in the northlands. As we speak, they are camped up-river building rafts and boats to navigate the Ginhonim to invade your kingdom. I beg you, do what Princess Delphinade has suggested, send a patrol to see for yourself, but act now by preparing a withdrawal. You will need as much time as possible to evade them. The goblin horde is merciless and evil, having been physically altered by the ancient magic that the Southland wields. I know of this firsthand as I have seen the black art's inception creating these beasts. We have all witnessed and fought against them." Baytel paused to let what he said sink in. "The lives of all your subjects are in your hands. Please. You must believe."

"Sire!" A guard ran into the drawing chamber. "Torchlights across the river!"

They all ran out of the chamber onto the balcony and looked across the black void of the Ginhonim River. It was a dark night except for the hundreds of torches high upon the opposite bluff.

"It will take a half day, maybe more a little more before they reach the low ground launch," said Nopel, assessing their situation. "It looks like hundreds, father."

Baytel followed the line of torches, knowing that for each torch there was a dozen goblins. They marched well past the bend of the river; the leading goblins were beyond the castle and already out of sight. The torchlight reflected off the Ginhonim River, illuminating the shadows against the forest, making them look larger than their already huge frames. Between the torchbearers, goblins carried rafts and crudely constructed boats fully prepared to launch their attack.

Looking down, Baytel watched as the people of Tiginset flocked to the battlements and towers to watch the procession. He sensed the terror in the crowd.

Baytel turned to King Forel, and asked, "The goblin troops will converge upon your kingdom tomorrow morning, King Forel. You now see what they are. Monsters. What will it be, Sire?"

The king looked hard at the vast horde of goblins. "You are right, druid. We cannot withstand such an army." He turned to Nopel and said, "Son, you are the heir to this kingdom. I am old and will not be long for this world. What I have to order will inevitably end what legacy I can give to you. I have defended this fiefdom my entire life. If I give this order, I will have nothing to pass on to you."

"Father, if we must evacuate, all we will be leaving behind is the castle. Tiginset and its king shall always remain in our hearts and souls. You shall do what you must to save your subjects and your fiefdom. What better legacy could you leave than the protection of the people who serve you? Tiginset shall prevail. That I promise with all my heart."

King Forel hugged his son and smiled proudly. "My order is to abandon Tiginset. But where do we go?"

Areus said, "By river, sire. To Kilhalen."

"Yes, that is wise," the king replied. "Delphinade, you coordinate the vacating of the castle and send runners to the farmers to retreat to the Ginhonim River. We shall fight as much as we can to give more promise for our subjects' escape."

"Me? Ordered back with the women and children?"

"Take hold of what you say, Daughter, for if we fail here, you shall be their queen and they deserve more respect than that from their reigning lord! Understood?"

She did not answer and stormed off the balcony and was gone from the chamber.

After a pause, as it appeared no one wanted to speak, Baytel said, "King Forel, may I suggest you assemble your army in the castle yard where we may, with your permission, enlighten your soldiers on how we are to battle these monsters."

Chapter 57

A layer of mist covered the Ginhonim River. The steady current flowed unobstructed at the part of the river where Baytel stood and he wondered if it was fast enough to transport the citizens of Tiginset away from the murderous goblins already swarming their empty castle.

The entire population of Tiginset had evacuated their homes and were on the ghostly river in boats, barges, rafts and whatever sturdy craft that could float. Women, children and the aged were launched first, with farewells from the soldiers who watched them drift silently away disappearing down the river into the fog. The Ginhonim River would take them to the great Awär River. Then the strong current of the Awär would carry the people of Tiginset westward until passing by the mighty kingdom of Kilhalen and their sanctuary.

In the short interval since witnessing the goblins march past, Baytel and his men had to that morning devised a battle plan and prepared Tiginset as best they could. The soldiers of the small fiefdom accepted their duties with fervent resolve, each willing to fight to the last, for they embodied renewed enthusiasm for their liege lord.

Baytel called for a final meeting of the select few to lead each division. The plan was in place and everyone had his orders. The main division of soldiers went down-river with ropes and as many arrows as each could carry. Telek orchestrated their preparation at a site where the river narrowed, cut between the granite bluffs soaring high on each side.

Telek was speaking to the soldier who carried messages to the main division. "You understand fully what to do?"

"Yes, sir, I understand completely," said the soldier, snapping to attention. Word had spread through the ranks of Tiginset fighters of Telek's plan and they were all quick to take the old soldier's orders.

"Then if you have no more questions, off you go."

The soldier hesitated, looking to his king and prince, and said, "My only concern is for King Forel and Prince Nopel. I would rather they be farther back with us than risk being part of the forward battle."

"We stay with the men in the front line," said the king. "We will be with you soon enough. You have your orders, soldier, move out and do your duty as stated."

Baytel brought the leaders together, along with Areus, and, with a stick, scratched a crude map in the sand at the riverbank. Pointing, he said, "The first strike force is hidden awaiting the goblin horde *here*. The rest are downriver behind us, here and here. Let's all get into position. Stay alert and be ready to launch swiftly."

The mist became brilliantly lit as the first rays of the sun broke over the bluff. To the southwest, mixing with the glowing white mist, black smoke descended over the river from the billowing fires of Tiginset castle.

Baytel looked at the black clouds and then into the faces of King Forel and Prince Nopel, the proud leaders of their fallen realm. They stared mute, sorrowful and angry, at the easy destruction of everything they held dear, and Baytel knew they would never find peace except to spend their fury in battle.

A short distance away were Telek, Adetin Gar, Dirk Ironwright and thirty bowmen.

The king fidgeted and addressed Baytel. "Are you quite certain of this Telek character?"

"Quite certain. His plan coordinates speed with efficient aggression and shock that should cause confusion in the goblins' assault. The first Tiginset force will launch its arrows into their front line, scattering them across the river. Then the first force will retreat to their boats, drawing the stronger lead goblins away from the main group. Then the second force, led by us, will launch our arrows into the backs of those goblins, turn and shoot at the slower main force, and paddle to join the first strike group in retreat down the river. The third strike force will let fly into the main goblin force and follow us, leading the remaining goblins toward Telek's trap. It will be a race to reach Telek before the trap springs, but with the current's help, we can do it."

"Will any goblins be on land?" asked Nopel, apprehensively.

"Let's hope not. The goblins will see we have escaped by river and assume it to be the fastest way of travel. They are unfamiliar with this region and will not know better. We use water to our advantage for, as I have stated before, goblins cannot swim," Baytel replied with as much confidence he could.

"Here they come!" shouted Adetin Gar. "The first strike force is leading, drawing them away. Notch your arrows and then ready another. The first volley is the most important so stay steady."

"May your arrow points reach these demons' lungs and extinguish the breath of evil," cried Telek, his oration bringing muffled shouts from the hidden bowmen.

The stronger members of the goblin horde swung into view.

"They're so many!" exclaimed one bowman.

Baytel said, "Once they are beyond the bend of the river the attack is at your command, King Forel."

The king raised his arm. "Ready your bows, men...wait...wait...now! Arrows away!"

Arrows flew with deadly accuracy as not one missed its mark. Terrible goblin screams of pain and anger echoed off the river bluffs. Another volley of arrows hit their mark and the lead goblin contingent writhed in the churning waters, dead, dying and drowning in a swirl of black blood and water.

"Another volley!" shouted the king, and the arrows left the bows in unison, each singularly accurate. Baytel declared: "To the boats, men. Hurry!"

Baytel launched with Gar, Ironwright and Nopel, followed by Telek and Areus with the king and three bowmen in another boat. Paddling the two boats into the middle of the river, they caught the current full and passed by the waiting third strike force.

Baytel kept an eye on where the goblins were positioned. With the arrows still sailing and his and the king's boats being pursued, they were leading the goblins perfectly into position for the next strike.

No sooner than Baytel had envisioned it came the simultaneous twang of hundreds of bowstrings, and the third strike force's arrows soared, filling the sky with deadly intent. The next sounds were screams of death as the arrows pierced the lead goblins. Then the third strikers turned and shot three more volleys into the main goblin contingent, and as ordered, took to their boats, and the chase began in full.

It was mayhem as the goblins screamed, paddling through the bodies of their dead and in reckless pursuit of the third strikers. Baytel paddled hard, constantly looking over his shoulder and seeing the plan working as he had hoped. Down the river Telek's trap was coming into view with a swarm of Tiginset men still at work finalizing the construction.

Baytel saw Telek's boat had fallen behind and shouted, "Hurry, Telek!"

"Aahgh!"

The yelp brought Baytel around only to see Nopel fall from the boat with a goblin's spear sticking from his chest. The young prince was drifting away and sinking. Baytel called to Areus in the adjacent boat, "Areus, the boy!"

Areus turned in time to see Nopel flailing in the water. Areus leaped in after him.

"Nopel!" a high-pitched scream came from Telek's boat. Unnoticed, Princess Delphinade had secreted into their company, and she dove from the boat after her brother.

"Delphinade, you little fool! What are you doing here?" yelled the king.

Baytel saw two goblin boats converging and shouted, "Telek, keep the king safe! We will go after the prince and princess!"

The two goblin boats split, one headed at Telek's boat and the other at Nopel and Delphinade. Baytel turned his boat and paddled against the current back toward them. Bowmen from a third boat killed two goblins before they reached Nopel but still more were converging on the swimmers. As Baytel's craft reached the goblin boat, Ironwright jumped into it, cutting one goblin in half with his delve-axe and facing another at the ready. Baytel maneuvered the boat so Gar could engage with Ironwright and he jumped into the goblin boat with sword drawn flashing brilliant in the fog and quickly helped dispatch the remaining goblins aboard.

Baytel saw more boats headed his way. Gar and Ironwright rejoined him and Baytel steered toward Areus and the prince and princess, who were caught in a side current and floated away toward shore. Then he looked back and saw Telek turning to come back and help.

Baytel waved him off, shouting, "No, Telek! Go! We will catch up to you!"

A moment of pause between the two boats held the air still. Telek was looking back apprehensively, and then he finally waved a good-bye and paddled away, joining the Tiginset force racing down-river.

Chapter 58

TELEK called out to the men in the boats, "Paddle, men! Put your muscle into it!"

Telek stole a glance back at his companions, seeing them in a heated battle with a swarm of goblins. A sudden burst of light flashed across the river as Baytel unsheathed his sword. It flared bright as he cut down goblin after goblin. Near Baytel were Gar and Ironwright fighting back to back, their unstable craft causing missed strikes and blunders, but neither was giving quarter. Ahead in the water was Areus guiding the princess and prince through the current; all were floating farther away, rounding a sandbar in the Ginhonim that took them into a small bay.

A hush settled over Telek's boat, as the men of Tiginset ceased paddling and trained their eyes at Baytel and the spectacle of magic upon the Ginhonim.

Baytel's power lay bare to all and King Forel asked, "What goes on here, Telek?"

Telek responded to the king's ear only, "King Forel, what I say was stated to me and sealed by oath to keep secret. Nevertheless, I will tell the truth behind what you see before you, for you trusted us and have a right to hear it. Baytel is more than just a Druid of the Citadel. He is the prince of the Kings of the North and in his hand he wields their talisman, the sword of the Kings."

The king said nothing and, as the rapids swept them down-river, Telek said, "Look, sire! They are drifting to shore with only a few goblin boats broken off from the main force following. They will vanquish those monsters that follow. Those men will see Nopel and Delphinade to Kilhalen alive. I would wager my life on it."

"I hope you are right, Telek," the king said, grimly. "They are my life and the life of my kingdom."

Telek turned back to the river. Just past the narrow bend, at a point not visible from up the river, thick ropes had been pulled across and tied to trees on each bank. Intertwined in the ropes the Tiginset workers had followed his plan perfectly. They had constructed a trough-like bridge at the water level high enough for a man to stand. The soldiers had filled the trough-bridge with dried leaf, branch and twig.

Telek made it to the bridge with the company of the first strike force. Men were waiting balanced upon the vines and hauled them over, boats and men, to the other side. He stood on the bridge for everyone to hear. "Fourth line bowmen to the front! When in range, shoot over the third strike force into the goblin front on my command!"

The third and last strikers afloat paddled around the bend. The goblins had gained and were close behind. All of Tiginset were shouting, encouraging their comrades to paddle faster.

"Second strike force to the trees!" Telek shouted and the bowmen climbed the large willows that stood on both shores of the bridge.

Telek watched the remaining boatmen approach the bridge. The exhilaration was nearly taking his breath away. This was what he loved—planning a battle in every minute aspect and seeing it unfold accordingly.

Telek called out, "Ready, bowmen?"

All of Tiginset shouted back with bravado.

"Fourth line bowmen, fire away!"

Their arrows flew over their paddling companions and into the goblin horde. The third strikers reached the bridge and clambered over it, dragging their boats with them.

Telek stood above the men, calling out another order. "The oil barrels, men, pour them on the bridge, every last drop."

Barrel after barrel tipped over the lip of the trough, soaking the dried kindling. "Saturate that wood, men, all the way across the trough. That's it, good. Well done."

A hail from the trees came. "Here they come!"

"Stay hidden up there. Your arrows are for the flying goblins only," warned Telek.

The king had climbed next to Telek and said, "They're making the turn, Telek." The king raised his sword and faced his subjects. "Tiginset!"

The men yelled back in unison, "Tiginset and victory!"

Telek looked across at the horde advancing. Their numbers were vast; all Tiginset looked on in trepidation. But they were a proud, sturdy, valorous bunch with courage in abundance and he felt pride in leading such men.

"Again, bowmen! Arrows away!"

The goblin screams echoed in the narrow river canyon as volley after volley flew. Yet still they came.

"Shoot into the center of their formation! I want them spread out across the river!"

The blue-green water of Ginhonim flowed black with the blood of the goblins as more were pierced with arrows. The stench of their dying flesh filled the air with a sickening odor, and still the goblins were unthwarted, paddling on through their dead.

"Good, men, now spread out your pattern, keep them stretched. Keep them from forming any wedge drives into the bridge. I want them to meet the barrier fully across."

Arrow after arrow penetrated the goblin front and Telek felt they were gaining against their numbers when all went deadly quiet except for the twang of a few bow strings as another contingent of goblins turned the bend, showing their entire force as it doubled before his eyes.

"Men, keep shooting while we retreat away from the bridge," yelled Telek as he jumped into the king's boat. "Ready your torches."

Tiginset fell back upon their boats, awaiting his signal. Then the goblins began reaching the bridge, crashing hard against it. The bridge lurched back as Tiginset watched goblin after goblin pound into it as masses rammed into one another, bunching together at least thirty deep and across the width of the Ginhonim.

Telek shouted over the clamor, "Torches! Now!"

The men flung them onto the bridge and flames shot up across the expanse. The fire caught the first goblins and then spread behind them, setting one another on fire. The fire became a conflagration, igniting row after row of crammed goblins as their flesh burst into flames, burning away their shells, and then their black blood completed their deaths.

Winged goblins took flight above the burning masses, but none could break away from the bowmen in the willows.

"Another volley, men, into their rear guard!" And another barrage flew into the horde.

The bridge was burning itself up and Telek knew it would give way soon. Arrows were decimating the horde and the fire leaped deep into their ranks, sparing none.

Telek sensed the time was right and shouted, "Ready, men! When the bridge gives way, we charge!"

The front boatmen drew their swords as the rear kept shooting. Then the bridge gave way, and Tiginset charged. Boat to boat they fought, floating in a mass of black blood and bodies. The clash of swords rang out. Shrieks of terror echoed in the canyon as the two armies converged.

Telek was fighting back against back with King Forel as they swept away the assailants, striking down monster after monster. Arrows whistled past, as the Tiginset bowmen fired with precise accuracy, hitting their mark. But the losses were great as the bodies of the dead, both goblin and Tiginset, floated in the now red-black waters of the Ginhonim.

The goblin numbers had dwindled, but what remained was still strong. The bowmen in the willows continued to shoot as more winged creatures took flight.

A screech from above brought Telek around to the king's side but he was too late. A winged goblin dove at the king and knocked them both into the water.

King Forel and the winged monster were tangled in a frenzied battle, swords lost in the water and both fumbling for daggers with arms and dreadful black wings merging.

Telek jumped after the king but was separated by too many bodies as he struggled to swim to the king. Then he saw the goblin's arm rise from the water and watched helplessly as the clawed hand plunged a dagger into the king's chest.

Telek climbed atop an upturned boat and hurled himself upon the back of the goblin, pulling his own dagger. He jerked back the head of the monster and drove his blade deep.

Letting go of the creature, he grabbed the stricken king, pulling him atop their upturned boat. He removed the dagger from his chest and held the king up.

"The king has fallen! The king is dead!" screamed the men of Tiginset. As their cries spread through their ranks, their fury and fight increased.

"Tiginset! Tiginset and the King!" they shouted, and with the cry of their dead king upon their lips they cut the goblins down with blade and arrow until, miraculously, the horde retreated away.

Telek ordered them to not pursue and allowed the current to take them all away from the desolation and death on the river. Silent in grief, the men of Tiginset drifted away from the remains of the bridge and soon the Ginhonim turned and the death scene disappeared.

Telek's thoughts trailed back to his companions of the quest. The last he saw of them they were in a battle with a small contingent of goblins and Areus was swimming to shore with the wounded boy and his sister.

Telek spoke to himself, as if his friends were beside him in the boat, "I will see you soon. All of you. At Kilhalen."

Telek took a head count of the Tiginset men who began the battle. Less than half remained. They floated upon the river, hurt and exhausted. With their king lying dead at the bottom of Telek's boat, their prince and princess lost, the Tiginset survivors were disheartened and bewildered.

"Telek, why is this happening?"

"What do we do without our king?"

"All is lost. King, prince, princess, all is lost. What will happen to us?"

Telek stopped paddling, giving all a chance to gather around him in the center of the river. "Men of Tiginset, we have fought an evil force from the Southland. This goblin horde was sent out to destroy your Prince Nopel. The Dark Prince Ravek and Vokat, the Red King, possess the dark magic and have begun to wield it against the northlands. They are preparing for war and will soon march north.

"You, Men of Tiginset, are the first to meet them in full battle and put them down. Be sure of the fact that there will be more battles to come. Now we must reach Kilhalen to tell of your misfortune and fight again to reclaim your kingdom."

"What is Tiginset without its king?" one man yelled.

"Your king is dead. He died bravely and the honor of Tiginset was his only thought. Prince Nopel and Princess Delphinade are alive."

"How are you so certain, Telek?" yelled another.

"I saw Prince Nopel and Princess Delphinade being pulled to safety by my friends. Among them are two Druids of the Citadel. Combined, these men are more capable than I, and will reach Kilhalen. Now let us join your families far down the river to tell of the heroics of their dead, and the legacy they leave for you to rejoice in. Take to your paddles, men, and let us leave this place so the Ginhonim River can cleanse itself of the Southland's evil."

Follow the ongoing quest of Druid Baytel and his companions in
Book Two of:

Druids of the Faerie
Baytel and the Goblin Horde

Acknowledgements

Artwork by: Robert Slajus

My earnest gratitude to my editor and friend
Alex Cruden for his wealth of advice and support.

Thank you to my family and friends for inspiration and encouragement.

And a special thank you to my daughters Camille and Claire, my muses.

CPSIA information can be obtained at www.ICGtesting.com
Printed in the USA
LVOW08s0149100516

487458LV00004B/198/P

9 781457 533396